Also by Therese Fowler

Souvenir

Reunion

Reunion

A NOVEL

Therese Fowler

BALLANTINE BOOKS · NEW YORK

Published in the United States by Ballantine Books, an imprint of The Random House Publishing Group, a division of Random House, Inc., New York.

BALLANTINE and colophon are registered trademarks of Random House, Inc.

Library of Congress Cataloging-in-Publication Data

Fowler, Therese.
Reunion : a novel / Therese Fowler.
p. cm.
ISBN 978-0-345-49970-7 (hardcover : alk. paper)
1. Man-woman relationships—Fiction.   2. Family secrets—Fiction.
I. Title.
PS3606.0857R48 2009
813'.6—dc22   2008055710

Printed in the United States of America on acid-free paper

www.ballantinebooks.com

2 4 6 8 9 7 5 3 1

First Edition

Book design by Li*z* Cosgrove

For Andrew, who reminds me that things always turn out
pretty much the way they're supposed to.

Love to faults is always blind,
Always is to joy inclin'd,
Lawless, wing'd, and unconfin'd,
And breaks all chains from every mind.

Deceit to secrecy confin'd
Lawful, cautious and refin'd
To every thing but interest bind
And forges fetters for the mind.

WILLIAM BLAKE

Reunion

Prologue

Her name was Harmony Blue. Harmony Blue Kucharski, *not Forrester, as it ought to have been by then. Unmarried, nineteen, she lay in her narrow bed in the smallest of the run-down rental's bedrooms. Her groans had already driven one of her housemates away, leaving only two people to tend her: The midwife, whose name at the time was Meredith Jones, and a teenage girl who wanted to be known as Bat.*

"I'm looking out for you," Bat said, sitting on the bed's edge and holding her friend's clammy hand.

Like all of the fledgling adults who came and went here, Bat was hardly capable of looking out for herself. But if her words had little impact—the young woman hardly cared what she said—the fact of Bat being there was real comfort in between the pains.

Harmony Blue, sweaty and exhausted, had once been described as "fetching." She tried to remember where she'd heard it, who had used such a word . . . Then she had it: an old farmer in Wisconsin, five or six years earlier. She'd been trying for the Miss Junior Dairy Maiden crown, despite never having been within milking distance of a cow. Entering the pageant had been her mother's idea, a chance for the two hundred and fifty dollar prize. Pink and white hair ribbons, the young woman remembered; ruffles at her throat and knees, a rhinestone tiara that was lost in the next move.

She looked at Bat's reflection in the mirrored closet door, at bony shoulder blades visible inside a black Duran Duran tour T-shirt, black hair cut asymmetrically, longer on the left and striped with one fuchsia swath behind her ear. Bat had style, identity, whereas she had neither. What she had was matted hair, a stretched-to-its-limits red sweatshirt, a swollen belly and rounded, pallid face.

Excepting the belly and the fullness of her face, she appeared to be the same untethered person who'd taken refuge here ten months earlier—which just went to show how untrustworthy an image could be, nothing but the visible bit of an iceberg that was otherwise out of sight. She wasn't the innocent she'd been when she got here. She was no longer quite so naïve.

She watched the mirror, saw her eyes narrow and her lips flatten as another contraction began and tightened, a cinched string yanking her entire body inward to its core. Then she was seeing nothing but the black heat of pain as Bat said, "Breathe, remember? Breathe!"

Slowly, her vision cleared, and the midwife examined her again. "Just about time to push," Meredith said. Meredith's face was thin but kind, and not so much older looking than her two companions', whose desperate faith in her was all too common.

Harmony Blue panted, avoiding the midwife's eyes and words and looking, instead, at the pink ceramic lamp on the dresser. A painted-on ballerina smiled serenely from the lamp's rounded base. The light shining through the dusty lampshade warmed the room the same way it had warmed the bedroom where the lamp used to be. Where her sister had been too, until adulthood—such as it was—had come for each of them.

She concentrated on the faded Journey poster on the wall above the lamp, positioned just as it had been in that other bedroom. "Don't Stop Believin'" they urged in one of their songs, but she'd failed them, and now look at her. Pregnant not by a man she loved, not by the man she loved, but by a guy she barely knew, a guy she could not have cared less about. Pregnant and then paralyzed by the mistake, tortured, unable to decide what she wanted to do. Keep it? End it? Indecisive weeks had turned to months, leaving her with a different pair of choices—and even then she'd had trouble choosing, until Meredith helped her see which way to go.

Meredith had supported her wish to give birth at home, where she would not be judged. Meredith was a facilitator—that was the term she'd used, a facilitator for the people on the other end. There was some money involved, not that it mattered. There was always money in these situations, according to Bat, who'd found Meredith through the friend of a friend. The new parents' offer to the girl, through some law firm, through Meredith, had been ten thousand dollars. For expenses, Meredith said. It would be a closed adoption. Anonymous. No strings. No names.

Bat squeezed her hand harder. "Why is there so much blood?"

Meredith, sitting on a stool at the end of the bed, leaned back and sighed. With her forearm, she brushed dark bangs back from her narrow face. "It's normal. Okay now, with the next contraction, take a breath, focus, and push."

Focus. Icy rain blew against the window just above the midwife's head, pattering, streaking. Focus. How was she supposed to focus when her belly was going to split wide open at any second? This accidental baby . . . the pain was her punishment, pain like a hot iron shoved into her lower back, proving there was no escaping stupidity. So she'd gotten her heart broken by the man she'd believed was perfect for her, so what? Other girls didn't deal with heartbreak by running away, by joining a group of directionless misfits like the ones she was living with. Getting high. Getting pregnant.

Getting over it was what she should have done.

She was over it now, though. In her time here, she had not spoken of her past, not to Bat, not to Will—who'd gotten her pregnant, she didn't care how much he'd denied it before he ran—not to any of the people she'd met. If she revealed her heartbreak, they would see her for the fool she was. They'd reject her too, she was sure. She had not spoken of her past, and she would not.

"Deep breath," Meredith said. "You're almost there."

"No," she moaned, holding her belly. "No, I can't." If only time would stop for a minute, let her catch her breath, let her spend a little longer with the baby there beneath her hands. It was true that she hadn't been sure, at first, if she'd continue the pregnancy. It was true that this baby owed its existence more to inaction than intent. Even so, they were good friends now. She'd tried to protect him—or was it her?—she'd really tried. A few more days as one entity. Maybe that would be enough.

"Push now." The midwife's face was lighted, eager. "Come on, here's the head."

She began to cry, knowing there was no stopping it, pain like a locomo-

tive pulling, pulling the baby on to its real life, its better life. She wanted that for this child, this unintended effect of too much fun, too little thought— same as its mother had been, and its aunt. She wanted this child to have intentional parents, who would make its life everything that hers hadn't been.

"Happy accidents" was what her mother had liked to call her and her sister, even after they had little to be happy about. When the girls reached puberty, the refrain became, "Just don't imagine I'd be able to raise yours. We can barely afford ourselves and, though God knows I try, I am not as capable as my mother." That would be their grandmother, Kate, who'd helped raise them. Until she died, and then they'd had to for the most part raise themselves.

"Oh my God, oh my God." Bat leaned over to watch the baby emerging, still squeezing her friend's hand. "Oh my God! You did it! Jesus! Check him out! It's a boy!"

A son. Good. Everyone wanted a son. He'd be especially loved by his parents. He was from questionable stock but the adopting parents didn't care. It was enough for them that he be white and healthy—he was healthy, just look at him, listen to that cry!—and free of complications. Meredith had assured her that this way was best, no strings for any of them. As soon as the adoption paperwork was filed and finalized, the original birth certificate would be sealed away, accessible only by court order. She would own her future again free and clear, as if he had never happened. No strings, no trail.

Meredith would be back later, and tomorrow, and again, if needed, in the weeks to come. Postpartum was the term she'd used. Any trouble and Harmony Blue was to call the number she'd called when her labor began, and Meredith would come. "If it isn't an emergency, don't go to the ER," the midwife had said.

Bat had nodded as though she, too, was wise, and said, "Not unless you want to have to answer a lot of questions."

She didn't. Not any. Ever.

"Not unless she wants to wait all day," Meredith said.

Now Meredith held the baby up, one hand beneath his buttocks, one beneath his head. "Do you want to hold him?"

"I do!" Bat said.

Harmony Blue struggled to sit upright. The pain was a shadow now, the way her belly was a shadow of what it had been just moments before. Her belly. Round but no longer bulging. A cantaloupe instead of a watermelon, and why was she thinking of fruit? Would the tiny thing sputtering there in the midwife's hands, that red-faced creature with blood drying on his new-born skin, would he love fruit the way she did? Would his parents one day tempt him with fresh pineapple and find he took to it like a duck to bugs? Her grandma, Kate, had always said that, like a duck to bugs.

Would he have her brown eyes, her slender fingers? Would he love to play Scrabble the way she once had? Before, in that other life that now seemed as far away as Sirius. Sirius was the brightest star, the most hopeful point of light in the sky. She had wished on it so often. Had begun, for a time, to be-lieve she'd been heard.

"Yes, I'll hold him," she said. Meredith cut the umbilical cord and tied it off. She squeezed drops into the infant's eyes, then wrapped him in a pale-yellow receiving blanket and handed him into her arms. He continued to sput-ter, but it was a halfhearted noise, as if he knew some sound was expected but really didn't want to make any further fuss. He'd be a good baby, she could tell already.

When the placenta was out and the contractions had subsided, stitches were put in place, plastic bags filled and tied and placed in the cardboard box Meredith had put by the door. Meredith picked up the box and left the room, saying she'd be back in a few minutes. "We'll do the paperwork, and then . . . I'll be needing to go."

After the door closed, Bat smoothed the baby's damp hair and traced his eyebrows with one finger. "You have to keep him. Don't you want to keep him? God, he's so . . . I don't know. I mean, wow!"

Harmony Blue recognized the feverish look in her friend's eyes. Speed, probably. She looked away, back to the purity, the innocence of the tiny boy in her arms. "He deserves better."

Meredith had quizzed her on her drug use when they met two months ago. How often? How much? She had quit once she realized she was pregnant, even as she'd still felt the need to disappear from herself. "Not too much," was the answer she'd given Meredith, "And nothing really, you know, bad."

Nothing from a needle; she'd heard of AIDS, she said—only to have Mere-dith look at her sideways.

"You know about AIDS, but not condoms?"

Guilty.

The baby seemed to be studying her. What did he see? Was her face, with its narrow nose and wide mouth and olive skin that tanned so quickly, being stored in his memory so that if he saw her one day he would know? Would she know him? Not that such a meeting would happen; the adopting parents, who she'd spoken with twice before making her decision, lived far from Chicago. They said they were West-Coast people who had tried every fertility treat-ment medical science had to offer. They seemed caring and kind—she'd thought so even just seeing the Polaroid Meredith had given her before they'd spoken, anonymously of course. Meredith the matchmaker. To the couple, she had given two photos of Harmony Blue—a close-up and a side view—to prove she was seven months along, she supposed. At forty and forty-three, the parents-to-be were a little older than she might have chosen, all things con-sidered—but that was why they were using a law firm, and Meredith: No agency would approve them. They had money, though, so why not use it to help out a troubled young woman and fulfill their single most important dream? Their compassion and their money meant this child would never suf-fer for her weakness.

She whispered to him, "Never."

They'd told her to take her time deciding—at least a day or two after the birth, so she would be sure she was making the right choice for her, and them. But, having finally made her decision, she'd told Meredith she wanted to get it over with quickly. She was strong, but not that strong.

Soon the front door opened again. She could see Meredith shake sleet from her umbrella and then pull it inside and prop it by the door. Terrible weather for a first trip out into the world, but children were resilient, her grandmother had always said so.

Wiping her shoes, Meredith reached into her trench coat's right pocket. She crossed the front room and came into the bedroom, saying, "Where do you want me to put this?"

The envelope was so fat that a rubber band had to bind it. All twenties?

The baby pushed a foot against her ribs reflexively, same as he'd done for months, only on the inside.

She shook her head. "I told you: no money."

"And I told you, you need it. Take it." Meredith's eyes were sympathetic. "Consider it payment for the hard work you just did for this family. Consider it a scholarship fund."

"Take it," Bat said.

Harmony Blue kissed the baby's downy head, letting her lips linger as if to imprint herself on him. He wouldn't remember her, not really. Thank God he wouldn't. Except in some quiet piece of his soul, where he would know she loved him.

"Have them start a savings account with the money."

Meredith came over and squatted next to her. "He'll have a savings account already. And everything else he needs. Don't be foolish."

"Too late."

Meredith watched her for a moment, then sighed and put the money in her pocket. "We'll talk about it again later. Let's do the paperwork."

Harmony Blue would not remember, in the years to come, much of what was on the forms she signed. She would remember instead the warm weight of the infant in the crook of her arm, the vision she conjured of the new parents' joy when Meredith delivered the baby for the second time.

Meredith tucked the papers into a folder and set them aside. She asked Bat, "Do you want to go over the care instructions once more?"

"No, it's cool, both of you can count on me."

"All right then," Meredith said. "Supplies are in the bag. I'll check on you later tonight. Meanwhile, use cold packs for your breasts if needed, and Tylenol every four hours. You'll be sore all over—"

"I know. Take him."

Meredith reached for her free hand, held it while she said, "Now I know what you told me, and I know we've signed the forms, but until I leave you can still change your—"

"Take him."

"All right then," Meredith said, reaching for the child. "It's a good decision. I want you to know that."

She could only nod.

Empty. Her arms, her belly. Now, quickly, she had to empty her mind, too, or be destroyed. Teeth clenched, she watched Meredith diaper the infant, watched her wrap him in a heavier blanket and put a cap on his head, watched her put him to her shoulder, watched her grab the file and leave the room and grasp the front door's knob. Meredith didn't look back; she'd done this before.

The door closed, and it was over.

Part 1

I do not like the man who squanders life for fame;
give me the man who living makes a name.

EMILY DICKINSON

1

In Chicago, the snow was falling so hard that, although quite a few pedestrians saw the woman standing on the fire escape nine stories up, none were sure they recognized her. At first the woman leaned against the railing and looked down, as if calculating the odds of death from such a height. After a minute or two, though, when she hadn't climbed the rail but had instead stepped back from it, most people who'd noticed her continued on their ways. She didn't look ready to jump, so why keep watching? And how about this snow, they said. What the hell? It wasn't supposed to snow like this in spring!

To the few who watched her a minute longer, it was conceivable that the woman in the black pants and white blouse could be the popular talk show host whose show was taped inside the building. Conceivable, but unlikely. Was Blue Reynolds's hair that long? That dark? Why would Blue be standing there motionless on the fire escape, looking up into the sky? Such a sensible, practical dynamo of a person—she certainly wasn't the type to catch snowflakes on her tongue, as this woman now appeared to be doing. And especially not when *The Blue Reynolds Show* was going to start in twenty minutes. Tourists who'd hoped for last-minute tickets were right this second being turned away, the studio was full, please check the website for how to get tickets in advance.

This snow, coming two days after spring had officially begun, had the effect of bringing people throughout the city to windows and door-ways—and to fire escapes, apparently. Though six to eight inches was forecasted, it was hard to begrudge snow like this, flakes so big that if you caught one on your sleeve, you could see the crystalline shape of it, perfect as a newborn baby's hand. And with tomorrow's temperatures rising into the fifties, what snow was piling up on railings and rooftops and ledges would melt away. It would be as if this remarkable snowfall had never happened at all. Much like the sighting of Blue—if in fact it was Blue—there outside her studio building's ninth floor.

The black steel fire escape stood out against the buff-colored limestone, an add-on when the building got transformed from bank to apartments in 1953. Now that it housed offices again, its fire escape made balconies for those lucky enough to have access along with their downtown skyline views. Like a switchback trail, the escape descended from the twelfth-story rooftop to the second floor, with landings at each floor.

The landing on which the woman stood was piled with a good three inches of snow, deep enough to close in on her ankles and soak the hem of black crepe pants. Her boots, Hugo Boss, lambskin, three-inch heels, were styled for fashion, not utility, and as she stood with her face upturned, she was vaguely aware that her feet were growing cold. Still, the pleasure of being pelted by snowflakes held her there. She could not recall the last time she'd been in, truly *in*, weather like this. And never alone, it seemed, and never focused, anymore, on the weather. Standing here, she had the exquisite feeling of being just one more anonymous Chicago dweller. Just a forty-ish woman on a fire escape in the snow, and not Blue Reynolds at all.

This snow made her want to be a child again so that, instead of going home to a bowl of Froot Loops eaten while she reviewed reports, she would be preparing to pull on snow pants and boots and head for the lighted hillside at the park, plastic saucer sled in tow. She would return home later soaking wet, with chapped red cheeks and frozen toes and a smile that would still be on her face when she woke the next morning.

Was such a day a memory, she wondered, or a wish?

She knew the snowflakes must be wetting her just-styled hair, spotting her white silk blouse, Escada, she'd put it on not fifteen minutes earlier. These thoughts, they existed outside her somehow, far enough away that they didn't motivate her to climb back inside her office window—

even as today's guests waited downstairs in the green room, nervous about meeting her. Even as the camera and lighting and sound and recording crews were gearing up for this last show of the week. Even as three hundred eager audience members were now taking their seats and would soon meet Marcy, Blue's right hand, Marcy who managed her life, who would tell them what to expect on today's show. They wouldn't expect a snow-wet, distracted Blue Reynolds.

Still, even when she heard someone tapping the window to get her attention, she stood there squinting up into the whitened sky. *One more minute. One more.*

The tapping, again.

"I know, I'm coming," she said.

Inside, the stylists and her producer and her assistants fluttered around her, clucking like outraged hens. *What are you doing, it's practically showtime! Look at that blouse! Are you sure you're okay?* No. She wasn't okay, hadn't been truly okay ever, that she could recall.

*W*hat expectation she saw on the faces of her studio audience when she took the stage! It wasn't her they'd come to watch; she never lost sight of that. Because *she* was a regular person who argued with her mother, who cleaned hair from her shower drain so that the cleaning lady didn't have to. She was a woman who failed to floss, who needed to clean out her purse, who paged through *People* at the dentist's office, just like most of them. They were here to see the woman who, upon seeing that magazine, could then book whoever interested her and interview them on this very stage. They were here to see the woman who sometimes made the cover herself.

On today's show were a sociologist, a high school superintendent, a Christian minister, and three teens—one boy and two girls. One of the girls was eight months pregnant. The topic was abstinence education.

In talking with Peter, *TBRS*'s producer, about this show, Blue had protested his suggestion that she open with an audience poll. Getting the audience involved in hot-button issues had in the past led to a *Jerry Springer*-like atmosphere she had to work hard to redirect. Peter said, yes, but think of the drama. "We *want* people to engage," he said. "And not only because it's good for ratings." She agreed in part; engagement was the point of it all, or was supposed to be the point.

He continued, "You saw the latest numbers. We're slipping—just a little, and obviously we'll bring it back up, but if we lose our edge right now, we lose our contract renewal leverage." Lower ratings also led to lower ad revenues, lower production budgets, more difficulty in booking guests who had the power to draw viewers—all of which then trickled down to lower salaries for everyone on her payroll. Lower salaries meant good people jumped onto newer, flashier, competing ships. Ultimately, she'd agreed to do the poll.

Standing at the front of the stage, she welcomed the audience. Three hundred faces of all skin tones and both genders watched her eagerly, fans from any and every place on Earth. Beyond, too, she sometimes suspected. While Marcy claimed there was an angel in every audience, Blue rather thought there was an alien, who would inevitably write in to rant about how offbase she'd been on a particular topic, even if that topic was the fifty best uses of phyllo.

"Let me introduce you to some typical teens," Blue said, and the two teenage girls appeared from the wings to take their seats behind her. Indeed, both girls were typical-looking, with long brown hair and eye makeup and TV-modest clothing bearing popular-brand logos. Both girls were white.

Facing the audience, she said, "Kendra and Stacey—who is eight months pregnant—are seventeen-year-olds from intact middle-class families. Their parents are professionals. Both girls are B-students, involved in extracurricular activities"—this drew a chuckle from some of the audience—"and both have made preliminary plans to attend college. The main difference in these young women's lives is that one of them attends a high school that follows an abstinence-only curriculum, and one attends a school where teenage sexuality is considered 'normal' and the students are educated accordingly. Abstinence is taught as one of several possible choices."

She stepped down from the dais and walked to the lip of the stage.

"With a show of hands: Which of you thinks Stacey, our pregnant teen, got the sex-is-normal message?"

About half of the audience raised hands.

"Now, who thinks Kendra did?"

Most of the other hands went up, as did the volume of voices, arguments already begun.

Blue waited a beat, resisting the urge to rub her face. Looking into Camera 4, she said, "The answer, when we come back."

She allowed the rumbling to continue during the break, hoping the audience would get it out of the way now; things were not going to get better.

Taking a seat between the girls, she looked at each of their nervous faces. "Are you hanging in there?"

Kendra shrugged. Stacey shifted in her chair and smoothed her pink maternity top. "I'm okay, I guess," she whispered.

In a moment, they were on-air again. Blue said, "With me today are Kendra and Stacey, Chicago-area teenagers who, like most of their peers, are dealing as best they can with the pressures of growing up in our increasingly sexualized culture.

"Before the break I polled the audience on which of these girls received the teen-sex-is-normal message from her school, and which was taught to abstain until marriage." She looked at Camera 2: "Brad, give us that tight view—audience, watch the screen."

She waited, knowing that on the screen behind her would be a close-up image of a girl's left hand, on which there was a silver ring. Brad nodded, and Blue continued, "This is known as a purity ring, representing adherence to the abstinence ideal: a vow of chastity, a promise to wait for the right man—or woman, because some young men are wearing them, too—and marriage.

"Girls, raise your hands."

Of the four hands now displayed, three were bare of jewelry, as they'd arranged ahead of time.

The silver glinted, of course, from Stacey's left hand.

Amidst the reactions of surprise from many in the audience, and sat-

isfaction from others, a skinny, dark-haired woman in the middle of the
room stood up and yelled, "Sinner! Hypocrite! Take off that ring!"

Stacey's face crumpled. "It's not wrong! I love him," she said, then
burst into tears.

And before Blue could stop herself, she did, too.

*A*fter refereeing fifteen rounds between the sociologist and the minister—had Peter chosen such a closed-minded, sanctimonious old man on
purpose?—Blue escaped the set the minute they were clear. Reverend
Mark Masterson, a tall, self-serious man with heavy jowls and bottle-
black hair, followed her backstage.

"Just what do you think you're going to accomplish by telling
teenage girls to go ahead and have sex?"

"Was that what I said?"

"You made that child out to be a hero."

He'd made no secret of his disdain for the facts and the statistics,
which were the substance of her supposed endorsement. Blue looked at
him coolly. "And you made her out to be a whore—I'm sorry, 'whore-
monger' was your word, wasn't it? I thought you were a minister, but
apparently you're a judge."

He frowned down at her, his height giving him an illusion of superi-
ority she was sure he made the most of. He said, "When I agreed to do
this show, I was under the impression that you had a conscience."

"And I was under the impression that someone who has committed
to serving his community would at least attempt to do so."

He straightened the lapels of his brown suit jacket and picked off a
spot of lint. "These are children we're talking about. They require firm-
ness and absolutes to shut down ungodly urges. Romans chapter eight,
verse thirteen, for example: 'For if you are living according to the flesh,
you must die; but if by the Spirit you are putting to death the deeds of the
body, you will live.' "

"So Stacey must die? That's a reasonable punishment."

"Now let's not be ridiculous. The Bible permits a certain amount of
interpretation."

Blue nodded. "So true. Excuse me." Giving him no chance to reply, she walked away quickly, shoulders pulled back, chin up, and shut herself in her dressing room. She'd known there would be no easy consensus on such a complex issue, but just once she would have liked to have the kind of powers needed to instantly transform a person like Masterson into a hormonal, love-struck teenage girl.

Blue was pulling off her boots when Marcy joined her, looking as fresh and enthused now, at four-fifteen, as she had at eight this morning. It was more than Marcy's white-blond hair ("Of course it's dyed," she'd told a woman in the audience during a commercial break. "Nature doesn't make this color . . ."), more than her flared-leg jeans and gray cashmere T-shirt. Marcy had what Blue's mother Nancy Kucharski called "a dynamic aura," grown even more dynamic since meeting Stephen Boyd, an industrial designer who was teaching Marcy ballroom dance. Passion created that aura, Nancy said. "It's good for the complexion, and not bad for the rest of the body, either!" Blue had to take her word for it—and an experienced word it was.

"Good show," Marcy said, as though things had gone just as well as the day before, when they'd hosted four champion dog breeders and four captivating puppies.

"Compared to what?" Blue stepped out of her pants and stripped off the substitute Escada blouse (there were two of everything, just in case) then put on gym gear and brown velour sweats. Or rather, a brown velour track suit, as they were being called again. The seventies were back, complete with Barry Manilow and Cat Stevens and Neil Diamond on the radio, which Blue didn't mind so much. The songs were reminders of a time when she was young enough to believe she knew where she stood.

"I'm serious. Except for that little . . . outburst, you really kept things under control."

Blue shook her head, still embarrassed. "I don't know what that was about."

"Empathy, maybe."

"Is Peter having a fit?"

"He's too busy working on a spin strategy. Stacey's still a mess though, poor thing."

"I suspect she's going to need therapy."

"*You* didn't."

"I did. I just didn't get any."

Marcy reached behind Blue to straighten her hood. "Speaking of misguided youths, your mother called. She's not coming to the Keys with us after all; she says she met someone and he wants her all to himself this weekend."

"Someone named Calvin," Blue said, more curious than surprised. "She apprised me the other day. He owns a bookstore—not the 'adult' type, a real one, but that's all I know. Did she tell you anything about him?"

"Only that they'll be by your place for drinks at eight tonight. She said to tell you don't worry, they won't stay long."

Calvin was Nancy Kucharski's third "boyfriend" since New Year's. He'd been there at her mother's place when Blue called last Monday night. The call had been brief, with Calvin waiting and Joni Mitchell crooning loudly in the background. Blue had a strong suspicion that Joni wasn't her mother's only throwback indulgence; the last time she'd visited her mother's apartment, the place had smelled vaguely of marijuana.

Her mother hadn't waited for the seventies retro movement to catch up with her; she'd continued to march as its poster child these three decades since. Her hair, left alone to evolve to a natural silver-gray, was past her shoulders and often braided. Her favorite earrings were small silver peace signs. She wore vegetable-dyed t-shirts to work in her rooftop organic garden, and she had recently pierced her nose. Probably she'd been smoking pot all along—maybe even grew it, organic and therefore wholesome—and where Blue was concerned was simply following their mutual and long-established policy of Don't ask, Don't tell.

Marcy dropped a manila folder onto the countertop in front of Blue. "This has your itinerary and Peter's final notes for next week. With spring break in progress, we're sure to have some great crowds. Oh, the first scuba class is set for Sunday at nine. I know you said you're not planning to dive, but I think you should. Key West has some of the best reefs in the northern hemisphere and you can't see them if you don't do the course."

Blue removed her makeup with pre-soaked pads—the sort of single-use product her mother hated—while skimming the itinerary. They'd leave Chicago early tomorrow, arriving in Key West at about ten. The whole crew would stay at the Ocean Key Resort, where, for her, a spacious oceanfront suite would make a nice home-away-from-home for the week.

She said, "I'm afraid I'll get the bends," a cover for the truth, that she was a lousy swimmer.

"Do you even know what the bends is?"

"Hey," Blue said, still reading, "now that my mom has bailed, why don't you bunk with me in my suite? It's two bedrooms. We can stay up late watching Owen Wilson DVDs. I was so embarrassed when we had him on last time and I had to admit I hadn't seen *Shanghai Noon*."

"I would . . . but I invited Stephen along, and . . ."

"Say no more," Blue said, closing the folder.

"Besides, you should really get out some, while we're there. I hear the nightlife is crazy good."

"Sure. I'll just hang out in bars and, I don't know, take home whoever's willing."

"If you did a little more of that, then—"

"Then what?" Her own answers: Then she might have had *multiple* fatherless children, as her mother did. A career of cleaning motel rooms and checking groceries and up-selling fruit baskets at a phone bank for catalog retailers every holiday season.

Then she wouldn't be cloistered in this building, in this life.

Marcy said, "Nothing, forget it. You should just have more fun, that's all. Life is short, and you've paid your dues."

Blue leaned over and took longer than she needed to tie her sneakers. "So, I'm off to the gym. Guess I'll see you—and Stephen—at Midway, six-forty-five AM sharp."

"Blue?"

She sat up. "Yeah?"

"What were you doing out there, on the fire escape?"

"The fire escape?" She looked out the window. The snow was still falling with vigor.

"Yeah," Marcy said, "you know, that steel thing, used for egress in the event of an emergency. Was there some emergency I should know about?"

"Branford called." The private detective she'd had on retainer for almost four years now.

"And?"

"And he has a lead. I don't have any details yet." She looked at Marcy and saw her at nineteen, saw her as Bat, heard her saying even back then, days and weeks afterward, that it wasn't too late to find the child. She could change her mind, she could track him down.

Now Marcy said, "Ah." That was all there was *to* say, so many fruitless years into the search.

"So, see you at sunrise."

2

Inside Blue's apartment was the life she'd been living for ten years, or seasons, as she'd learned to call them. Ten seasons of ratings pressures and growing competition, the challenge of keeping a laser-sharp focus on *what daytime audiences want,* but trying to do it on her terms. "Style and Substance," was the headline of her recent *Elle* interview. That was the goal. Sometimes they achieved it.

Ten seasons of expanding success. The apartment's structural remodel had come after season two, and the color scheme back then . . . what had it been? Pale blue and lavender with light woods? Or was that the following incarnation? She could no longer recall. Only that the décor had been updated four times—every two years, the way some people traded up vehicles. The apartment needed to be current, Marcy said, because Blue sometimes entertained there. Marcy handled it all just the way she handled most of the other details of Blue's life. Saint Marcy, Blue often called her, and Marcy would say, "Ha! Not after the life *I've* led."

It was all talk, though, had always been all talk with her. The worst Marcy had done was what they were all doing that year they'd shared the dilapidated house. Taking on new names—Blue had tried out Skye, after the heroine of a book she'd read, but became Bubble when her belly began to round—inventing themselves, dabbling with drugs, with sex (though she'd quit both when her periods quit) . . . and while some people might consider them hell-bound for their behaviors, Blue wasn't convinced. She and Marcy and their various housemates had been young, rudderless, sure of their invincibility and the idea that they had so much time ahead of them that they could waste it freely, using home-made bongs and listening to Prince. So much time that even the biggest of mistakes would sooner or later melt away and be forgotten, like tonight's snow after tomorrow's sun.

The apartment was newly decorated in what Blue thought of as Twenty-first Century Lodge style. Though the work was completed weeks ago, the scent of fresh paint and new wool rugs persisted, in a pleasant, low-key way. The place looked marvelous, all warm woods and natural stone and leafy plants throughout the wide-open space. Marvelous and unused. Marvelous and bereft. An *Architectural Digest* spread, after the magazine's crew had gone.

In her bathroom she pulled off the elastic that bound her hair. *Highlighted chestnut*, her stylist called the color, *with hints of honey and cinnamon,* as if her head were a pastry. "Wholesome" was the word the media often used to describe her, suggesting that somehow her nut-honey-cinnamon hair and her long-legged tomboyish build explained her success. They'd changed their tune a bit when she made it onto the *Forbes* list. Now she was wholesome and driven, wholesome and savvy, wholesome and well connected and well dressed.

Style *and* substance, how surprising, how unusual!

A woman who made her living on TV did not, strictly speaking, have to be attractive to succeed, but if she wasn't, the media loved to say so. Hence the hour she'd just spent at the gym, an hour for which she paid a ridiculous amount of money in order to get exclusive time with Jeremy. An effective hour, though, repeated five times each week (up from the three that used to do the trick); she was in top physical form. If while doing stretches, crunches, leg lifts, she sometimes thought of Jeremy's sculpted body making better use of hers, where was the harm in that?

Her bathroom's new wallpaper, an amber grass-textured weave, kept bringing to mind a Hemingway story—not one of the novels they would be promoting on the show next week, but another, about Mt. Kilimanjaro and a couple waiting for rescue at a nearby camp. The short story, a tale of regret, had been a favorite of Mitch Forrester's . . . and Mitch had been a favorite of hers.

As she washed her face she recalled Mitch reading her the story one evening, early in their short-lived relationship. He'd been pensive— something to do with his ex-wife and the difficulty he was having in get- ting to see his son. "There are only so many chances to get things right," he'd said, but she hadn't understood very well at the time. She'd been barely nineteen, sure that life was a broad and endless series of chances. After all, didn't they live in the land of opportunity, where success in business, in life, in love, was no accident of birth but could be *made*? Wasn't Mitch in charge of his own destiny? What was there to regret at his age, twenty-seven? He could have a new wife. (*Her.*) He could have new children. (*Hers.*) For two promising months she had done a very ef- fective job of ignoring anything that contradicted her vision, and then he'd set her straight. And then . . . then, he'd set her free.

Less easy to ignore, these days, were the lines in her forehead and the tiny sunbursts spreading, now, from the corners of her eyes. Her soften- ing jawline. Thinner lips. Less easy to ignore was her makeup artist's in- sistence that the miracle of Botox was her salvation. Easier, though, if she quit looking in the mirror. She pressed the light switch and left the room.

She now had the entire sixth floor of this historic art deco building. It was more space than she needed, by far—as if that mattered; what did need have to do with her life anymore? Here it was just her and Peep, her tabby Maine Coon cat. He slept most of the time, and she was gone most of the time, so their pairing worked out well.

With the apartment's lights still off, the falling snow looked like a shimmering veil outside the east-facing windows. In daytime, that view included Lake Michigan as seen between downtown's towers. Out the north side was a view of slightly lesser buildings, one of which housed the studio. The apartment was swept and dusted and vacuumed weekly, the floors polished monthly—and before and after every cocktail party. The refrigerator was stocked, the wine bottles circulated, all by a Marcy- directed staff that Blue never saw.

She went barefoot down the hallway to the kitchen on marble floors the color of bitter chocolate. Why colors seemed so often to be named for food she wasn't sure. Her kitchen cabinets were crème brûlée, and her granite countertop was confetti orzo. The wall color throughout all the main rooms was something to do with squash: pale summer squash? Light butternut puree? Whatever. She wasn't Martha Stewart.

There was time, yet, for Froot Loops before her mother and Calvin arrived. She poured a bowl and ate it standing at the counter, Peep lurking at her ankles until she put the milk dregs down for him to finish. Ten 'til eight. She had better put some socks on; her toenails were ragged, and who knew what kind of garbage this Calvin guy might decide to report to *Perez* or *TMZ*?

She could hear her mother's voice chastising, telling her to *relax already*. Right, relax. Re-lax. "Chill," she said, heading back down the hallway. That her mother wanted to introduce this latest companion suggested he was, in Nancy's estimation, higher caliber than most. Even so, after years of exposure to the public's appetite for gossip—guilty, herself, of spreading it now and then—Blue preferred to be overly cautious. Live by the sword, die by it.

Calvin K., as he was introduced to Blue, was in every visible way her mother's counterpart. Silver hair, pierced ears, rangy and kind-looking. According to her mother's earlier account, they'd met at the co-op on Lake Park one Saturday morning, buying organic vegetables. Calvin had an endearing passion for rutabaga.

"Calvin, meet my oldest, Harmony Blue—or just Blue, if she prefers."

"She prefers," Blue said. "Is it Calvin Kay, K-a-y?" She'd need to know in order to have him checked out. Her practice of getting background checks on her mother's companions was another of the subjects neither of them spoke of, or not to one another at any rate.

"No, it's the letter *K*, for K-r-z-y-z-e-w-s-k-i," he spelled it out, then told her it was pronounced *sha-sheff-ski*. "Like Coach K, at Duke? It's Polish. Ya'd think someone would anglicize it, but there you go."

"Well," she said, taking her mother's coat, and his, "Good to meet you, Calvin K."

"Hard to beat *Kucharski*, huh?" her mother said.

Which was why Blue had chosen Reynolds.

Though Calvin's accent had already answered her next question, she needed something with which to make conversation. She did not, after all, know a single thing about rutabaga. She said, "Are you a Chicago native?"

"Nah, Winnebago. I came here in ninety-seven, I guess it was, to run a bookstore in Hyde Park—my brother's. He had colon cancer."

"Oh, I'm sorry. Is he—"

"Gone? Yeah. Saw that special you did on it, though. I appreciate that."

Her mother, hair down, wearing a formfitting Impressionist print top and jeans, told Blue, "We watched the show today. Calvin's been a fan for years. What was with the tears? Do you have a cold?"

"A cold?" Blue closed the closet door and led them into the living room. "No, I'm not sick."

"When you were little, I would always know when you were coming down with something because your emotions would be all over the map. Could be early menopause—are your periods irregular? Are you having hot flashes?"

"No! Really, Mom, it's nothing," she lied. "I'm tired is all. Hey, I have some of that red wine you like; can I pour you a glass? Calvin?"

After they'd settled onto the L-shaped sectional, Blue listened while her mother brought her up to date on her sister Melody's latest. For as intertwined as their lives had been as children, she and Mel had a tenuous connection as adults. Blue relied on their mother to keep her current about Mel, while Mel had their mother and the tabloids to keep her updated on Blue, either of which she seemed willing to regard as reasonably authoritative. The question now was whether their mother or the media would be first to alert Mel to her on-air outburst.

Currently, Blue's mother was saying, Mel and her husband Jeff were leasing out two hundred tillable acres of their central Wisconsin farm to

Green Giant and, using the rent income, intended to buy themselves an RV. With their sons both grown and out of the house for the first time, they were planning to spend the coming summer touring the country, one KOA campground after another until they'd crossed off all twenty-nine of their sightseeing goals. "They've never traveled; Jeff refuses to fly."

"So they're gonna knock 'em all out at once, eh? Carpe diem," Calvin said.

"I can't get over how differently you and Mel turned out," her mother went on. "No way can I see you in an RV—or on a farm, for that matter." She told Calvin, "She's never been one to settle for what's ordinary."

Blue shook her head. "That's not true."

"No?"

"No." She craved ordinary. Grocery shopping. An afternoon in the park with a blanket and a book. "If you mean my career, you know that a lot of my success is owed to luck."

Calvin chuckled. "A pretty good run of luck, then."

"You laugh, but I'm sincere. I started out as a production assistant. I never saw myself hosting a talk show; I wanted to do the news." If she threw herself into her work as though it was a life raft, if she appeared to be far more dedicated than her cohorts, that was only because she'd used work to fill the empty spaces that others filled with spouses or children, with bar-hopping or hobbies or sports.

In her defense she added, "I had Froot Loops for dinner."

"You just made my point," her mother laughed. "How many times have you been there, to the farm?"

"I don't know—three?" She knew exactly. Each exhausting visit had seen her treading the narrow line between tolerance and envy. In spite of Blue's support of her sister's choices and admiration for everything Mel and Jeff had accomplished, Mel was still inclined to defensiveness. It seemed her every sentence began with a version of, "I know it isn't as glamorous as *your* life, but . . ." Blue hadn't been there in years. She'd wanted to attend the boys' high school graduation ceremonies but Mel insisted her presence would detract from the events. "No offense, but we just don't want it to turn into Blue Reynolds Day." The sad thing was, Blue couldn't fight the logic. She'd sent each boy a generous check and invited them to visit her at will.

"You know," her mother said, "we should all get together soon. Then Calvin can see for himself what I mean." She turned to Calvin. "My girls don't think alike, and they don't look a bit alike, either. Melody's taller, kind of stocky, with wide blue eyes and a little bit of a cleft chin. She's been blond since she was a toddler."

"My oldest son's my ex-wife's spitting image—well, bigger nose and more facial hair now, ya' know—while my daughter's me to a tee. Could be true for yours—one like you, one like their dad."

"Not that we'd know if that was the case," Blue said. She hadn't meant to sound bitter but the words, once out, had an edge. "We don't know anything about him."

Her mother looked at her over the top of her wineglass, then finished her sip and said, "For your own good, and what difference would it make if I'd told you every detail? He was gone even when he was in this world, no practical use to me and none to either of you."

Which Blue was sure was true, but she had been there on those long Sunday afternoons when her mother played Fleetwood Mac's "Go Your Own Way" over and over again on the console stereo. (*Loving you isn't the right thing to do / How can I ever change things that I feel?*) Watching her mother towel off after a shower, she'd stared at the black script $\mathscr{L}$ on her mother's right hip and wondered, Lou? Leonard? Larry? Lance? The absent presence of $\mathscr{L}$ in their lives had gnawed at them all.

"I did the best I could with you; God knows I wasn't very sensible in my younger years."

Calvin said, "Who is? All I got to show for my early adulthood is five years' experience driving a fuel-oil truck, and a perfect memory of the words to every Crosby, Stills, and Nash song there was at the time."

Her mother started singing "Teach Your Children" and Calvin joined in. Blue shook her head, but a part of her, a reluctant, soft part that she liked to forget she had, was captivated. That her mother sang

well was no surprise; her singing had always been the cue that Blue and
Mel could ask for bubble gum money or, later, new jeans. The surprise
was in how her mother and Calvin harmonized so well, and with such
obvious mutual pleasure, and in exactly the manner Blue had wished for
as a child when she'd watched *The Sound of Music* and imagined that for
her mother there could be an add-on father. Their Maria would be a
long-haired, soft-souled Peter Fonda sort of guy.

If the likes of Calvin had come along back then, everything would
have turned out so differently . . . There would be no past to hide away,
no lost son to track down.

Branford has a lead.

But she could not think about that right now.

"Something to eat?" she asked, heading to the kitchen without waiting for an answer.

Through the kitchen window, Blue saw that the snow was slowing
and, out against the dark horizon, whole floors of lights still glowed in
the skyscrapers that separated her from the vast black of Lake Michigan.
Who was working this late? Who, like her, had little reason *not* to work
any and all hours, or was so disconnected from those reasons that getting home at nine o'clock, ten, had become par?

She refilled wineglasses and brought out another bottle, along with
cheese, bread, olives. Her mother was in the middle of a tale from Blue's
childhood.

"Now this would've been around the time Mom died," she was saying, "so who knows what those girls were thinking, we were all such a
mess, but I came home from work—was it the Laundry, then? No, no, I
remember, I was cleaning houses in this snotty part of Milwaukee, for
women who filled their days getting their poodles groomed. Anyway, I
finally got home and there were the girls, in the kitchen, very serious-
looking, water and flour and paper towels spread *everywhere*."

Blue remembered too; she'd been ten, Melody nine. A spring
evening shortly after they'd moved to Jackson Park, on the south side of
Milwaukee, when Mel, on a let's-test-the-new-kid dare, had climbed
their new school's flagpole just after school let out. She was already near

the top when Blue came outside—not that Blue's protests would have stopped her—knees wrapped around the pole, one arm waving to the growing crowd of kids below. Blue's mouth was just opening to yell, "Be careful!" when Mel lost her grip and fell backward, skimming partway down the pole and then landing hard on her right side. The school nurse—Blue couldn't recall her name or even quite what she looked like—thought the arm was probably broken. But when she failed to reach anyone at Nancy's work number, she had reluctantly let Blue persuade her to take Mel home.

Blue remembered how grown-up she'd felt, how capable, standing there somberly in front of the nurse, Mel equally somber, not even crying. If Mel had been hysterical, the nurse would never have let them leave. But faced with two little girls who swore their mother was going to be home soon, was probably on her way that minute and that was why the nurse couldn't reach her, the nurse let them go. "You tell your mother Melody needs to see a doctor *today*," the nurse had said, making Blue promise.

"I was *thinking* that Mel's arm was broken," Blue said now. "So I was making a cast."

"Oh, the two of you," her mother laughed, "with wet flour clumped in your hair and Melody practically mummified."

"Cute kids," Calvin said. "Resourceful."

And Mel's arm *was* broken, and needed surgery, and their mother had been forced to take a second job to pay off the hospital bills.

"Resourceful—oh, you don't know the half of it!" her mother said, pouring herself another glass of wine. "There was one year when Miss Harmony Blue here was so determined that I should have a cake for my birthday that she took Mom's old car while I was gone—oh my God, she couldn't have been fourteen—so that she could get the cake mix and be back home in time to surprise me with it already made, frosted, everything."

This was after they'd moved to Homewood, outside Chicago, where a friend had offered her mother a job at a florist's—a good fit, finally, for her mother's earthiness, but their apartment had no grocery store in close walking distance. Blue had driven that car, a worthless Chevelle with rusting, busted-out floorboards, quite a few times before she was licensed to drive. To buy peanut butter and saltines when there was nothing left in the house to eat. To track down her sister, times when Mel failed to come straight home from school.

Once, during her senior year, she'd driven all the way into the city in the middle of the night to rescue her mother from a parking deck where the "good" car, a '77 Ford LTD, had broken down. To rescue her from a date, downtown, with a man who had turned out to be "too corporate" for her mother's tastes. That time was in the dead of winter and the Chevelle's heater didn't work; she'd driven hunched over the steering wheel, shivering, wiping the windshield every few minutes to keep it clear. Wishing her mother had not missed the last train. Vowing she would not live this way forever. At a stoplight she'd waited, peering out the side window into the vast black sky. There was Orion's belt and there, there was Sirius, and she had said, "*Please* get me out of here."

And it had been the very next day—she would take this as a sign—when her high school English teacher, Mr. Forrester, told her that his wife was looking for someone to work for her part time. Receptionist for a commercial realty office, where she'd have time to keep up with her homework. The pay was half again what she'd been making cleaning cages at a pet store. Then there was the added benefit of potentially more chances to see Mr. Forrester's handsome English professor son, Mitch, who she had first seen when he visited their class in October to encourage them to pursue liberal arts degrees when they all went off to college. He had to know that fewer than a third of them would go to college at all, and those who went would go mostly on scholarship, choosing professions such as accounting and engineering—practical, good-paying occupations that would free them from repeating their parents' worries about how to pay the gas bill and still buy groceries. Liberal arts degrees were for people who could afford to be idealists. An hour in Mitch's presence that October and she'd decided that, affordable or not, she wanted to be one. She took the job.

Calvin checked his watch. "We got a nine-fifteen reservation," he said. "Point me to the restroom, and then, Nancy, we better scoot."

As soon as he was down the hall, her mother leaned close to say, "He's The One." She was nodding as she said it, eyes bright.

Too much wine. "You've known him for a week," Blue said.

"Almost three, actually. Doesn't matter. When you know, you know."

"*I* know you're being brash." She, Blue, had been brash a time or two, so she knew what it looked like, how it sounded. *She* had imagined, once, that she *knew*.

Her mother stood and stared down at her. "Harmony Blue, I did not get to fifty-nine years of age by being completely stupid."

"That's not what I'm saying." Blue got up and began gathering the plates and glasses. "Just, think about it. The money—"

"*Your* money, is that what you mean? He's not seeing me because my daughter's rich and has generously padded my own accounts."

"It wouldn't be the first time."

"He has his own money—and a little thing called integrity." She held up her hand to stop Blue's protest. "Yes, I know, some of the others were lacking. Irrelevant. I was sowing my oats."

For four decades in all. A lot of oats in Nancy Kucharski's bag. "Fine," Blue said, going into the kitchen. "Still, these things take time to play out. You need to see how you feel about him after you've been together a year or two—"

"How old am I?" her mother demanded.

Blue set the dishes in the sink and turned. "Mom."

"How old am I?"

"Fifty-nine," Blue sighed.

"How many of my friends have died in the past ten years?"

"I don't know . . . three?"

Her mother held up six fingers. "Cancer, cancer, stroke, drunk driver, cancer, heart disease. Now tell me I should suspend my judgment for a year or two."

"You're as healthy as I am."

"Today." She kissed Blue's cheek and left her standing in the kitchen.

Calvin joined Blue while her mother took a turn in the bathroom. "I'm glad to get to meet you," he said, and when he smiled there was no evident avarice, only the refreshing sense that, in his eyes, she was equally Blue Reynolds *and* Nancy's daughter, or perhaps even more the latter. His pale gray-blue eyes made her think of Huskies, those reliable sled dogs of the Inuit. She wanted to like him. So much as she knew him she *did* like him. He could sing. He owned a bookstore. He paid her mother more attention than he paid *her*. If her usual discreet inquiry into this man's background proved out, well, that would be a start.

What a strange concept, her mother in love after all these years.

"All right then," her mother called, heading for the foyer. "Have a good trip to the Keys. Watch out for pirates."

"And sharks," Calvin said as he and Blue joined her.

"And I love you," her mother added, kissing her forehead.

Blue watched the elevator doors close after them with tears welling—envy? Longing? She wasn't sure, and didn't want to think about it. By the time she was back inside her apartment, she had willed the tears away.

3

*O*utside Mitch Forrester's Chapel Hill office window, the trees were a green haze of new leaves, the only real color on this gray, rainy morning. Spring weather had a solid hold on North Carolina, as was evident by the number of students who'd been showing up to class in shorts and flip-flops this last week before spring break. It was scheduled late this year, so they were more than ready. Today would be a mess of dripping plastic ponchos and wet umbrellas, slick floors and poorly attended classes.

An oak tree's branches brushed his second-floor window. He'd been startled more than once by scratching sounds, nights he'd sat here on an old slip-covered couch reading journals or grading essays, nights when he'd thought all was calm outside. Shut away in the English department, he'd be unaware of the storm rolling in until the wind began rising, the trees swaying like so many lithe dancers in one of those troupes his ex-wife, Angie, had liked dragging him to see. Now he saw the rain stream off the tiny narrow leaves without paying it much attention, as what he was hearing on the telephone preoccupied him.

"Let me see if I understand correctly," he said, returning to his desk. It was piled with scholarly books whose pages had long since yellowed, books with cracked spines and worn corners and opinions, within their pages, that were hardly credited anymore. By contrast, *Dr. Seuss's Sleep Book* was faceup with a note stuck to the front, reminding him to bring it for this afternoon's tutoring session with a third-grader named Chris; after hearing Mitch's story of how his son Julian had *loved* the book when he was a boy, Chris had grudgingly agreed to try reading it himself. A potted purple orchid with a name Mitch could never remember sat atop four copies of his most recent publication, a slim book that considered the role of women in Ernest Hemingway's fiction. The legendary author hadn't been too successful with women, a problem Mitch unfortunately shared.

He said, "I'll need some sort of filming permit from the city *along with* whatever I arrange directly with you folks there at the Hemingway Home, yes?"

The man on the other end of the phone call, a volunteer with a gravelly voice, said yes, he believed so. However, he said, September was thick into hurricane season and if Mitch came then, he was taking his chances.

"I know—my parents live there in Key West. But I appreciate your advice. Unfortunately, I'm working against a number of factors, one of which is my, er, crew's availability, and my own. I only have the fall semester to pull this project together. As I said, I'll be down tomorrow and hope to start getting things in order; can you give me the name of the person to contact about permits?" When he had the information jotted in his date book, he thanked the man and hung up.

Literary Lions, his under-construction biopic series about classic American authors, had seemed uncomplicated when he'd first come up with the concept, which he envisioned as ideal for public television. The money he might earn was likely to be modest, but as a tenured professor, he was doing fine. And as Julian had reminded him recently, he already had a lot more of everything—time, money, security, opportunity— than most of the world's citizens. Mitch had admitted this was true, and said, "Now do we sing a chorus of 'We are the World'?" It was a nervous tic of a joke, he knew it even as the words left his mouth. Julian had been generous about it, though, saying, "Sure, Dad—you start."

Mitch propped his feet on his desk and leaned back. His old leather chair squealed with the motion, testifying that, while tenure equaled job security, there were no luxuries in the academe. If he could make *Lions* fly—the image made him chuckle—he would reward himself with a new chair. That *if* was a big one, however, and *uncomplicated* was proving to be a bit enthusiastic on his part.

To begin with, writing the script for the first episode, the *pilot,* as it was called, was more challenging than he'd anticipated. He'd imagined it as something like prepping a lecture for twenty students. However, a few torturous nights of script writing had proven that a low-stakes lecture was nothing like crafting an entertaining and informative hour-long program for a million viewers, all armed with remote controls.

Okay, maybe a million was a little zealous, to start. Thousands, though—surely he could count on thousands.

The script was coming along.

Overcoming his anxiety about inviting Julian to direct and film the pilot had been difficult, too. It required actively facing the fourteen-year-wide chasm in their relationship, which had been only minimally bridged when they were together at the hospital in Miami last fall after Mitch's father had a stroke.

In the hospital corridor that day, without the usual buffer of his parents and an occasion like Christmas or graduation, it had been hard to know how to greet Julian. He'd wanted to hug him, something he hadn't done since Julian was a pre-adolescent, but sensed the desire wasn't mutual. He patted his shoulder instead.

"Dad's going to be all right," he said, "but it's really nice that you could get here." Julian had been at the beginning of his Afghanistan assignment then; traveling to Miami had taken him the better part of two days. The strain showed in his tired eyes—or was that strain from his work? Mitch worried about his living conditions and his safety and his diet, and whether Julian had found the comforting companionship of a woman—none of which he felt entitled to ask about. So he said, simply, "How are things?"

"Busy. You?"

"Oh, fine—busy." He searched for something more to say as the silence dragged out. Then, inspired, he'd blurted, "Hey, one of my grad students is a portrait photographer on the side."

"Oh?"

"I thought you'd find that interesting. A lit major who's also a pho-tographer." He knew he was trying too hard, knew his eagerness would be plain on his face. He was one of those people whose expressions translated every thought, every emotion as it happened.

But Julian wasn't looking at him. "Sure, interesting," he'd said.

"So . . . are you getting a lot of work?"

Julian nodded. "Too much."

Julian's chosen career was in documenting human tragedies, people who were victims of governments, of bureaucracy and neglect. That day, Mitch had stood there next to his mature, experienced, world-traveler son and for the first time felt just slightly lesser in comparison. A strange feeling—chagrin and pride and envy, none of which had any place in a Miami hospital ICU ward when a man they loved was laying ill a dozen feet away—and yet there it was.

"Good that you could get here," he'd said again.

Before he found the nerve to call Julian a few weeks later, to ask for his help with *Lions,* he'd tried to anticipate all possible objections. There was Julian's lack of interest in the subject matter—Hemingway, Julian had declared once during a Thanksgiving dinner at Mitch's parents' home, was too depressing. And Faulkner, God, spare him from ever reading Faulkner again! Even back then, as a sixteen- or seventeen-year-old, Julian hadn't wanted to read about problems; he'd wanted to read about solutions.

Then there was the lack of funds from which to pay Julian very much beyond basic expenses, and his fear that his low-pay offer could be interpreted as disregard for the value of Julian's skills, given how Mitch had so steadfastly resisted Julian's photojournalism career choice. In Mitch's limited experience, Julian was an emotional minefield, and while he didn't blame him for it—blamed himself, in fact, he also didn't relish treading there with no detector.

So when Mitch finally did place the call, he did it after two shots of whisky, then rushed through his pitch, making the project sound as ap-pealing as possible, braced for resistance, for disdain. That he'd gotten neither was still difficult to believe.

He was both anxious and eager to see Julian, to spend some quality time with him, as the saying went these days. He was both anxious and eager to get the project underway, to open people's eyes to the joy and value of literature. But . . . suppose *Lions* didn't ultimately win the interest of PBS. Suppose he invested so much—his time, his money, his ego—only to see the door slammed in his face.

He stood up and went again to the window. There were worse things than rejection, worse things than disappointment. But he'd had enough of both.

A knock on his open door startled him, and as he turned toward the door, he stumbled slightly and reached for the bookcase for balance.

"Mitch!"

"I'm fine," he said, holding off Brenda McCallum with a raised hand. "You surprised me is all."

"You looked—"

"No, really, I'm fine. See?" He did a few soft-shoe steps on the bright Cuban rug to prove he was not about to end up as her husband had last April, in this very office. Craig McCallum, fellow professor, best friend and biking buddy, had suffered a brain aneurysm and died on Mitch's small sofa while they'd all waited helplessly for the paramedics to arrive. Today was Mitch's fifty-first birthday; Craig had been just fifty.

Brenda continued to watch him. "I saw your door was still open. Aren't you running late?"

"Yes, but they won't start without me," he joked, and gathered the books he needed for the morning's ENG 620: The Twentieth-century Novel. His fifteen graduate students, if they were all in attendance, would be seated around the conference table, most with their noses buried in *The Age of Innocence* because they'd failed to read all, or any, of what was to be discussed today. His late arrival would not be troubling.

Brenda was frowning at him. "What's going on? You look funny."

"Thanks for that vote of confidence."

"You know what I mean. Odd."

"Really, nothing at all. Just lost in thought. I've been on the phone with a guy in Key West, about how to shoot part of the *Lions* pilot there at the Home and Museum. I'll fill you in later." He squeezed her shoulder and nodded for her to precede him to the door.

She took his hand. "Mitch . . ."

"Why don't we get lunch when I'm done?" he said, letting her keep hold for a moment longer. "I'm in the mood for barbecue, how about you?"

In part because he was so distracted, he devised an exercise for his students that would take most of the class period. While they sat in groups of three or four outlining literary elements in the novel and discussing possible authorial intentions, he stood at the podium thinking about Brenda. Things were warming up between them, certainly. If he was ambivalent, well, that was to be expected. She was not only Craig's widow; she was the chair of the English department. As his friend Tony had put it, if Mitch wasn't careful, Brenda could easily have his balls in a sling.

Better, maybe, to think about Hemingway.

After decades of teaching, Mitch knew his ideas about literature weren't going to change the world. Oh sure, he'd managed to impress his colleagues a time or two or three, he'd won teaching awards, he'd set at least a dozen students on the path to prominent literary scholarship. He'd also faced down a handful of annoyed undergraduates over the years who demanded to know what the *point* of it was. Who cared about evaluating whether Hemingway's prose was more effective than Faulkner's? What difference did it make that Hemingway had a tough time as a soldier, that even with the respect and awards—a Nobel for literature, for God's sake, plus the devotion of a forgiving wife (or four)—he'd pointed a shotgun at his head and killed himself? What about what was happening to ordinary soldiers *now*, friends of theirs, in Iraq in the nineties, in Afghanistan and Iraq again today?

He'd nodded his agreement. He'd said, yes, my son feels this way too. There was no convincing some people—or he was not persuasive enough to convince them—that they would find their positions right there in the texts if they just gave the books a chance. Wharton, Hemingway, Faulkner—they had it all: passion, romance, existential questions, the human condition imbued in every story. "Give it a chance," he'd say. "Give me a break," was the answer he usually got. Or, what Julian had said that day some fourteen years ago: "Get a life. That's what *I'm* going to do."

But what Julian hadn't understood then was that not everyone was interested in, or equipped to travel, *his* chosen path, either. Some people were spotlights, some were reflectors. The world needed both. Yes, he'd pushed Julian too hard at the time, he saw that later. He'd been too passionate, too eager, too single-minded; he hadn't recognized how Julian was already so much like him—and still was. Just not in the ways he had wanted him to be.

Well, he'd mellowed. Which didn't mean he was any less passionate about literature's relevance. *Literary Lions* grew from his urge to demonstrate that relevance in a new way . . . and, if he was fully honest, demonstrate his own relevance as well. Since Craig's sudden death, he'd gone around feeling as though he had one foot in the grave. What was his legacy, other than a collection of articles, a couple of books read by approximately fourteen people, two failed marriages, and a strained relationship with his only son? With *Lions,* he hoped to rectify the past and revise his outlook for the future.

A future that appeared to want Brenda in it in ways he'd hardly imagined.

"Dr. Forrester? *Dr. Forrester?*" A student's voice penetrated, finally.

"Sorry—you caught me daydreaming about, um, spending spring break in Key West," he said. "What can I do for you?"

"Well, I was going to ask if Archer's mistaken perception of May is a good example of dramatic irony—but I like your new topic better."

To celebrate Mitch's fifty-first birthday, he and Brenda joined two other couples at Mez, a new "green" Mexican restaurant Brenda wanted to try. Deirdre and Corbin he'd known since moving to Chapel Hill: she taught human genetics, he taught physics. Mitch met them at a UNC basketball game. The other pair was Tony and Gemma, both college administrators whose friendship stretched back to a time when he was dating Angie, who'd worked with Tony in the recruiting office. The couple's friendship was one of the few things he'd kept when he and Angie split.

Deirdre raised her margarita and said, "Here's to Mitch. Good to see you made it another year, and that you're making it with Brenda—oops, I didn't mean that like it sounded!"

"To Mitch," the group echoed.

"To making it," Tony added.

By the third pitcher of margaritas, their dinner plates were cleared and Mitch was discussing *Lions* with much less reluctance than usual. According to some in the English department—not Brenda, but others— the idea of such a series was seditious: Literature was not *video*, for crying out loud, and never the twain should meet. Just look at what Hollywood had done to *Frankenstein*! It hardly mattered that he wasn't attempting to adapt any of the works. They felt he would be making their world common, and that would never do.

Corbin, however, was all about demystifying the universe, especially when the tequila was doing its work on him. "I think the show's got serious possibilities," he said.

"It does," Brenda agreed. "Mitch is so knowledgeable—and so popular! It never fails, his classes fill on the first day of registration."

Gemma said, "Serious, like, he gets millions of dollars and moves to Hollywood?"

Everyone looked at Mitch, who shook his head. "Not likely."

Corbin preferred his vision. "It's happened."

"To whom?" Brenda scoffed, left eyebrow raised just as it often was during faculty meetings.

"All kinds of people. Just look at all the shows where a chef or a decorator or a geographist—"

Tony snorted. "A *geographist*? What the hell's that?"

Deirdre said, "A historicist of places—"

"These experts," Corbin said, "*supposed* experts sometimes— *attractive,* supposed experts, right? These people get a break and then, boom! They're superstars—like Steve Irwin, for instance. Simon Cowell." He nodded at Brenda. "It happens."

Mitch said, "I just want to share some literary love." Tony clinked his glass to Mitch's.

"Seriously," Deirdre said, "you're wa-a-ay more attractive than Simon. I can see it."

Brenda shook her head. "That's not realistic. If he went into it with those kinds of expectations—"

Gemma said, "Somebody refill her glass!"

"No, come on, I'm just trying to be the voice of reason."

"Who wants reason, for crying out loud?" Gemma stood up, nearly tipping the table. "We want fame, and money!"

The patrons around them cheered.

Corbin, laughing, said, "Okay, okay, but I don't know that we're winning the birthday boy enough points to score later, so . . . how about those Tarheels?"

Talk turned to the team's recent performance in the ACC basketball tournament, but Mitch's tipsy mind stayed stuck on Corbin's last statement. Would he "score" later? Of course he wanted to, even as he was unsure how wise it was to take his revised friendship with the woman who was also his boss—more or less—to that complicated level. She was lovely, and more desirable than he'd let himself acknowledge when Craig was alive. Want was not a question. Neither did it mean, though, that they would—or should—sleep together.

Did she want to?

His questions ceased when he felt her hand on his thigh. His libido took over for his brain, making it much easier for him to later accept the birthday present that she was saying, softly, close to his ear, waited for him when they were through.

4

*A*fter climbing the jet's steps and greeting the flight crew Saturday morning, Blue took a seat in the spot she preferred, left side, just in front of the wing. The jet, customized to the most demanding celebrity standards, wasn't hers. She could not do it, could not transform the numbers on her accounts statement into one of these sleek white and silver aircraft. They'd chartered this Gulfstream G500 for the week, a $65,000 expense. That was far less than the $50 million or so she'd pay to purchase one. How many times could they charter luxury jets before they even approached that figure? She was too tired to do the math, but surely it was many, many times. Buying one seemed wasteful—and imagine what Melody would say if she owned a Gulfstream, when Mel and Jeff still drove a '95 Chevy pickup.

In a meeting last year, when Jim, her business manager, spoke about capital investments and appreciable assets and tax advantages of ownership, Marcy had said, "*Buy* one. What else are you going to do with the money?"

"More of what I'm doing already." An assortment of charitable endeavors selected and implemented by Jim's partner, who briefed her about them monthly. Trust funds awaiting her nephews on their twenty-fifth birthdays. A bottomless account for her mother—and for her sister if Melody would see past her pride to accept it.

After ten years in syndication and almost as many spent watching her finance manager diversify her holdings in a series of double-up ventures, of seeing her net worth mushroom with the energy of an atomic blast, Blue still could not quite match the numbers to her life. She could not quite believe—even as she inhabited them—what those numbers meant in concrete terms. If she had known things could turn out like *this*, chartered jets with hand-stitched leather seats and burnished walnut tables, silk twill pants suits and everyday diamond earrings, twenty-eight full-time employees whose houses and cars and designer martinis were bought with paychecks she signed . . . If she could have forecasted her success the way her old WLVC-TV colleague Carl Newman forecasted the weather, she never would have given up her son.

—Or so she liked to think, when the truth was that she wouldn't have stepped onto even the first rung of this ladder if she'd had a child. The whole idea of working as a television journalist was about avoiding *Harmony Blue Kucharski* by keeping her attention on anyone, on *every*one, else. If she had not given up her son, an uneducated single mother with little support and no prospects is what she would have been. Worse off than her mother at nineteen, the child worse off than the child *she'd* been.

Yet the doubts persisted. How could she really know what her life with a child would have been like? She had never even tried—but, why would she have chosen to try when she'd known that her mother couldn't help her out? Why get attached to a child whose life you could only ruin? In that hand-to-mouth life there would be no time to love the child properly, and all that would come of it would be a kid who hated her and hated his life, she'd been sure of it.

But what if . . . what if she had gotten hooked up with the social services she now knew would have given her—them—options? Someone could have directed her, surely *would* have, if she'd been brave enough to expose her foolishness to someone who, unlike the midwife, had no directed agenda. If she had not been too embarrassed, too proud to go looking for unbiased help.

Well even if she had, she'd still have been a lower-class single mother whose good intentions simply could not come close to providing what that upper-class adoptive home could. Did. Love by itself was not enough to make everything come out happily, she didn't care what all those feel-good movies claimed. She'd loved her son—loved him so much that she had sacrificed her relationship with him. It was the right thing to do.

She was pretty sure.

She snapped her seat belt closed. Stupid conundrum, why couldn't she let it alone?

Sometimes, when the heartache and guilt overwhelmed her, she pared off a piece for her mother, whose own questionable decisions had led to hers, and for Mitch, because if he'd hung on to her there would have been no other man, no accidental son. Still, the remaining portion was too large to swallow; she could only cover it with a pretty napkin and act as if it didn't exist.

She would not be able to keep it covered, though, if the ravenous media sniffed it out—which could happen only if one of the few people involved decided to capitalize on insider knowledge. This was the fear that dogged her in her quiet moments, had been dogging her ever since she'd contracted to do *TBRS*, the fear that had grown in proportion to her success.

If she'd had that ability to see into her future and to feel the way the guilt, the fear would bind her, she would have announced her history at her first employment interview. *I'm not proud of myself*, she might have said, *but I may as well tell you* . . . Except that there had been no benefit to telling; all the benefit lay in keeping the truth of who she was and how she lived out of sight, where it couldn't affect the way people perceived her. She'd been using the strategy all her life.

The risk now, after having long ago established a child-free bio, was in being outed as a liar and a hypocrite. Her most ardent fans, the ones who watched her every day, who knew her so intimately (they thought), would feel betrayed—and to paraphrase an old saying, hell hath no fury like a fan scorned. Especially these days, when the Internet gave anyone with access to a computer a giant-size megaphone with which to vent. Others would delight in ridiculing her. Her competition would pounce on the opportunity to knock her out of first place—or worse. The show would suffer, maybe even fail, and then what? Who would she be if she was not *Blue*?

Only a court order could expose her son's original birth certificate, and until her son had come of age a little more than three years ago, only his adoptive parents could seek such an order—and if any of them did, she would know about it when it happened. That was the law. She would receive notice, allowing her to protest or protect or defend. Of the few people in her past who might know both who she'd become and what she'd done first, only Meredith and Marcy were credible. Meredith, she hoped, would continue to put ethics ahead of self-interest, as she'd presumably been doing all this time. And Marcy? Well, self-protection was certainly not the reason Blue had kept Marcy close all these years, but she did rest more easily having her in sight, and happy.

The law that protected her was the same law that protected her son's identity. Hence her hiring of Branford, whose job it was to find another route to the answer—not so that she could make contact, necessarily; just so she could *know.* That it was proving so difficult for Branford to find the midwife, the answer-keeper, was sometimes disheartening, sometimes reassuring, depending on which emotional lens she happened to be looking through when she let the thoughts idle in her mind.

She looked out the jet's window, where six-inch-deep snow glowed pale pink as the sun approached the horizon, delineating the taxiways and runways, which were wet but clear. The day's first commercial flights were already stacked up down the field, and the steady rumble of morning traffic noise was punctuated every few minutes by the roar of jets lifting off for New York and Minneapolis, St. Louis and San Diego, Raleigh, Denver, Las Vegas, Seattle. One of those jets, full of morning business commuters and eager vacationers, might, in a few hours, be landing in a city close to where her son would be waking up.

She'd played this imaginary game so many times over the years. At first she had imagined a snuggly infant in a soft blue sleeper, held in the arms of a woman who looked out her window upon San Francisco Bay. Then it was a toddler in footed pajamas, and Puget Sound. The parents and the midwife, Meredith, had said west *coast* but, over time, Blue realized this was a generic descriptor; the family might as easily be in Sacramento or Olympia or Salt Lake City. And who could say whether they'd moved since then—or whether they'd truly been there to begin with?

Blue would wake up and, as she padded through her Chicago apartment, think of a dark-haired little boy waiting for the school bus with a Power Rangers lunchbox clasped in pudgy fingers. She would open the curtains of her New York City flat, and imagine a gangly boy hauling hockey gear into an ice arena for early morning ice time. She would sit on a stool as a stylist readied her for a *Vanity Fair* photo shoot, and see a teenager, hair falling into his eyes, choosing jeans and a Hollister sweater for senior pictures.

This morning she thought of a young man with slender hands and long eyelashes, still asleep in a posh private college dorm. With the life his parents had provided him, the care, the education, he could be at Princeton or Harvard or Notre Dame. In a coincidence too ironic to want to consider, he could this moment be across town at Northwestern University.

Northwestern, where Mitch Forrester had been teaching when she met him. If her son had been Mitch's son, if her wishes on Sirius had been granted . . . well, everything would be different, wouldn't it? She would still be Harmony Blue Kucharski—or perhaps she'd have taken Mitch's name; she'd practiced writing it both ways during those few short months when she'd seen her wishes edge tantalizingly close to reality. And instead of touring the Hemingway Home in Key West in front of a camera crew as she would do on Friday, she might have toured it with Mitch, whose aim it had been to become the preeminent Hemingway scholar. Mitch, who in effect had chosen to take refuge from the turmoil in his life with a dead literary idol, rather than a living young woman who idolized *him*. Well, it was his choice to make; it would be interesting to know if he thought it was the right one.

At the sound of Marcy's "Good morning," Blue looked up to see her, puffy-eyed and yawning, as she sat down in the seat opposite Blue. Stephen, so tall that his messy black hair brushed the aircraft's ceiling, was right behind her. He took the seat across the aisle from Marcy and reached for her hand. Both of them looked sleepy, tousled, as if they'd climbed out of bed and straight into Marcy's limo. Of limos, black Lincoln Town Cars with full-time drivers, they had four: one each for Blue, Marcy, and Peter, and one kept at-large, for ferrying guests.

Blue would have preferred not to witness Marcy and Stephen's bed-head coziness. But she smiled as though she found them adorable. "Morning. Looks like good weather for travel."

"Do they have coffee ready?" Stephen asked, stroking one arm of his seat with his free hand. "Nice leather. I'm desperate for some caffeine."

Marcy was nodding in agreement. "Vanilla-double-espresso-whipped, now *that* would be fab-u-lous," she said. She rubbed her face and pulled back her hair. "But holy Christ, it would be so much easier to just pop a pill."

Blue flagged the flight attendant who waited in the galley pretending not to stare. "Easier," Blue agreed, "but not as tasty."

"Lower calorie, though," Marcy sighed. "And fast-acting, which I could use. Peter called me at five fifteen, insisting I log on to YouTube."

"You—?" Blue started, then she knew. "The bit with Stacey and me, the tears, right?"

Marcy nodded. "It's viral. You know how it goes. Peter sounded like he could use a tranquilizer."

"Vultures," Blue muttered.

The attendant came over and Blue requested coffee while Stephen stretched out his legs and crossed them at the ankle. He said, "Speaking of pills, last night Marcy was telling me all about the good old days."

Blue shot Marcy a look of disapproval.

"We were doing tequila teasers," Marcy said, her half-smile an apology. "A little practice, you know, for Duval Street. I told Stephen how we roomed together in our little house, and maybe got a bit wild a time or two. Nothing serious," she said. Blue caught her look of assurance and relaxed a little.

"Oh, well, that's true. We did have a wild time or two." Or fifty. If she could recall those early months' adventures, she might be able to count them. "You know how kids are when they first leave home." Naïve. Stubborn. Self-destructive—those were Blue's personal adjectives. Not that she was about to say so, and Marcy had better not, either.

Stephen, apparently, was chatty in the morning even without the benefit of caffeine. He asked Blue, "So why did you change your name?"

"Do you know what my mother named me?"

"Yeah, *Harmony* Blue . . . Kucharski?"

"There you have it," she said.

It had been years since anyone aside from her mother had brought up the name change, a change made legal so long ago that neither the media nor the public thought to question it. Her given name was not so awful, despite how she'd felt about it when she had to explain it to yet another teacher, principal, classmate. Back then, she'd been embarrassed to admit she'd gotten the name because her mother liked the anemone, *harmony blue*. Later, during what she and Marcy now referred to as "the recovery period" when she'd set her sights on working at WLVC, they'd agreed it just wasn't a name for television.

Stephen said, "It's cool, isn't it? You're Harmony and your sister's Melody. Harmony and Melody. You should've been singers, or songwriters."

"Now why didn't I ever think of that?"

"Marcy says your mother is a trip."

"Marcy ought to know." She took most of Nancy Kucharski's calls. The two women were as close as blood relatives. Closer, probably; they didn't share any baggage.

Marcy said, "It's a flower. Blue's named after a flower."

A sturdy, pale blue-to-violet flower that had grown in the shade garden of her grandmother Kate Kucharski's postage-stamp yard. That was the way Kate had described it to Blue, *postage-stamp*. Near that garden, Blue's mother, the adolescent Nancy Kucharski, daydreamed away her summer evenings—until she started meeting boys who had cars. And, at some point, a particular boy whose name began with *L*. Taking advantage of her mother's overindulgent parenting style, young Nancy had launched her dating life at fifteen and, except for two pauses to gestate and deliver two daughters, had never stopped since.

The story Blue had liked to hear when she was young began not with teenage Nancy but with baby Harmony Blue, being delivered to the little house by a stork, Kate always said, which Blue had imagined as a white-feathered version of Big Bird. But the little house was too small; soon they moved to a bigger place, an apartment with three bedrooms. The stork brought Melody there.

In the evenings, when her mother was out and Melody was already asleep, Blue had urged her grandmother to tell her again about the home she'd been brought to as a newborn. When Grandma Kate described the yard of that house that way, *postage-stamp*, young Blue imagined a million little squares pasted down where grass would have been. A broad, level, gymnasium-sized spread of stamps, some of them as exotic as the ones that appeared on her mother's airmail envelopes. The ones from "guys" who wrote from wherever the U.S. Army had assigned them after something called a draft. Germany. The Philippines. Vietnam. Was one of those guys her father? Was the *L* from Cambodia the *L* tattooed on her mother's hip? Did that explain the absence of a man in their home, when almost all the homes around them had mothers and *fathers*, not grandmothers?

"Don't you worry about that father stuff," her mother told her once, face close to the mirror while she darkened the mole on her right cheekbone, a mole matching the one that had just appeared on Blue's five-year-old cheek. The *L* was covered that night by brown polyester bell-bottoms and a cheap gold-colored hip chain that draped low. Her mother rumpled her hair. "You two are my precious little gifts from God."

Blue had tried to believe that being a stork-delivered package straight from heaven made her superior to other children, children whose fifties-era ranch homes looked just like the one they moved into next, but whose families inside those homes did not. Those were common children. Normal children, who had normal families. What she knew, though, was that they were what she would never be, never have. What use in hoping otherwise? What use in puzzling over a black tattoo that was covered up almost all the time?

She'd made a valiant effort to be like her mother, like Mel. Nothing fazed them. Mel's first tattoo, done when Mel was sixteen, was a wreath of words around her upper arm that read "Frankie Say Relax." Blue had been as impressed with the act as with the sentiment. If Mel could be so bold, why couldn't she? At the library, she paged through books with tattoo designs and slogans. She drew one on her ankle in permanent marker, a vine with heart-shaped leaves, then hid her work beneath her sock until the ink wore off. The truth of it was that when she was alone she sometimes still hummed "When You Wish Upon a Star," and waited for all things to right themselves, the way they surely would.

Voices from up near the cockpit told Blue that Peter and his wife had arrived. "Are we on schedule?" she heard him asking. She imagined him holding a stopwatch and waiting to tell the pilot, *Go!* If she was lucky, he would stay up there; she had no desire to hear him fret aloud about tears and ratings and ridicule.

The flight attendant brought coffee in stoneware mugs, delivered from a cloth-draped tray. "What else can I bring you? We'll be wheels up in about five minutes."

"I don't know," Marcy said. "Blue, do you want anything?"

"No." Or nothing that could be stocked on board, at any rate.

Janelle and Peter joined them in the cabin. "Did Marcy tell you?" Peter said. His round face was flushed and he was rubbing the top of his balding head, his habit when stressed. "YouTube, *Perez*—we cut it from our time-delayed broadcasts but it doesn't matter, it's everywhere. We're telling everyone that your dog died yesterday morning, okay?"

"I don't even have a dog."

Peter looked at her as if she was simple. "Work with me here, Blue."

*A*fter cruising over what from Blue's east-facing view looked like an infinite expanse of ocean, the Gulfstream bumped through clear but turbulent air and landed at the Key West airport, three hours ahead of when the crew would arrive via commercial airline. That airline provided *TBRS* with free freight and free airfare for the equipment and its users, for which Blue would thank them at the beginning and end of each broadcast in the week to come. That was how it was done. Endless backscratching—so much that sometimes her back was raw from it.

"Jesus, there's nothing *to* this place," Stephen said, looking out his window as the jet taxied toward the terminal.

Blue leaned to look and saw a long stretch of shell-pink building that could pass for a warehouse except for the presence of two small jets and a gaggle of single-engine aircraft tethered close by. She said, "What were you expecting?"

"I don't know, something like Honolulu, maybe. Something that doesn't look like we're going to have to unload our own gear."

"God forbid," Peter said from his seat behind Blue. "We wouldn't want to overwork our *guests*."

Blue told Stephen, "I'm sure it'll be fine." Yes, the airport was small, nondescript, but what was not to like? A thousand feet past the terminal was the Atlantic Ocean, sea green and gleaming, brilliant in the midday sun. Plus, there were palm trees; she'd always thought palm trees worth any amount of trouble, even unloading one's own bags from the belly of a multimillion-dollar chartered jet.

A contingent of Key West folk was waiting to greet Blue as she descended the plane's steps into the midday heat. A stout man of about forty came forward, his flowered shirt's buttons straining such that it was obvious he'd bought the shirt fifteen or more pounds ago. Several photographers circled them, jockeying for position.

The mayor extended his hand. "Welcome to the Conch Republic!"

"Thank you, Mr. Mayor," Blue said, remembering his face from her prep file, but forgetting his name. It wouldn't matter, Mr. Mayor always worked—or Ms. Mayor, as the case sometimes was. "It's so thoughtful of you to take time out from your full schedule to meet our plane."

"Oh, it's no trouble. I speak for everyone here when I say we are delighted to have *The Blue Reynolds Show* in town. Whatever I can do to make your stay more enjoyable, you just let me know. Anything. I mean it. That's a promise."

Blue smiled her public smile, clearly delighting the man, who beamed in return. She said, "Yes, I will, I'll let you know."

Outside the terminal a few minutes later, Peter stood at the curb where a battered, empty Toyota was idling in spite of the NO PARKING signs. He said, "Do you think the mayor could find out where our limo might be?"

Marcy took out her phone. "I'm sure I stored the number in here . . . they must just be running late . . ."

Blue stepped away from the group and leaned against a pole to wait, letting the heat and the salt smell of the air be her real welcome. She closed her eyes, just for a moment, and savored the illusion of invisibility she'd once believed in when she was small.

There'd been a lot of waiting during her childhood, mostly waiting for her mother's return—from a date, from a new-town-scouting trip, from a dead-end job. Melody, passive and untroubled, watched a lot of TV, entertained by *Mork and Mindy* or *Remington Steele*. Blue, anxious, distractible, had better luck with books.

Without the interruption of commercials or the finite images of someone else's interpretation of a story, she could more easily fit herself into the romance or drama unfolding inside a book's cover. She filled empty hours, when her homework was done and the paper plates from dinner were cleared from the coffee table, with stories of clever women who won over reluctant bachelors. Women who defied parents or society in order to follow their hearts—inevitably to romance, and often to fame and wealth. Or women who traveled to exotic places in astonishing jets and were greeted by mayors who were glad to do their bidding. What a glamorous life, and so far removed from reality that she never thought to jump the chasm between her vicarious thrills and the methodical plotting that living such a life would require.

No, what she'd planned for was far more predictable and achievable: When she and Melody were both out of school, she would use what she earned working for Lynn Forrester to put herself through college and become a high school English teacher. She'd assign her students the books she was growing to love under Mr. Forrester's guidance: books about Mark Twain's river life, Willa Cather's prairies, and of course the battlefields and savannahs and islands that featured in Hemingway's troubled imagination. At eighteen, she hardly understood the causes of Hemingway's torments, but she had an instinctive feel for the tragedies in his stories. What is tragedy, though, at eighteen? It's romance, and it was romance that had been fixed in her mind that fall after she met Mitch. Romance, and a steadfast determination that, whatever she did, she would not allow her life to turn out like her mother's.

That, at least, had gone as planned.

5

$\mathcal{M}$itch sat on a bar stool in his parents' kitchen, looking at the shopping list his mother, Lynn, had just handed him.

5# potatoes
5# shrimp
8 lobster tails
Lemons
Romaine
Tomatoes, onion
Cornmeal
Butter (unsalted)
2 Key Lime pies—Blond Giraffe

"A person could gain ten pounds just reading this list," he said. "There are only four of us, you know."

His mother, who'd begun rearranging things in her crowded freezer, leaned around the door to squint at him critically. "I think you'd better stop at two or three pounds. You're officially over fifty now, and you know, the older you are, the stickier those pounds get."

"Tough to stop when I'm around enablers like you," he said. "You want me to buy *two* pies and also show restraint?"

"We need two," she said, going back to her task. "While you all were in the pool, I invited the girls from next door."

"The girls" would be the new neighbors, Kira and Lori, who he'd met soon after arriving this morning and who had wasted no time in telling how they'd met each other (at Fantasy Fest) and, thanks to some very savvy stock trading on Lori's part, could now afford to call the place home. They'd also wanted to know everything about *him*. The things his mother hadn't already told them, that is. Things she said she didn't know. For example, how serious were he and his traveling companion, Brenda? She looked like such a nice woman, they said, from the glimpse they'd gotten through the flowering hedgerow. Was she really a professor of Victorian literature? "Indeed she is," he'd answered. "And she just published a wonderful book on Lewis Carroll—Duke University Press, you should pick it up." They'd looked at one another with suppressed laughter in their eyes. "No, seriously," he'd said, "it's really good."

"I was wondering," he asked his mother, "why did you tell them about Brenda?"

"Oh, you know how it goes. We hang out in the kitchen, we make a pot of tea, we chat, things come up. They were curious. We're all curious."

"Hmm." In fact Mitch, too, was curious. He'd known Brenda for sixteen years, but there was no telling what would happen now that they'd gone ahead and dipped their toes into more intimate waters. Well, a little more than their toes, which was going to take some getting used to. The only reason he'd told his parents was as forewarning that Brenda, who they'd known was joining him for this visit, would now also be sharing his room.

Not once, while she was his best friend's wife, had he coveted Craig's nights with her. Not once had he mentally undressed her, let alone imagined more—though he had certainly noticed her curves and the appealing play of freckles on her skin, the times he'd seen her in a swimsuit. Taken more notice after he and Angie split, true. He'd noticed every attractive woman at that time, the start of a six-year stretch of single life dotted with oases of relationships with women who were more reluctant to get involved than to get *busy,* as the saying went. Call him old-fashioned, but he liked to truly know a woman before he and she took their clothes off together.

He was proud of having made only one embarrassing, clichéd, mid-life mistake: last year, with a twenty-four-year-old graduate student who was also his teaching assistant. An aspiring writer (they were all as-piring writers), her quiet demeanor belied the specific and vivid tell-alls she posted on her Web log, or rather *blog*—he was still playing catch-up on the evolving vocabulary. Her good judgment was lacking, true, but at least her writing was skillful: she'd written a post that said he was "suf-ficiently endowed, and capable with all the tools in his toolkit," which, revealing as it was, was still nice to know, and he was also "tender, re-ally; a credit to his gender." His colleagues had enough ammunition with which to ridicule him, they didn't need purple prose, too.

Brenda had not, however, been any kind of prospect until she was suddenly widowed. Their new closeness might owe more to shared grief than shared passion . . . except, after last night it was clear the passion wasn't lacking, not in the least. Was she just using him as a stand-in? Was she going to wake up tomorrow morning, or maybe Sunday, or next week, and realize he was only superficially like Craig?

Fine time to worry about that now.

He scooted his stool back and stood up. "So then," he said, folding the list and putting it into his pants pocket, "the girls are joining us for dinner. Anyone else?"

"No—oh, except they're bringing the baby, so you better pick up some Cheerios, and some apple juice, too."

He smiled. "Mom, I think they'll have the baby's needs covered."

"Probably, but you never know."

Mitch's father came into the kitchen, having changed his swim trunks for plaid shorts in red tones, which he'd paired with a blue tropical-print shirt. His crew-cut white hair was spiked and shining with hair gel. "What don't you know?"

"More like what *you* don't know," Mitch said, shaking his head. "About matching."

"And what *you* don't know, about style and attitude. Let's hit the road."

Mitch looked down at his white golf shirt. It *was* boring. "Soon as Brenda's changed," he said.

His father sat down at the table. "Right, right, Brenda. How about you two?"

Mitch shrugged. "We'll see how it goes."

"I understand that," his father said. "I hear it from the damn doctor all the time." About the progress he was making, and was expected to make, recovering from his stroke. He was doing well, tackling the challenges of speech and motor control with determination born of stubbornness. The remaining challenge was in how they were all supposed to deal with what the neurologist could only describe as "crossed wires"—the highly technical term used to explain how it was that his father now and then slipped into another man's persona. And not just any man: astronaut Ken Mattingly, who his father had known as a teenager while living in Miami in the fifties and whose career he'd followed ever since. The delusions were disconcerting, to say the least. One minute his father was Daniel Forrester and then, with no outward sign, he was the astronaut, only with Daniel's memories conflated with what Daniel must imagine Mattingly's life had been. Mitch found it maddening—he never knew who he'd get when he called—but his mother was actually entertained. "Gives me a little variety," she'd said.

"Listen," she said now, closing the freezer. "Get the lobster and shrimp from Rusty's, over on Stock Island—Daniel, you can direct him—and you know what? Forget buying cornmeal, just bring home some of their conch fritters."

She stood with her hands on her generous hips, surveying the kitchen as though looking for something that had just snuck away under her nose—the most iconic image he had of her, dating as far back as he could remember. Then she said, "Oh! Dad told you about *The Blue Reynolds Show* being in town this coming week, yes?"

Did his pulse jump a little with those words? If Blue Reynolds remembered him at all, it would be for things he wished he could take back. He said, "No, he must have forgotten."

"I did forget, damn it!" His father slapped the tabletop. "But how about that, eh Mitch? The one you let get away."

Brenda's footsteps were audible as she came down the hall from the guest room they were sharing. The same one he'd shared with Angie. It didn't matter that he was now fifty-one and twice divorced, he still felt awkward about rooming with a new girlfriend in his parents' home. That they had known Brenda for a decade and a half was no help; they knew her as Craig's wife, now widow. She was his colleague who taught works by the Brontës and Dickens and Carroll, not a woman he slept with. Did any of them feel as weird about this as he did?

Brenda stopped in the doorway to the kitchen. Her short auburn hair was dry, and she was wearing a summery black knit dress with a neckline that plunged a little farther than was usual for her. "Who did you let get away?"

"Blue Reynolds," he said, attempting to sound casual, as though he also had Kate Capshaw and Kim Basinger in his past. "Only she wasn't Blue Reynolds back then."

"*You* dated Blue Reynolds? When?" She couldn't have looked more surprised if he'd told her he had moonlighted as a porn star. So much for sounding casual.

He repositioned a mango atop a bowl filled with fruit. "It's not a big deal—and it was a long time ago."

"Twenty-three years," his father said.

Mitch was stunned. "You can remember *that*?"

His father shrugged.

"Blue Reynolds, really?" Brenda said as Mitch took his parents' car keys off the hook near the counter. "You never told us—or me, at any rate, that you knew her."

"It never came up." Even Craig hadn't known. "Shall we?" he asked, holding up the keys.

He hoped Brenda didn't think he'd hidden the information deliberately. In truth, he'd never thought his short relationship with Harmony Blue, as she was called back then, was worth divulging to anyone, especially since she'd become *Blue*. What point was there? Sure, it would make great cocktail party fodder, but he'd be barraged with questions he either didn't enjoy answering or had no answers for.

They had been young—or she had; too young for the complexities of his life at the time. He should've known better than to keep dropping by his mother's office over that first winter, ostensibly to lend a hand with some rearranging and remodeling of the office space. There was something innately compelling about Blue, though, even back then. She was somehow both tough and vulnerable, somehow experienced and innocent, and lord, she was pretty. Their nine-year age difference was not *so* huge. He was not *Lolita*'s Humbert Humbert, for God's sake.

If he'd been teaching during the summer session, that year after she finished high school, or if Renee, his first wife, hadn't hauled Julian off to Maine for two months, he'd have been too busy to notice her. As it was, he'd gone from the intensity—or more like the insanity—of juggling a teaching load of three classes, his research, Renee's demands and fits of jealousy, and erratic fatherhood, to the yawning expanse of days as wide open as the rolling farmland outside the suburbs, where he sometimes rode his bike. Harmony Blue Kucharski, with her love of reading and Scrabble, had been a welcome distraction that summer. She was the subject of pleasant daydreams during the little downtime he had in fall. By winter, he'd convinced himself that she was old enough to become something more.

He didn't want to discuss, with Brenda or anyone, how he'd led Blue on—with respectable intentions, but still—and then broken her heart. And he didn't want to discuss the domestic drama that led him to break things off. He didn't want to talk about how he'd waited until his U-Haul was packed and he was leaving for North Carolina before he stopped by Blue's house, to apologize for being so harsh with her at the end. His coldness had been an act, to discourage any hope that they would get back together. He felt awful when her mother reported that she was gone. "She needed her own space," Nancy Kucharski had said, shrugging. He knew this was right; she did need her own space, some separation from everyone who had relied on her too much.

So he'd moved on. That's what you do when you're powerless to fix what's broken. You bury yourself in your work. You focus on your goals. You eventually find another woman who you think is right for you, and try not to be conflicted when *the one you let get away* shows up several years later on your living room television every afternoon, transfixing your second wife—along with almost every other life-form free at that hour. You move on, because if you don't, you end up like Renee: tormented, pessimistic, alone. You end up with no career, dependent on others to give you your worth.

He'd had things to do with his life then, and still did. A wise man would right now put aside all thoughts of that girl of the past in favor of thinking about the woman of his present. With any luck, they'd be able to get his *Lions* business accomplished without further reminders of that past. The island might be small, but a celebrity and her entourage should be enough of a spectacle that he could see them coming and avoid them entirely.

6

*J*ulian Forrester's BlackBerry buzzed in his pocket, reminding him he was due to phone his grandparents, but he ignored it and kept his attention on his two good friends who stood, hands joined, at the center of what was ordinarily the mess tent. Through his camera's viewer, he studied the pair. They looked something alike: both had short black hair, both were lean, both had skin darkened by a sun that seemed to shine more harshly on the kinds of people they served—except on this evening, when that same sun, heavy now on the western horizon, was lighting their faces so beautifully it was as if their marriage really was being sanctioned by God. They gazed at each other as though they shared a delightful secret. He pressed the shutter release, capturing their look if not their thoughts.

"Wow," Brandy whispered, close to Julian's ear. Her warm breath gave him a shiver. "They are so in love."

Love. He'd seen the look on other faces: mothers in Darfur whose children were finally getting a nutritious meal; fathers, as they watched a child finally grown strong enough to kick a soccer ball across a dusty yard . . . *That* made sense to him. What Alec and Noor had, though, was for the most part beyond him. If not for his grandparents' enduring, happy marriage of fifty-four years, he wasn't sure he would buy it at all.

A minister, his camouflage uniform somehow neatly pressed despite the heat, spoke sincerely about the obligations Julian's friends now faced. Trust, intimacy, and devotion, every day, forever. What an incredible ideal. Who could meet such obligations, especially these days? He approved of trying—ask anyone, they'd say he was willing to give most things a try. Fried caterpillar. Lamb's brains. Cliff diving in Croatia in the dark. Marriage, however, was almost certain to have a much worse and more enduring outcome than any of those stunts; he would leave that to the truly courageous.

He focused the Nikon, pressed the button as Alec pulled Noor close, pressed it as Noor tipped her face upward, pressed it as Alec's lips met hers, pressed it as the kiss became two wide smiles and the couple turned to face the crowd.

The forty or so guests inside the tent applauded. It was done. Noor and Alec were now a single entity where before they had just been a great guy and a smart woman who did the kind of stuff he did: ramble around the planet trying, in their meager ways, to undo the damages of fate and luck. What little they did manage to accomplish—provide water and food and medical care and sanitation, give the people a presence, a face, a voice—had to be enough.

Today his efforts were being made in Afghanistan, just as they had been for the last seven months, while tent camps for refugees continued to multiply and spread across the south desert like a plague. Before here he'd worked in Bangladesh, Malawi, Croatia, Darfur, Mississippi, Indonesia, Bosnia . . . all beginning with Chechnya in early 1995. His history was a blur of turbulent flights and iffy food, desperate children and chaos. He felt like thirty-two going on sixty.

His collection of photos and video and the documentaries he'd shot all preserved the stories that had begun to merge in his memory. One tent camp after another. One starving family, one mother dead of AIDS, one village torched, one empty-eyed girl working as a sex slave, one boy with hands lost to machetes—his memory was overflowing with the atrocities he'd documented with a succession of cameras that had, so far, seemed to protect him from any serious harm. He'd gone to sleep hungry countless nights. He'd been shot at, he'd been cursed—literally, if not effectively. In Bosnia three years back, a disgruntled Mafia type had cut off his left hand's little finger and threatened his thumb if he didn't leave Sarajevo that day (which, as soon as he was bandaged, he did). That was the worst of it for him, though. He was lucky.

Interspersed with all that were moments like the ones now unfolding in this tent. Weddings, and births; lives begun and lives saved; hope restored. Events like these kept him going. A person could be only so skeptical when they'd witnessed the expressions he was seeing on his friends' faces right now. He didn't, however, hold out much hope of wearing such expressions himself. Just before he'd packed out from his previous assignment, in Kabul, his now-ex-girlfriend announced that he was "congenitally incapable of permanent connection." He hadn't told her much about his parents, so she had no idea how accurate a statement that was.

The wind kicked up, flapping the tent's walls and roof, blowing in the fine grit no one much noticed anymore, though it was murder on his camera equipment. He spent nearly as much time huddled over his stuff, cleaning it with tiny brushes and ear swabs, as he did putting it to use.

Alec walked over and clapped him on the shoulder. "Can you believe she actually went through with the wedding?"

"Hell, if I was a woman, I would've locked you down myself a long time ago—so yeah, I can believe it."

"I'm not sure *I* can," Alec said. "What does she see in me?"

"A lot of what you see in her, but with a mustache."

Alec laughed. "And speaking of facial hair . . ."

"I know," Julian said, rubbing his beard. "I needed to shave three months ago."

"And a haircut wouldn't have hurt, in honor of your best friend's wedding day."

"Love me or leave me," Julian said.

As Noor joined them Alec said, "I'm afraid it's gonna be both."

"What will be both?"

"Loving Julian, and leaving him—it's what we have to do as soon as the sun comes up again." He kissed Noor, looking at her in a way that made Julian's belly feel empty. Alec turned back to Julian and said, "But you're still planning to ship out soon, right?"

Julian nodded. "Back to Chicago for a couple weeks, then I'm doing that troop embed in Iraq—should be interesting," he said, "assuming they don't stick me with a bunch of paper-pushers." He sighed. "It's hard to get good access, you know? I was born in the wrong era—I should've been working in 'Nam."

Alec said, "With that hair and the way you worship Hendrix, you'd fit right in. Hey, so maybe you'll join us again after Iraq?"

"Not that I wouldn't like to, but I'm doing the thing with my dad." Noor tilted her head, a question. He explained, "Shooting the pilot episode of a biopic series, which he hopes he can sell for television. He wants to be a TV star."

"Me too," she said, smiling.

"Nah, you're too beautiful for that," he told her. "And too smart."

"And you're too sweet. But seriously, if I could get on TV and get people motivated to sacrifice a little of their Starbucks money for the greater good, trust me, I would."

Alec said, "So hurry up and become a star, what are you waiting for?"

They were joined by more friends, and then the dancing started, with music coming from an old boom box they'd bought at a Gereshk market. Julian stood off to the side and snapped more photographs while couples stood pressed together, shuffling their feet on the gritty plywood floor. For this first dance, Alec and Noor had chosen the Nickelback ballad, "If Everyone Cared."

Julian hummed along as he aimed his camera at one swaying couple, then the next, then the next.

If they could love like you and me
Imagine what the world could be

A theme song for the bunch of them, wasn't it? A little somber, maybe—better, though, than the usual Shania Twain selection you often got at this kind of thing.

The minister walked over and put a beer in Julian's hand. "Good party," he said. He was not much older than Julian—mid-thirties, an Army officer assigned to the camp nearby. "Did I hear right, they're honeymooning in Africa someplace?"

Julian nodded. "Noor's going to save some elephants for a change."

"Me, I'd head for someplace wet. Hawaii would be good, but I'll take anything with a coastline."

"I hear you. My grandparents, they live in Key West. It's great. I'll be there in September." The thought was a trigger, reminding him that he was due to call.

He and his grandparents had an unusual relationship. He'd seen little of them when he was very young; his mother had been possessive of him, and bitter about the divorce. Often he'd overheard her talking about *Daniel and Lynn,* her tone derisive or wounded, depending. When he'd thought of them, it was in her manner—they were either *your grandparents,* very formal, not at all the familiar Grandma and Grandpa his mother's parents were to him—or they were *Daniel and Lynn.* He'd been imprinted like a duckling, so that, even as he got older and his father wrested back some control, when he saw them they were still Daniel and Lynn.

Over the past several years, his contact with everyone outside his daily circle had become sporadic. That is, until his grandfather had a stroke. It was eerie how in the space of a few words (*Honey, listen, I don't want to alarm you, but Daniel's in ICU . . .*) his world had been frozen in place. With different, unluckier words, it would have been altered forever. Funny how he'd witnessed just these kinds of disruptions to other people's lives for so many years, never fully appreciating how impactful they could be until he'd gotten that call. Now he made sure to talk with his grandparents regularly, and with his mother. She had nightmares if she didn't hear from him, she said. She had nightmares anyway.

He took his BlackBerry from his pocket, saying, "Excuse me just a minute," before stepping out into the cooling night. With laughter and music spilling out behind him, he called his grandparents.

"Hi, it's Julian," he said when his grandfather answered.

"Oh, you just caught me on my way out—good timing! How's our boy? Steering clear of scorpions, I hope?"

"So far, so good."

"Let me get your grandmother. Lynn!" he called. "She's chopping . . . something. We've got your dad here, and Brenda. *And* the neighbors coming over for dinner later. A regular fiesta."

Julian imagined his grandfather was dressed for one. "Is Brenda the woman from his department?"

"Yep. They're definitely simpatico now."

"Oh? That's good. I guess."

"I guess too. He'll get it right sooner or later. Maybe sooner. Here's something interesting: An old flame of his is in town this week."

"That so?" Julian had no idea who this might refer to. The specifics of his father's life and his father's history were even now hardly real to him. They were reports, they were anecdotes about a man whose identity had once been so confusing to him that he'd had to stop caring. Was Dr. Mitch Forrester, PhD, the callous skirt-chasing liar of his mother Renee's recollection? Was he the ardent tries-too-hard sometime-father of his own? Maybe he really was the well-meaning but overwhelmed nice guy his grandparents had spoken of in voices thick with sympathy. Back then, he'd had no way of telling who was right.

The reports and anecdotes he'd heard in more recent years had for a very long time been sufficient. Was his dad alive, healthy, still teaching literature? Good enough. Remarried, divorced again, what difference? He, Julian, had gotten busy *living* life while his dad was apparently treading water. He, Julian, had been experiencing the world his father accessed only through TV and books and newspapers. Who had time to read when there were lives to be saved? Or if not saved, documented, and that was something.

Admittedly, this had been a skewed attitude, aggressive, defensive, and he'd gotten his upbraiding for it one night while in Bangladesh, after he'd just spent eighteen hours documenting the Cyclone Sidr damage for *Newsweek*.

Image after image, hundreds of frames of devastation, a few of which would be used so that the folks at home could say, *Aw, that's awful,* then turn on the TV and cry over some lost-dog story. After he finally finished, he'd tried to sleep, but the day replayed in his mind in a continuous loop. He was aware, not for the first time, that it was getting harder to believe in the value of his work. There was no end to suffering, no end to disaster. His efforts were the equivalent of spitting on a forest fire.

He'd gotten up and gone in search of rum. Rounding the corner of the mess tent, he stumbled when a hand tried to grasp his leg.

"Please," he heard from the shadows. He turned to see a thin man struggling to stand, arms wrapped around his middle—broken ribs, most likely. The man stepped into the security light's circle and Julian saw a gash in his cheekbone, blood and dirt thick on his skin and in his hair.

"Please," the man said again, this time pointing.

"What is it?" Julian asked. No comprehension. He tried one of the few Bengali expressions he knew. "Kemom achhen?" *How are you.* A feeble effort when the answer was apparent.

"Please," the man urged.

Julian went for an interpreter, a flashlight, and a medic. The man's father, he soon learned, had gone missing in the storm, and the son had just located him after days of searching through soggy rubble. The injured pair had made it to a spot about a half-mile from the Red Cross camp, where Julian and the medic found the father missing most of one leg and surely half his blood supply as a result. The man was propped against a log, barely breathing, pulse thready—but he was savable, thanks to his son's lamp-cord tourniquet and willingness to carry him who knew how far to get help.

The son had searched, found, saved, and carried, and then when he could carry no more, crawled for help. Julian had heard the words in the rhythm of his footsteps as the group made their way back to camp in the too-still night: *Searched, found, saved, carried, crawled . . . searched, found, saved, carried, crawled . . .* Would he have done as much for his own father? He wasn't sure.

After getting back, he'd gone to the medical tent with his camera and taken photos of the son sitting at the father's bedside, giving blood, and having his cheek stitched on the spot because he wouldn't leave his father again.

When Julian finally got his rum, he used it to ease his shame.

When several months later his father asked if he was interested in shooting the *Literary Lions* pilot—maybe the entire series, depending— he saw the opportunity for what it was: a bridge.

He agreed to work for expenses only, to have his pay deferred until *Lions* sold, if it did; not an ideal set-up, but in this case, the working conditions were stellar: he'd get to spend time in Key West, rooming, as he'd done in his high school years, in Lynn and Daniel's guesthouse. He'd get to do a different kind of filmmaking, stretch his professional muscles a bit. And see what waited across that bridge. He was nearly thirty-three; it was time.

About the "old flame" Daniel had just mentioned, Julian said, "So who is it?" just as his grandmother got on the phone.

"Hello, sweetheart! I expected to hear from you earlier. Isn't it getting awfully late there?"

"I'm at a wedding reception. I just stepped outside for a minute to let you know I haven't been eaten by sandworms."

Daniel said, "The old flame is Blue Reynolds."

"My father knows Blue Reynolds?" The name and reputation were familiar, though he couldn't say he'd bothered to watch any of her shows even when he had access to a TV, which wasn't often. Best he could tell, she and her daytime TV kin represented everything that was wrong with Western culture.

His grandfather was explaining, "He knew her back when she was hardly more than a kid. They had a thing. We thought it might get serious."

"Really?" This was news . . . or was it? Hadn't his mother once just about gone over the edge about his dad's supposedly shameless affair with a teenager? "How old was I?" he asked.

"Oh, nine or ten, I guess," Daniel said. "I wonder if he still likes her."

Lynn scoffed. "Honey, even taking Brenda out of the equation, that was more than two decades ago."

"So? I loved *you* two decades ago, and I still love you today. Think of it, J," Daniel said, his tone reminiscent of times when they'd be out kayaking through the mangrove islands and Daniel would get to talking about how pirates had hidden treasure among the tangled roots. "Your dad could pair up with a famous celebrity."

"Julian's using international minutes," Lynn said. "Now, Julian, when will we see you next?"

"September. I have ten days left here, then I'll be in Chicago briefly before Iraq—gotta stop in, water my plants before I go again."

"Good thing you don't have a cat," Daniel said.

"Why would I need one when you've got six?"

"Four," Lynn said. "Say, do you want to talk to your dad? He's just gone out to the car but I can grab him."

"Nah, I have to run. I'm on duty—wedding photographer."

"I'll bet that makes a nice change."

"You know it."

Daniel said, "So I'll keep you updated on the Blue Reynolds business," and Lynn began chiding him about whose business he was supposed to mind.

Time to get off the phone. "Listen, I love you guys. Send more brownies any time the whim strikes—just send 'em to Chicago, okay?"

"I expect the whim will strike soon," his grandmother said. "We love you, too. Be careful."

"I always am."

He ended the call, holding his phone to his mouth for a moment before dropping it back into his pocket.

Out ahead of him, bright security lights lit the admin compound, the collection of tents for sleeping, for showering, for treating the walking wounded and the sick. There was little activity at the moment; the clinic was closed and almost everyone except essential staff was gathered in the tent behind him. But in ten hours, the clinic tent would be surrounded again by a line of misery. Women and children, mostly, whose needs would overwhelm the available resources before noon. *This* was life in the world today; he could not get excited on his father's behalf, especially over someone as superficial as Blue Reynolds.

A shout of "Hey, where's our photographer?" brought him back to the present.

"Right here," he said, stepping back inside. "Who's got a smile for me?"

*L*ater, Julian lay on his cot, the drone of power generators all there was to hear now that the party had ended. He could hardly remember a night in recent months when a diesel engine wasn't singing his lullaby. Rarely, though, did he have to hold on to his cot's frame to keep it from spinning—well, seeming to spin. Those champagne cocktails Noor kept pushing on him had a surprising kick.

Home was officially his apartment in South Chicago, not too far from where his mother was living—alone, still, and that seemed unlikely to change. How long since he'd spent a night in his own place, where the night sounds were of toilets flushing, of babies squalling, of couples arguing—or *not* arguing, the way Noor and Alec would be *not arguing* right now, alone together in her small tent at the edge of the compound.

He stopped in at his apartment two or three times a year, ran the faucets, washed the windows. There were no plants (he'd been joking with his grandparents) and no pets. Nothing live or dependent, which usually felt like a good truth but right now made him sad. Too much champagne.

The apartment was his property, free and clear—had been his mother's parents' home when they were living—and though people were forever telling him he should rent it out, he liked knowing it was always there waiting for him just as he'd left it. It anchored him, the way his Key West room had done throughout his teen years. If not for Daniel and Lynn and their willingness to take him in, who knew in what direction his life would have gone? He had been an angry kid, a confused, resentful one. If not for their patient support, the cot he was sleeping on now could be a metal one in a prison cell.

Images of the just-finished party played in his mind. The happy couple. Erica and Cameron and Laticia and T.C. and Brandy (especially Brandy) in a kind of bump-and-grind conga line. He should've joined them. Maybe if he had, he'd be holding on to Brandy now instead of the cot frame. Maybe they, too, would be *not arguing* as the generators droned on. They'd be oblivious to the noise and the heat and the knowledge of how hard they would work tomorrow, in as good a way as he'd ever found.

7

From a Key West guidebook Blue found, left behind on a stool at the hotel's Sunset Pier restaurant where she was seated for lunch Saturday, came an entrancing description . . .

> The Florida Keys, it is said, are an island string of enchantments. Here, the daylight lasts a little longer, its light a little softer than in northern climes. Once-disenchanted women dazzle amidst vibrant blooms and clear tropical waters. Men who have forgotten how to breathe discover that their lungs and their tolerance have expanded. Nighttime brings skies strewn with glitter, and dreams so benevolent that you want them never to end. The tropical breeze, perfumed with frangipani and oleander, has been known to bewitch many an incautious visitor.

She'd like to see that glitter-strewn sky. Maybe tonight she'd slip out and judge for herself. When had she last seen the stars? Chicago's lights, New York's, London's, all attempted to steal the glitter for themselves. The cities' lights pretended to be the equivalent of the heavens, keeping everyone's eyes on their earthbound attractions. Trendy shops, restaurants, theaters, clubs, posh high-rises, light-strewn bridges, fountains, statues, all winking, *Look at me! Why look upward when it's all right here?* If her hotel's compound wasn't too lighted, she might even have a good night-sky view from her patio, which in daylight gave her the most astonishing outlook over water so ridiculously turquoise that it was as if Walt

Disney had concocted it. From where she was sitting now, near the end of the pier, at a lime-green table beneath a teal-colored umbrella holding a violet menu, the entire turquoise landscape—waterscape, rather—was like the crowning touch in a digitally enhanced movie scene.

A sleepy-looking waitress, who Blue could tell didn't recognize her behind sunglasses and with her hair pulled up, led Peter, Janelle, Marcy, and Stephen to the table. Blue slid the book into her bag, but not before Peter noticed it.

He said, "I hope you're studying up for Monday's show."

Marcy sat down at Blue's left and picked up a fuchsia menu. Janelle's was lime green. Marcy said, "Or maybe she's reading *Find A New Producer in Only Twenty-four Hours!*"

The waitress pulled a fifth stool over to the table and said she'd be back for their drink orders. Blue waited until she was gone, then said to Peter, "Okay, bring it on: What do you want to know?"

"Size of the island."

"Eight square miles."

"Length of the Keys string."

"One hundred thirty miles, give or take."

"Date of secession?"

"What, you mean the Conch Republic business? I don't know . . . 1984?"

"Eighty-*two*," Peter said. "Ha!"

Marcy rolled her eyes. "All right kids, let's move on to the really important business, that being, are there daiquiris on this menu?"

Peter said, "We just got here, and already you're partying?"

"I'm on vacation."

"You are *not* on vacation. If memory serves, you have to liaise with that nice mayor at three o'clock. He's put off bowling so he can encourage you to spend even more of the show's money while we're here."

"Yes," Marcy said, reading the menu, "and to that end, I'll pay the eight dollars for a daiquiri. I might even have two."

Janelle, long inured to what Marcy called Peter's *short-man attitude*, asked Blue what her afternoon plans were.

Blue said, "I'll be reviewing my Key West factoids."

For two hours after lunch, she did just that, sitting on her suite's ocean-front balcony with a docked cruise ship in sight and Peter's extensive notes on her lap. History, legends, dates, names . . . when she was sure her eyes would cross and stay that way if she read another dry word, she put aside the folder and picked up the guidebook again.

$\mathcal{B}$y four o'clock, street life had slowed to a strolling pace—even a napping pace for a few unselfconscious fellows. Venturing out from the hotel, Blue saw one man propped against a shadowed alleyway wall, another in the shade of bougainvillea that was thick with red flowers. Even with the late-afternoon languor, she was on the lookout for people who were themselves on the lookout. People well aware that you never knew when a celebrity would show up in a place like this. As a case in point, when Blue was chatting with the hotel clerk before setting out, the clerk reported that guests had seen Gloria Estefan, Leo DiCaprio, and one of the Hilton girls just in the past week. With colleges and universities all over the United States on spring break, the celebrity watchers would be thick, the clerk said.

"I expect you're right," Blue had replied. "They'll have a grand time this week: we've got Meg Cabot on the set Monday, Jimmy Buffett on Tuesday, and Ernest Hemingway on Friday."

The girl looked impressed, and then confused. "But—wait, are you sure? I thought Hemingway was dead."

The guidebook claimed that at this time of day, many tourists—celebrity and otherwise—lazed under thatched cabanas called chickees, or at the counters of tin-roofed bars like the one Blue passed a block from her hotel, where four shirtless men with crude tattoos on their backs were singing Jimmy Buffett's "It's Five O'clock Somewhere." In Greenland, if she had her geography right.

Dressed as she was, in oatmeal linen walking shorts and a white tank top, she could have been any woman with a ponytail and large dark sunglasses. By most external measures she was hardly different from the woman just leaving Fairvilla with two large bags. When Blue passed the store she saw in their display window, beneath lingerie-clad busts with prominent nipples, a sign declaring that no one under eighteen was allowed inside. Those bags, then, would be filled with lots of amusements for grown-ups.

Okay, so she and the woman had less in common than she'd thought.

Still, like that shopper, she was youthful-looking and slim in that way middle-aged women could be if they worked hard at it. Without the benefit of expert hair and makeup, she was average-looking, or perhaps a little prettier, but nothing more. If she were now, say, an English teacher vacationing in the Keys, teacher-Blue might get an appreciative look, maybe even a wolf whistle if she leaned over where a certain type of man could see her. That would be the extent of getting noticed. As it was? As it was, she would put money on there being a photo of her wearing oatmeal linen walking shorts and a white tank top, ponytail, sunglasses, posted on some celebrity gossip website before California's sunset, and in glossy newsstand print before the week was out. Exposure came with the territory, the same way box seats at Wrigley Field did, and offers of exquisite jewelry for the Emmys, on loan. And how absurd was it that the very things a person with her income could afford were, in so many cases, the things she now got for free?

With map in hand, she left Front for Simonton, stopping across from a building with a façade that reminded her of the Alamo. She read its sign, *Blond Giraffe Key Lime Pie Factory*, perplexed as to what giraffes and key limes had in common. Whatever it was, Peter was sure to quiz her on it later.

Farther up the street, she stopped in front of a small shop, an old cottage with pink clapboard that glowed neon bright in the afternoon sun. Arrayed on the tiny front lawn (*a postage-stamp lawn*) were metalwork birds in dazzling enameled colors: coral flamingos, posed in one-footed sleep; some black and white birds with large orange bills, prying at oysters; goldfinches perched on swaying daisies. Some were stylized, some realistic, and all of them were remarkable. She went up the short sidewalk and onto the porch, glancing inside through the open doorway. Smaller works were displayed on shelves and in cases, and hung suspended from the ceiling by fishing line. A bright, multicolored bird atop a pedestal display caught her eye and drew her inside.

The shop encompassed the entire cottage, save for a small room at the back, probably what had once been the kitchen. The space was narrow and long, with only a few small windows. Underfoot were wood planks, freshly painted yellow to coordinate with the windowsills. Display cases and shelves held more birds, plus T-shirts and hats, jars of sauces, packages of candies, polished seashells, a vivid collection of dolls made entirely of fabric. She approached the display she'd seen from outside, noting with pleasure that she had the place to herself.

Unlike the upscale shops she was accustomed to, no music played, no strategic spotlights lit featured items, and no one approached her with a too-eager inquiry on whether they "might be of assistance." The companionable sound of wind chimes on the porch, ringing with the light breeze, was all she heard as she took a closer look at the sculpture.

The bird was small—no larger than her fist—and made to sit on a branch, with deep green leaves offsetting it. Its shape was finchlike, but she'd never seen such a finch. Indigo head, scarlet breast, green wings, yellow back. A rainbow bird. A Gay Pride bird? A striking, appealing bird, at any rate.

"Painted Bunting," said someone from the back of the room, startling Blue. She looked that way and saw what she'd missed when she came in: a diminutive black woman seated in the corner behind a crowded table, most likely reading the book she was just setting down.

"Oh. Thank you." The feeling of solitude evaporated, and Blue smiled to mask her disappointment. "It's beautiful."

The woman stood up and walked over. She moved with such grace it was as though the air around her didn't stir. "You've never seen one?"

"So they're real? No, I haven't seen one. Do they actually look like this?"

"Oh yes," the woman said. Her voice was low and warm, a calming voice to match her calming expression, and the calming earth-toned pants and woven shirt she wore. "If you'd come down a month ago, you

might have caught a glimpse. This is the male. He is the most spectacu-
lar songbird you'll find in the northern hemisphere."

"But I'll guess not in Chicago," Blue said. "I live in Chicago."

"Oh, hon, I know you do."

Of course she knew. "Are you the artist?"

The woman nodded. "I come here from Dominica in, oh, 1963 I
guess it was. My husband, he was a pirate." She drew out the last word,
pi-i-rate, reminding Blue of her mother's warning from the night before.

"No kidding?" Blue said, stroking the bird's wing with her index
finger. "I thought all that pirate business was finished in, you know, the
nineteenth century."

"So it might seem," the woman said. "But it's still happening. People
just don't see things when they don't want to look. Like little children,
we cover our eyes and say, 'I don't see it, so it must not be there.' "

"You have such beautiful things here," Blue said, an attempt to
change the subject. "You're very talented. I'm going to take the Painted
Bunting here home with me, and I want to look around some more—he
might like a companion."

"Yes, he should have one," the woman said, lifting the bird from the
pedestal. "We should all," she continued as she carried it to the checkout
counter. "Don't you think?"

What Blue thought was that the woman was striking nerves—proving what she already knew: that she, Blue, was stressed out and oversen-
sitive, and needed a real vacation. Hiatus could not come too soon.

As she browsed, she was aware of the woman's steady gaze. Well,
when didn't people stare? She tried to ignore it as she moved from one
sculpture to the next, considering whether she should buy one for her
mother's birthday in June—a job usually accomplished with a phone
call to Marcy, like so many of her personal tasks these days. Years, more
like. God.

A Wading Heron? A pair of orioles on a copper birdbath? Or this, a
large, regal red bird with a straw-like, curving beak?

"You brought it all with you," the woman said.

"I'm sorry?" Blue looked up from the glossy, black-beaked bird, which was made to stand in a two-foot-wide cattail marsh.

"All of it. You brought it here. Most don't."

Blue fought off her initial reaction, that uncomfortable sensation that her thoughts were somehow discernible, that people could see through her mask of capability and accomplishment, see how weak and scared she was. She'd endured a lot of such moments in her life, enough to know that the feeling was only anxiety, that the woman was not referring to her burdened mind, but to the production crew with their cameras and cables and soundboards, the light towers, the reflectors—all the things that made Blue look and sound good when nature would have it otherwise. She said, "I guess I did. That's the way it works, you know."

"Does it work that way?"

Blue reached for her ponytail, took out the elastic, shook her hair, then began to bind it up again as she said, "What can you tell me about this bird? I've never seen one like it."

The woman stared a moment longer, lips pursed, then said, "I think your mother would enjoy that one, yes, the Scarlet Ibis; you decide, and I'll go in back and find a box," leaving Blue standing with her mouth open. She had not mentioned her mother.

"On second thought, just the Bunting," she called.

When the woman was out of earshot, Blue muttered, "No one can read minds." Saying the words aloud gave them more weight, more reassurance.

There was an easy explanation for what seemed like clairvoyance: When the woman knew the show was coming to town, she'd studied up on her Blue Reynolds facts, easily found on the Internet. Blue wouldn't be surprised if there were sites devoted solely to birthdays of celebrities' family members. The woman had recognized her when she came in, watched her while she looked around just now, and simply made a lucky guess.

It had to be something like that. Her pulse slowed, but the sensation of vulnerability, like an aftertaste, remained.

8

*M*itch encouraged his father to narrate their tour around the island, from fish market to grocery store to pie shop. Brenda, who found Daniel completely charming, was the ideal audience for a man who'd become a teacher because, he said, he liked to hear himself talk.

"Turn left here," Daniel directed, as they headed back from their last stop. "We'll go give you a peek at Mallory Square, where some of the cruise liners dock—it's impressive, the way they dominate the waterfront. The *Enchantment*'s about to sail, so things'll be quieting down a little. You wouldn't believe the circus, when these ships first put in."

Mitch didn't bother to remind his father that he and Brenda had seen cruise ships before, that they had sailed on them twice with their spouses of the past. Those had been good trips, kicking around San Juan, spelunking in Curaçao . . . In the Bahamas, Brenda had loved the Royal Victoria Gardens, while Angie complained that she hadn't gone to the Bahamas to see grass and trees, both of which were plentiful in Chapel Hill. She had a good point. Still, Brenda had seemed to bloom amongst the blooms there in Nassau. Her perspective was, Who had time to notice such things at home?

And here was something he'd forgotten until just now: The next night, while he and Craig sipped whiskies in the ship's casino, Craig had been compelled to tell him how versatile Brenda was in bed—on the night before, and in general. Uninhibited, as if all her study of Victorian morality had worked as a warning. "Whatever the case," Craig said, elbowing him, "I'm damn lucky for it!" Mitch had been embarrassed; that kind of candor was for lesser men, for locker rooms and seedy bars. That said, he had to admit he now felt lucky too.

"We're on the northwest corner of the island here, and if we went down to the opposite end, on Whitehead," his father was saying, "that's where you'd find the southernmost point in the continental U.S. Now Hawaii, at about nineteen degrees south latitude, has the southernmost point altogether—I tried to compare them from the Shuttle on my final trip, just to see for myself, but the fact is, both are pretty much invisible from orbit."

Mitch glanced over his shoulder at Brenda, to see whether she'd noticed his father's slip. She smiled at him and shrugged. She was a tolerant person, the type to take lemons (of which there were many in academia) and make not only lemonade but also lemon bars and lemon drop martinis. A good trait. He really did like her. He might even love her, the way you loved any friend who'd stuck by you for so long—which could become something more, sure it could.

Would Craig sanction him and Brenda as a couple? Was he up there in English professor heaven nodding in approval? Mitch wasn't the best of her prospects; while he was considered good looking, he wasn't as accomplished or well-connected as some other single men he could name, which made him wonder—again—what drew her. He supposed she simply *liked* him, always had and, like he with her, now liked him . . . more.

His father, still chatting away, was saying, "Maybe Mitch will take you over there—to the point, not to Hawaii—well, maybe Hawaii, too—but anyway, don't be fooled by the touristy claims. It's not the honest-to-god southernmost point, even on the Key. That's over farther west, on Navy property."

"How interesting," Brenda said. "You have such a wealth of knowledge about Key West—I'm glad Mitch brought me along."

Mitch liked the rapport his father was forging with Brenda, even if at times it was Ken Mattingly who forged it. Whereas Renee had been . . . tempestuous, and Angie had been . . . flighty, Brenda was sensible and solid, attractive, dependable, kind. She'd make an ideal daughter-in-law, if it ever came to that.

"Oh, there she is," his father said. Mitch, looking seaward down Front Street, saw the cruise ship, *Enchantment of the Seas,* rising majestically from behind the small buildings at the corner.

Brenda said, "That's her? How can you tell?"

What do you mean, how can you tell? Mitch was about to say as much when his father answered, "I watch her every day—and don't forget, I taught her senior year English class. Even hiding behind those sunglasses, she has the same posture, same ponytail."

Mitch, catching on, spotted the woman—and hit the brakes, stopping the car abruptly.

The posture. The ponytail. The girl—now woman—he should not still regret wounding, but did.

In that moment it was as if she was nineteen and walking toward him on the Lakefront, that cold Saturday afternoon when he'd ended it. She'd had to have been expecting bad news, given that he'd told her they "needed to talk," and yet she'd been there, she'd shown up to face whatever song he was about to play.

As abruptly as he'd braked, he pressed the accelerator again and they lurched past Blue Reynolds.

No one spoke. The silence was worse than any outburst of surprise or criticism would have been. As he drove down Duval, the pressure to *say something,* to explain himself, grew oppressive.

What was the big deal? He'd been surprised is all.

Why didn't his father speak? The man was never silent. Mitch glanced over at him, dredged up, "Have we forgotten anything?"

"How to drive, maybe?" His father was grinning.

"The apple juice!" Mitch said, grasping the words as if they were a rope that would haul him out of sinking sand. "Did we get the apple juice?"

Brenda, voice calm, flat, said, "Yes, we did."

"Oh, okay, good."

Silence.

Then she said, "Is it true that 'Key West' is really a bastardized translation of the original 'Cayo Hueso,' or bone key?" And though Mitch was unsure whether her question was forgiveness or diversion, he was relieved when his father bit, launching into a colorful recounting of the island's history that lasted until well after they had returned to the house.

9

Blue had been perhaps a block from the hotel, where she intended to drop off her package, when she saw a sedan stop abruptly some fifty feet ahead of her. She'd barely gotten a look at the man in the passenger seat before the car lurched forward again, zipping past her and around the next corner. She stared after it. The man had reminded her strongly of Daniel Forrester—older than she recalled him, but of course he would be older, in his seventies by now. The question was, what would he be doing in Key West?

The possibilities occupied her as she continued on to the hotel, careful not to meet any passerby's eye. So far, she'd evaded detection—the artist excepted—and prayed her luck would hold. Maybe Daniel was on vacation, or visiting friends. Maybe he lived here—with Lynn, she hoped; they were such a wonderful couple, and judging from what she'd seen so far, there were worse places to retire to than Key West.

Inside the hotel's nautical lobby, she left her package with a clerk, a pale young man with Rasta braids held back by a bright green shoestring. "Would you go ahead and send that up to my suite? Thanks a bunch." The narrow, secret streets of residential Old Town she'd read about in the guidebook were calling to her, and there would be no time for exploring once her staff got organized and the show's wheels began turning once again.

"Of course, Ms. Reynolds. How are you enjoying our town?"

"So far, so good—the warm weather is such a treat. We left Chicago with six inches of snow on the ground."

He nodded. "I'm a Nebraska native. Used to be a computer pro-grammer—my dad's idea of the right job for me. A lot of the residents here are people who quit their jobs and ran away to Key West, to live *la buena vida*. Corporate people, CEOs even."

"How could you just drop everything that way? Just . . . leave?"

The clerk shrugged. "You only live once."

His words, common as they were—clichéd even, nonetheless stayed with her as she left downtown, walking along the short blocks, the his-toric cemetery as her goal. Instead of thinking about the show or her mother or Branford's search, she would try to live fully in the moment, the way Thoreau had advocated. Or was that Socrates? Both, maybe.

As she walked, she paid attention to the picket fences and low stone walls that delineated more tiny front yards. She noticed the folded-fan shape of one of the few plants whose name she knew: palmetto. She noticed a dragonfly, its iridescent body, its gossamer wings. "Gos-samer," she said, just for the pleasure of it. The word made her think of fairies.

The houses sat very close to the street, but when she looked past them she could see deep rear lots, some of them thick with trees and shrubs and bursts of colorful blooms. It was surprisingly quiet, a few blocks in. The three or four humans she saw were children who, judging from the way they ignored her, were pleasantly underexposed to televi-sion talk shows. The rest of the beings whose paths she crossed, or that crossed hers, were roosters and lizards and, in one case, a dog.

Despite the guidebook's claim, until she was here she hadn't believed that the air could be as perfumed as it was. The salty breeze she ex-pected; this trip was not, by far, her first time near an ocean. When, though, had she ever done as she was doing now, simply walk around a place and *see* it? And *smell* it? When had she done *this,* stop at an old wrought-iron gate laced with a flowering vine—jasmine?—to press her nose into a small yellow flower? What a heavenly smell . . . If she thought she could get away with it she'd sit down right here and keep her nose in these flowers for the rest of the day.

When she stood back from the gate, a sign posted on the nearby stone wall—coral stone, it was—caught her eye. She pushed her sunglasses up onto her head and read, *Offered by Claskey and Shefford,* and a phone number.

"Really . . ." She looked past the gate and into what was a small but lush courtyard so thick with green that it dazzled her. Perhaps because it was a corner lot, the yard was a little wider than some she'd seen. Not huge by any standard; no bigger than the one her grandma Kate told of, at Blue's first home, when you took into consideration that a narrow garage had shared that lot. Here there was no garage. There were trees. And shrubs. Ferns. Vines. Flowers. Bricks. Pots.

Here in this yard—a garden, really—were short palms and tall ones, wide-leafed shrubs and shrubs with such small, intricate variegated leaves that each seemed its own work of art—and vines *everywhere.* It was Eden, left untended after Adam and Eve had gone. Were those lemons hanging from a crowd of green in the far corner? And what sort of tree was the one with hairy-looking bark? There seemed to be a pond behind the tree; she craned to get a clearer view, but there was too much in the way.

The house that belonged with the yard was, as far as she could tell, reasonably sound. A story-and-a-half cottage—a *conch cottage,* she remembered—with an attached open carport, wide sloping rooflines, and a wrap porch. Its narrow wood siding was a faded yellow. What few windows she could see were uncovered, and there was no furniture on the porch. Maybe the place was vacant . . . She reached for the gate's latch and glanced around. Seeing only a hen nudging her fluffy chicks onto the curb, she opened the gate and stepped through.

If the place was occupied, she'd have to quickly become *Blue Reynolds* again. Her anxiety was sharp and surprising, as full-fledged as in the moments before she'd gone on-air for the first time. *Will I remember how to be Blue?* She walked up the cobbled brick path, up the six wooden steps onto the wide porch, five paces to the door . . . Without waiting to analyze *why* she was standing on this porch, facing a stranger's door with no prescribed agenda, she made a fist and knocked.

Now she could feel her pulse throbbing in her neck, her heart hammering her ribs. "Ridiculous," she whispered, listening for motion inside the house. Waiting . . . waiting . . .

If someone answered the door she'd say . . . she'd say . . . what would she say? *Nothing like the truth,* her grandmother's voice advised, as clear and real as if Kate was standing next to her on the porch.

Grandma Kate had been such a good person. A chain-smoker, a terrible money manager, too soft on Blue's mother, but caring and good-hearted. She'd caught Blue in a lie once, overheard her fabricating a heroic father for the benefit of a girl who'd moved into the apartment across the hall. Blue and her new friend were playing outside, in the scrubby yard below the windows of Blue's first-floor apartment. She remembered being aware that her grandmother was sitting near the open window even as she told the girl about a father drafted into the army, sent to Cambodia, taken prisoner—but still alive, they were sure, and no one should give up hoping for all POWs to come home safely; President Ford was even that minute getting everything straightened out. She remembered waiting for her grandmother to interrupt, to call her out, remembered feeling both shame and relief when nothing happened. Only later, at bedtime, did it get brought up.

For all that your mom has done things not everyone approves of, she's honest, you know? No matter what, she tells it like it is.

I know, Grandma. I just don't like how it is.

Harmony Blue, the truth is always easier in the long run. Lying will leave you as worn-out as the soles on a cheap pair of shoes.

Blue thought again of her grandmother's advice, and knew it was right. She'd been tired for years.

If someone answered the door, she'd say . . .

"I'll just say I love the house and wanted a closer look." Everything did not have to be so damn complicated.

A sudden screech from close behind her made her jump. She turned to see a flash of red feathers as a macaw winged through the canopy of trees, and onward. What next? Wild boars? Alligators? Who knew Key West had a little bit of *Wild Kingdom* going on?

She was smiling as she turned back toward the still-closed door. It seemed that no one was coming, so she braved a peek in one of two windows looking in from the porch. The room was empty. No furniture, no rugs, no curtains. Just a broad expanse of wide-planked floor, slashed by a shaft of sunlight that had cut its way through the foliage. Beyond this room, through an arched doorway, was another empty room.

Empty. Unoccupied.

For sale.

Her pulse slowed, and with her calm came a light breeze that stirred the leaves. *Go ahead,* it seemed to be saying.

"Oh, sure." First, the artist was a mind reader, then her grandmother was talking to her, and now the leaves were speaking, telling her to buy a house. "Harmony Blue, you are not right," she said, stepping down from the porch.

She went around to the carport, where an old coaster-brakes bike like the ones she'd seen parked all around downtown leaned against the wall, connected to it by cobwebs. In back of the carport was a patio; from here, she peered into the house through a sliding glass door and saw a small kitchen with Formica counters and sixties-era appliances. Older, maybe. The floor was wood in here, too, scratched and gouged from decades of active use. Very unlike her kitchen at home. She imagined a little boy with tanned skin and honey-blond hair lying on his tummy on the floor, pushing a toy car between chair legs while his mother peeled and sliced a mango, to be eaten out here in the shade.

From the patio, she stepped onto a path leading into the garden. She knew already that she was going to hate leaving this serene spot, that she would truly, tangibly miss it. Still, she had to leave; certainly she couldn't do what the hotel clerk said so many others here had done. She couldn't ditch her career for a collection of palms and bromeliads and, what? Orchids? She recognized this pink flower, too, hibiscus.

But she could, if she wanted to, purchase an occasional escape.

She went outside the gate to check the realty sign, and then she called Marcy.

"Hi," Marcy said, "I was just about to call you. Have you been kidnapped? Where did you go?"

"Listen, I need you to call this number," she read it from the sign, "and, whatever price they want for the house on the corner of . . . of . . ." she located the street sign and read it to Marcy, "I'll pay it. It's empty; I want to take possession immediately—while we're here in town, if possible." If she waited, she might change her mind. She knew herself: practical, cautious—she'd talk herself out of it if she had to wait.

Marcy said, "You don't even want to negotiate the price—of a *house* that you, what, just saw, in a town you've been in for like seven hours? Have you lost your mind?"

Blue leaned over to smell the jasmine again, considering the question. The prospect of spending summer hiatus right here gave her butterflies, and why was that? It was just a house. In Key West, true, but what did she know about the place, beyond the guidebook, this walk, and Peter's notes? She shouldn't feel so giddy. *Had* she lost her mind? No, she thought, suppressing a laugh that felt like a gulp. Not lost; quite possibly *found*.

She said, "You're always saying I should live a little. Anyway, please just get the details—actually, never mind, I'll call and see if they'll meet me here." She'd have the agent bring a purchase contract and they could do the paperwork inside.

"*Blue* . . ." Marcy was laughing. "This is crazy!"

"Crazy!" she agreed, and bent to sniff the jasmine again.

"But hell, why not? I want to come see it! Oh, but first, here's why I was calling you: Someone named Daniel Forrester left a message for you at the hotel's front desk."

So it *was* Daniel she'd seen in that car. How about that? He must have seen her, too—maybe he had told the driver to stop, and then thought better of such sudden contact. Maybe he thought he should follow official channels instead.

Marcy was saying, "He claims you know him. Let me quote from the message, here: 'Harmony Blue, please join Lynn and me for dinner tonight if you are free. Seven thirty, come as you are.' How do you think he got your name? What won't people try, huh?"

"No, I do know him—*them*, I should say. Or, I did, a long time ago. He was my English teacher, senior year, and Lynn's the woman I worked for after I left the pet store. Before I moved in with you."

Here was a rare *apropos* opening, when she could naturally tell Marcy the whole tale, her stupid story of schoolgirl naiveté and heartbreak. She'd kept it secret at first because she hadn't wanted Marcy to think less of her. Then she kept it secret because it was easier than admitting she'd kept a secret from Marcy in the first place.

The truth.

She might be able to just work it in, casually. She was glad Marcy couldn't see the sheepish, cringing look she knew must be on her face as she added, "I, well, I dated their son, Mitch. He was older, divorced; he had a young kid. He dumped me, and that's why I was so depressed back then."

"I figured it was a guy," Marcy said. Blue waited for more, for an accusation, for some sign of irritation, but Marcy apparently had no issue with her waiting two decades to reveal these details. Blue didn't know what to make of such an anticlimax. Finally she just said, "Yeah. Men."

"So it could be a little awkward, seeing them," Marcy said. "Do you want me to return the call and make your excuses?"

Standing there with her hand still resting on the gate, Blue's first impulse was to say *Yes, do.* Keep the past in its place—because even if the Forresters didn't say it aloud, they would be thinking of how she had simply disappeared from their lives. They would be recalling an anxious young woman who must have seemed overly eager to please. She didn't want to be that woman again, even for a moment; she didn't want to see that woman reflected in their eyes.

And yet . . . she couldn't quite say it. Why be so cowardly? She *was* free tonight, and while things had ended badly with Mitch, that had nothing to do with Lynn or Daniel. They'd been so good to her. Like second parents—like *first* parents, really. She'd missed them. Maybe this was happy fate.

"No, I think I'll accept." And as she said it, she smiled, a smile as wide as the well-known and well-loved version so familiar to the world. Wider, perhaps. And then she began to laugh.

10

$\mathcal{A}$fter speaking with Lila Shefford, of the sign, Blue sat down on the porch step to wait for the agent to arrive. Two million dollars was the asking price. Lila had not known, at first, that she was telling this to her, to Blue Reynolds, and so she'd justified the price, citing the large lot, off-street parking, original wood floors, good rental history, and new tile roof. "Great, I'll take it," Blue had said, leaving Lila momentarily speechless.

Two million dollars. "Two million," Blue said now; even aloud, the number was meaningless. She could spend twenty, or two hundred, and never really miss it—not that she would spend so much, or even truly could, if by *could* she meant *was capable of*. She, personally, was nowhere near that. What she was capable of was letting people who spouted ideas and ambition manage her business interests. She had holdings—stocks, real estate, publications—that she knew only by their summaries in her annual report. She, personally, was great at two things: hosting her show, and delegating. The nagging thought that she could be more, could do more, had a permanent roost in her conscience; she kept it fed with bits of *someday soon,* and wondered if someday was going to come.

Marcy called back to say the Forresters' address was a house on Eisenhower, "near the Garrison Bight, whatever that means." She offered to bring Blue a change of clothes, if time ran out.

"A bight is some kind of inlet. Don't bother with the clothes, I'm fine like I am. Maybe I'll have you call me a cab, though, if it comes to that.

I'll check my map for how far Eisenhower is from here." She hoped to be able to walk over there; Old Town was such a pleasure. She felt ordinary here. She felt real.

She'd bought several properties over the years. The loft in New York, the London flat. A Montana ranch—which she could not help thinking was a celebrity cliché. She rarely went there, and lent it out to almost anyone who asked. Peter and Janelle summered at the ranch with his two brothers and their wives and kids. Montana was beautiful, and she did enjoy being there. Yet there was something too wide open about the place, something that made her feel she needed to watch her back.

This, though? This close garden of tropical everything was a place where she felt right at home; no doubt it would be on her mind whenever she was anywhere else. She could already imagine how much fun it was going to be to get a landscape designer to help her sculpt the jungle before her, shape it—but not tame it, not entirely; its wildness was its appeal. Already she knew she wanted to have fish swimming in the rock pond, and one of those charming chickees over on the west side, by the wall, and strings of tiny white lights on the lemon tree.

Sitting here on the porch step, she could envision those lights, lights like the Forresters had strung through the pine swags that decorated their house that New Year's Eve when what had been a friendship, a flirtation with Mitch, became something more.

1985, it was. About to be 1986 in the same way she was about to be nineteen, at the stroke of midnight. She'd made two wishes for that birthday, and the first of them had already come true: she was there at the Forrester's. The second wish? The second wish depended on Mitch being there too.

He'd been twenty-seven, two years out of his PhD program and a very junior professor at Northwestern. Twenty-seven sounded old, but he was in tune with people her age because he spent his days exploring literature with them. His nights he'd owed, when he could persuade his ex, to a nine-year-old boy she'd heard about but had never seen.

Lynn, who she'd grown very fond of in the year they'd been working together, had told her the whole story: The winter before Mitch finished high school, he got his girlfriend Renee pregnant. She was from another school; they'd met at a party. "It wasn't true love," Lynn said. "These things rarely are. But he wanted to do right, so the weekend after graduation, he married her. Julian was born in August, and they all played house for a couple rocky years while Mitch was an undergraduate. Then Renee, sure that Mitch was screwing around, kicked him out—and even though he wasn't cheating, he *went*." Lynn shrugged. "Julian is a quiet boy, earnest as they come. I wouldn't trade him for the world. But I can't help thinking that, all things being equal, they'd have been better off if Renee hadn't left the whole birth-control matter up to Mitch. How many times have I told him that good intentions make a lousy defense?"

Now Blue watched a trio of small white birds flit about in the trees. Parakeets? Finches? Maybe she'd get one of those bird-identifier books while she was here.

"No, no maybes: I *will* get one." Unlike Mitch, she'd follow through. You had to start with the small things, right?

Back when she'd heard that story from Lynn, she hadn't faulted Mitch. She'd seen Renee as conniving—a plotter who was willing to get pregnant just to snag him. Her opinion changed, though, when she feared the end of her relationship with him was coming and she began to wonder what *she* could do to keep him. A woman in love—especially a very young one—could so easily be blinded by desperation. If Renee really had entrapped Mitch, she'd gone too far, yes. But was what Blue got herself into after Mitch cut her loose any less appalling? At least Renee's son knew his real parents, was raised by them. Having two separate homes was not ideal, but surely it had to be more ideal than knowing that neither parent wanted you, that you'd been given away.

Or maybe her son didn't know. If Branford's lead was solid, she might soon have a chance to find out. She knew this, intellectually. In her gut it still felt unreal, impossible.

Ah, but that New Year's . . . everything had seemed possible.

She'd been elated by the invitation: finally, a chance for Mitch to see her not as his mother's receptionist, not as a nice girl with an over-worked, eccentric mother and a sister who needed to be leashed; not just a young woman with her heart filled with hope at one day winning his. Surely there were lots of those types in his life.

Her second wish, the one that powered her through her anxiety at showing up at the party alone was simple: one kiss, from Mitch, at midnight.

How awkward she'd been . . . Unused to wearing high heels and snug dresses, she'd opened the old Chevy's door and climbed out into the snowy street. The door groaned as she pushed it shut, and she was grateful no one was outside to hear it. Suddenly she was certain she was wrong for the event: too young, too unimportant—definitely too poor to dress well enough to match the luxury cars already lining the street, not to mention the enormous homes all around her, though she'd tried her best. Her dress, sleeveless yellow taffeta with a tight bodice, was a dance-scene dress she'd "borrowed" from her high school's theater wardrobe after a stage production of *Grease*, for which she'd been a stagehand. She'd been waiting three years to have an occasion suited to the dress, never imagining that the first opportunity would far outclass it.

Rock salt crunched beneath her feet as she walked up the long side-walk from the street. She stamped snow off her strappy, open-toed shoes, stupid for winter but the best she had, hoping that when the plows came past, her car wouldn't be blocked in. Not that getting stuck there would be so awful.

Overhead, the suburban sky was the darkest gray, soft like silk vel-vet, with snow falling in gentle, lazy flakes. She'd pulled her coat close, hoping she'd be able to take it off before anyone noticed how tatty it was. How she would've laughed at herself if she'd known that one day she'd be dressed for free by Oak Avenue shops, in return, of course, for crediting them in her broadcasts. That she would go from worrying about what the scores of guests inside a single house would think of how she looked, to worrying about what the Greater Chicago viewing area would think of how she looked, to being watched, studied, parodied, criticized—and yes, on occasion praised, too—by media and viewers worldwide.

Would people point and chuckle behind her back? Would they think her breasts were too big? Her dress too tight? Her hair too oily, when *glossy* was what she was trying for? Would Mitch think she looked pretty? Did she dare hope for *beautiful*? No; such hope would be tempting fate. Pretty, then. And she *was* pretty—she could see that now, and maybe she saw it then, too, if obliquely; after all, she did buy sparkly stockings, and steam press the dress, and spend two hours on her hair and makeup. Melody and their mother, crowding the little bathroom to prep for different party dates, had been as astonished as they were impressed.

And she did walk up to the massive, arched doorway of the Forresters' home, a doorway that seemed half as wide as her entire house, a doorway that, along with the rest of the structure, demonstrated to Blue what had up until then been only disparate numbers on contracts she filed in broad metal cabinets—numbers that were Lynn's commissions from sales to mall developers and tower builders and collectors of architecture by van der Rohe and Jenney and Sullivan and Wright. And after standing for a moment in the cold, still air with snow on her shoulders, her breath rising in silver clouds, her heart stuck in her throat, she did pull her hand from her pocket and ring the bell.

When at first it seemed that no one would answer, she thought she might turn and hurry back to the car, save herself from the possibility that she would leave there later as a fool. Then the door opened and there was Daniel. Fifty-something at the time, he wore a black tux with a yellow plaid bow tie. The tie's pattern had shiny silver threads that shone in the porch light. She'd never seen him in anything so fancy. He clapped his hands once and said, "Well, Harmony Blue! Come in, come in."

She stepped into the foyer, grateful for the enveloping warmth. "Hi, Mr. Forrester." Though she'd seen him daily for an entire school year, it was awkward, both of them dressed up, neither of them ready to discuss literature—or *she* wasn't. Probably he could recite Twain in his sleep if required.

He took her coat, handed it off, and said, "So it's just you?" As in, had she brought a date?

"Just me." Her voice came out smaller than she wanted.

He leaned over and kissed the top of her head, an affectionate gesture she was sure must have owed to champagne. "Happy New Year. Now come on, let's get you mingling."

Lynn's line of work brought her friendships with every kind of professional. Retail developers, sandwich-shop owners, hospital administrators, the mayors of Chicago and its suburbs north, south, west, and central. Blue knew many of the guests as voices on the phone, a few by sight; they looked transformed, that night, by the elegant tuxedos and chic gowns. As Daniel steered her across the room, she was impressed to see Morgan Cole, the statuesque WLVC-TV nightly news anchor, among other high-profile Chicago personalities.

Lynn was standing near the buffet talking with her uptight assistant, Deb. "Harmony Blue, you made it!" Lynn said. "You look amazing. Wow!"

Blue shrugged, embarrassed but delighted, too. Lynn was the most dynamic woman she'd known in her young life, so different from her mother that the two women might as well be different species.

"Where'd you find that dress?" Deb asked.

Blue, recalling the theft, couldn't meet her eyes. "It's, um, my sister's. Melody bought it at The Limited, I think." The Limited had been the height of fashion to Blue, who could not have imagined she'd one day wear Prada, have couture designed just for her, auction off that same couture for charity. She'd said, "*You* look really great—both of you, I mean."

"This," Lynn said, indicating the silver beaded sheath she wore, "was hand-sewn. Can you imagine? And you think office work is tedious!"

Deb surprised Blue by saying, "It *is* tedious—but Harmony Blue, you're doing a great job. I love your dress. And your hair's gorgeous tonight, too. I wish mine curled like that. Oh—there's Mark Poole; I need to ask him about those contracts."

Deb, charitable? What else could it mean but that her wish had a chance?

She watched Deb go, taking the opportunity to scan the room for the face she was longing to see, was *always* longing to see. Her crush on Mitch wasn't so sensible; he was older, divorced, an assistant professor, a *father*. But he was also charming and smart and kind. And she'd thought maybe she was reaching for an ideal she wasn't entitled to, but at least she wasn't like Melody, always coming home reeking of smoke, glassy-eyed and dismissive. Was it so bad to have stars in her eyes, to want to one day tell her grandchildren how, on the stroke of her nineteenth birthday, a prince gave her one magical kiss?

And then what? they would ask, all of them eager to know more about the story of their own histories.

Well, she would say, *the prince finally realized he was madly in love with her, and made her his princess.*

Blue had stood there listening to Lynn talk with Mary Conner, a facilities manager for Marshall Field, about the rising per-square-foot costs in the Loop. She'd nodded now and then as if she were a Realtor-in-training. Her mind, though, had been on Mitch, and the hour (*nine fifteen*), and her wish's odds of coming true.

When she saw him, he looked like a prince. His hair, almost as dark as hers, was mussed a bit and fell onto his forehead. Rakish, she thought the word was—not from English class this time, but paperback romances. He wore a tux like most of the other men, but with a brilliant blue bow tie and vest. Even in the low light of twinkling strings and glowing candelabras, his eyes shone blue. Like the Earth from space, she thought. Like Lake Michigan from the Hancock building on a sunny afternoon. As blue as she felt each time they parted.

How silly she'd been, how young . . .

If she hadn't been there that night, though, if she hadn't been so wound up about Mitch, she wouldn't have met Morgan Cole, who would later become her mentor. Morgan was glamorous and warm and smart. She kept the whole circle of listeners enthralled with a tale of how, as a new reporter, she'd done a story at the Brookfield Zoo and was accosted by both a chimpanzee and the chimp's trainer. The anchorwoman's laugh was like a Christmas bell to Blue: cheerful and resonant with hope and pleasure. Blue would remember this later, when, *postpartum*, she went searching for a new life to escape into.

But that night, with Mitch close enough to touch if she were to let her hand follow her desire, she'd felt that all was right with the world. When she glanced at him, caught him looking at *her*, she knew, just *knew*, that she would see her wish come true.

Daniel Forrester asked her to dance and she did, imagining herself as Cinderella, Daniel as the king. The string quartet played, and Blue spun, dizzying circles that made her laugh. She loved this party, she loved the Forresters, she loved this house, this life.

Mitch cut in. "Dad, may I?"

"If you must," Daniel said, putting her hand into Mitch's.

Mitch looked down at her. His eyes were so inviting she wanted to dive into them. "Thank you, Harmony Blue, you've made my night."

"Me? What did I do?"

He laughed and held her tighter. "It's not what you *do*, it's just that you *are*." It was enough to make any girl swoon.

The quartet stopped playing, temporarily, at five minutes to midnight.

"Let's get some cool air," Mitch said. He took a bottle of champagne and she followed him past the buffet, through the kitchen, through the mudroom, to the back door.

He opened it and she said, "Wow, look at the snow!" It fell heavier than before, an audible rain of snowflakes, confetti tossed down by the Nordic gods of winter. She thought she'd never heard anything more pure.

This was the moment she'd waited for: the moment when she, now girded with just enough champagne to shore up bravery, could tell him her wish.

"You know, it's my birthday tonight."

"What, really? Why didn't you say so before?"

"Well, technically it's not for"—she checked her watch—"two more minutes. At the stroke of midnight, I'll turn nineteen. And I have a birthday wish, too."

"Do you, now? Are you going to tell me, or do I have to guess?"

"I did have *two* wishes," she said, feeling somehow bold and shy at once. "I got the first one already."

"Which was?"

"To get invited to this party."

He nodded. "And the second?"

The buzz of the party grew louder and she looked behind them, into the house. "I think they're about to count down."

"I think so," Mitch said. He set the bottle in the snow.

"Do you want to—?" She inclined her head toward inside.

"No." He took her hands in both of his. "I'm glad you came tonight, Harmony Blue. To be honest, I wasn't looking forward to the party until Mom said she'd invited you."

"Come on," she said, heat rising from her neck to her cheeks.

"I mean it. I know it's complicated." He'd looked past her, into the night. "But *you* . . ." He smiled and shook his head.

Chanting from inside told them that midnight was only moments away. Together, they counted down with the crowd, eyes locked, snow falling mere inches away from them.

"Happy New Year," she said, at the same time Mitch said, "Happy Birthday." He drew her in, closing the space between them, closing his eyes. She closed hers, too.

They kissed, a sweet, tentative first kiss. "That was my second wish," she said.

He'd nodded, looking pleased with himself, with the moment, with her confession. "I guessed."

She asked, "Now what?"

"Now . . ." He looked uncertain, but then he said, "Now, we have some more champagne."

Blue was smiling at the memory when Lila Shefford arrived and let herself in the gate. Blue stood up to greet her. "Hello—thank you for dropping everything to do this today. I believe it's the start of something very good for me."

11

Mitch loved his parents' house, with its wide-open rooms and towering ceilings designed to help cool the space during those long, hot days before central air-conditioning. Ceiling fans turned lazily in every room. He laid the dining table with the "good" china, a set of delicate white stoneware featuring hand-painted oleander blooms and branches, thinking of how the place never failed to remind him of *Casablanca*. He loved the film; wasn't Bogart's Rick Blaine a real Hemingway sort of hero? The night after he'd split with Blue he'd gone home and watched *Casablanca* on tape, consoling himself with assurances that he, like Rick, had made a noble sacrifice for the benefit of a good woman. He'd drunk scotch and, when the movie ended, fallen asleep on the couch musing about a fantasy meeting of himself, Hemingway, and Bogart knocking back drinks at a little Chicago bar he'd liked to frequent at the time.

His mother joined him in the dining room. "Thank you for getting this going. Where's Brenda?" she asked.

"She volunteered to take the baby for a walk while the girls, as you call them, get ready to come over."

"Nice of her. She's a giver, isn't she?"

"She is," he said, not keen to discuss her just now. His reaction at seeing Blue had put her off a bit—understandably. After they'd helped put away the groceries, Brenda had drawn him into the hallway and asked him whether there was more to that than surprise. He'd told the truth: there was not. How could there be?

So rather than continuing on the Brenda subject line, he told his mother, "You look great." Which she did. She wore lavender silk pants and a sleeveless white blouse, silver hoops at her ears and a silver cuff on her right wrist. She'd turned seventy-seven on her last birthday, but her gently lined face looked ten years younger. Her hair had gone pure white over the last few years and she'd left it that way, declaring that it set off her silver jewelry much better than the dyed blonde look she'd worn for so long. She was barefoot.

"Thanks. You clean up nice yourself—I like you in blue. Which, speaking of *blue:* Dad tells me you saw Blue Reynolds on Front Street."

"We did," Mitch said, marveling at the way his mother's mind worked. *Vibrant,* everyone called her. Nothing escaped her notice or her interest, and was often recalled through associations, the way she'd just done. Earlier, Brenda's chin-length hairstyle had reminded her of a story about a dress she'd bought in 1974.

"You should've stopped."

He had. Sort of. "I guess . . . but, we had groceries, and, you know, I'm sure people bother her all the time."

"You're not exactly 'people.' I'll bet she'd be glad to know you're here. The *Paradise* says they're all staying at the Ocean Key—why don't you call?"

"And say what?"

"Well, I've found that *hello* often works, to start."

When he was dating Blue, his parents had been aware of his relationship but elected to keep out of it. The only advice he'd gotten from them was, "Think about the trouble you've had with Renee," which could have meant *Don't get Harmony Blue pregnant, too,* or it might have meant *Protect Harmony Blue from that mess.* He'd finally decided it meant both. After he'd broken things off, they'd accepted his decision without much discussion—until a day later when Blue quit her job without notice and disappeared. Then his mother had grilled him, and what could he say? Blue had seemed to take the break-up with admirable composure. None of Renee's histrionics—which was a relief, but which also made him doubt his decision long after it was too late to do anything further about it.

He was teaching at Carolina when his mom called one day, maybe two years after, and said she'd seen Blue doing a brief on-the-scene report for the WLVC-TV news. "So she's fine," he'd said, glad to know things had turned out well for her, and his mother had answered, "So it seems."

Now she straightened a place setting. "Isn't it interesting that Blue's never been married?"

He thought so. Everyone thought so. Late-show hosts often speculated about it: she was the female George Clooney, they said—among other less charitable things. He said, "You're not imagining that has anything to do with me?"

"No," she laughed, "I may read the occasional romance, but I am pretty sure that a woman like Harmony Blue has not remained single for two decades because she's pining for some man. Even a man as wonderful as my only son."

"Thanks—I think." She must be right. To imagine otherwise would take more hubris than he'd ever had. He did wonder, though, what kept Blue from committing, given that she'd once been a believer. The moment he'd made the decision to end things, he'd prayed that Blue would quickly find a better fit than he'd been, trusted that she would. She'd been a girl who deserved much better than she got.

"Well, maybe she has someone," he said, "and it just hasn't made the gossip pages. Maybe she's really discreet."

His mother shook her head. "What you don't know about the entertainment world. But you'd better learn, if you're going to succeed with *Literary Lions*. You should call her. I would do it myself, but I don't want to make either of you uncomfortable. Call her. Reconnect. I'll bet she knows all kinds of people. She could open doors."

"I can open my own doors, thanks. I'm not going to call her just because we both happen to be here in town at the same time."

"You, my darling, favorite son, are a hopeless businessman. You have to take the opportunities providence tosses in your path."

Mitch let her comment go unanswered. Providence had not been all that good to him, or not, at any rate, in the ways that mattered most.

"What a life she must lead," his mother went on, taking crystal water goblets from the hutch that flanked the table. "She's successful, she's beautiful, but think of the effort it must take to stay looking like she does, especially as she gets further into her forties. Little wonder young women are so troubled these days. They're under such pressure to measure up to Blue and women like her—to appear to do everything perfectly, to look perfect, to overachieve . . . I'm relieved that neither you nor I ever had to raise daughters."

Mitch had to laugh. "Mom, you epitomize the do-it-all beautiful, successful, perfect woman."

She went around to Mitch's side of the table and kissed his cheek. "I'm flattered you think so, but listen, there's a difference: I always dressed and acted the ways I did because I wanted to, because it was 'me.' And I chose my career because I loved the work, and I was good at it—and because your father is so wonderfully domestic that I trusted him with the household stuff. I never felt like I *had* to do anything except be myself."

"And you've done an admirable job of it. So," he said, "is there anything else I can help with?"

She surveyed the table. "No, I think we're good. Enjoy the peace while it lasts."

He went into the den, intending to do as she said. This den had none of the woodsy, masculine character of the one in his childhood home, but it was every bit as welcoming. A round floral rug covered the white-washed wood floor and anchored the rattan furniture. The walls held shelves filled with souvenirs of the sea: starfish, sea biscuits, conches so large you could lose a small dog inside them . . . and there were photos, some of which shamed him, though he never let on. They were in many cases photographs *of* Julian—with Mitch's father, piloting the thirty-foot cabin cruiser he and Julian restored during the four years Julian lived with them, for instance—or *by* Julian, some of which had appeared in national magazines like *Newsweek* and *Audubon* and *National Geographic*. The professional work, these wonderful, remarkable photos of orphans, of landscapes and birds, would not exist if he had succeeded in raising Julian the way he'd wanted to. He'd had in mind a bookish fellow who would share his passions—as smart as Julian was, maybe even a Literary Lion-to-be. He'd been unwilling to believe Julian genuinely wanted something different, and for this he owed his son an apology, long overdue.

Soon, Brenda and the neighbors came in, and the house was buzzing with the voices of women, their conversation peppered with the occasional declarative "Ha!" that Annabelle, Lori and Kira's daughter—fourteen months old, he learned—was enamored with just now. Annabelle toddled from one cupboard door to the next, opening each, then closing it, then opening it again, apparently delighted with the activity as much as the contents.

"What will they do when she's old enough to talk?" he asked Brenda as the two of them carried platters into the dining room.

"What do you mean?"

"Which one is 'mom'? And what will she call the other one?"

Brenda laughed. "I don't know. Ask them. They'll tell you anything—everything, in fact, that you could want to know. Did you know, for example, that Kira has a doctorate in electrical engineering, but since moving here she's decided to try professional photography?"

"She'll get on well with Julian, then."

Brenda looked at him with concern. "I hope you will, too."

"I'm doing what I can. I brought him on to my project, didn't I?"

"You did, but you two haven't talked about anything of substance—unless you've forgotten to mention it to me."

He shook his head. "No. He's busy. I'm busy. We'll deal with all that when we're here in the fall." She gave him her raised-eyebrow look and he said, "Let's not worry about it right now."

The doorbell chimed. "I'll get it," he called to his mother. "Are you expecting a delivery?" Since his dad's stroke they'd been using a do-it-all service, for cleaning and errands and, in his father's case, the occasional whim for crab-and-avocado-cream ceviche, when his mother was out and his father could cheat a little on his usual low-fat diet.

When he opened the door, there was Blue Reynolds.

Her expression was as naked with surprise as his must be. Her recovery, however, was quicker. She said, "Well, Mitch Forrester, I had no idea you were here."

"I—yes—it's spring break. I'm visiting my parents."

She nodded. "So I see."

She must also see, now, that he was at a complete loss as to what to do next. "I—you look great," he managed.

"Thank you." She glanced away, her embarrassed smile making her look so much like the Harmony Blue who had charmed him so thoroughly. "Time's been pretty good to you too," she said.

"Yeah? I . . . thanks." He stared. "We heard you were going to be in town, but I'm just so surprised to see you *here*."

"Oh." She appeared suddenly worried. "I was told that Daniel called my hotel and invited me to join him and your mother—" She looked past him into the house, where a quick glance over his shoulder told him they were being observed by Brenda and Lori, and the baby, now holding tight to Lori's leg. Blue said, "Along with a few other guests, I see, for dinner."

His father, lord. The man hadn't said a word—had forgotten, maybe, that he'd extended the invitation. Or had deliberately failed to confess it.

"Okay. Sure. That explains it then. He didn't say." Realizing he was still blocking the doorway, Mitch stepped backward. "Please, come in." She did, and he turned to introduce her. "This," he pointed, "is Brenda McCallum, and then this is Lori—I'm sorry Lori, I don't know your last name—"

"Goldberg," Lori said, her eyes as wide as her daughter's just now.

"Goldberg," he echoed. "She lives next door—that's her daughter Annabelle, and her, er, partner, Kira . . ."

"Moreno," Kira called from the kitchen doorway, where she and his parents now stood.

Blue stared at Annabelle as if the child was a novelty, her expression curious but also hesitant. Then, abruptly, she looked up at the women as though remembering there were others present. "Hi," she said simply. "I'm Blue Reynolds."

The gathering took on the feel of a party, something like a conference after-celebration where the esteemed guest elected to come out to the bar with the devoted attendees. It was tough to be subdued and natural while feeling awestruck, so no one tried. Instead, they grouped together in the kitchen and smiled and laughed about everything Blue said—though it wasn't a lot, and stared when they thought they wouldn't be caught at it. Even Mitch could not help feeling dazed. This dinner party, her presence in this kitchen, in this house, in this town—it was all so vivid and yet so unreal.

His father brought up some crisis on yesterday's show, something about Blue crying over a guest's emotional outburst. "That poor girl got the better of a lot of us," his father said.

Blue twisted her wineglass where it sat on the counter in front of her. "It was the end of a long week—"

"And your poor old dog!" Lori said.

"My dog—? Oh. Oh, yes, my poor old dog. My pets mean so much to me. I just don't always show it so openly." Lori patted her arm in solidarity and Blue said, "Tell me, does little Annabelle here have any furry companions at home?"

When they'd finished off a good amount of wine and all the fruit, they made their way to the dining room. His mother, beaming like a proud parent, sat at Blue's right and said, for at least the second time, "I can't believe Daniel invited you without telling me!"

"And I almost didn't make it," Blue said. "This is crazy, but . . ." She proceeded to tell them how she'd found the house and decided to make on offer almost on the spot. "Well, not really an offer," she laughed, "more like a plea—'I have to have this house,' I said. Really, I must seem insane." A chorus of protests followed. "No," she said, "it is pretty odd. I'm not impetuous—in my line of work, impetuosity can get you into a lot of trouble."

Kira and Lori agreed, citing several notable examples of celebrity catastrophes before Lori stopped mid-sentence to say, "Oh—I hope we didn't just trash any of your friends!"

"Tell us about the house," Kira said. "I bet it's that two-acre walled estate, am I right? The one that looks like a little Taj Mahal?"

"Or the oceanfront Victorian," Lori guessed. "God, I wish we could have afforded that one."

Blue was shaking her head. "No, neither. It's just a little cottage with this wonderful yard, maybe a quarter-mile from here."

The pair stared at her, perplexed, while Mitch's father stood up with wineglass in hand and said, "We're practically neighbors, then." He raised his glass. "Welcome—"

" . . . to the Conch Republic!" chimed all the women, except non-resident Brenda, who sat looking bemused.

Ah, Brenda. She hadn't moved from his side since Blue's arrival, and seemed to be watching him closely. Not that he was doing anything wrong—why would he? That he still found Harmony Blue—*Blue*—attractive and was enjoying being around her did not mean he was going to ditch Brenda and attempt to win back Blue. If that was what was in Brenda's head, she was letting her imagination carry her off.

That said, he might slow down his wine intake in case his own imagination was inclined to travel the same path.

Brenda raised her glass. "To new beginnings."

Likely she was as fascinated by Blue as the neighbors were, which made him feel a little freer about his own reaction to having Blue six feet away. She *was* still Harmony Blue Kucharski; her mannerisms—the way she lasered her attention on whoever was speaking, for example—hadn't changed. No question, however, that she was also a great deal more than the girl she'd been when he knew her. Watching her, he understood more clearly than ever the term *larger than life*.

After the topic of conversation had turned to how full they all were, they cleared the table and then settled in the den, where Brenda spoke up with a question he suspected had been on her tongue since Blue arrived.

"So, Blue, I'm really curious: How did you go from being Lynn's re-

ceptionist to being—to getting where you are today? It must be a remarkable tale."

Blue glanced at him, then her glance ricocheted back to Brenda, so
quickly he couldn't be sure anyone else would have noticed. He wanted
to assure her it was okay, that Brenda knew about their past.

Their past. He and *Blue Reynolds* had a past. He let the thought fill
him up in a way he'd not allowed before, and it made him buoyant. Or
maybe that was the wine.

"Well, I don't think anyone was more surprised by my career path
than I have been." She outlined—surely for the ten thousandth time—
the path she'd taken. It began with a meeting she arranged with Morgan
Cole, she said, explaining to Brenda, Lori, and Kira who Morgan was.
"We'd met maybe two years previously—"

"At New Year's!" his mother said.

"Yes, that's right, at your party."

Mitch had the sense that this bit, the party, was not embedded in her
standard story. Neither, he soon realized, was any mention of the period
of time that came after his mother's employ and before her meeting with
Morgan—she skipped right over it, didn't even look his way to see if
he'd noticed that she had left a gap. Yet he was positive the omission was
deliberate. Why? Clearly, now was not the time or place to satisfy his
curiosity on that account. Later, though? Maybe if they got a minute or
two alone he'd ask. Where had she gone when she ran away? Who was
she with? A friend? A man? Someone he'd known at the time? How
badly had he broken her heart? He let the questions pile up like a stack
of unopened party favors you weren't sure you were going to like.

Blue was saying, "I had the idea, then, that I might like to be a TV reporter. Morgan took me under her wing, and that helped me get on-air
much faster than I might've otherwise. The assignments were mostly
crap. I did a lot of minute-long interviews with, you know, the fire chief,
police officers on the scene of whatever crisis, the mayor's assistant's
assistant—you name it. If there was a cat in a tree, I was there getting
the story."

That was the most she'd said all at once since arriving. Could be the wine was working on her, too.

Brenda, who was now so relaxed by the wine and the food that she leaned her head against her chair's back, observed, "Those treed cat reports must have been exceptional."

"I don't know about that," Blue laughed. "My next stint, as entertainment reporter, was better. Morgan told me, 'Anyone can look at a camera and talk. Make it personal.' I just took her advice, and the rest followed from there."

Mitch knew, more or less, what "the rest" was: anchor at WLVC, then a morning talk show in Kansas City, then her own show in Chicago, then syndication and world-wide popularity. She was one of those people who seemed to have *the touch*. Certainly she'd had it, if in an undeveloped way, with him.

Brenda said, "You make it sound easy, but I'm sure it took a lot of determination and effort to get where you are today."

"I was fortunate to be working with smart, experienced people who were always on top of the trends. *TBRS* was not my brainchild; I wanted to get on at *60 Minutes* or *Nightline*."

Mitch couldn't imagine that version of Blue. "But you're a natural at what you do. People loved your show from the start—"

"And up you went, like an Atlas rocket!" his father declared.

"Well," Blue said, "maybe a fast elevator."

"I'm hopeful Mitch can find that elevator for his new project," his mother said.

Mitch gave her a warning look. "Mom, really, she doesn't—"

"What project is that?" Blue asked, turning her gaze on him.

A gaze like a spotlight. He blinked. "Just a little thing I'm doing, a biopic thing."

Brenda's nudge told him what he already knew, that he had just undersold his idea, but he couldn't be the aggressive self-promoter he knew he was supposed to be. Not to Blue.

His mother said, "He's being modest. It's a whole series, really brilliant—he hopes to sell it to one of the major cable channels."

"To PBS," he corrected, frowning at his mother. "But yes, a biopic series."

Blue nodded. "Featuring . . . ?"

"Oh. Featuring the greatest American authors. Hemingway, of course—" That sounded presumptuous. *Of course,* as in, *you remember.* He added, "I mean, given that he was a Chicago native who later lived here, well, it seems fitting to start with him."

She said, "And are you still teaching his work?"

"Some. I do a series of American authors—Williams, Wharton, Twain, Faulkner. You know." He felt his cheeks growing hot.

"Hence this biopic *series* idea," she said, smiling in that way she did, that way she'd used to whenever she saw him coming into the office. *I'm so glad you're here.*

His mother said, "Mitch, show her the prospectus you showed Dad and me."

He loved his mother, but she was a steamroller. "Mom. You're putting her on the spot—"

"No, it sounds really interesting. I'd be happy to take a look."

"I appreciate that, thanks, but—"

His mother said, "It can't hurt for her to take a peek. Maybe Blue will have some good insights."

He looked at Blue, and she nodded.

His father thumped the arm of his chair. "Oh, get it over with," he said.

Mitch retrieved the prospectus from his bedroom, returning to find his father telling Blue about the aftereffects of his stroke.

"Lynn keeps saying I've taken on a new persona, but I think she's the one who's addled. You tell me: do I seem any different to you?"

"Not a bit," Blue said. Her expression was fond. Mitch might even say wistful.

He handed her the prospectus. The five-page, plastic-sleeved document looked flimsy in her hands, more a brainstorm than a plan. "It's really mostly a sketch at this stage . . ."

"You'd be amazed at how often producers buy a project based on a sentence," she said, reading the intro, then opening to the next page. "Comparatively, this is a book."

"All right, then," he said, though it didn't feel all right. It felt pushy. He sat down again, wishing the air-conditioning would kick on.

Brenda said, "Are you a fan, Blue? Of Hemingway, I mean, or any of the authors in the prospectus?"

"You know, I don't think I've read a single one of them since high school, or thereabouts."

Thereabouts. Mitch remembered.

Blue read with obvious concentration while the chatter flowed lazily around her. Brenda, next to Mitch on the loveseat, took his hand in hers. "She seems interested."

"She's being polite," he said. Everything he'd eaten this evening sat now like a lead ball in his gut. He couldn't look at Blue. Instead, he watched Brenda watch her.

"Impossible to tell for sure. She doesn't give much away, does she?"

Annabelle drew his attention as she toddled after one of the brindle cats, a hand extended forward as if certain to catch the cat's tail in due time. The cat allowed her pursuit, equally certain he would evade her hand. One of them had to be wrong, and yet across the room they went.

"Well," Blue said, laying the pages on the coffee table. "This is ambitious."

He nodded, certain he knew what was coming next: The project was too big in scope, not interesting enough to attract viewers outside academia—

"I love it."

"What?"

"I do, it's really timely, and I think you're the perfect sort of host."

"You do? I—er, thank you." He was stunned.

"But if you don't mind me giving you some advice . . ." she said.

His mother said, "He doesn't mind at all."

"There's lots of interest in the literary classics at the moment—which is why we're doing our own Hemingway piece on Friday. Given the production cycle, your best chance to get this picked up is now. It's almost April, and the networks will be buying shows in June."

"I'm really only interested in PBS," he said.

"Well, even just PBS, then. So, what I'm thinking . . ."

Everyone watched her, hung on her words as though all their fates were tied to them. She might as well have a wand in her hand, poised for spell-casting. Or had the spell already been cast? He would have to say so. Or was that only the wine?

"How close are you to having the pilot ready?"

"Not until fall," he said. "But you're saying that might be too late."

"Less ideal, let's say."

Suddenly, what had seemed like a careful plan felt flimsy and amateurish. Doubt flooded him. He knew nothing about production cycles, nothing about filming or funding—he knew literature, and authors, neither of which qualified him to run a TV series. He said, "There's no way I can do the pilot before September. My son, you might remember, Julian—he's a documentary filmmaker now, and a photographer—"

"Most of what you see on the walls here is his work," his mother told Blue.

"He's running the technical end of the project, and our schedules don't match up until then."

Blue was looking at the photographs around them. She pointed to a large matted and framed print. "That looks so familiar—was it published?" The image was a close-up of two young girls, five years old at best, staring out from between the limbs of some fallen trees. Mitch had a copy on his office bulletin board.

"It's the one we call 'The Orphans'; it was a *Newsweek* cover," his father said. "Indonesia, after the tsunami."

Lori said, "Haunting, isn't it?"

Kira settled Annabelle on her lap with a bottle. "The boy's got an eye."

Blue watched them, seemingly captivated by the toddler's wide green ones. She said, "He does . . ."

She stood up, then, to take a closer look at one of Julian's bird photographs. A Red-billed Tropicbird, Mitch had been told, cruising at about fifteen feet above Sugarloaf Key as the sun was going down in the opposite sky, behind the photographer. The contrast of the large, white bird, its bloodred bill and foot-long pair of tail feathers set against the blue-violet sky, made for a kind of artistic drama Mitch had not appreciated when Julian was younger.

"You know," Blue said, "if your only hold-up is technical . . . maybe I can help." She turned to face him, looking so much like her younger self that he blinked twice, to verify his vision. She said, "We're here, we have all the equipment and technicians—what would you say to shooting the pilot this weekend?"

"I . . ." What could he say? He'd love to. But he didn't have a finished script, he didn't have permits, he didn't have a real clue what he'd do with the footage after, nor who he'd go to with it when it was done. All these were details he was still working on, or leaving to Julian.

"That's awfully generous. I'd take you up on it if it wasn't so important that Julian be involved in the project." Which wasn't a lie after all.

"Mitch," his mother said, "Julian's getting ready to leave Afghanistan—he might be able to rearrange his plans and join you."

Blue turned back toward him. She smiled, and he felt suspended in a bubble of pleasure. Surely they all felt it, it was irresistible. "Now that sounds worth a try," she said.

"Yes, but . . . Julian is . . . well, he's not exactly difficult . . ." Mitch paused.

His mother said, "He can be a little rigid at times."

"Right," Mitch said. "Stubborn—which can be useful. He's accomplished a lot."

Daniel agreed, adding, "Gets it all from his grandfather."

"Well," Blue said, putting an end to the digression, "you won't know if you don't ask him. What do you say?"

Mitch glanced at Brenda, whose expression mirrored the one worn by the calico cat sitting in the windowsill across from him. Not a bit helpful, and secretly judging. She would advise him to wait, he was sure.

Blue's expression, however, was soft and encouraging, taking him back to a winter afternoon at his apartment, when she was lying on his couch, and . . .

"You have to try," Lori said. "You can't pass up your best shot."

It pained him to answer. "I can't put him out that way." This was a ship that was going to have to sail without him. "Thank you Blue, but I can't see it working out."

"*W*ow," Brenda said later, sitting next to him on the edge of their bed. "That sure was an interesting evening."

He was still trying to process everything, with a brain that was aswim in wine and nostalgia. He said, "Yes, yes it was."

"Nice of Blue to make that offer. Imagine what a sellout you'd be branded if you'd taken her up on it."

"I don't see," he said, taking care to enunciate clearly, "how using her equipment and such would be selling out. Do you?"

"I'm certain it would lead to further involvement, which I suspect is what your mother has in mind."

"My mother," he said, scooting back onto the bed and stretching out. The pillowcase was cool and smooth against his neck, perfect. "She is a businesswoman through and through. She makes things happen."

"Obviously."

"I keep telling her *Lions* is meant for PBS, not, lord, MTV."

"There *is* some middle ground, you know."

He sat up on his elbows, suddenly compelled to ask, "Did you like her? Blue, I mean?"

Brenda looked surprised. "I—sure. She's lovely."

Yes, yes she was.

"What do you suppose she's really like?" Brenda said. "You know, when she isn't being fawned over by zealous fans like the neighbors— and your dad." She laughed. "Did she seem anything like you remembered?"

More. She was everything she'd been as a young woman—engaging and intelligent, always upbeat, always generous—but with the appealing patina of wisdom and experience, like copper after a few seasons of exposure. He said, "Kind of."

"Mm. Well, I don't know that I'd trade places with her. I have enough on my hands with our bunch at the university."

He closed his eyes while Brenda went to use the bathroom, musing over whether she was right, that Blue's offer would have, if he'd taken it, been only the start. Taking advantage of providence, as his mother had put it, was not akin to selling out. You only sold out if you gave up control for money—which he wouldn't do.

Too bad the timing was off. He liked the visions now swirling through his imagination, visions of a successful start, enough funding to craft a show that people really loved. Immersion in the books, in the research. When he'd done all the great Americans, he could expand into British literature—not his field, but he'd be delighted to learn. Visit London, take trips into the countryside—he could do walking tours just as Shelley and Coleridge and . . . and . . . and his memory of British literary trivia was failing him . . . and, well, as they'd done with the others, whoever they were.

He called toward the bathroom, "Who went walking with Coleridge and Shelley?"

Brenda answered, "Coleridge and *Wordsworth*. And his sister, Dorothy. How much did you have to drink?"

Enough to make him think he should at least call Julian and feel him out.

He heard Brenda come back into the room. "Hey," he said, opening his eyes, "I think I'm going to—" He stopped. She wore a different nightshirt from the one she'd had on last night. Shorter. Lacier. Her thighs were bare, as were her shoulders. A tantalizing scent of something floral and spicy caught his attention as well.

"You're going to what?" she asked, raising her eyebrows in that other way she did.

"Never mind," he said. "I'll tell you later."

12

"Well?" Marcy asked, when Blue found her seated with Stephen on the balcony of Hot Tin Roof, the Ocean Key's restaurant and lounge. On the pier below, a three-piece band played reggae music. The breeze was lighter than earlier in the day, barely stirring the bits of hair that had escaped Blue's ponytail during the short taxi ride back from the Forresters'.

Blue nodded to the people gawking at her from the tables nearby, and sat down. Another ship had put in, taking the *Enchantment*'s place, its lights adding to the waterfront's inviting glow. She felt a bit glow-y herself—the effect of the wine, the company at dinner, the prospect of the new house, everything.

"Well, it was a really nice time."

"Excellent. Let's get you a drink." Marcy signaled a waiter.

"Just one, then I'll leave you guys to your beautiful, romantic evening."

Stephen said, "Hey, congratulations on the house deal! It would be so great to live here. If you're feeling generous . . ."

"She's already paying for your transportation, your room, your food, and your martinis," Marcy said. "Now you want a house, too?"

"Yeah, why not?" He laughed. "What I ought to do is find some work here."

"As long as Marcy remembers where *she* works," Blue said.

"I remember that there's always vacation."

The waiter came by and Blue asked for Chardonnay. "Which would

you like?" the waiter asked, holding out a wine list. He looked fright-
ened when Blue waved it off and said, "You pick."

"She's easy, really," Marcy said, grinning her dismissal. "Now, tell
me everything."

Blue inhaled deeply, exhaled. Where to start? "Well . . . I wasn't the
only dinner guest. In fact, Mitch answered the door."

"No shit."

Blue shook her head.

"Who's Mitch?" Stephen asked.

"Old friend," Marcy said. "Did he *say* anything?"

"No, and he didn't pass me a note, either," she laughed. "He's here
with his girlfriend. And the neighbors were over too. We had lobster and
conch fritters and salad—"

"None of which I give a damn about."

"Really, I don't have a lot to report. It was just nice to see the Forresters again." Surprisingly nice, where Mitch was concerned. Not at all
how she would have imagined it, if she'd been willing to indulge that
sort of possibility.

"Not weird at all?"

She shook her head. "It was like a homecoming." A homecoming
where everyone suffered a peculiar amnesia about how they had parted.
Was that what time could do, if you let it?

"Mitch is teaching literature in North Carolina . . . And this is cool:
he has a biopic series he's getting ready to make—"

"Of course he does."

"It wasn't like that at all," Blue said. "It's a great idea. Unfortunately, for him to have any real shot with it, he needs to film a lot sooner
than he'd planned. So, I offered the use of our crew for this weekend."

Marcy sat back and cocked her head, as if seeing Blue in a new light.
"Now was that wise?"

Was it? She had no idea. Her habitual reticence was out of service.
"No matter. He turned me down."

Stephen said, "*That's* what wasn't wise. Is he clueless?"

Blue shrugged. "He seemed . . ." *reluctant* "committed to his existing plan. I told him the offer stands." *Call me if anything changes,* she'd said, standing with him on the front porch, awaiting the cab. She'd noticed his scent, like Irish Spring soap and a touch of chlorine, not familiar but pleasant. *I'm glad things turned out so well for you,* he said. *You seem happy.* She'd felt happy, standing there. Comfortable, the way she'd always felt around him.

The waiter came with Blue's wine, waited for her to taste it, and was clearly relieved when she said it was good. "You made his night," Marcy said as he left. She rubbed her bare forearms. "Stephen, doll, would you mind running for my sweater? I'm feeling a little chilly."

"You bet," he said, getting up right away.

When he was gone Blue said, "*That* wasn't obvious."

"He's had four martinis. He won't notice. Now, I gotta say it: What are you thinking? Is this one of those 'no hard feelings' moves, or is it, dare I ask, the start of a 'second-chance' bid?"

"I told you, he's here with his girlfriend."

"Uh-huh."

"Who is smart and attractive, and really nice."

"I'm sure."

Blue shrugged, but couldn't hide a smile as she sipped her wine. "Okay," she said. "It could be both. I *don't* have any hard feelings, not really, and I can think of worse things than a second chance. He still looks good, he's kind, he seems passionate about his work. I feel like . . . I don't know . . ." Like she didn't have to worry about being *Blue.* Like he could be counted on to value her for her. Like she could tell him the parts of her story she'd held back, earlier, and he would understand. He had a son. He'd be sympathetic.

She said, "One of the neighbors told me the girlfriend is brand-new, so it wouldn't be like I was a home wrecker."

"But just think of the free publicity we could get if you were."

"Peter would birth a cow," Blue said. "Anyway, I have no expectations. For all I know, he might elope with Brenda tomorrow."

"But you hope not."

"I honestly don't know what I hope." She gazed out at the black nighttime sky, the starry horizon that appeared to go on without end. Sirius was just visible, low among the glitter. In about a month, it would disappear from the northern hemisphere to bestow its power on yearners in the southern. Blue's wish came to her in a word: *Ease.*

She looked back at Marcy. "He seemed to be glad our paths crossed."

"Nice," Marcy said, smiling. "So maybe I should call you 'Stella.' "

Blue had to think about this. "What, because we're at Hot Tin Roof? Stella wasn't in *Cat on a Hot Tin Roof;* that was Williams's *Streetcar.*" Either way, she couldn't see the connection.

"No, not Williams. McMillan. *Her* Stella went down to the islands and 'got her groove back.' "

Blue laughed. "Ah, now I get it. I never read the book—or saw the movie, either. Maybe I should try to find one or the other while we're here. Take a lesson."

"Looks to me like you're doing all right just following your instincts."

"We'll see."

Stephen was returning. Blue stood up with her glass in hand. "I'll take this with me. You two have a lovely night, and I'll catch up with you when you're back from the dive class tomorrow afternoon."

"Stay out of trouble," Marcy said.

"I'm going straight to my suite, don't worry about me."

When she'd navigated the labyrinth of hallways and was back in the suite, she left the lights off and opened the patio doors. The ocean, turquoise in daylight, was as black as the sky and dotted with its own stars, the colored lights of boats. Earlier tonight, Kira had told of a nighttime dive out at the reef. An hour-long sail to some remote spot, then into the water with masks, fins, and tanks, and only handheld spotlights to orient themselves. Kira had found the experience of following a tiny corridor of light while sea creatures swam out of sight all around her fascinating; Blue thought it terrifying. *This* was how she liked to appreciate the ocean: from a balcony, with a glass of wine in hand.

She pulled the elastic band from her hair and stood at the rail taking stock. A house. An unintended reunion. And maybe, maybe a second-chance long shot that, if it paid out, might right a lot of wrongs in her life. Not all of them, but some. Right some wrongs, and make the future something to look forward to. She had no idea how she really felt about Mitch—too soon for that—nor could she say whether he felt anything at all about her. She did know that she liked the prospect of feeling really good about him, and that was enough for tonight.

Part 2

If I am not for myself, who will be for me?
And when I am for myself, what am I?
And if not now, when?

RABBI HILLEL THE ELDER

13

*W*hen his phone rang, Julian was assisting in the clinic tent, which this time meant letting a malnourished boy getting shrapnel removed from his legs play with an old point-and-shoot digital camera.

"Go ahead, take it," Brandy said. "I've got this under control."

He knew she did. He asked anyway, "You sure?"

"Yeah, go." Her smile was impersonal, distracted. Already the separating had begun, even though he wouldn't pack out for another week. That was the way of it, and he wasn't sorry, not really. Only sorry he hadn't connected better when they'd had the time.

He took the call. "Julian here."

"Hi, J, it's Dad."

His father's voice sounded odd. "Is Daniel all right?" he asked, walking toward the supply lockers where it was relatively quiet. Not another stroke. Or worse.

"Yes—everyone's fine. It's just that, well, there's been a turn of events regarding *Lions*. Possibly. It's like this . . ."

Julian listened. *This* was an unexpected opportunity—no, not just unexpected, remarkable. A lightning strike of good fortune, or almost. *If* his father could get his script in order right away. *If* the city would grant permission—which Blue was certain they would. *If* after they finished, the editing could be done quickly. "She's offered us the use of her production lab to do it. We'll have a much better chance of success this spring, so I'm thinking, let's accept—if you think you can get here by this weekend."

"Whoa—*this* weekend?"

"I know it's short notice. Your grandmother said you're leaving soon anyway, so I just thought—"

"Hold on. Blue Reynolds says this spring is ideal, but what does she know about it? She hosts a talk show."

"She does a lot more than that, J. And English used to be her favorite subject."

Like that made all the difference. "All right, say she does know. There's always next spring. We'll have most of the series done by—"

"Interest is at its height," his father said. "Producers are looking for ways to capitalize on it right now. And while she hasn't said it outright, you understand, there's reason to think her production company may even have interest."

"In literature."

"In a smart, fresh biopic series. They'd have a lot of clout with PBS—or possibly one of the cable networks."

"So you'd sell out?"

His father sighed. "Not at all. It wouldn't hurt us to think a little bigger, though. She offered the use of her crew, their gear, everything."

"Is this really how you want this gig to go? A rush job?"

"It's worth a try. Time's of the essence."

Julian watched the activity in the room in front of him. A dozen doctors and nurses, a sea of dusty, grungy, dark-haired people whose eyes beseeched and accused, depending. Wasn't it always?

"So I'd have to be there by *Saturday*?"

"Where are you, exactly? Is it difficult to alter your travel plans?"

Julian rubbed his chin, which he'd shaved clean this morning. "I'm at a refugee camp outside Gereshk. It's in Helmand." Silence. "South-central Afghanistan."

"I'm trying to place it. Has it been in the news?"

"Not likely. The camps aren't exactly a hot topic." One more reason for Julian to be here. Most of his work would go into a website and book project meant to raise money, and consciousness.

"In any event, I'd reimburse your plane ticket change fees. I have to be back to work the following Monday, but like I say, Blue offered to let you do the editing at her studio in Chicago. I expect you'll be eager to get home."

Home. He made it sound so . . . common.

This altered plan was not an impossible one; he did have the time, the flexibility. Still, he said, "I don't know. Doesn't sound like they need me." Like *his father* needed him, to be more accurate.

"Maybe they don't, but I do. I know this changes things a bit, but I thought it would still be nice to work together."

Would it? Julian was as unsure about that as he'd been after he'd agreed to do it. It *might* be nice. It *might* be a new sort of hassle that would put another tense decade between them. They had never teamed up for anything, not even a last-minute homework assignment.

When Julian didn't reply right away, his father continued, "I'm willing to stick to our original plan if you prefer."

Would he stick to it? Would he, just on Julian's say-so? The possibility made Julian weirdly uncomfortable, pleased and angry at once. Where had this understanding been, this generosity, when he'd wanted it so badly?

"I appreciate that," he said. "It's really your call, though, to do a rush job or not. I'm not even sure I can make the logistics work. Let me check into things and I'll get back to you, all right?"

"Yes, absolutely. That sounds good. Let me know—as soon as possible, obviously."

"Will do."

"Great, okay. And . . . well, take care." They hung up.

The child who had his camera was crying now. There was only so much that distraction could accomplish.

Pretending to still be occupied, Julian held his BlackBerry and acted as if he was engaged with it, pressing buttons, scrolling. What he saw on the small screen, however, was the reflection of fluorescent lights suspended overhead and, when he angled the screen, a pair of dark, conflicted eyes, the eyes of a fourteen-year-old boy whose mother was about to check into a psychiatric hospital. The eyes of an eighteen-year-old young man whose father refused to accept his passion for photography. The eyes of a weary thirty-two-year-old who had seen more than his share of conflict and wanted to finally resolve his own.

The idea of leaving here for Key West appealed like the prospect of a whisky shot sometimes did, something quick to steady the nerves. Neither Chicago in very early spring nor his mother at any time of year held great appeal. The islands, though? The islands had captured a piece of his soul in the four years he'd lived there. Every return since then was a reunion.

He sat down on a footstool. Island life in the Keys. It wasn't quite what the tourists saw. Or rather, it was that, but it was that and so much more. Yes, sand and sunshine, coconut palms and gentle turquoise waves. Women in skimpy sundresses. Impetuous tattoos of rainbows or hibiscus or the skull and crossbones. Sunburned scalp as seen through cornrows. Drunken sex with strangers—even for him, once.

Excepting that mistake, for him Keys life was a less hedonistic morning paddle among the mangroves, where he might find a snowy white heron standing in sea grass, plucking breakfast out of the shallows. It was wahoo or tarpon or bonefish filleted under the watchful eyes of pelicans. It was a dive to a reef teeming with ocean life, or a visit with Christ of the Abyss, who refused to answer the questions Julian brought to the barnacle-encrusted shrine.

He knew you had to stay longer than a few days or a week in order to see past the glossy brochures about swimming with dolphins, to go deeper than the gay PrideFest celebration, nightlife on Duval Street and the sights from the Conch Tour Train. You had to stand on a painted wooden porch watching tropical storms roll across the Atlantic from West Africa, feeling the wind-lashed rain. To really know Keys life, you had to be on a first-name basis with the weaver who sat, every evening, at the intersection of Caroline and Whitehead. You had to inhabit the rhythms of tides and sun and storms, and listen to the ghosts whispering from behind the banyan trees.

Who was this Blue Reynolds, that she thought she could stop by his grandparents' house and upend everyone's plans with her insider advice? Was her standard—and by extension the standards of all the TV-show production types—so low that she really thought they had a better chance with a quickie effort now, as opposed to a quality product later? If so, he shouldn't be surprised. Reality TV shows were his answer incarnate.

So many people in such a hurry over things that mattered so little . . .

Julian saw one of the translators coming toward him, and slipped the BlackBerry back into its customary pocket. He'd go to Key West next weekend, he'd make it work. If *Lions* morphed into a broad collaboration, God knew when—or whether—he would have another opportunity to spend time with his father. He'd shoot the pilot and show Blue Reynolds how things *should* be done. His father would see that he was equally capable of making a Darfur documentary or a bit of literary infotainment about an author who, like so many of the people Julian had known in the Keys, really just wanted a good drink and to be left more or less alone.

*F*riday afternoon in Key West was the middle of Friday night by Julian's internal clock. He longed to be horizontal. The sunlight trickling through the palms overhead felt soft but somehow unreal, unreal as the scene before him.

He understood organized chaos, but usually the people milling about him (in this case, on the sidewalk in front of Hemingway's house) were not dressed in expensive cruisewear, in name-brand flip-flops, in golf shirts that cost more than some Afghans earned in a year. They did not usually have bright smiles and wide-brimmed hats, three-hundred-dollar sunglasses, careless sunburn, careless lives. They did not often speak English and take pictures of celebrities with cameras that rivaled some of his—all of which were locked away in his grandparents' car for the moment. He missed the customary weight of having one hanging from his neck.

Somewhere nearby, frangipani was blooming; he breathed deeply and got, too, the scent of warm coconut. Someone had been sensible enough to put on sunscreen.

The rugged brick wall enclosing the compound was too tall for most people to see over. A dozen or so resourceful tourists had brought milk crates or folding chairs or bicycles—propped against the wall—to stand on. A pack of others pressed together at the wall's entrance. Lynn was there now, talking to a big man who stood behind a makeshift metal gate. Her straw hat was as wide as her shoulders and banded by a sleek satin ribbon of deep violet. She certainly didn't lack presence.

His grandfather spotted a friend who watched the commotion from across the street. "There's Carlos—you remember, we play chess on Tuesdays? I'll be right back."

"Sure thing," Julian said, waving to Carlos. He went to a middle-aged woman who stood on a folding chair. The backs of her legs were painfully red. "Can I take a quick look?" he asked. "Just for a minute, I swear. My dad's in there."

She stepped down and Julian took her place, looking where the rest of the crowd did: at the front of the two-story tan box of a house, where lime-green shutters and a black wrought-iron balcony made a backdrop for his father, who stood before the cameras talking animatedly about the house's history. Blue Reynolds, in a rose and white floral dress and crocheted white cardigan that begged to be photographed—it was the texture, the lightly tanned skin in the gaps—watched his father with rapt attention.

And snagged his own.

Seeing her in the flesh, in three living, breathing dimensions, he understood why his father had wanted to alter his plan. Even from fifty feet away, she was magnetic. What was it? Her trim curves, wavy hair, broad smile, intelligent eyes—they *were* intelligent, he had to admit—were not traits she alone owned. She was built like many women he knew; some he'd known very well, in fact. And yet there was something more going on with her . . . Something he felt in his belly, and lower. Something he knew already he would need to ignore. Even if she weren't older (eight years? nine?), even if she hadn't once dated his father, she was no prospect for a guy like him. Her reach extended far outside their bit of shared history and in-common hometown—where, of course, she was revered as though she were Chicago's own Olympic goddess. Watching her, he could smell her influence like a scent overlaying the coconut and frangipani.

"Wait another minute or two, they're about to take a break," Lynn was whispering from near his elbow, "and then you can go say hello."

She and Daniel—or he should say *Ken,* for the moment at least—had brought him here to *The Blue Reynolds Show on Location in Key West!* directly from the airport. Ken wasn't sympathetic to his lack of sleep or the six flights in his recent history, *six,* not all of them smooth, that got him here to this last inhabited island in the string of Keys. Astronauts, Ken said, had to do a lot more on a lot less. "Take Apollo 13, for one vivid and personal example," he said, and proceeded to recount how long he and Lovell and the rest had gone without sleep so that they could save not just the lives of three excellent men but also NASA's reputation and its congressional allowance. "Aw, quit yer whining," is what Ken said, with an affectionate slap on the back.

Although this alter ego of Daniel's expressed the same opinions Daniel held, Julian preferred the original, preferred "Daniel one-point-oh," as Lynn often referred to him. Julian didn't have a past with Ken Mattingly. Ken wasn't the life preserver he'd clung to in those first months after his mother was admitted at old Northwestern Memorial. How many nights had he sat in the den next to his grandfather, fiercely glad to be there and not in Chapel Hill, while at the same time fiercely wounded by what seemed his dad's indifference to his having chosen to stay in Key West? Daniel, maybe sensing this, had filled his head with trivia about the islands and the currents, about pirates and developers—who were in many cases one and the same.

Though eighteen years had passed, he recalled too well the day he'd come home from baseball practice and found his mother sitting on the tub's edge in her underwear and bra. The water was running and she held her wrists above the stream, letting her blood course down into it.

The police had been kind to him despite his angry fear, a supportive female officer sitting silently beside him in the ER until his grandparents arrived, followed an hour later by his father. The man had seemed a stranger to him, and responsible, somehow, for the razor blade and the blood.

Two days of discussion and debate among the adults had followed. The outcome: *Mom needs some help.* No shit. *She'll be in the hospital for a while. I'm teaching, so we think maybe you should go to Key West for the rest of the summer, then see how things are.* It wasn't until November, however, that his father said, "You're welcome to come live with me . . ." leaving the next word, "but," unsaid, yet Julian had heard it. Screw that.

Had it really been there?

While living here as a teen, he could hardly set out from the house with his grandfather without getting a history lesson. Even today, Ken wanted to talk about how World War I aviators trained at the nearby Navy base, terrorizing the residents with their daredevil antics much the way he, Ken, had, he said, in his early days at NAS Pensacola. Yes, it was Ken's story, but it was a story just the same.

About his dad, Julian now asked, "How'd he get on the show?"

Lynn said, "It's the funniest thing; on Wednesday night, I guess it was, we were all eating at A&B, and they decided he should be the tour guide for today's show. Thought having an actual scholar would give the piece dimension, I think Peter said."

"Peter?"

"Her producer."

Her being Blue, obviously. And hadn't they all gotten awfully friendly in a short space of time?

A sleek black cat lounged on the path near his father's feet, tail whipping against the ground in an irregular rhythm, as if to show who was truly in charge here. If Daniel had his facts straight, more than ten thousand travelers visited Hemingway's island home every year to see where "the iconic alcoholic," as Daniel liked to call him, had written *For Whom the Bell Tolls,* as well as opened his home to polydactyl cats like this fellow. Julian admired the cats, six-toed and normal alike, and in some limited ways he admired Hemingway. The stories held up, he'd give them that. How could he not admire the work when he was named for one of Hemingway's characters? A minor one, from "The Snows of Mount

Kilimanjaro," but legendary. A Hemingway nod to F. Scott Fitzgerald. This is what came of being born to an English professor who was himself an English teacher's son.

He watched Blue turn to face one of the cameras and say, "When we come back: We go inside Papa's house, and reveal the truth about what he went through while living here in this island paradise."

She held the camera's eye until a technician called, "We're clear."

"Come on." Lynn grabbed Julian's hand and pulled him down from the chair, then led him past the metal temp fence.

"Look what I've got," she said, striding over the snaking cables without a thought. Julian kept his eyes on her feet until they'd cleared the hazards without incident, then looked up to find they were almost nose-to-nose with his father and Blue.

Quickly, Julian extended his hand to shake his dad's, heading off any possibility of an embrace. "Good to see you," he said, and then was immediately sorry to be so stiff.

"And you," his dad said warmly. "Here, meet Blue Reynolds. Blue, my son Julian." He actually sounded proud.

Up close, Blue practically hummed with energy. "Hi, Julian, I'm very glad to meet you," she said. Her dark eyes were wide, sincere, welcoming. She had a slightly raised mole on her cheekbone that might or might not have been made flesh-toned by makeup. A pretty woman, but not a knockout. Not, looking only at the powdered, lipsticked surface, *that* remarkable, really.

Right.

He shook her extended hand. A firm clasp. Strong. Woman in a man's world and all that. "Yeah," he said, wanting to keep hold of her hand. *Fool.* "Same here."

Lynn patted Blue on the arm. "I just wanted him to say hello. We'll get out of your way now."

Blue smiled at him, her eyes curious and somehow vulnerable. His stomach dropped, a strange and not altogether pleasant sensation in the way it was a betrayal of his better judgment. She looked away, saying, "All right. Will you two be joining us when we've wrapped things up here? Mitch, you and Brenda are going down to Mallory Square with some of the crew, to start with, yes?"

"We are. She hasn't seen the spectacle yet."

"Right," Blue said, "and then some of us are going to grab dinner and drinks someplace where we won't be mobbed."

"Join us," his father said.

His grandmother answered for both of them: "I can't, but I'm sure Julian will." Then she grabbed his hand to lead him back to where the crowd waited.

He would have given a different answer, but in an odd, probably masochistic way, he didn't mind.

What he'd intended to do, needed to do, was sleep. Sleep, however, was a need he was accustomed to ignoring. It was obvious that if he wanted to get any time with his father in the next forty-eight hours, he would have to do what Alec had advised him at the beginning of their first assignment together in Bosnia: "As you'll learn quick enough, you have to go along to get along." He'd figured it out, trial and error, losing only the one finger in all these years, instead of his life. A lot to be said for that.

Whatever was unfolding here, he knew he could handle it once he got over his jet lag. Blue Reynolds did not have to be a trip wire, not if he didn't allow her to be. Caution. Patience. Determination. He possessed these traits, even if they didn't seem to be quite as accessible at the moment as he'd like them to be.

The other thing he'd learned to do was divest himself of expectations. He and his father weren't going to undo a lifetime of mistakes and misapprehensions in a weekend, or a week, or a month. Success sometimes had to be measured in small increments. It hid, very often, in the small gains: a pinky lost but a thumb saved, a father's white-flag offer accepted, a cold beer on the waterfront at sunset. What was his life about, if not proving that much could be made from little?

14

"*He* seems pleasant enough," Blue told Mitch as they waited out the last thirty seconds of the commercial break. More telling was what she didn't say: that she thought Julian Forrester was beautiful. Startlingly, disturbingly beautiful. Thick dark hair, strong forearms, long fingers she couldn't help but envision stroking a woman's face—her face, in fact, before she caught herself.

And his eyes. They were darker than Mitch's. Violet, almost. Deep, unreadable, magnetic . . .

Enough. There was no time, no space for such a distraction right now. It was nothing. A chemical reaction. Meaningless.

Even so, she felt a flush creeping upward from her neck, and prayed her makeup would hide it. Good that Mitch was watching Julian and Lynn as they left the grounds.

"Julian's great," he said. "And really talented—you saw some of his stuff." His expression turned worried, and he sighed as he faced her again. "I hope everything goes well this weekend."

"It will," she said with more confidence than she felt. "He's here, isn't he?"

"I see you're still an optimist." Mitch's smile returned, and in *his* eyes—his familiar, friendly eyes—she saw again what she suspected she'd been seeing throughout the week: a spark, if not an outright flame. A bit of light and energy she feared Brenda had seen as well. Even so, his being attracted was a nice thought, a satisfying thought, like fate coming around full circle and rewarding her—in a small way, yes—for the heartache he'd caused her in the past.

She got the cue that they were down to the break's final ten seconds. "All right, ready? From here we head inside and all you have to do is answer those questions we scripted. Good?"

He nodded, and they were back on-air.

The Hemingway home was as interesting as all such places are. Pieces of legend that capture the imagination. She'd been in Anne Frank's Amsterdam hiding place, she'd walked the Vatican's halls, she'd spent three nights in the Playboy mansion—alone in her suite, except when Marcy was there; they'd watched *Sleepless in Seattle* one of those nights, something romantic, sweet, a palate-cleanser of a movie.

The more you revered the legendary resident whose home you were in, the more awed you were by being in the same space where they'd once stood, slept, cried, loved. As she and Mitch moved from room to room, up to the writing loft and then into the garden, she felt the house become the theater of drama that Mitch saw. Saw the author as a brilliant, conflicted man who sat in *that* chair, drinking scotch, three glasses before dinner every night. A four-time husband who, despite the bouts of depression that grew worse as time wore on, ascended the wrought iron stairs—a curved staircase originally, Mitch said, as they climbed the straight, tourist-friendly risers—and wrote stories showing the salvation love *could* bring. *Might* bring, if character or fate allowed. She listened to Mitch talk about how the author had strolled along the garden pathways here, pondering Robert Jordan's path in *For Whom the Bell Tolls*. Right here under the waving palms and towering bamboo, a story, a literary classic, had grown and bloomed along with Pauline Hemingway's plants.

And then they were up to the show's close. Blue stepped away from Mitch (they always closed with only her in the frame) and outlined their schedule for next week.

"Thank you all for spending this week with us here in the islands. Hasn't it been amazing? I've had a terrific time and can't wait to visit again." Sooner than she would reveal on-air. All she needed was for thirty million people to know she'd just bought a house here. Word would trickle out soon enough, despite her request for Lila Shefford's discretion, despite the purchase being in her holding company's name rather than her own.

"Don't forget to join us back in Chicago on Monday, when we'll be talking to Dr. Dean Ornish about heart health, and then Tuesday, Carrie Ann Inaba will show us some calorie-burning dance steps that will not only tone your tush but jazz up your love life, too."

She read her *thank-yous* from the prompter so that no one was forgotten, and with that, one more episode of *TBRS*, one lovely, surprising week's work in Key West, wrapped.

The crew cheered. They were eager to get back to the things they'd come here for, to the diversions, thoughts of which had preoccupied most of them for the months leading up to this week. There was always so much stress over location broadcasts, so many things that could go wrong. This trip, though, had been a breeze—an ocean breeze. She felt the corners of her mouth curl upward at the thought. In addition to having gotten full cooperation from local officials, a hearty welcome from locals in general, steadily ideal weather, and the surprises of a new house and old friends, she'd felt her optimism returning. Like the beans her first-grade class had grown in clear plastic cups set on classroom windowsills, it seemed all she'd needed was fresh soil and sunshine. She smiled at this thought, too. Instead of a green bean, she was a Blue bean—and Julian was nothing more than a passing cloud.

Instead of mature and professional, she was silly.

As Mitch came up to her, she glanced at Marcy, expecting a thumbs-up for the show and getting a concerned look instead. *What?* Blue mouthed, and Marcy gestured for her to come over to the porch.

Blue told Mitch, "Hey, there are some things I need to take care of before we get the party underway, so I'll have to catch up with you later, all right?" Maybe they'd get lucky and Julian would decide not to join them. Her initial reaction to him suggested that would be best.

Mitch fidgeted with his wristwatch, twisting it as he said, "Oh, absolutely. Of course."

"You were fabulous," Blue assured him. "Really. More than we bargained for by far." He was so easy to be around, so accommodating. "A real pro," she said.

"I'm delighted to hear it," he said, and looked it.

The spark again. It wasn't right to fan it, not here and not yet—if at all. She'd watched Brenda sticking close to him all week; her attachment was obvious. That Mitch was less attached was apparent too. Still, the call was his to make. All she would do was try to let him see that she would welcome his attention.

So she smiled warmly. "I'm delighted to say it." She looked past him, to where Marcy waited, frowning. "Marcy's getting impatient, so I'll say so long." She left him there, certain he was watching her go. Pleased that he was watching her go. Sorry, just a little, that he was watching her go. She liked Brenda.

"All right, spill it," she told Marcy as she stepped onto the porch.

Marcy handed over Blue's phone. Making sure no one was within earshot, Marcy said, "It's Branford—I mean, he's not on the phone this *second,* but he says he needs to talk to you *ASAP.*"

Blue's breath caught, and she coughed. "Did he say why?" As the words left her mouth, she knew how stupid they were. He was forbidden to tell anyone anything, would not even tell *her* anything until she'd repeated their agreed-upon code of authenticity, which changed after each conversation. He'd created a master list in the guise of a fifty-question geography worksheet, which she glanced at each morning. If not for the weight of their business, she would find the whole system ridiculous— found it ridiculous anyway, something right out of an old B-movie thriller. Still, it worked.

Marcy said, "You don't think he—?"

Blue raised one shoulder, a half-shrug, her voice trapped by the pressure in her chest. If this *was* the call she'd been waiting for all this time, if her son was suddenly found, she had some choices to make. Knowing where he was would lead to needing to know *how* he was, *who* he was beyond name and occupation. Would he be open to meeting his birth mother? Did he even know he had a mother other than the one who'd raised him? If he knew, or when he found out, would he want to know who she was, how she was, where she was?

Did she have any right to put the questions to him?

Her chest felt tight. Was she breathing? She didn't feel like she was breathing. "I'll call when we're back at the hotel."

"Just so you know? He sounded—that is, he said it's urgent."

"Urgent? But . . ." But she wasn't ready for *urgent*, didn't have her answers yet.

As often as she had imagined her lost son, she'd imagined his parents reaching out to her, wanting her to meet him again. An innocent play-date drop-in. *This nice lady's name is Blue, honey, say hello.* Or face-to-face at the Field Museum, maybe, when his family visited on vacation. A short introduction in front of dinosaur Sue, followed by an ice-cream cone on the outside steps. Or maybe the two of them would meet in his parents' front room—those well-off adopting parents would be the sort to have a front room, impeccable pale carpeting, antique pianoforte with Grandma's oval portrait framed in cherry hanging above—and if all went well they'd move to the less formal family room, because of course she was part of his family, and wasn't that wonderful?

The more successful she'd become, the more difficult the scenario became. A Chicago news-reporter mother was not the same as a syndicated-talk-show mother, was not the same as an international TV personality multimillionaire mother. The absurdity of the situation paralyzed her; how could she go to him as Blue Reynolds? *Honey, it's time for you to meet your birth mother, say hello to Blue Reynolds. Ms. Reynolds, my son Collin.* Or Ray. Or Brice. Or Benjamin. Or Sean. The absurdity of not knowing her own son's name paralyzed her. He was not, of course, *hers,* except that he would always be hers, she could not help her possessiveness. He was *of her.* Nonsensical did not begin to describe the pathways of her thoughts.

What she was conscious of in the thirty minutes it took to divest herself of assistants and officials and get driven back to the hotel, was the way her heart raced. Her urge to lean forward in the car as though that would make it go faster. Her sweaty palms. And yet when she was finally alone in her suite, she stared at her phone's keypad for agonizing minutes before she could press the buttons.

The line rang and she waited, one hand pressed to her belly, her eyes on a single dark-green leaf of a plant too shiny to be real. If Branford had found him, she didn't have to do anything right away. Once found, he was not likely to be lost again. She could wait a day or two. A week, even. She didn't have to do anything at all. It should be enough to simply know.

She heard a click, a pause—a canned voice advising her to leave a message.

15

The Green Parrot was full of salty types, locals. They looked like illiterates, many of them: uncombed, unshaved, probably also unwashed. Mitch, wearing the same pressed slacks and golf shirt he'd worn for the show, drew not the looks of recognition he thought he might get after having just been on live TV a few hours earlier, but suspicious stares. Maybe they thought he was a cop.

Brenda, on the other hand, drew approving nods; women in low-cut knit tops were always well-received in a place like this.

Julian had suggested the bar, saying the "important TV people" would fare better here than in the more obvious tourist-clogged places. Those TV people who, he'd noted a half-hour earlier, were missing all the fun of the sunset celebration over at Mallory Square. They'd watched the sun disappear into the ocean amidst a crowd that cheered two young men juggling flaming torches, and Julian had said, "Of course Blue Reynolds can probably buy her own sunset, suited to her schedule."

Mitch was surprised by the negative tone. "I think you've got her wrong, J. She's not a diva."

Julian shrugged. "Her world is fake," he'd said.

Julian, in a faded green T-shirt from a Dublin club, fraying shorts, and flip-flops, fit right in with the other Green Parrot customers. He stopped near one corner of the square bar that dominated the center of the room and turned around.

"I'll see if I can get us some space in the back." He pointed to the other end of the room, at a second bar that took up the short back wall.

In the area between the two bars was a pair of pool tables and a group of heavily tattooed bikers, whose gleaming Harleys Mitch noticed were precision-parked outside. More bikers were pulling in; the chest-rumbling chatter of the engines through open-air windows drowned out all other sound before abruptly cutting off.

While Julian went to talk to the bartender in back, Brenda pointed out a large portrait hanging behind them. It was the cartoonish face of an ugly blond male. She said, "He looks like a pedophile."

A man seated near them said, "That's Smirk."

"Of course it is," Brenda laughed. "And that?" she asked, pointing upward at a puffy thing that resembled a gigantic sea urchin strung with green Christmas lights.

"Parachute."

"Just in case?" she asked the man, who nodded.

Julian was back. "We're all set."

Brenda excused herself to use the bathroom. "Order me a Mai Tai," she called as Mitch followed Julian to the back.

"Teacher's and soda," Mitch told the grizzled, tattooed bartender. To Julian he said, "That was Hemingway's drink."

"I am aware," Julian said.

The bartender filled a highball glass and set it in front of Mitch. "Maybe you want to take it over to Sloppy Joe's," he growled. "I've heard told the Big Man liked it there."

Julian was laughing as he said, "We'll also need a Mai Tai and a Corona, lime."

"Forgive me," Mitch said, sitting down on a bar stool just left of center. "I forget that you had so much Hemingway exposure here."

"Don't worry about it." Julian sat down, his back to the bar. Mitch turned so that he faced outward too.

"Seems like a different lifetime, those years when you lived here." He remembered being anxious about Julian's well-being, but the memory was distant, more knowledge than feeling. Despite his intentions and despite what was right, Julian's life had always been peripheral to his own, and those few years were no different in that respect. He'd only been grateful that his parents were willing to be parents again that year when his tenure was being considered. As much for Julian's sake as his own, he couldn't risk being passed over. Once approved, his career would finally be safe from Renee's problems—he'd intended to bring Julian to Chapel Hill by Christmas. Julian's decision to remain here in Key West had hurt, but he'd understood. Or tried damn hard to understand.

He said, "A different lifetime, and a lifetime ago."

Julian took his beer from the bartender, pushed the lime into the bottle's neck and, thumb over top, tipped it upside down then righted it again. "Tell me about it."

Better to find a new topic. "So, it's been a whirlwind week here." He shook his head. "I can't believe I was just on *The Blue Reynolds Show*." Everyone said he'd done a great job, that he'd been genuine and authoritative. The only criticism came from his father, who said he should've worn something more colorful.

"The start of your fifteen minutes," Julian said.

"Maybe. I can say that being on-camera is more fun than trying to get grad students motivated at nine AM, before their caffeine kicks in."

"Working with Blue Reynolds isn't all bad either, I'll guess."

The remark was innocent enough, but Mitch heard an edge in Julian's tone—or thought he did. Criticism? Challenge? Suspicion? Could Julian sense his guilty conscience? Because the truth was that working with Blue was so very much the opposite of bad. When she'd turned that gaze of hers onto him this afternoon, he'd felt as though he was—for that moment at least—the most important person in her life. He'd felt as if everything he did and said and thought mattered to her. As if the time they'd been apart was two weeks, not two decades. It was delightful, and worrisome. He liked her too well.

He said, "No, it isn't all bad. She's very good at what she does."

Brenda came out of the bathroom and stopped at one of the pool tables to talk to a tall man whose long black hair was held back by a pink bandana. A roses-and-daggers graphic covered his entire left arm. They appeared to be discussing the game in progress, Brenda suggesting a move that would get the seven ball around the twelve and into the far pocket. She knew all the moves and was a skillful player, too, routinely beating Craig and him when they'd played in the rec room at her house. Those had been good times, the three of them gossiping about their colleagues and debating postmodernism's effect on the literary canon.

"You going to dump her, then?" Julian asked.

"What?" Mitch turned toward him, startled. "No. Why would you say that? Am I acting like—"

"Relax. I was just wondering."

Just wondering. Just wondering because Mitch's enthusiasm was too obvious? "No, no, we're good," Mitch said. "Everything is fine."

Brenda had been supportive of his decision to shoot the pilot this weekend. Craig's sudden death was itself enough of a motivator to choose sooner over later, they'd agreed. Then he'd been invited onto the show, and then Blue had mentioned she would come by the shoot tomorrow to see firsthand what he was about. All good, they'd said.

His mother was certain that Blue was coming to the shoot because she intended to discuss *Lions* with her team at Harmony Productions. Brenda rather thought she intended to hook him up directly with someone at PBS. For his part, he thought she might just want to be sociable one last time before returning to Chicago. He wasn't sure which scenario he preferred. He downed half his drink at once.

Julian said, "So, Brenda likes Mai Tais. What do you suppose America's Favorite Talk-show Host drinks?"

"No idea." Should he know? Julian was looking at him like he expected a real answer. "We'll have to wait and see when they get here."

"Hope it's soon. I'm starving."

They planned to order ribs from Meteor Smokehouse next door—the island's best—and eat while they listened to whatever band was playing. There was always somebody worth hearing, or so Julian claimed. Mitch had to wonder if Julian's insider knowledge was being shown off for his benefit. As if to prove how right Julian had been to choose to stay here after Renee's breakdown. As if to prove that despite Julian's globe-trotting, Key West was his rightful home in a way Chapel Hill never could have been. Julian, it was long apparent, would not have thrived in the genteel, traditional university atmosphere—and Mitch would not have let him loose in the free-for-all arts scene that existed outside academia's gates.

There was irony for you.

Brenda had taken a pool cue and was demonstrating the angle needed for the shot. She looked great, as she did in all the summertime outfits she'd dug out for the trip: colorful skirts inches shorter than the skirts she wore for work; tops that showed off small-but-still-decent breasts. And backless sandals with short heels, a kind of shoe he'd never seen her in before. Sexy shoes. She seemed to be redefining "widow," and getting younger in the process. The biker took the cue and lined up the shot as she'd directed; the ball went in and the other bikers cheered.

Brenda bowed, then joined Mitch and Julian at the bar. "Did you see that? I'm a hero."

"Very impressive," Julian said. He had his BlackBerry out.

"Checking email?" Mitch asked.

"Thought I'd read the script once more. You did a good job of cleaning it up."

"Thank you." He'd spent a lot of the week revising and rehearsing, alone in Julian's old guesthouse bedroom. "Did I tell you Blue plans to come by the shoot tomorrow?"

Julian looked up. "No."

"Yes, well, she might have some useful insights for us."

"Is a Blue Reynolds version of *Lions* really what we want?" Julian said.

"That's not how it would go, I'm sure. I should mention that your grandmother thinks there's a chance Blue might get Harmony Productions involved—which would be incredibly generous."

Brenda said, "You're forgetting there would be money in it for Blue, too, if things worked out."

Julian reached across Mitch to tap his bottle to Brenda's glass. "My sentiments exactly."

"I'm not forgetting," Mitch said. "I just don't believe that would be her motivation."

"One has to wonder, then, what her motivation would be." Brenda's tone was unmistakable.

"She can have any man she wants," Mitch scoffed.

Brenda nodded. "Yes, that's my point."

Mitch changed the subject, asking Julian whether he'd had a chance to talk tech with any of the crew while they were over at Mallory Square.

Julian said he had. "But I'm sticking with what I planned."

"Is that a good idea? I mean, don't you think—"

"Yes, it is," Julian said, "and no, I don't."

"Okay, I was just asking. These guys, they do this every day, and—"

"Nine," Julian said, as a woman wearing the shortest shorts Mitch had seen since the seventies joined the bikers at the pool table.

"Nine what?" Mitch said.

"Documentaries. I've done nine full-length documentaries. Direction, cameras, lighting, sound. I understand production values. I understand a literate audience. I'm here," he said, pausing to take a drink, "because you believed I could do the job. So let me do it."

"I didn't mean to offend you," Mitch said. "I know you're qualified. It just seemed like an opportunity, that's all."

Julian looked at his watch. "I'll go grab menus. If they aren't here in five minutes, I'm ordering without 'em."

Brenda said, "Me, too," and gave Julian a reassuring smile.

As soon as Julian was out of earshot, Mitch said, "I can't tell if he hates me, or Blue, or life, or what."

"He's just worn down right now."

She was probably right. Still, he worried that Julian would alienate everyone around them, and Blue in particular. A fine thank-you that would be.

Julian was still gone when the group arrived, Marcy and Stephen in the lead, Blue behind them, Peter and his wife last. Blue looked distracted but lovely, wearing the same thing she'd worn this afternoon.

"Leave a spot for Julian," Brenda said as they moved the bar stools into a loose circle. Blue, who had been about to sit next to Mitch, moved over one.

Peter was full of praise for Mitch and the show and the entire week's work, dominating the conversation. "Best we've had in months, hands down," Peter said. "Next week's mail will be a big improvement over what I hear has been coming in this week."

Marcy said, "It hasn't been all bad. We got as many letters commending Blue as damning her."

Blue said nothing.

The band began its warm-up as Julian returned, a waitress trailing him. Mitch saw him assess the seating arrangement and frown before sitting down. The waitress began handing out the menus, her hand shaking when she gave one to Blue.

Marcy took a menu and told the bartender, "A bottle of tequila— Who's in?" she asked the group. Stephen and Peter raised their hands.

"Water for me," Blue said.

"You are *not* drinking water. Set her up, too," Marcy said. "You need a drink."

Blue looked at Marcy, then at what the others were having. She nodded toward Julian and said, "That looks good."

Julian's frown deepened and Mitch thought, *Oh Christ*. But all Julian did was raise his bottle high enough for the bartender to see, and say, "One more like this."

*W*ith the music so loud, conversation was all but impossible except with the people closest by. For Mitch that meant Brenda who, after a light dinner and four drinks, was calling the ongoing pool games with animated play-by-play analysis, and Julian, who had eaten well and drank even better. He'd said little to Mitch, and nothing to Blue. Brenda caught Mitch glancing at him for probably the fifth time in twenty minutes and said, "Quit worrying."

"I'm not worrying," he said, though of course he was, and of course it showed.

The pink-kerchiefed biker was waving Brenda over. "We're doing teams," he called, "and I need a good partner!"

She was out of her seat before Mitch could suggest maybe it was time to head home. When she pointed at him with a questioning look, he shook his head, thinking it was wiser to stick close to Julian. In a minute she had recruited Stephen and Peter, too, and the bikers were urging Blue to play.

"Thanks, but no," Blue called, standing up. Two women with leather-wrapped braids and bikini tops to match took pictures of her with their cell phones.

Mitch just caught Blue's words as she asked Marcy something about walking back to the hotel. Marcy looked at Stephen, and Mitch could see she was torn—things were just livening up. Mitch wondered if he could—or even should—offer to go with Blue. He wouldn't want Brenda to take it wrong . . . Maybe if he was quick . . . He tried to envision how far they were from her hotel—

"I'll go," Julian said, laying a twenty on the counter. Mitch swung around, sure he'd heard wrong in the din of the ending song and the applause that followed.

But Blue was saying, "No, stay. It's fine, I'll get a cab."

"You'd end up waiting longer than it takes to walk," Julian said. "I was leaving anyway."

She hesitated, then said, "Okay. That's—well, that's a generous offer, thanks. Marcy, just catch up with me mid-morning, or whenever you get up, okay?"

"Will do. You feeling all right?"

"Fine."

"Yeah?"

"Yeah."

"Okay then," Marcy said. "Julian, make sure she doesn't get kidnapped by pirates."

Julian nodded. "She's safe with me."

16

$\mathcal{N}$ow here was something Julian never imagined himself doing: walking up a dark Key West street at eleven o'clock at night with a woman whose yearly income exceeded some countries' gross national products. Such a thing was a conceptual impossibility—and yet, here he was. Here *they* were. A slightly tipsy, past-his-limits man and a too-attractive, slightly older woman. It was beginning to drizzle, which didn't seem to trouble her—a surprise. He should not be here, not tonight, not alone. His offer had been knee-jerk, good manners besting good sense. It wasn't at all about wanting to be alone with Blue. That would be absurd.

If he *had* imagined doing this, he wouldn't have thought it would feel as awkward as it did. They'd walked three blocks so far, and, even away from the noise of the bar, she hadn't said a word. So he hadn't spoken either. Here in the dimness of Whitehead Street, there was only the sound of their shoes on the sidewalk, distant laughter and music, the odd dog's bark, the tiny peeps of chicks in hedges, and the continuous hum of night insects—a sound like soothing music, a symphony compared with the night noise he'd grown accustomed to.

He thought she'd be talkative. Weren't talk-show hosts supposed to be super-friendly, inquisitive types? She hadn't done anything he'd expected tonight—sit near his father, horn in on Brenda's turf, talk incessantly about herself, that sort of thing. In fact she'd hardly spoken to anyone. If he hadn't known, he might have thought Marcy was the celebrity in the room, or Stephen, with his Nordic features and the stories he was telling of designing restaurants with Jamie Oliver.

Glancing at Blue's profile, he wondered if she had written him off as uninteresting, beneath her notice or attention.

Well, what if she had? It was no sweat—except that he *was* sweating. She walked fast, and he was unused to the humidity here after so long in the deserts of the Middle East.

Her phone rang and she stopped suddenly, looking at the display. Her eyes were wide and worried when she faced him. The phone continued to chime. "I have to take this," she said.

She moved away from him, closer to a towering banyan tree whose branches spanned a hundred feet or better. "Ketchikan," he heard her say into the phone, then, "Really. What was the cause of death, did it say? . . . I hope you do. Keep me posted."

She didn't turn back to him right away; in the darkness he couldn't see whether her stillness was contemplation or grief so he waited, unsure of what he should do. Then she turned around and said, "Sorry for the interruption."

"No trouble." That was it?

They were at the end of the block, two more to go before reaching the hotel, when she stopped again. "Would you mind if we take a detour?"

He checked his watch. Things were barely getting started on Duval. For him, however, it was . . . too many hours past his bedtime for his brain to be able to do the math. "Why? Where did you need to go?"

"Nowhere, really. Never mind—I forgot that you're on Afghanistan time. You must be desperate to get some sleep."

"I'm pretty beat," he admitted. "But I did catch a few winks between"—which flight had it been?—"Zurich and Miami. I'm doing all right." Sort of. The image and feelings the word *sleep* conjured were beginning to take on a hallucinatory quality. Still, seeing as they were already walking, and it was such a nice night, and she looked so appealing in that white openwork sweater . . . "So what's the detour?"

"It's stupid," she said, pulling her hair up with both hands; she held it there with one while she fished in her skirt pocket and found an elastic band. As she fixed her hair into a ponytail, she continued, "See, I was out walking the other day, and I fell in love with a house—so I bought it. Maybe you heard?"

He hadn't. "Nope. I guess they didn't think to tell me. You went for a walk and bought a *house*?" Not a hat, not sunglasses, not some cheap shell jewelry or a fake parrot on a metal hoop.

She nodded. "I'm not an impetuous person, either."

"No, no, clearly not."

"You're laughing at me."

"It *is* a sort of improbable statement, coming from a woman who went for a stroll and spent a couple mill while she was out."

"I know. Do I sound even crazier when I say I couldn't help myself?"

No; this love he understood. "Not so crazy," he said. With his foot, he nudged a toad and watched it hop a few inches, then stop. "I used to want to own a place here until I realized that, with the way prices have increased over the years, I'd have to sell my soul in order to afford it." Which implied that she'd sold hers. And hadn't she—she and pretty much everyone else in show business? He believed so, but it was hard to reconcile that belief with the evidence of *her*, damp, fragrant, present.

He said, "I didn't mean to say *you* sold—"

"Don't worry about it."

For a long moment, neither of them spoke. He scratched his chin, thought about whether he should let his beard grow back, what the differences were between toads and frogs, whether or not the mist would turn to rain and drench them, or affect the shoot—anything to avoid analyzing his desire to extend his time with her. Alec would probably tell him he just needed to get laid.

Blue said, "Anyway, I wanted to go . . . visit the place, just for a few minutes. I sign the papers tomorrow afternoon, but I haven't seen it at night, and I just thought—"

"That it might be smart to check for obnoxious neighbors who blast their stereos at full volume?"

"Right, or—"

"Zombies?"

She laughed, and the sound penetrated, giving him that empty-belly feeling. He nudged the toad again, harder, popping it into the grass.

"I hadn't thought of zombies."

"Huh," he said, "well you should. In fact, I'm pretty sure my high school math teacher was one."

"Oh, you went to high school here?"

"I did." Tough years, long past. "So where's the house? Let's go have a look."

"Okay, great—let me just take off these shoes." She took them off and was immediately two inches shorter. "That's so much better. Who invented heels, anyway? Bluebeard?"

"Napoleon, I think."

As they walked, she asked him about how he'd come to live with Daniel and Lynn. Last she'd known, she said, he was living with his mother in one of the Chicago suburbs and seeing his dad whenever his parents could work things out.

"Which was like never," he said, surprised that he'd wanted to answer. "Then Dad got the job at Carolina and moved to Chapel Hill." After which his mom declared his dad to be a self-centered, uncaring son of a bitch who would abandon his own son.

Julian recalled knowing even then, at age ten, the term "bipolar," given that his mom regularly declared she was *not* that, no matter what anyone said. He remembered, too, that he'd fought with her the night of her outburst, defending his father while at the same time secretly fearing she was right about him. "You made him want to go!" he'd yelled. "He had to get away from *you*!" He couldn't tell, though, how much of his father's alienation was her doing. Was she reacting to rejection? Wasn't the divorce all because he wouldn't be faithful, that he couldn't keep his eyes, and hands, off the college girls? Or was all that in her imagination, as his father claimed? Had he taken the new post because he, Julian, had so much trouble connecting with him whenever they *did* spend time together? And how was he supposed to be able to judge?

But none of that mattered now. Nor did Blue's role in those events, if she'd had any. But he couldn't help asking, "Did we ever meet?"

"No," she said. "There weren't too many opportunities."

Why was her answer such a relief? It shouldn't matter whether they'd been acquainted back then, her a teenager, him a kid who tried to forget reality by reading C. S. Lewis and Mark Twain. She was never going to think twice about him—or if she did, it would be as his stepmother, the way Daniel had suggested. He needed to wrap his brain around that and forget this odd pleasure he felt in having her so close. A physical reaction. Suppressable.

Maybe.

She continued, "I never saw you. It was just your dad, and your grandparents. They were . . . I was . . ." She sighed. "I didn't have the greatest childhood either. But anyway, I lost touch with all of them until just last weekend."

She was so unlike his image of her that his mind was filling with questions, yet he couldn't just start barraging her. Maybe if he shared first, she'd share, too—it's what they always told the kids in the camps to do when they were trying to make friends.

As if.

He said, "Well, there's not much more to my story. I lived with my mom until the summer before I started high school. She—you never knew her?" Blue shook her head. "She has some issues," he said. "She's doing pretty well now, but back then she was really at the end of her rope.

"Her parents had died a few years earlier—not at the same time, but within a year or so of each other. So when she hit bottom, I came here to stay for a while." He kept it simple; Blue's sympathy was not what he was after. He shouldn't be after anything, except maybe some charitable contributions—why did he need to keep reminding himself? Why wasn't he in bed, sleeping off his journey and the beers and whatever was making him so much less sensible than usual?

Blue paused, turning to look at him when she asked, "Why here and not your dad's—or would you rather I didn't ask?"

"This was just a better choice for me." He took a step, and she moved along with him.

"Key West must have seemed like a teenage boy's paradise."

"Sure," he said. No need to tell her that his choice had been a test: if his father wanted him to live in Chapel Hill, he'd fight his decision to stay here. When that didn't happen, Julian could only conclude that the offer to live in Chapel Hill had been made solely out of duty. It hadn't occurred to him that maybe he'd been so convincing in his argument that he'd be happier here that his dad had *believed* him.

"So you stayed here until you went off to college?"

"Not college. I did more of a trade internship." Extensive lessons with a photographer in Miami—and then he'd signed on with the Red Cross and taken a space-available military flight out of Homestead Air Reserve Base, bound for Chechnya.

They'd reached the corner where her soon-to-be-vacation-home was located.

"I assume it's this one," he pointed at the house closest to them, the only one with no lights burning, inside or out.

She rested her hand atop the gate. "Yep, this is it."

He studied the shadowed structure, the dense, black jungle of a yard. She was lucky to get the wide lot. "Looks great. If you need some inspiration, you should tour some of the gardens in town while you're here."

"Yes, Lynn suggested that too. Now *she's* quite a gardener. I'm thinking of trying to grow some pineapple, like she's done."

"Her friends say she has not only a green thumb but green hands."

"I can see why," she said, nodding. "Beautiful place. I love the pool, and they have a charming guesthouse."

Where he should be sleeping right this very moment.

"It's so quiet here, so normal . . ." She turned and examined the houses around them, taking longer than he expected, as though her mind was elsewhere. He watched, curious. She said, "Can you believe I saw a macaw here the other day? Scarlet red—it was gorgeous. Just flying right through the trees!"

He nodded. "I've heard of people turning them loose here. Beautiful birds, aren't they?"

"Yes—and the painted bunting. I just bought a sculpture of one. Do you think I'll get any here, in the garden?"

"In late winter you might. You like birds?"

"I—well, I guess I do. I just never gave them much thought before coming here. Do you? I saw that picture you took of the . . . the . . ."

"The frigate bird?"

"Right. Frigate bird. Odd name, but amazing photo—you really have a talent." She looked away as she said this, the way a shy woman might.

"Thanks," he said, rubbing the knuckle where his finger used to be.

She opened the gate. "Anyway, I'm going to just step into the garden here . . . Do you want—"

"Nah, I'll wait here," he said, because he *did* want, and that was a problem.

"Okay," she said, so easily that he was sure her invitation had been nothing but politeness. And why would it be more than that? He could take a good bird photo, so what?

She dropped her shoes by the wall, saying, "I'll just be a minute." Then she stepped past the gate and disappeared into the shadows.

He sat down on the curb to wait, resting his arms on his knees, his chin on his arms. The scent of jasmine was strong. He closed his eyes and breathed deeply. Would it always transport him, as it was doing now, to his teenage summers? Long days empty of purpose, when he longed for everything he couldn't name and rejected everything he could?

He pushed away the memory, thinking instead of being here, on the curb of a house that would soon be occupied by Blue Reynolds, of how bizarre it was to have her walking barefooted through the wild garden just behind him. How it was only thirty-six or so hours ago that he was sitting on the edge of his bare cot, packing his gear, imagining her as a lovely-but-fire-breathing dragon. Obviously she was no dragon. If anything, she was more like a lamb.

A very, very wealthy lamb. A lamb with a hugely popular television show. A lamb who might yet gambol her way into the Forrester pasture, but not in any way he would find endearing.

17

$\mathcal{F}$ive AM came too early for Blue. The alarm clock made a startling reminder that during the few hours she'd managed to sleep, Branford had been en route to some small West Virginia town where Meredith Harper—not Jones, he'd learned—had died from pancreatic cancer. The obituary said she'd moved there with her husband and daughter twenty years earlier. The husband died a few years later, the daughter was apparently still unmarried. He planned to drop in at the daughter's unannounced. "I find it's the most effective strategy in these kinds of situations," he'd said.

She shut off the alarm and pulled a pillow over her face, held it there, then threw it onto the floor.

If she'd slept even three hours she'd be surprised. And what time she had slept was spent in the repeating loop of a dream she'd had before. She'd been at her mother's childhood home, her own first home, the one with the tiny yard. Or it seemed to be that house; she had no true memory of it, had only ever seen bits of it in faded three-by-three Polaroids.

In the dream, she lived there with only her grandma Kate; always they were rolling out pie dough. Blue's palms were tight, dry, coated with flour, and everything she tried to grasp slipped from her hands. A pie tin, a glass of water . . . She tried to turn doorknobs but couldn't. Her grandma leaned over the table, rolling, rolling . . . her blue polyester pants were loose across her thin backside; Blue knew she was ill, and tried to phone the doctor, only to have the phone slip and drop to the floor.

Sometimes the dream ended here. Other times, like last night, she would dream that she was waking, a thick confusion where she discovered she was in her mother's bed and her mother was still out. So she'd turn over, go back to sleep, and wake again, but not really wake, and her mother would still be gone.

So the alarm was a relief, but the reality it brought was an anxious one. What would Branford learn? Would it get her any closer to her wish? Every possibility seemed equally possible and improbable. When would she hear from him next? And what if some radical terrorist group succeeded in nuking major U.S. cities, knocking out all communications before he called? What if it already had, and the news just hadn't made it here yet?

"Now *that's* likely," she said, sitting up and untwisting her nightshirt. Even if no one else on the island was tuned in to the larger world—which if the Green Parrot's crowd was any indication, was not as far-fetched as it might sound—Peter would be. With his earpiece phone and his does-everything palm device, he was like a walking media receiver. Janelle said he was up and checking the news at five o'clock all seven days of the week.

The image of an entire nation of media junkies in chaos remained with Blue as she used the bathroom and then went to the armoire to choose clothes for the day. Linen shorts again, and maybe the violet tee . . .

Violet, like Julian's eyes.

Julian. He was not at all what she'd been expecting. He seemed like an old soul, maybe because he'd seen so much. Too much, probably, but she admired him for it. And while he'd been reserved—even antisocial—at the Green Parrot, he was much less so afterward. She's been expecting *difficult, rigid, stubborn,* but got funny and thoughtful instead.

She chose a sea-glass green shirt and closed the door.

There were worse places to ride out a crisis than the spit of land she was on right now. Imagine, no cell phone service, no television, no radio . . . nothing but warm days under blue skies, a horizon of palms and sea . . . she hadn't tried coconut milk yet, but it might be good; she was open to it being good. Here, on a lounge chair with the sun browning her usually protected skin, there was a chance she would be able to forget everything that bound her to the mainland. In the shade of her new home's trees, she could while away the days with fresh pineapple juice and all the books she'd been wanting to read since forever.

Of course, everyone she cared most about would be safe—her mother (and Calvin, to keep her mother happy); Mel and Jeff and the boys; *her* boy, wherever he was—because she'd know if something had happened to any of them, the same way the Baltimore woman she'd had on the show last spring had known the precise moment her twin brother was killed in a small plane accident. Blue had been skeptical of the woman's account when Peter first brought up the program idea, but it had proved out.

If you were paying attention, the woman claimed, you could tune in to all kinds of things. Music on nearby radio stations, TV broadcasts, even other people's thoughts—not mind reading per se, but "perceptive awareness," she'd called it. Blue hadn't said so, but she'd had one somewhat similar experience of her own: Three years before, she'd fallen asleep on a flight to London and dreamt of a grand house with a lake view, a white canvas tent set up on a clipped lawn, a party underway; a young man in cap and gown stood on the flagstone walk, welcoming an old man in a fine navy suit. It was nothing like her usual dreams—no story, no muddled emotions. She'd awakened certain that she had seen her son, a vision, not a dream. She was so persuaded of this truth that a week later she'd hired Branford, to prove it.

Whereas last night's dream persuaded her of nothing except to drink less before bed.

She phoned down to the restaurant for room service. Grapefruit juice and a hard-boiled egg would do. Then she checked her email, half hoping Branford had jumped protocol and sent her some kind of optimistic update. *Made it to West Virginia, found M's daughter waiting up with files in hand*. He hadn't; in fact, everything in her inbox was work-related, except for one message from her mother. The subject line read, "Gone Fishin' " and there was an attachment. Probably junk, but with her mother, she never knew for sure. She opened the message.

We had a whim. See pic. Much love.

The attachment, a photo, showed her mother and Calvin sitting side-by-side in a painted gondola, a canal stretching out behind them. Her mother's hand trailed in the water.

Venice. Their whim was *Venice*.

What was their world coming to, when her mother was running off to Italy with a man she'd only just met at the same time Blue was spending two million dollars on a house she'd only just seen? A house she'd visited last night in a dreamy mist, with a man she would not think about further. A house only a half-mile away from Mitch's parents'.

She hoped she and her mother both knew what they were doing.

When her breakfast arrived, she was showered and dressed and ready, more or less, to face the day. She would spend the morning helping Mitch with the *Lions* pilot in whatever ways she could, then meet Lila Shefford at the closing attorney's office at one. They'd expedited everything. Her own lawyer had overnighted the check; all she had to do was show up and write her name a few times, and then Lila would hand over the keys. Just like that, she'd own her fifth home.

Melody might be willing to stay at this one. That Jeff didn't fly had been Mel's excuse for why they had never accepted her offers to use any of her homes when she wasn't there. Blue was sure, though, that Mel preferred to avoid feeling like the poor relative, unable to enjoy what Blue had because she was preoccupied by what she and Jeff had not. Mel couldn't have any objections to staying in a charming, unassuming house in Key West; despite its cost, it was no finer than Mel and Jeff's house, and half the size. An ideal place for a couple who could finally vacation without their children.

How good it would feel to call her sister that minute, share her excitement about the house and offer the use of it. She wished she felt she could make such a call. Wished Mel were not so threatened by her success. Why did Mel undervalue the riches of her own life—steady, true Jeff; two well-adjusted sons; a close-knit community that gathered often for fish boils and festivals and fund-raisers? Melody had a good, honest life, something to feel proud of.

In the beginning, Blue had been eager to share every success with her sister. When the show went into syndication and she bought her New York loft, she'd called Mel and Jeff to offer its use to them, thinking Mel would leap at the chance to stay free in New York. Before the farm, before Jeff, Mel had dreamed of designing edgy clothes, living in Greenwich Village, seeing shows off-off-Broadway and eating Chinese food every day. It was this goal, Mel had liked to say, that got her through the boring-ass days of her senior year. Then she'd met Jeff, and Jeff dreamed of owning his own spread, and Mel was so impressed with Jeff that she adopted his dream, dirt, weeds, worms, and all. Blue, though, was sure Mel hadn't forgotten the appeal of New York. The day Blue's offer on the Soho apartment got accepted, she'd call Mel and said, "It's just a few blocks from where you used to want to live, remember? You and Jeff can stay there anytime you like—see the shows, order Chinese take-out—"

"I'm sure happy for you and that thirty-million-dollar salary raise you just got," Mel said. "But *People* hasn't run *my* story yet, on how we haven't had rain in three months. It's a dust bowl up here. Do you know what drought like this does to the beans? To our income? We'll be lucky if we can keep the fuel oil tank filled this winter."

"Oh. I didn't—I mean, look, let me send you some—"

"I'm not looking for pity, and we don't need anyone's charity, Harmony Blue. We've got this far on our own, you know; two hundred acres isn't a hobby farm."

"It's not charity. I have more money than I need, so why not—"

"I'm glad for you. Enjoy it. I gotta go."

Mel was right to be cranky, Blue understood that. In her eagerness, she'd failed to see her sister's point of view, failed to appreciate how widely the gulf had opened between them. She'd tried to be more considerate since then.

Unless something had changed Mel's attitude—and Blue worried that years of plentiful rainfall and, now, a good lease deal with Green Giant wasn't enough for that—this new house would, in Mel's eyes, be just one more bauble for Blue's collection. One more thing Blue didn't need, one more extravagance highlighting their wildly divergent paths.

Suppose Mel knew the truth about what Blue *didn't* have, *couldn't* buy . . . ?

Then she'd know what a fraud her big sister was. Better to leave it alone.

"Onward," she said, tucking her phone in her pocket and taking her egg to eat on the way.

Cloud cover filtered the morning sunlight, softening the lines of the shops and houses of Whitehead Street. The flora—she would have to check that guidebook, learn some plant names—seemed saturated with color. If she picked a leaf from a shrub and squeezed it, surely green would ooze through her fingers and drip onto the cool pavement.

From the sidewalk in front of the Hemingway Home's entrance, she saw Julian standing in the open side yard, his back to her, adjusting a tripod. Balanced atop it was a small video camera—smaller by far than what her crew used. She couldn't see Mitch yet, nor any of her crew, though the presence of light towers and a pair of screens suggested they were nearby.

"Good morning," she called as she reached the porch.

Julian turned, glanced at her, looked away. "Good morning."

"Did somebody drop the ball? My crew was supposed to set you up with our camera equipment."

"This was all I wanted," he said.

"Oh. All right. Where's your dad?"

A shadow of displeasure crossed his face, so quickly she wasn't certain it *was* displeasure—not certain it was a shadow, for that matter. "Inside," he said, nodding toward the house. A colorful rooster strutted by them in the grass.

"Everything ready to go?"

"Yep."

"Great," she said, wanting to end the exchange. Yet she continued to stand there, searching for something more to say. Just to be friendly (she wanted to believe this explained the urge) after the favor he'd done her last night, the pleasant hour they'd shared. "Did you manage to get some sleep?"

"Some," he said. His hand rested, still, on one of the tripod's knobs.

She had the feeling he would like her to move along, if not leave altogether. Fine. That was fine with her. "Well, good," she said. "I'll just, um, go in and say hello."

"Okay."

A quick look behind her as she opened the door confirmed her feeling that he not only wasn't watching her, he was engrossed in getting the camera set—not that such a simple camera could take that much effort.

Inside the foyer was Mitch, one of her crewmen, and two museum volunteers, all four of them with Styrofoam cups in hand. Mitch's face lit up when he saw her, provoking her to smile, too.

He said, "Good morning!"

"Hi," she said, nodding to the other three. "I see you've all fortified yourselves."

The mustached volunteer, who she knew from yesterday was a regular porch-sitting Hemingway look-alike, held his cup aloft and said, "Cuban coffee—don't tell me you're not hooked."

"I'm supposed to avoid all caffeine," she said, though the rich scent was making her want to revert to old habits.

"Good God, that's inhumane."

This morning she could not agree more. "So, what's the schedule? Looks like Julian's just about ready, out there."

Mitch said, "He was out the door before I even got up this morning. Did everything go all right last night?"

She looked past Mitch, to the tall screened doors of the living room, and Julian outside. "Yes. Fine."

"Glad to hear it. He seemed a little antisocial, and—"

"No, really, he was pleasant." There was that word again. "And you? Did you all have a good time? Who won the pool tournament?"

"God knows. By the time we left, no one was keeping track of anything except who would buy the next round."

"You don't look any worse for the wear." He looked very good, in fact. Engaging. Warm. The Mitch she remembered from long past.

He said, "You look very nice yourself. That color's good on you."

The look-alike volunteer said, "Can I get in on this mutual admiration society?"

"I will admire you very much," Blue said, "if you can tell me where to find a cup of that coffee."

Outside, Mitch positioned himself in front of the house while Julian double-checked the lighting and sound. Blue, now fortified with a cup of coffee herself, took the opportunity to assess him more fully than she'd done this week. He looked nervous at the moment, but he was without question more handsome than he'd been in his late twenties. As with so many men, the silvering of his temples and the lines around his eyes gave him character and dimension.

Julian, she noticed, looked almost nothing like Mitch. His eyes were darker, his hair was darker, he had fuller lips, a more pronounced nose, and bigger bone structure overall. Both of them were attractive; Mitch, however, was camera-ready.

He noticed her watching him and smiled nervously. "Any tips?"

"Try running through the first bit without the camera on," she suggested.

Mitch wiped his hands on the back of his pants. "Okay—good idea. J, just stand there but don't film, okay? I'm going to run through the intro."

He started, sounding confident for a moment before beginning to stammer. He stopped. "Shit, that was pretty lousy. Let me try again." Again, he began well, then lost his concentration.

"Hell, I'm never going to get this right."

"Maybe not, but you'll have treated us to every swearword in the process," she laughed. "Here, let me show you something." She went to him and stood arm-to-arm, looking out toward the camera and avoiding Julian's eyes.

This close to Mitch, she could smell soap and fabric softener, feel the heat of him through his shirtsleeve. An odd intimacy she couldn't process just now. She pointed at the camera. "Okay, that's your favorite student, the most promising kid you've had, ever. Give me a name."

"What? Oh—um, Alicia. She's astonishing, a prodigy, really; only twenty and almost done with her PhD."

"Great. That's Alicia, and she's hanging on every word you say, right? She's *so* glad she got to come to Key West and see where her literary idol came up with so many remarkable stories. She's waiting for you to dazzle her." She looked at him, modeling confidence. "Okay?"

Mitch's face relaxed, and he smiled. "That's brilliant."

Blue backed away, out of the camera's range. "I know. Do it."

Julian said, "I'm going to shoot. In case he gets it on the first try."

Mitch looked up into the trees, breathed deep, looked at the camera, and nodded.

This time, he was far more convincing. When he finished, she said, "Hey, that was terrific. Now, have another swig of that coffee and do it again."

"Again?" Julian said. "That was really solid."

"It was. Now that he knows he can do it, he'll be even more engaging on the next take."

Mitch said, "Maybe we should move on and then come back to it later if there's time. I don't want to waste half our day on the intro."

She disagreed. "I'm not saying your prospective producers won't watch the entire pilot, but look: If the first ten minutes don't absolutely persuade them that you're the guy and this is the show, you might as well not shoot the rest of it. Maybe that's not fair, but that's how this stuff goes."

"That's showbiz for you," Julian said. He leaned down and put his eye to the viewer. "Ready."

Blue gave Mitch a sympathetic smile. "Remember: Alicia's waiting for you to prove she was right to choose Carolina and you over, um, what, Princeton? Harvard?"

He nodded and started again.

She watched, satisfied that he was warming to the task. Everything about this project looked promising. Julian had lit the set expertly, lending brightness without glare and making Mitch appear engaging. Mitch sounded clear and knowledgeable, a man enamored of his subject.

She wondered if she was irritating Julian with her direction. Even if she was, the outcome was proving her right. Just as Morgan had once advised her, no viewer would care about her words unless she pulled that viewer right through their television and into her world, whatever and wherever it might be. People thought it was easy—*she'd* thought it would be; she'd thought that all she had to do was face the camera and talk without flubbing the report. When she'd tried it that way, the results were snooze-worthy. It hadn't mattered that her hair was lustrous and her body lean, as unmarked as it had been before she'd gone off track and had a child. It hadn't mattered that when she looked in the mirror, she saw herself as a *contender.*

I will be Diane Sawyer, she would say. *I will be Barbara Walters.* Even so, the results of her early assignments declared that she would remain a junior reporter whose best jobs were found-pet stories and the recounting of the minutes of suburban town hall meetings. Something needed to change.

Morgan's advice had been for her to visualize the camera as one ideal viewer, someone she wanted to impress. She had visualized Mitch, a fact that now had a new, strangely fateful significance. That moment leading to this moment—was there not a strong message in all this that she should be attending to?

She would think, *See what you're missing?*, giving the camera her best intense look. *What you could've had?* If he hadn't dumped her, she would never have abandoned her good sense. There would have been no pregnancy and no adoption and no desperate need to reinvent herself as someone who *mattered.* In an alchemy of energy, she'd transmuted her anger at him, at herself, into determination. If she would never become a Forrester, then she would become something far grander. If not a princess like Cinderella, then a queen, like Elizabeth. She would use success not as revenge but as refuge.

It had worked.

Just as her advice to Mitch was working now.

He finished, and she applauded. "Give that man an Emmy."

He bowed. "That felt great," he said, as the crewman joined Julian to begin disassembling equipment and moving it indoors.

"You have the knack." Certainly as much as most of the rest of television's hosts, and, with practice, maybe he'd develop a persona that viewers would tune in for regardless of their interest—or lack of interest—in Herman Melville or Robert Frost.

"Thank you for being here, for shortcutting this for me in yet another way."

She said, "It's nothing." It was becoming quite apparent, though, that it was *something*, more than just a good distraction while she waited on Branford. What, though?

"Really, Blue. This is awfully generous. After how I treated you—"

She waved away his concern. "Twenty years ago. Things didn't work out, so what? It happens all the time."

"Especially to me," he joked.

"So why shouldn't I help out an old friend, if I believe in what he's doing?"

"Some women would as soon pull out their own manicured fingernails."

"Well, I guess I'm not them."

"No," he said, "you are definitely not like other women."

A negative, in her view. It was time for a change. "With your permission, I'd like to see whether my team at Harmony might have some interest in the series." The offer was genuine, and if it created yet another thread of reconnection in the process, that would be more evidence for her developing theory. "What do you think?"

Julian approached, the camera under his arm and the tripod in his hands. As he pushed past them, he said, "Get one of those light towers, would you?"

Mitch waited until Julian was inside, then said, "I'm overwhelmed, Blue. This has been quite a week. Nothing is turning out at all the way I'd imagined it."

18

$\mathscr{A}$t three o'clock Saturday afternoon, Blue was standing at the gate of her newest house, keys in hand. She had felt no trepidation in signing the paperwork, none in turning over the check with its seven figures. So why were her hands trembling now?

Rain fell, light but steady, pattering the umbrella she'd taken at Lila Shefford's insistence. The commission Lila had just earned from this one sale was literally ten times Blue's first-year salary at WLVC; the woman could afford to give away an umbrella. Blue was glad she'd taken it and walked the seven blocks. She was part of Key West now, an actual homeowner. No car ride would convey that feeling the way a walk over wet pavement, across—or through—puddles, past crowing roosters and a soaked but jovial mutt could, and did.

The gate's latch slid easily. The gate itself moved easily, swinging wide open, inviting her to take ownership. She wiped her hand on her shirt and stepped onto the brick path. One step, another, until she was clear of the gate. She pushed it closed behind her.

A soft clicking from above drew her attention; there, beneath the sheltering umbrella of a banana-tree branch, sat a brilliant red macaw.

"Well hello," Blue said. "Make yourself right at home."

The bird cocked its head at the sound of her voice, then went back to preening its damp feathers.

She walked the rest of the way to the porch, stepped up, closed the umbrella and leaned it against the wall. The light was low here, close, and she fitted the key into the lock, wondering who else had done exactly the same thing in exactly this same spot, and whether they, too, had felt safe, protected as they turned the knob and knew they were home.

For the better part of an hour, she went from room to room slowly, looking each one over, noting the wide moldings at baseboard, doorjambs, ceilings, windowsills. The millwork, all hand-done in the very late 1800s, looked as though it would endure several centuries to come. The floors, too. Lila had said the flooring was made up entirely of reclaimed wood from wrecked European ships; this parlor floor, then, upon which she was standing, might well once have been a tree that shaded a valley cottage in Switzerland, or a stone farmhouse in an English copse. Later, it had been sawn, sanded, shaped into decking on a vessel that had carried people across thousands of miles of ocean—many times, probably—until some unfortunate night when the odds caught up with it. A storm? A battle? Who had been on the ship then? Who had lost their fortunes, who their lives?

"There are stories here," she said, and her voice filled the small room.

Then her phone rang.

The caller's number was the one she'd been waiting all day to see; her heart lurched. "Hello?"

"You know the code?"

She had to think. "Oh, Louisville, right?"

"Sorry for the delay. I had a small crisis at home—my daughter jumped off a swing and broke her arm when she landed."

Blue sank to the floor and sat, legs folded. "But she's all right? Do you need to go back?"

"No, she's fine. Just wanted me on the phone with her while she waited for X-rays and all that."

"So then, did you meet the woman, Meredith's daughter?" Surely her heart would drum a hole through her ribs if it beat any harder than it was beating now.

"Well, her pastor showed up about two minutes after I did. It was a hard sell, getting her to agree to talk with me later, once she knew I was there to inquire about her mother's records. I had to double my first offer." He sighed. "I wonder if I'm losing my touch. Maybe I should retire. Do you think?"

She could not care less if he retired, as long as he did it after his work for her was done. "Did you go back yet, or—?"

"Just left her place three minutes ago. Spotless, but depressing. You know the type? Small, dark, shades always pulled so the neighbors can't see her watching HBO or something."

"And?"

"And she's got the records. Well, she can get them, I should say. Some of them for sure—I guess the mother's basement is piled with file boxes—but she didn't know how far back they go. And of course she couldn't say how long it would take, but she promised she would search for records from the date range I gave and get back to me."

Blue pulled her knees to her chest. There were boxes in some basement in West Virginia, one of which might hold the answer to years of anxious suspense. Her medical file, possibly with the adopting parents' names written down somewhere, or maybe typed out, dark, precise revelations on white paper. Possibly along with their address.

Possibly along with nothing.

No strings. No trail.

"Okay, well, we're closer," she said.

"That we are. And look: If she won't cooperate or there's nothing there, you could still try going through the courts. If you were willing to go public, obviously."

"That's just not a possibility." Her throat felt tight, and she swallowed to relieve the pressure.

"I know, I respect your position," Branford said. "I was just saying. I hate to think of you wondering forever. So okay, I'll keep on it, and maybe have something concrete for you real soon. No promises, of course."

"Of course." Never promises.

A beep sounded in her ear. "I have another call." Her mother, the display showed. "I need to take it," she said. "Keep me posted."

"Absolutely."

Her mother's first question was, "Did you see my email?"

"The gondola picture?"

"Yes! Isn't that so cool? Venice is . . . well, it's not without its odor problems—cool, breezy weather is best. But even so, the city is *amazing.*"

"Are you back home?"

"No—we have a Monday morning flight. I just had to call to tell you, I'm getting married!"

"You're not."

"Yep I am. We are. Calvin proposed . . . let's see . . . twenty-four minutes ago. We were—well, I'll spare you the details—but I will say, he promised me a ring when we get back, because, you know, he knows a guy or something. Right now I'm going to call your sister, then Calvin and I are going out to get matching tattoos. I'll tell you everything when I'm home, but I wanted you to know right away."

"Mom—"

"Calvin's dressed, I have to run. Much love."

Much love. Blue tossed the phone and watched it slide over the bare floor, stopping in front of the tiny fireplace. She hadn't even had a chance to tell her mother about the house.

She pushed her legs out in front of her, then lay back, feeling the cool wood where it contacted her shoulder blades, the back of her head. With palms spread and pressed to the floor, she looked up at the smooth ceiling. Its blankness soothed, the visual equivalent of the warm milk her grandmother had made for her when she was small.

Kate, her grandmother, had believed that three was a spiritual number. "Not only because of the Trinity, though there is that proof," she'd say, but also because three was Nature's number. The sun, the moon, the stars. Air, water, land. Red, blue, yellow. "Paper, rock, scissors," Blue had said once, wanting to contribute her own wisdom, and her grandmother had laughed so hard that tea had come out her nose.

News always came in fits of threes, she'd said. If Blue had been paying attention, she might have anticipated her mother's call, or something
like it. First was the Forresters and Mitch, second was Branford—and
now, third, the engagement.

Her mother was getting married.

It was lucky the cosmic number wasn't four.

Part 3

Where so many hours have been spent
in convincing myself that I am right,
is there not some reason to fear I may be wrong?

JANE AUSTEN

19

After spending most of the week at Harmony Studios editing the *Lions* pilot, adding historical footage and graphics using software he could only dream about before, Julian was taking Thursday off to see his mother. He rolled out of bed, put on a pair of gym socks and an old University of North Carolina sweatshirt, and turned up the heat. Soon the radiators were ticking with the promise of warmth—unlike the early April weather pattern, which was treating Chicago to a continuing wave of arctic chill. Spring was taking its sweet time coming to the Midwest. He was almost looking forward to leaving for Iraq—not that his trip was going to be any kind of tropical vacation; the temps would, however, be warm. Hot, in fact, and windy and dry.

Better that than this cold, and the sloppy, slushy dregs of winter still hanging around the streets and alleys, plastered to curbs and the bases of signposts. If he had any sort of view from his place—a view, say, like the one Blue's office was said to have (she hadn't asked him in, had hardly spoken to him, in fact)—he might be more eager to stay. A great view, a good reason, and the absence of crisis that was sure to follow his visit with his mom this afternoon. Once he told her what might be in store with *Lions*—and he had to tell her so she wouldn't later accuse him of keeping secrets—she would be spitting venom for who knew how long. He would be glad to go riding around in armored vehicles, wearing night-vision goggles, glad to be sleeping, once again, on a cot.

When the coffee finished perking, he poured a cup and leaned against the counter. A series of heavy thuds sounded above his head. *Whump. Whump.* Pause. *Whump-whump.* He waited; the rambunctious four-year-old boy upstairs was slamming cupboard doors, he was pretty sure. Another thud, this one louder by far than its precursors, and then a wail that said the kid had jumped or fallen from the counter and was hurt. Julian waited to hear the mother, a twenty-year-old he'd heard was about to be evicted, come tend to him, then heard her yelling from her bedroom, the room right above his own. The boy yelled back, *I wasn't!* and continued to cry, but less sincerely. Julian opened the broom closet next to his refrigerator, took the broom out, and used the handle to rap against the ceiling. He did it playfully, tapping a rhythm, and knew he had the boy's attention when the crying stopped. He tapped again. A silent moment—and then the boy tapped back.

He picked up his mug and went to shave.

In a half-hour he was dressed and standing on the train platform with other clean-shaven men. The younger ones carried leather-look briefcases and wore suits that approximated the suits of the men they hoped to one day replace in jobs at banks and law firms and insurance agencies. They had the *Sun-Times* or *Wall Street Journal* tucked under their arms and spoke to seemingly no one using earpiece phones, a scene reminiscent of some of the science fiction he'd read as a teen.

He was decidedly unambitious looking, he knew, in his jeans and running shoes and down-filled vest. More like the trio of teens who appeared to be cutting class than like the strivers. Like a guy who didn't have any direction beyond boarding the train and getting off somewhere nicer. Only the camera resting against his chest delineated him—and that as tourist, because who else would think there was anything to photograph here on an old platform at eight-fifteen in the morning?

He lifted the camera and aimed it past the southbound track, at the sagging wooden stairs clinging to the backs of stained brick buildings. At the top of one flight, maybe four stories up, was a Red-tailed Hawk perched with talons wrapped around the rotting wood rail. The breeze ruffled its neck feathers as it turned its head. The hunting would be good here, done between the rumbling arrivals and departures of commuter trains. Where there were humans, there was garbage, and where there was garbage, there were rats. There wasn't a city he'd ever been in where this wasn't the case, and where he hadn't gotten some great close shots of hawks and owls and ospreys.

Alec had a theory, after seeing his urban-birds portfolio during a Chicago layover a few years back: "You identify with them," he'd said.

"What, with the birds?"

Alec nodded. "I think so. These raptors are loners with keen eyes, and they like to stay above it all, zooming in on their targets when the time's right."

"Okay, smart guy, then explain my other bird shots." He'd pulled out another fat portfolio album and opened it randomly. "Here. Arctic loons in Bosnia."

"Loners, divers."

"Okay—bad example." He flipped to another page. "Canadian geese. I have some terrific geese shots."

"You don't give a rip about geese. That was practice."

That was true.

This hawk stretched its wings and he snapped a series as it readied to dive, and then it was gone. He capped his lens just as the platform began to vibrate with the approaching train.

His mom was waiting in her car at the Evanston station. She waved eagerly when she saw him; today was a good day, he could see it in how bright her eyes looked. He hated to change that with his news.

"Hi, sweetheart," she said when he got in the car. "It's so nice to see you ahead of schedule."

"You look great." He kissed her cheek.

"New earrings." She twisted her head so that her silver-and-turquoise earrings swung, bouncing against a jawline that had drooped over the years. She was still attractive, times like this when she felt up to showering and dressing in what she called "out" clothes, wearing jewelry and makeup, too. She looked like any other fifty-something woman—maybe a little harder worn, if you looked closely at the deep lines in her forehead, the creases beside her nose and mouth. Who escaped trouble, though? Hardly anyone. There were a lucky few—like Blue—but the rest of the world had to struggle, on one level or another. Some on every level. There was no justice, and possibly no God, though he would dearly love to think otherwise.

They drove to her house, the house where he'd lived for most of his early years. It was a split-level on a small lot, the maples grown forty feet tall now, their bare branches etched across the sky above the dandelion-filled yard.

She pulled up to the garage and parked. "Do you think you can get the gutters done before you leave?"

"What, today?"

"Yes, yes today—actually, let's do it first thing. We'll borrow Marvin's ladder, you can run the hose up there. I think I have a robin nesting up front, above my bedroom window, and that's just a catastrophe waiting to happen if she lays eggs."

"Okay, sure." He understood impending catastrophe, had lived in a perpetual state of it for as long as he could remember.

"I hope it's not too late already. Or maybe you could move the nest . . ." She went on talking about the pros and cons of relocating the nest while he unreeled the hose and then went to Marvin's, next door, for the ladder. Finally he said, "Mom, let's take it one thing at a time, all right? Let me get a look. Maybe there's no nest at all."

There was a nest, but no eggs. So while she was unhappy about ruining it, thwarting the robin's hard work, she felt the action was justified. Ultimately, they were doing all the birds a favor, she said, watching him throw debris from the gutters onto the still-brown grass.

She said this again two hours later, when he sat down for lunch of grilled cheese and tomato soup.

"Absolutely," he agreed, dunking his sandwich.

"They'll build someplace else, someplace safer."

"They will."

"I'm so glad you could get that done."

Her look of relief was so real it pained him. How was he supposed to now tell her that his father's life might soon become exponentially more wonderful than it had been before—which, compared to her life, was so cushy already? The prospect of PBS was one thing; a big-budget commercial production would be something else altogether.

He could wait, see what actually panned out . . . But putting it off any longer was its own recipe for disaster. Best to just give the bitter pill and commit to hanging around until the effects wore off.

"So, Mom, remember that thing I told you I would be doing with Dad this fall? The TV project?"

"What, that Hemingway thing?"

"It's Hemingway and several others. A whole series is what he's got planned."

"Okay." She cleared the dishes and turned on the water to wash them right away.

He got the dish towel and stood beside her. "Right, so, I stopped off at Daniel and Lynn's before coming home—"

"You didn't tell me that."

"No, well, it was just for the weekend. Really, it was completely last-minute. Dad was there to check out some Hemingway-related stuff and, coincidentally, Blue Reynolds was there—"

"Doing her show on location, I know. I saw some of that! They had Jimmy Buffett on—he did that funny song, the cheeseburger one."

"So, it turns out she and Dad go way back, and, long story short, she thought she could help him with the series—"

"Way back to when?"

"What? Oh. I guess to when he still lived here in Chicago."

This information stopped her questions for a moment. She stood very still, looking at him but *not* at him, then she said, "No; the show's just ten years old, they did an anniversary special last fall."

"It was before the show, when she was pretty young, Daniel said. Anyway," he pushed on, wanting to get her off whatever anxious track she was poised to go down, "Blue's production company—"

"Harmony. Her company, it's called Harmony Productions, the logo's at the end of every show. Wait—" She put her hand out. "Just hold on."

Oh hell, here she goes.

"Don't tell me *she's* Harmony Blue . . . something. It wasn't Reynolds . . . but what was it? Something Polish or Italian . . ." She looked up. "Right? Am I right? Harmony Blue is her real name?"

"I gather," he said, puzzled by the tack she'd taken. What did this have to do with anything?

"She was the one he was dating the winter before he moved," she said, nodding. "I can't believe I never put it together before—but why would I? God, it was at least a dozen years later . . ."

"What was?"

"The show. And I didn't start watching until, oh, maybe the fourth season. It never even crossed my mind—the 'Harmony' Productions, and the 'Blue' . . ."

Julian was sure she was about to discover her way right off a cliff—but instead, she drew him back to the kitchen table. "Come sit down. I have to tell you something I should have told you a long time ago."

Nothing had been going right that winter when he was ten, she said. She'd slipped on the icy back steps and broken her wrist just before Christmas, which meant she couldn't work (she was doing temp secretarial work then) which meant she couldn't pay her January bills until at least February, which would lead to trying to catch up February's and failing to cover March, April . . . who knew where it would end? Yes, she got child support and his father was paying half the mortgage, but she didn't have a stable income let alone a career; *he, Julian* was her career, and he was being difficult, too. Always wanting to know when he could see his father, making her feel so inadequate, making her angry at Mitch, making her want to punish both father and son, even though she knew it was wrong.

She said, "Why did *he* get to be your favorite, that's what I couldn't understand. So, you know, I thought, well, if you saw less of him and more of me, you'd remember how much fun we had together when you were little, before you went to school."

"Mom . . . I didn't—I mean, it wasn't like . . ." He stopped. What was he supposed to say?

"No, honey, listen, it wasn't you. I'm trying to say, I did the wrong thing, but that's how I was thinking at the time."

Sometime in January or February, his father had come over unannounced. Fed up, but calm. He had a right to see his kid *every* weekend, it was part of their divorce order and if he had to, he'd bring in the sheriff to enforce it. What was her problem anyway, he wanted to know. *He* had gotten on with his life long ago, he told her, and she ought to get on with hers. Date. Go back to school. Something that would take her out of the walled world she'd built for herself.

"I demanded to know who he was seeing—as if I had the right, you know? I made a lot of noise about how his choices affected your well-being, and they did, but really I was just seething with jealousy—seven years after our divorce, and I still wasn't over it. Oh, I was awful." She'd made him tell her everything about the woman. A nineteen-year-old who worked for Lynn, whose name was very odd, she'd thought. Harmony Blue, like a flower child, a hippie with no morals and no shame.

She'd latched on to that image, she said, and even though his father assured her that this young woman was in every way a good person and would be a good influence on a young boy, she had made him out to be a pedophile.

"I told him I would get a restraining order, can you imagine? I'd go back to court for full custody and demand supervised visitation. Oh, I was awful, waving my cast around and threatening that if he kept carrying on with a *child*, he'd never see you again."

She put her hands on the table, leaned down and pressed her forehead to the Formica. Julian stared, unsure what to do, what to say. It was awful, what she'd done to his dad, to Blue—who must have been devastated. It was awful all the way around.

With her head still down, she said, "I'm sorry."

"It's okay."

"No, no, not *okay*." She sat up again and looked at him. "Not okay. It gets worse. I blabbed it to the head of his department, to the dean, to everyone at Northwestern whose name I knew. I said they couldn't trust him, that I knew for a fact he'd slept with several of his students.

"It was pure vindictiveness, not a bit of truth. I was . . . way out of balance. It's not okay, but, it's done. The counselors have always said, accept the crime and its unchangeability. Then accept that from this minute, I can choose a crime-free life."

"Mom, you're not a criminal."

"Oh no?"

He shook his head, though with less conviction than he'd intended. So many things were coming clear to him now. "That's why Dad moved, then?"

"That's why. His boss said they couldn't risk any scandals. Anyway," she sighed, "I've done better since the breakdown. Haven't I? No, I know I have."

Which was true. No "crimes," or none that he knew of, in any of the years since. She'd accepted his decision to remain in Key West even after her release from inpatient treatment; she'd supported his career choices; she'd ranted a lot less about his father . . . and she'd made a life for herself, with her support groups and her work. He still worried about her—it was ingrained—but he didn't fear for her, and that was a small grace they could both appreciate.

"You have done better," he said. "So. Do you want to know the rest, about Dad and the TV thing?"

"Yes, yes, tell me. Is Harmony Productions going to produce his show?"

She looked so sincerely eager that he wanted to ask, *Are you on new medication?* He held his tongue and told her it was possible.

"I suppose they'd pay him a lot of money," she said.

"I suppose they would."

"Good."

New medication, or his real mother had been abducted by aliens and this look-alike was her replacement.

She was nodding as she said, "I always wanted to meet her. Blue, I mean."

"Maybe you can." He told her they'd made the pilot, and that he had another day of editing ahead of him before his father arrived Friday

evening to review the finished film. "Come by the studio and I'll introduce you."

"Oh, no, I couldn't—not now, when I know what my actions did to
her. God, she must have been heartbroken when he ended it—don't you
think? I can't meet her now, I'd be mortified! What she must think of
me . . ." She looked like she might cry. Then she brightened a little, saying, "Did you know she's donated something like twelve million dollars
to Illinois mental health programs?"

"No, I guess I didn't." He tipped his chair back onto two legs as he
fit this new information about Blue into the puzzle she still was to him.
A sought-after celebrity; a business mogul; a focused, professional television personality; the girl whose life had been upended by his mother;
a generous philanthropist . . . She was many things.

Yet in his mind she was primarily the quiet, barefooted woman who
loved Key West so much that she'd bought a house there purely on impulse. On instinct. If a man wasn't careful, he could fall for a woman like
that.

She was much more than that, though. Too much more, when he included *possible prospect for his father.* How possible? Hard to tell. The
wind did seem to be blowing that way, though.

His mother sensed it too: "Wouldn't it be great if now your dad
could put things right with Blue?"

"No." He sat up, banging the chair's front legs on the tile floor.

"No? Why not?"

"I—well, that is . . ."

She gave him a penetrating look. "Don't you think he's entitled to
some happiness?"

He avoided her eyes. "Of course I do."

"You're *jealous,*" she said, and when he glanced at her again, her eyebrows were raised.

"I'm not. I'm—I'm concerned."

"I don't think so. Look in the mirror, Julian Forrester. I know that
expression, God knows I saw it on my own face enough times. You want
his attention all for yourself, is that it? Or wait—is it *hers* that—"

"It's fine," he said, standing up and returning to the sink. "If that's what they want, then it's fine." He grabbed the sponge and started scrubbing a bowl that didn't need to be scrubbed. "It's good. It's all good."

But it wasn't *all good*. It was in fact no good. Waiting for the train back into the city, he pointed his camera at his fellow travelers' feet and photographed loafers, sneakers, pointy-toed high heels, and allowed himself to think it through. He did want his father's attention, up to a point. The real trouble was, he also wanted Blue's, wanted it viscerally. His want was a hunger.

Well, he'd gone hungry before. "Deal with it," he muttered as the train pulled in.

20

$\mathcal{I}$t took most of the week following the Key West trip for the crew to get over their sunburns and hangovers and for *TBRS* to return to its clockwork flow. Blue was glad when Friday afternoon finally arrived so that she could begin to unwind. There had not been a single day this week when they weren't running right up to the edge with some issue or another. The worst had been on Tuesday, when a severe thunderstorm knocked out their power and their generator system failed to start up immediately. The *joie de vivre* from Key West fell apart quickly when so many dollars were at stake.

Second worst was Julian's presence—or that was Blue's unspoken opinion. Everyone (herself included) found him more engaging and interesting than even the most comely of the interns they got each season. Even amidst the chaos she was acutely aware of him being there, down the hall from the main studio, editing the *Lions* pilot exactly as she'd offered. The offer had been meant to help Mitch, to give her more opportunities to think about *him*.

Julian was a distraction. Unwelcome. Unsettling.

Today, same as every day this week, she'd left for the gym at the earliest possible moment. When she got there, Jeremy had her weigh in.

He frowned when he saw she was still two pounds heavier than she was supposed to be. "How much water did you drink today?"

"I have no idea. Not enough, I'm sure."

"All right then, I want you to do eight ounces right now, and I'm adding fifteen minutes of cardio."

"No time for extra cardio," she said, taking a bottle of water from the cooler. She went to the elliptical machine, where she always began. "I have a six-thirty appointment."

"It's two pounds, Blue. I can see them clear as day on your hips and belly."

So could she; she just couldn't bring herself to care about them as much as he did. The extra couple of pounds made her hip bones seem . . . friendlier. While Jeremy programmed the machine, she said, "Let's just stick to the usual," and pretended she didn't notice him shaking his head.

Halfway through her workout, she was ready to quit. Two-thirds of the way through, she did. "That's it, that's all you're getting out of me today," she said, toweling her face. She ignored his protests as she went to shower, allowing the diva moment to play out only in her head: *I don't pay you to lecture me. There are five hundred people waiting in line for your job.* It was satisfaction enough.

As soon as she was dry and dressed, she was returning to the studio to meet up with Mitch and, unfortunately, Julian, for an after-hours welcome tour. She'd brought her favorite broken-in jeans and a lime-green Key West T-shirt, hoping the color would lift her up.

Her mother was always talking about clothing color and its effect; this week, her talk had been tailored to the developing wedding plans. Blue and Melody would have the choice of fuchsia or yellow bridesmaid dresses—one daughter in each color, no fighting. Nancy would not be dissuaded by Blue's worries that she and Calvin were rushing things. "Remember how on an impulse last week you paid two million dollars for a tiny, dated house?"

"That's money," Blue had said. "It's different."

"I heard how you described that place. It was love, and so is this. *Embrace* happiness, don't resist it. You might not live longer, but you'll live better."

Embrace happiness. That's what she was trying to do, and everything was getting all muddied up.

She arrived in the studio's lobby as Marcy was on her way out. Marcy stopped and set her shoulder bag on an armchair. "I was just about to call you. Julian says Mitch is stuck at the airport—his airport, that is. His plane's been sitting on the tarmac for two hours and now they're going back to the terminal. He may not be able to get here tonight. Meantime, Julian's in the lab. I said I'd send you in."

"Why did you do that?"

Marcy frowned at her. "Why wouldn't I?"

"Never mind. Where are you off to?"

"Dinner and dancing." She did a twirl with an imaginary partner. "It's unbelievable, I feel like I'm twenty-five again. If your man gets here tonight, give me a call. You can come join us."

Blue said, "My man? Let's not jump the gun, here."

"Oh, let's."

"He's in a relationship I'm not certain he wants to be out of, and I'm—I just feel so . . ."

"So . . . ?"

Blue set her bag down and unbuttoned her suede jacket. "I love the idea of reconnecting with him. He looks good, he's kind, he's smart. There's not a single thing about him I dislike . . . Maybe I've forgotten how to be eager about a man." Whereas she was perfecting the practice of being anxious.

"I doubt you've forgotten. You'll see."

"It used to be so easy—didn't it? Remember how it was when we were living in the rental house?"

"And where that got you," Marcy said.

"Besides that. Guys were always coming by, we were always laughing—"

"We were always stoned."

"We were having fun. I need to find that groove you were talking about that night in Key West."

Marcy kissed her on the cheek. "Step One is admitting you have a problem."

"What's Step Two?"

"Umm . . ."

"Believe in a greater power," Julian said from the hallway behind the reception desk, where he was walking toward them.

"Right," Blue said. How much had he heard? She began to ad-lib, "So, Marcy, tell Peter to go ahead and, er, book Britney for that week. In November. Fall sweeps, you know." She smiled at Julian, praying Marcy had caught on.

Marcy said, "Gotcha." She headed for the door. "Blue, don't forget you have that museum thing tomorrow. Your dress is already done—did you see it? It should have been delivered yesterday."

"Which dress is it?" She could barely recall that she had an event the next day, let alone what she was wearing to it.

"The black Balenciaga. With the fringe and the sequins—it's that sexy above-the-knee look you do so well."

"Not if what Jeremy says is true."

"Which is—?"

"That I'm liable to start mooing at any moment."

"Cut back on the grass," Marcy said with a wink. "Okay, I'm off."

They watched Marcy leave, watched the security guard lock the doors behind her.

"Jeremy?" Julian asked.

"My personal trainer." Why did saying it that way sound so pretentious?

"He's an idiot. You look healthy and beautiful."

Though he'd said it plainly, a statement of fact, she felt herself blush. "Thanks. Any further word from your dad?"

He shook his head. "Doesn't look promising, though."

Which left her here with Julian, who looked as intense as usual and as appealing as ever in blue jeans and a white button-down shirt, untucked. Except for security, the lobby was empty around them. She picked up her bag and held it in front of her like a shield. "Think he'll be happy with the finished pilot?"

"I think so." He didn't offer to screen it for her, and she didn't ask if he would.

"Good."

"Yeah." He pushed his hands into his pockets and began to say, "So I guess I'm going to—" just as Blue was saying, "I have some work I'd better—"

"Oh— My phone's buzzing, hang on." He took it from his pocket and answered. "Hello?"

She listened, knew it was Mitch when Julian said, "Not at all, huh? What about tomorrow? Well, even if not, it's a digital file; I can send it to you electronically and we can talk while you watch." A long pause, then, "Actually, she's right here. Sure, hold on." He handed the BlackBerry to her, saying, "He wants to talk to you."

"Hi," she said to Mitch. "The luck's all bad tonight, huh?"

"My plane's grounded and I can't find another flight. Strictly speaking, I guess I don't *have* to get there at all. But," she heard him draw a deep breath, "I thought it might be nice to get together," he said in a rush. "So if you have time tomorrow evening—"

This was a surprise. "I wish I did. I have some benefit gala for one of the museums, Marcy just reminded me."

"Ah. Well, I own a tux—as you may recall."

"In fact I do." She turned away from Julian and began walking toward the reception desk. "I didn't tell them I'd be bringing a guest, but—"

"I was kidding; I'd never foist myself on you that way."

"No, I know that . . . but, if you think you'd like to join me, why don't we plan on it?" Dinner and dancing. A pretty dress, a tux . . . The association with that long-ago New Year's party was irresistible. "Let me call you later with the details, all right? Will you be home?" A coded question for, Will you be with Brenda?

"Call me at home, that'd be great."

"I will." She turned around, saying, "I have a few things I need to do while I'm here, so let me give you back to Julian." She handed off the phone with a quick wave to Julian, and walked away without looking back.

When she got to her office, she closed the door and leaned against it. The wall of windows displayed Chicago's skyline, lights glowing against the darkening sky. It was a wonderful view, and familiar. There was safety in what was familiar. Comfort, too. Though she may not have spent time with Mitch over the past two decades, he'd existed for her, he'd lived inside that soft space of memory reserved for first loves. The way he'd sounded on the phone suggested she occupied a similar sort of space for him.

She had not been his very first; that was one of his high school girlfriends. The one before Renee, who'd broken his heart and left him vulnerable to Renee's more insidious affections. Heartbreak. It was a catapult, launching people into ill-advised actions and unfortunate outcomes; didn't she know that too well?

With the perspective of distance and time, she understood better why Mitch had rejected her—the timing was all wrong. If the past two weeks had shown her anything, it was that the timing was now all right—or nearly. For all her doubts, fate seemed to be persistently lining them up.

Step Two: Believe in a greater power.

She had not been a believer. Maybe it was time to put her faith in that force and let go.

21

Mitch was out of bed at four thirty AM for his rescheduled-for-noon flight. It had taken him forever to get to sleep last night, then when he did finally sleep, it was fitfully and for too few hours.

He'd had no business suggesting he go with Blue to the fund-raiser tonight. The words had jumped out of his mouth like oil from a fry pan—and Brenda was none too happy about the resulting burn. He'd done the right thing, confessing to her when he'd called to say his flight was canceled. "I have to tell you," he said, "I think maybe something is going on with Blue and me." He told her about the date he'd made and she said, "How am I supposed to compete with that?"

In his mind, no contest existed. There was Blue, distinct and luminous, and there was Brenda, as lively and engaging a presence in his life as the books he loved. To compare the two women was like comparing Hemingway to Nabokov; he admired them both, differently. He told Brenda this, and she'd said, "Good luck sleeping with either one of them."

Then there was Julian, whose terseness on the phone last night after hearing Mitch's plans made it clear he was no fan of Blue's, and didn't think Mitch should be, either. He'd said, "This whole situation is out of hand. You shouldn't have taken her offer to help with *Lions,* and you shouldn't be going with her to that party."

Mitch wasn't entirely surprised—this was Julian, after all. "Look, J, I appreciate your concern, but I disagree."

"Suppose for whatever reason no *Lions* deal works out," Julian said.

"You get resentful, she thinks you used her, she blackballs you—there are any number of scenarios. I don't like it."

Julian's displeasure was like storm clouds gathered and waiting along the horizon. Mitch was keeping an eye on the horizon. Watching it with his peripheral vision. Glancing at it, from time to time, over his shoulder while running headlong into things like altered filming schedules, options possibilities, and museum benefit galas. You didn't have to hide from iffy weather, you just had to keep tabs on it.

Today's flight departed on schedule. Smooth air in a clear sky, the Carolina foothills falling away beneath him. He spent the two-hour trip reading *Newsweek* and *Forbes* so that tonight he would be informed and articulate on more than the matter of symbolism in "Hills Like White Elephants."

By three o'clock central time, he was sitting on Julian's ancient, dusty sofa watching himself on a thirteen-inch laptop computer monitor. It had gotten damaged when Julian was traveling and no longer displayed any red tones. He looked like Martian Mitch in the jungle; the effect was sobering.

"Don't worry. It'll play fine on any functional monitor," Julian was saying. "The LCD and plasmas will make you look more life-like even than life. Focus on the content. I can always go back and cut or add, or rearrange. I think, though, that it's pretty solid."

Mitch agreed. Julian had taken the basic footage of him in the Hemingway Home and woven in Key West images, interview footage, archival audio and video, anything he could find that they could use without having to pay.

"It's brilliant," Mitch said when it was over. "Forget still photography—you should focus on this, you're a genius at it."

Julian closed the laptop and stood up. "Thanks—I think." He was barefoot and unshaven and wore a clay-toned T-shirt with a Hebrew phrase on the front. *Kol tuv*, it read, which he'd said meant *Everything Good*.

"I didn't mean that like it sounded. I was trying to say how impressed I am with your work. I can't think of a thing I want to change." Except how difficult it still sometimes was to communicate with Julian; he was so literal. "What time is it now?" He squinted at his watch. "Almost four . . ." Blue's driver would be there at six. "I need to shower, and I've got some spiffing up to do if I want to look like a suitable date for Blue."

Julian looked tired, or just moody, maybe, standing there picking at a callous on his palm. "She's mortal like the rest of us, you know."

"It's not that. Well—it *is* that, a little, but it's more about how we haven't spent any real time together in twenty-plus years. I feel like I know her, and yet I also feel like I don't." They'd each led very full, very different lives after all. "And," he laughed, "it's been forever since I've attended any kind of a dance."

Julian went into the kitchen, saying, "Did you remember to buy her a corsage?"

"Oh, damn, am I supposed to?" He had no idea what the social protocols were these days. Literary gatherings, or the ones he attended at any rate, demanded little more than a sports jacket, a bottle of red wine, and familiarity with the most current issue of *Southern Literary Journal*.

"Dad," Julian said from the kitchen doorway, "that was a joke. I highly doubt this is a corsage-type event."

"No, you're probably right. Still, flowers would be good, don't you think?"

His son shrugged and turned back to his task. "I've got some Chivas. Want a shot?"

Mitch shook his head. "But I'd be eternally grateful if you'd hunt down a little bouquet while I get ready."

Julian poured whisky into a tumbler and took a sip before answering. "There's no place to buy flowers around here, sorry."

"Are you sure? I mean, you've been gone awhile. Maybe there's—"

"Nope."

"Not even a grocery store? All my local stores have floral departments."

"We're in urban South Chicago."

"Well, even so, there must be a florist near here."

Julian shook his head.

"You're certain? What about, I don't know, one of those little side-walk vendors?"

Julian's expression was unreadable. His tone, when he spoke, was careful and cool. "Why are you so desperate to bring her flowers? Not only do you already have a great girlfriend, you're here getting all worked up about trying to impress a woman who has seen it all. Who *has* it all. You could give her flowers every hour all day long for a year and she'd only find it quaint. You're an English professor, you earn eighty thousand a year. Nothing you can bring her, nothing you can *do* for her, is going to make any serious impression."

"You don't know her—"

"*You* don't know her, you just said so yourself. You *knew* her, for a little while, twenty-three years ago. You knew Harmony Blue Kucharski—and then between you and Mom, you pretty much screwed her over."

It was as if the barometric pressure had plummeted, pulling all the air out of the room.

"What exactly did your mother tell you?" And why had she told him anything about Blue? When had she made that connection?

"She told me everything, the whole ugly mess. That she bullied you into dumping Blue, and that instead of fighting back with the truth, you let her win. You broke a girl's heart—a girl who must have really ad-mired you, really loved you, or why would she be doing so much for you now?—broke her heart because you were a goddamn coward."

"You don't understand what was at stake," Mitch said, trying to keep calm. "Your mother didn't care about the truth. She wouldn't listen—"

"Then maybe you should have told someone else! A lawyer. A judge."

"I already had so much to deal with. When you're a junior professor, it's all you can do to keep up with your teaching load, your research, meetings—I really did care about Harmony Blue—about Blue—and that's why it seemed kinder to cut her loose, rather than subject her to all that. I honestly thought that would put an end to all the trouble."

"It was a *Band-Aid*, for Christ's sake. Could you not see the bigger picture?" Julian's voice was tighter now, thicker. "Could you not see that the only person who would benefit from your 'kindness' was *you*?"

"That's not fair," Mitch said, clenching his hands together. "I thought I could placate your mother—"

"Who you should have known by then was implacable! But no. Instead, you dumped Blue, and when that didn't work . . ." Julian's voice caught, then broke as he finished, "you dumped *me*."

"I . . ."

What could he say? Julian was right.

Julian had been staring at him, but now he looked away—not so quickly that Mitch couldn't see the angry tears.

"J, listen," Mitch began, wiping the tears that welled in his own eyes. This was hard, harder than he'd imagined it would be if—when—he and Julian finally had it out. Who said time healed all wounds? Time hid them is what it did. It lulled you into believing that none of what happened in your past mattered as long as today was good. It made you think that the past was too slow to possibly catch up to *now. Rest easy,* it lied.

He lowered his head and breathed deeply. "I—I'm sorry."

Silence.

"I'm so sorry. You're right. It's true. I should have fought back. I was scared that she'd make things even worse—not for me, for you. I'm not . . . I'm not good at confrontation. She was the mother, she had everything on her side. It was a really difficult time . . ."

He'd known so little about how to *do* life then—his, or any. How to be a husband, how to be a father, how to be more than a guy who had hamstrung himself and a girl by getting her pregnant in high school. His parents had said it didn't have to ruin his dreams, and they were right, it didn't *have* to: if he had taken the energy he'd been using to create Professor Mitch Forrester and put it into a custody fight, a righteousness battle, he might have become something truly impressive indeed.

He sat up and looked at Julian, who stood backed against the door-jamb, hands in pockets, head down. "I ended up losing everything I cared about. And as for Blue . . ."

Julian looked up expectantly.

"I hated hurting her. She had a tough life as it was. Never knew her father, practically had to raise her sister while their mother worked eighteen-hour days . . . I don't know, I still think she was better off without me."

"But not anymore."

Mitch nodded. "I have to think we got reconnected for a reason. Maybe all this—*Lions,* you, this date—maybe it's my chance to redeem myself with both of you."

He got up and went to Julian, his hand held out. Julian took it, and let Mitch pull him into a hug. "Forgive me," Mitch said, holding Julian tightly.

"It's done," Julian said, his voice gruff but soft. He wiped his eyes, then stepped back and pulled the hem of his T-shirt down, pointing at the front. "Everything Good."

Mitch nodded.

"Right. Okay. So . . . I guess you better get in the shower," Julian said. "Blue . . ." He stopped, coughed, then nodded as if coming to a conclusion. "Blue's not gonna want a guy who smells like that sofa."

It took a while for the water to get hot, so Mitch took his tux shirt out of its packaging. He didn't know what he'd have done if the tux shop hadn't opened at ten, if they'd had nothing on hand. Maybe he wouldn't have come to Chicago at all. Opportunity would have passsed him by, leaving him as distant from his son as ever. As far from Blue as ever, too. But the shop *was* open, and they did have what he needed, and now here he was, standing at the threshold of a new start—which just went to show that things worked out pretty much the way they were supposed to.

In the shower, he stood and let the water beat against his neck and shoulders before using Julian's soap and shampoo. The soap was travel-size, the shampoo bottle miniature as if to highlight that his son had lived his whole life in transition.

He hummed, a nervous, tuneless sound as he went quickly from the bathroom back to the guest bedroom. The room had an old double bed, and the same chenille bedspread that had been on it when he and Renee had bunked there a few times instead of trekking back to their apartment in Evanston. She'd been hugely pregnant then, and he'd been mostly terrified and reluctant, too far in to back out.

A very long time ago, that was.

The tux fit well enough, for which he was thankful. He might not stand out among the crowd, but he felt sure he would at least fit in. God knew who else would be at this gala, being held in the "ridiculously enormous" home of one of Chicago's billionaires. *One*. Of their *billionaires*. Blue had sounded so casual about it all—which only made him more aware of how different their worlds were. Julian was right: he didn't know her very well, not this version. She was still Harmony Blue, but in the same way a butterfly was still a caterpillar.

She'd said, "The house is so overdone you won't even believe it. Italianate to the hilt. Statuary, toilets, everything."

"You've been there?" he'd asked.

"A few times."

"With a date?"

She'd laughed. "A time or two. Why?"

"I want to make sure I measure up."

"Then don't eat with your fingers. Oh, and speak optimistically about the Cubs."

A last look in the old silvered mirror and he was satisfied that he'd done his best. "Julian," he called, leaving the bedroom.

He got no reply. The kitchen was empty, and the living room, too. On the dining table was a key and a note—*See you tomorrow . . . J.*—and a vivid, fragrant flower bouquet.

*J*ust before the chauffeured Lincoln was scheduled to pick him up, Mitch rode the elevator down to the building's lobby. The flowers (he recognized tiny roses and lilies but not the purple or white blooms) were clutched tightly in both hands. His heart ached, yet, over Julian and was racing, now, for Blue.

Since the moment he'd seen Blue on Front Street, he'd felt unmoored. He had never imagined he'd meet up with her again, and couldn't have foreseen her interest in his project, her willingness to help—and to let him accompany her tonight. What should he expect to come of their date? What was she expecting of him? Good conversation, certainly. A sociable, amiable, companionable partner who wouldn't embarrass her, no doubt. Those things alone made him anxious enough; they were nothing, however, compared to his questions about afterward.

The way he felt tonight was not so different from the way he'd felt way back on the night of their first real date, a few days after that New Year's Eve party. If their romance was real, was it sustainable? Did he look his best? Would they end up in bed? He'd wanted to, yes; he just hadn't known how ready he was to deal with everything that went along with it at the time. The same was true now, if it came to that.

There was no way it could come to that.

But supposing it did?

"We're grown-ups," he said as the elevator bumped to a stop. Grown-ups could figure these things out. If the rumors that she'd slept with George Clooney were true, Mitch didn't want to know.

The limo waited at the curb, as did the driver.

"Good evening. Nice tonight, isn't it?"

Mitch nodded. "Lovely." It was cold for April, but the sky was clear, a deep sapphire fading to black. He could see the first stars.

The car was immaculate. Quite a change from his own car: a basic Toyota cluttered with folders and notebooks.

If his life were like Blue's, instead of driving himself to Southpoint Mall when he needed new shoes, he'd be driven to Michigan Avenue. There would be no squeaky desk chair, and he'd have no concerns over fully funding his retirement.

Not that he had it so hard. He'd never struggled, not really. His parents had money; all his life Mitch had lived comfortably, never hungry, never needy. They'd paid his tuition to Northwestern, paid for the Evanston apartment, freeing him and Renee to try to make a marriage and a home. Money had never meant much more to him than a means for funding his passions—for education, for a literary life. It was all he'd ever wanted. Hand-stitched Italian loafers, nice as they might be, would not make reading Tolstoy a more pleasurable experience.

22

The Balenciaga dress did make Blue look sexy. It fit like the body glove it was, showing off her legs, accentuating her waist, making her breasts full but not fleshy. Her hair fell onto her back in glossy waves that only a $450 stylist could craft. She would appear to be exactly the celebrity the public believed she was.

Usually, attending these kinds of events required little effort beyond superficial preparations: hair, nails, leg wax, makeup (done concurrently with the manicure, a time-saver). A wonderful couture dress. A teardrop sapphire against her breastbone, suspended from a fine silver chain. The resulting effect let her be in public—let her *be public*—thoughtlessly, in the most literal sense of the word. It took no thought, inspired no fear, and preserved her persona. Tonight was not so different. The extra effort was all mental, was all about Mitch.

She carried her shoes into the living room and sat down facing the windows, next to Peep. He stretched and rolled over onto his back, inviting her to scratch his belly. She obliged. Did Mitch like cats? She couldn't recall. Lynn and Daniel clearly did, so perhaps Mitch did too. "No worries, Peepster," she said. "Love me, love my cat. Tough chick, aren't I?" Peep's response was a deep, growly purr.

How different her life might be if she'd been tougher sooner. Tough enough to stick out Mitch's rejection, to keep getting up and going in to Lynn's office even after she lost hope that Lynn would ever be more than her boss. Why hadn't she been able to face the world, chin out, the way she made herself do later? Where was all her steadfast determination then?

When she first moved in with Marcy, she'd packed a few boxes and left a note. *Dear Mom: I'm moving in with a friend, don't ask where, as I'd prefer not to say right now. I just need to get away for a while.* She'd believed at the time that she was *making a statement.*

"Yeah," she told Peep, "a statement of stupidity."

Lake Michigan was the darkest blue today, the sky above it the color that Mitch said North Carolinians called "Carolina Blue." If he had taken her with him to North Carolina, *she* might now be *Carolina Blue.* Remade in a way that might not have allowed her to sit here looking out over a city that celebrated her as one of its greatest assets, but which might have given her something resembling a normal life.

And while it was true that a young man who was at this very moment living, breathing, perhaps studying or working or laughing as he tossed a Frisbee or kissed a girl, existed only *because* she had run from the pain of disappointed dreams, it was hard not to feel sorry for herself, for what she'd lost or, more accurately, never had.

A little more faith in herself might have made all the difference. Where would that faith have come from, though? The one thing upon which her entire worth was based—that Mitch had fallen in love with her in spite of her frizzy hair, her unsightly mole, her fatherless history—had been blasted apart by his rejection.

In the first week after, she had hardly been able to get out of bed. Melody would get up after hitting the snooze alarm three times, saying groggily, "You going to shower first?"

And Blue would roll over, putting her back to Mel.

Mel would leave the room, then, a little later, come back to see if Blue was going to get up. "Aren't you going to work?"

"Leave me alone."

Hours would pass, Blue sleeping away some of them, then waking to feel crushed again. Mitch did not love her enough. Daniel would not be her father, the grandfather of her children. She would never be a Forrester, never tell her children and grandchildren the story of that New Year's Eve.

The travesty was that she'd done everything so deliberately right.

She'd kept her sister out of jail, kept food in the refrigerator, made it through high school with decent grades. She'd found a good job, she worked hard, never called in sick when she wasn't. She'd avoided pointless relationships with immature guys, she'd held out even as Melody, pre-Jeff, was giving in with a different guy every week. She intended to earn some good fortune because, damn it, she wanted out of that dead-end life.

It had seemed to work. She'd fallen in love with a man who had all the decent qualities a girl could ask for: He was educated, he earned a decent living, he was from a good family with parents who treated her like a woman who was worthy of their son.

She had believed, for a couple fairy tale months, that the high road would lead her to the kingdom. Love, it had seemed, really could conquer all.

"Not," she said. Peep looked up at her and blinked.

Running away had been the worst possible choice, that was more obvious now than ever. At the time? At the time, she'd decided it was the solution to all her problems.

She'd had a very different solution in mind the day she dragged herself out of the house and out to the 7-Eleven store for a newspaper. There, however, she'd run into Marcy. Marcy, in all black, with her punk haircut, an Adam Ant T-shirt hanging off one shoulder.

"Hey, Harmony Blue! Long time no see." Not since the two of them had worked together at the pet store. "How's the new job? Or should I even ask—you look like hell."

"I'm—I was sick."

"Nothing contagious, I hope," Marcy said, stepping back.

"No." And thank God; she wouldn't wish her misery on anyone.

Making a little more effort to seem less hellish, she'd said, "So, what are you up to?"

"Just stopped back home to borrow money from my old man. I needed a snack before I head back to my place." She held up an open bag of Cheetos. "You?"

"I'm enlisting."

"Come again?"

"In the Army. They need a few good men."

Marcy said, "You're female."

She shrugged.

Making an obvious show of looking around the store, Marcy said, "No recruiters here." She popped a cheese puff in her mouth. "Hey," she said, chewing thoughtfully, "Why don't you come hang out with me today? It's not that far—a little place off the Dixie Highway in Harvey."

Not the greatest part of Greater Chicago, Blue had recalled. "I'm buying a paper. The recruiters run ads," she said, needing to demonstrate she wasn't crazy.

"I think we might have a newspaper laying around."

Blue considered this. "I could save the fifty cents."

"Right." Marcy steered her toward the door. "Maybe put it toward your share of the rent after you move in with us."

"Yeah?"

"There's room. You look like you could use a change of scenery. But you'll have to call me Bat. It's what I go by now. Cool, right? It's because I'm mostly a night flier."

Marcy. Even then she'd been genuine, unfettered; not a candle in the dark, a colorfully lighted Christmas tree. It wasn't Marcy's fault that, once free of rules of any kind, even those Blue imposed on herself, Blue had swung way out past caution and reason. Marcy hadn't pushed her to do anything except let go of the grief she had declined to explain. If Blue chose a chemical method to help rid herself of Mitch, if she jumped right into bed with Will, a guy whose greatest ambition in life was to ride his motorcycle around the entire perimeter of North America (as if that were possible) well, that was her business. They were nineteen. In their live-and-let-live world, being of age was a springboard into full adulthood. They'd seen it in their earlier lives: anything goes.

At the end of that first day, she'd handed Marcy two quarters. "Here you go, Bat. I'll get you the rest after the bank opens tomorrow."

Now her net worth was closing in on seven hundred million dollars. That fifty cents, for all that today it represented a single droplet in an ocean of money, had bought her some really good times. Yes, trouble, too, but before then, she'd had fun. The real thing. Craziness and laughter and camaraderie, the intoxicating pleasures of unabashed, uncomplicated sex. It had not been all bad. Now? Seven hundred million was an uncountable number, a long row of zeros that added up to precisely nothing.

Peep stood, arched his back, then jumped down and trotted to the kitchen. At the base of the refrigerator he sat down and mewed once, a request.

She looked at her watch: 6:40. "You're early—but I'm about to be late. Here," she set out his food and poured a splash of milk into a saucer for him. "No Froot Loops leftovers tonight, I'm afraid."

Watching him lap up the little bit of milk, she thought how lovely it must be to live this cat's life. Some would say that she was just as spoiled, what with her staff, her housekeepers, her business manager—and Marcy, God love her—plus all the freebies people sent in hopes she might give them the slightest public mention. If the public thought her life an endless series of spa visits and shopping, interrupted for a brief hour to do her TV broadcast, they were hugely mistaken. Excepting her visit to the Simonton Street gallery, she hadn't been shopping since one mad-dash afternoon just before Christmas. As for spas, the closest she'd been to visiting any lately was when perusing them late at night on the Internet. Actually going was a low priority, a pleasant daydream she could squeeze in between meetings and galas and other mandatory social events.

Now, though, she had Key West to dream of. Who needed a spa visit when they had such a house to return to between engagements?

"You're going to like it at our new place," she told Peep. "Good sunlight, and lizards to chase!—or watch." She stroked his head, noting his graying whiskers. What a comfort he was; she really ought to give him more attention. A bit of milk was a poor substitute for hours together on the couch. There must be a good bookstore in Key West; when she got back there, she'd stock up for the summer. Peep would see so much of her he'd think he'd gotten a new keeper.

"What do you think? We'll drink out of coconut shells, and our lemons—make that *my* lemons, or what a sourpuss you'd be, ha—get it? Sour puss?"

Peep looked at her, licking milk away from his mouth.

"*My* lemons will come straight off the tree." Not out of a top-end stainless steel refrigerator like this one. She didn't even know the name of the person—the woman? the man?—who shopped for her lemons, who arranged them so neatly in a hand-glazed bowl, which some other nameless, genderless person had purchased.

Suppose that tonight she and Mitch did pick up where they'd left off so long ago. Suppose they could spend the upcoming summer together, lazing in lounge chairs on her patio, reading aloud from whatever book of stories he loved these days. She'd bet a good chunk of what was in her bank accounts that he'd be willing—maybe even happy, to watch *Pride and Prejudice* with her. And they could invite Daniel and Lynn to dinner once a week, catch up on the latest Key West residents' dramas—maybe Daniel would be able to manage his boat again by then, and they'd do sunset cruises around the mangrove islands.

"I can think of worse things," she said.

*M*itch waited in the lobby holding a bouquet. "Flowers!" Blue said. "How thoughtful of you, thanks." She held them to her nose. "They smell heavenly."

"They do. You can't imagine what I went through to get them," he said.

"Oh?"

He shook his head and didn't elaborate.

As they drove to their destination, a North Shore estate that, when she was small, she'd thought was a castle, Mitch talked about how well the *Lions* pilot had turned out. She listened and was pleased, but was also distracted, by a familiar musky aroma that wasn't the flowers, and wasn't her hair spray. She was just about to ask him to identify it when it struck her how she knew it: it was Julian's scent.

Never mind.

She left the bouquet behind in the car when they stepped out onto the pale cobblestone drive, then climbed wide stone steps between carved stone balustrades, entering the house through a doorway that could accommodate a small yacht. The hosts' house was as she'd described to Mitch, the huge marble foyer filled with the sounds of conversation and orchestral dance music. A twelve-foot-wide crystal chandelier dappled light down onto everyone beneath it. Mitch shook his head and said, "People live like this?"

"Probably they use three rooms at the end of one wing," Blue said, nodding to anyone who caught her eye as they made their way inside.

By sight she knew few of the people they encountered, though when introduced their names were all familiar. *Real estate,* she briefed Mitch, sotto voce. *Hotels.* In contrast, everyone recognized her. *Blue! So lovely to see you. Loved your Jimmy Buffett interview!* She always used this contrast to her advantage; in conversation, it was safe to assume that the people she spoke with believed they knew all about her, so she made the discussion all about them. *Are you a Buffett fan? Which song is your favorite? I'll be sure to tell him.* They felt flattered and important, and she revealed nothing—except tonight, when she revealed a man in her life, "my old friend, Dr. Mitch Forrester."

"You must feel so conspicuous," Mitch said when they'd made it into the ballroom.

A waiter stopped and offered champagne. They each took a glass, and Blue said, "No, but I'll bet you do."

"Lord yes. How can you not?"

"I'm used to it," she said. This satisfied him. The real answer was more complicated. She didn't feel conspicuous in such a crowd because she understood that when people saw her, they almost never saw *her.* She was a sort of tourist attraction that everyone wanted to stand by and have their picture taken with, hardly taking notice of the attraction itself. If this made her feel a little empty sometimes, devalued, it also made her feel safe.

Mitch seemed to be holding his own nicely with this crowd so far, which was promising. As past companions had noted, it wasn't easy to be *Blue's sidekick*. Four times Mitch was asked, "And what do you do?" as though he might confess to being her tennis instructor. He had returned the volleys with aplomb: "I'm an English professor and Hemingway scholar. You must have missed seeing me on the show."

She said, "How are your dancing skills these days?"

"Passable, I'd guess, though it's been a while. Would you like to dance?"

"Let's finish our champagne first. If I'm not mistaken, it's Louis Roederer, *Cristal*."

"It's wonderful—and expensive, no doubt."

"They could fund a dozen college scholarships with what they've spent on it tonight."

"But if it gets guests to part with their money for the museum . . ."

"We would anyway. Most of us already have. In fact, most of us were unaware of how much we gave until someone briefed us on it, in some cases right before we got here." She hadn't known until this morning. A half-million.

"So this is mostly an excuse to have a party," Mitch said.

No museum fund-raising gala was complete without a bevy of society photographers, all hand-picked for their skill at knowing the hierarchies of who must be photographed, then who should be, then who shouldn't be, and finally, who should be encouraged to be photographed with whom. The tiny bursts of flashes while she and Mitch moved, better than passably, over the polished dance floor were no surprise. The surprise came several dances—and glasses of champagne—later: Mitch's kiss, at the end of one beautiful waltz.

"I've been wanting to do that for weeks—since you showed up at Mom and Dad's for dinner."

"Have you, now?"

"Well, I'm not saying I knew it at the time . . ."

"How does Julian feel about your being here?"

Mitch sighed. "He's worried about my mixing business with plea-

sure. Whereas Brenda thinks I'm throwing her over just so I can go dancing in billionaires' homes with America's Favorite Talk-show Host—all
caps; that's Julian's expression for you, not mine."

"Oh?" This was deflating; Julian thought so little of her?

"It's not really a sneer—I know it sounds like one, but he's just that
way, you know?"

"He can be any way he wants," she said, taking a fresh glass of champagne. "I'm more concerned about Brenda. *Are* you 'throwing her over,'
then?" Oddly, the thought made her sad for the woman, who she'd genuinely liked.

"I wouldn't put it in those terms . . . but, suppose I was?" he asked,
just as the announcement came that seating for dinner had begun.

"We'll have to talk more later."

He proved popular with the other partygoers. She took every opportunity to introduce him as both a long-time friend and a likely biopic
host, ensuring *Literary Lions* would get its start—though he seemed unaware of the scope of the game being played. She coached him along:
"That woman in the white silk is on the *Tribune*'s board, and helps organize the Printers Row Book Fair. Very well-read." And, "The man by
the window to your left is a major patron to Northwestern's Alice Ka-
plan Institute for the Humanities—new, since you left there. I've heard
he likes John Dos Passos; I've also heard he likes boys."

In many ways it was nice to have a date like Mitch, who was a novelty among this kind of crowd. If there was another person on the estate
(staff excluded) who earned less than a million dollars a year, she'd be
surprised. In this fishbowl, Mitch was a pretty striped minnow, holding
still enough that everyone could admire him.

Yet when she pulled him aside at ten minutes to eleven and said
they'd be leaving on the hour, her main feeling was relief that the
evening was ending. The night was not quite turning out to be the re-
play she'd envisioned yesterday. She was distracted. The atmosphere
was different. Snow was not falling, flashbulbs were not the equivalent
of twinkling light strings, and she was not . . . seeking. Or, possibly, not
seeking Mitch.

The fantasy she'd been entertaining when she invited him along tonight was exactly that: a fantasy. This was no magical New Year's Eve, for all that it was imbued with *auld lang syne*. Yes, she'd danced with Mitch and enjoyed his company. He was handsome and funny and as interesting as ever. When dessert was being served (mixed spring berries, mint leaves, imported cream), he'd enthralled the group at their table with the tale of Hemingway's Montana car accident and resulting broken arm, surgically repaired with kangaroo tendon. The resulting pain and recovery time led, Mitch said, to several brilliant short stories but was, he thought, "the beginning of the end."

The difference was that even with dancing and dinner, she in a pretty dress and Mitch in a tux, much of what she'd done this evening was work. The difference—and it was to be expected, after all, and was not necessarily a *problem*—was that she was not nineteen, and not in love.

$\mathcal{P}$redictably, the media didn't care about Blue's current age or emotional truth. The following morning even the *Trib* ran the photo in color: Mitch kissing her in a way that, when captured on film, looked much more significant than it was. She studied it. It could be real. She could let it be real.

Marcy called at seven. "Good morning. 'Spring Fling for Beautiful Blue?' You do look beautiful. Killer dress."

That wasn't the *Tribune*'s headline. "What are you looking at?"

"I'm online. This is *TMZ*, but you and the 'Noted Hemingway Scholar' are everywhere. Here's another one: 'A Blue Clue: Is It Love?' *Peter's* loving it, I know that; he said now no one will be thinking about the crying thing. Things must be improving fast."

"It looks that way, doesn't it?"

"It looks very sweet, in this photo. Do you have time to fill me in on what came after?" Marcy asked, a leer in her voice.

"Yes," Blue said. She took a bowl of grapes from the refrigerator and sat down at the counter.

"Well?"

"Nothing. That's what happened. We left at eleven, did a kind of play-by-play roundup on the ride to Julian's, where he's staying, I dropped him off without going in, and then I came home and went to bed."

"That's it?"

"If you want to talk porn, call your boyfriend."

"He's right here. Boyfriend," Marcy said, "Blue's story is boring. You got anything better?"

"I'm hanging up," Blue said.

Her phone rang again a few minutes later. Mitch.

"Good morning," he said. "I hope it's not too early. I left Julian sleeping—he has a long day ahead of him—"

"Why's that?"

"He's off to Iraq today. When I got in last night, he was waiting up to say they asked him to come sooner—so really, the timing of things has all worked out perfectly for him. Anyway, I'm out getting coffee and the paper—have you seen it?"

"It's right here on my counter." Next to the coffee she'd made, which was not as good as the Cuban, but necessary today.

"What do you think? Romantic, isn't it? I felt like Prince Charming at the ball last night."

"I'm glad you enjoyed yourself. Listen, pictures are all over the place. If you haven't prepared Brenda for this, you'd better call her soon."

"It's all right. We spoke Thursday night."

"And?"

"And . . . she said she already had a sense this might happen, and she wishes us good luck."

"Surely not as kindly as that—and who could blame her?"

Mitch said, "Blue, I'm a pretty easygoing guy . . . I don't mean to avoid all conflict, exactly, but I sure don't court it. It's time I was a little more . . . deliberate in my choices, and I have to say, it seems like we have a shot here."

Despite her misgivings, it did seem that way. Last night was not a fiasco; she'd had as nice a time as she ever did at those sorts of events.

Could restarting their romance be this easy, then? A coincidental meeting in Key West after twenty-three years, a dress-up date, a kiss, a photo, and public approbation? Was this strange bubble of calm she felt surrounding her what fate felt like when you knew the moment it was happening?

"Blue?"

"Can you hold on a second?"

She pressed the phone against her thigh and looked again at the photo. His words hung before her like ripe fruit she could reach out and pick, if she was hungry enough. Too much emotion made things murky and unpredictable, made people behave inadvisably. This was straightforward and clean and easy. Mature.

She could do this. It was a perfect setup, the nearest to a sure thing that she could ask for. She put the phone to her ear again. "Sorry about that, my doorman was buzzing me—my mom's here to talk about plans for the shower I'm throwing her next weekend."

His voice was soft when he said, "You must think I'm a fool—who but a fool would have let you get away the first time?"

"If only there were glasses for hindsight."

"I'd buy those. Life is complicated, isn't it?" he said.

"To say the least."

"Consider this my attempt to simplify matters. The media already thinks we're serious, so why not?"

What would it mean to open her mouth and let her wishes, all of them, escape into the care of someone else whose singular goal was to see her happy? Was that what he was offering? Was that what she wanted from him?

With far less certainty than she would ever show him, she said, "Why not."

"All right then," Mitch said. "All right. So I'll call you tonight, after I get home."

Right after she hung up the doorman did buzz, letting her know that her mother was on her way up. For the first time since her mother had declared her intention to marry Calvin, Blue got a whiff of their excitement and liked the smell. She wasn't going to kid herself; what she felt for Mitch wasn't what her mother felt for Calvin. The dynamics of the two relationships were as different as she was from her mother. She liked the idea of being settled, though, and who better to be settled with than a man like Mitch? She was excited for her mother, and hopeful that the feeling would bleed over into her new romance, given a chance.

She had plenty to feel good about in the meantime. Hiatus was coming. Her house in Key West was waiting.

23

With all of what mattered packed into his two bags, Julian walked through his apartment shutting off lights, double-checking the thermostat, locking the windows, shutting off the water main so that the dripping bathroom faucet didn't waste a village-worth's supply of water while he was gone.

His camera gear had its own two cases; those were packed and locked and waiting on the kitchen table. Though he was bringing three cameras, probably he'd be reduced to using a single one for most of his work in Iraq. Close quarters and frequent movement pretty much guaranteed that once they left the base he'd be traveling light. He was taking extra gear anyway, now that he'd given himself some time to go roaming before the assignment began. There were still several Middle Eastern birds he hoped to spot, birds he hadn't seen in Afghanistan; with Iraq at roughly the same latitude and of similar climate, much of the bird population would be alike.

In particular, he was looking for the rare Red-backed Shrike, known by its eponymous back and thick black eye stripe, and then also the Blue-cheeked Bee-eater, with its black-in-white eye stripe, rufous throat, pale blue face, blue rump, green wings. A true beauty that wintered in Africa but should, by now, be back. Wouldn't Blue be impressed with that one?

Not that it mattered to him one way or the other.

His father came into the living room, pulling his suitcase behind him. "All set?"

"Yep."

"Here, look at this . . ." His father handed him a section of the newspaper. On the front was a photo of a kissing couple.

"Ah," he handed it back quickly. "So the flowers worked."

His father smiled. "You'll have email access, right? I'll send you Blue's email address in case you think of anything more to put into the prospectus. I'm hopeless with the technicalities."

"My BlackBerry is pretty much an everywhere tool, so, yeah. I should have email, and phone, too. No telling if I'll be able to *answer* . . ."

"About that. You're going to have to be hard-nosed about not following the troops into any gun battles—you don't have to prove your manliness. I mean, you only have nine fingers left. Seems like you'll need most of them for your work."

"Nah," Julian said, playing off the light tone his father was trying for, "I bet I could get by with maybe six, depending which six they were."

"I'd feel better knowing you won't be taking the chance."

"Dad, I'll be fine. I've been in a lot of ugly places, I know what's what."

His father nodded. "Just . . . just promise me you'll be careful."

"I will be," he said. "You, too."

*E*n route to Iraq, he did his best to clear his head of all domestic nuisances. None of it made a difference to the way he lived his life, after all. Until a few months ago, he had hardly given his father a passing thought—and Blue Reynolds none at all. Then he'd agreed to do *Lions*. What he ought to be occupied with was whether to buy the new Nikon lens he kept hearing about. That, and what the troops in Iraq liked to do when they were off patrol. He should be thinking of how to finagle another assignment to Bangladesh, to Hanoi, to one of the research stations in Antarctica—he'd never been to the bottom of the Earth. Though, really, what was there to photograph? Penguins, maybe. Whales. No matter, he could find something.

The U.S. air base in Iraq looked more or less like every other desert base he'd seen, so much so that once he was standing on the tarmac, he didn't bother to do more than lift his camera and scan his surroundings. No need to document more dun-colored landscape, more Humvees, more razor wire, more army-green cargo jets, more tired young men with thick necks and haircuts so high and tight that in contrast he looked like a hippie. Maybe he looked like one regardless, if hippies sometimes wore photo vests with their jeans and zip-side boots.

Behind him, a woman's voice: "Are you Julian Forrester, the photographer assigned to our unit?"

He swiveled and saw a surprisingly attractive woman. Thick blond hair bound up under an army cap that couldn't quite disguise it, long slope of a nose that went well with the slope of her waist to her hips, apparent even within the bulky tan camo fatigues.

"I am," he said, letting go of his camera while he reached to shake her hand.

"Lieutenant Jenna Davies. I'm the battalion's liaison officer."

"Good to meet you."

"Same here." Her dimpled smile was an exclamation point.

"How long have you been in-country?"

"Four months. Interesting work, but I miss trees, you know?"

"Where's home?"

"Oregon. But who knows when that will be true again?" she said. "We've got some in-briefing tasks to get through before I turn you over to the battalion commander. Come along this way."

He fell into step with her. She talked as they walked through the camp, pointing out the essentials. Her voice was high—distractingly, so that he paid attention to it, and to his curiosity about how she'd come to be an Army officer rather than some other type of professional dressed in a skirt suit and heels that would, he was certain, show off the long slope of lean calves.

A woman with her looks electing to serve in the military was an incongruity that interested him. A sexist-sounding question, he was aware. He wouldn't ask it. If he did, though, he'd mean no disrespect. *She* interested him—just not the way she might have if he wasn't unwisely preoccupied with a different beautiful and interesting woman.

Who right now was surely preoccupied with thoughts of his father.

Just before Lieutenant Davies led him into the HQ tent, a flash of color caught his eye. He stopped and squinted, shading his eyes to see better: a bird, but which one, and where had it gone? He scanned the near horizon of temporary power poles, wires running from poles to tents, poles to tents—there, it had landed on a wire some fifty yards out.

"Hang on," he said, stooping to get his telephoto lens out and onto the camera while keeping one eye on the bird. Then he found it in the viewer, focused, shot. Half a dozen more frames. The bird leaned around to preen its wing, then turned obligingly so that he got a clear shot of its back. The hazy sky behind it was a good contrast for its vivid colors, and before he had the lens packed away again, he was envisioning a triptych made with this bird, the shrike, and the colorful Indian roller, all done in black mats with olive-wood frames.

"That," he said, pointing, "is a Blue-cheeked Bee-eater. It's a migrant."

"Do you know the names of all the local birds?"

He looked at her, the way her so-blond eyebrows were raised in a giveaway is-he-a-geek? expression. "Plants, too," he said. "And fish. And the capital cities of pretty much every country including the post-Soviet ones."

"Wow," she laughed. "Impressive."

Her eyes were an amazing color, like thick ice beneath bright sunshine. Assuming she signed a release waiver, he'd have magazine editors falling in love with her in no time. He imagined a caption: *The New Face of the U.S. Army?*

"Right this way," she said.

24

*A*s if Blue didn't appreciate it fully, on Wednesday Peter reminded her four times just what a coup it was to have Robert De Niro on this afternoon's show. And she *didn't* appreciate it fully, because while she was trying to keep the show's focus on the press-shy actor, he was determined to turn the tables.

She'd just asked him how he was doing. "Forget how *I'm* doing," he said, that bit of New York gravel in his voice. They sat in identical armchairs that were angled to let them face each other and the audience. "I saw your prom pictures in the *Post*—you're the one making news. Is there a slide you can put up?" he asked Peter, who stood next to a monitor in the wings. The audience cheered.

Blue shook her head at Peter and said, "Now come on. Who I'm dating isn't newsworthy. Tell me what's happening in Tribeca."

"You should bring the new guy around and see what's happening firsthand. We'll have lunch at the Grill. What's his name?"

Blue ignored the question, asking, "How's business at the Grill?" The audience laughed, loving the banter.

"No, come on now," he said. "I'll need to know it when I see him, right? He looks like a good kisser, by the way."

Cheers erupted, and someone yelled out, "His name is Mitch!"

"Yeah? Mitch? I like it."

Blue sighed. There was no winning against his charm and the audience's energy. She said, "Dr. Mitch Forrester, he's an English professor,

I've known him for a very long time, and it was just one date, okay? Now Bob, how about we at least mention that you have an exciting new film coming out . . ."

Backstage afterward he said, "I hope I wasn't too hard on you. You never talk about yourself. People, they like to know your life is good, that you have some happiness in it."

"You're right. But now you owe me another visit so we can talk about you."

"I meant what I said. Come out to New York—come for the Film Festival. It's a great time."

"I'll check my schedule," she said, hugging him before they parted, certain he was just as aware as she that neither of them had committed to anything.

Next on her schedule was to check in with her sister and find out whether Melody preferred to wear fuchsia or yellow for their mother's wedding. She understood that the task was less about accommodating their mother's ceremony-design scheme than it was a scheme to make Blue and Mel converse about something. Anything. Their mother had said, "Weddings are about bringing people together for physical and spiritual connection—or reconnection, as the case may be."

How effectively she and Mel could connect over dress color remained to be seen. In a perfect world, the matter of a fuchsia dress or a yellow one would be at most a secondary concern for a pair of sisters who had, for what felt at the time like endless years, kept one another away from the abyss. They could see what might await them over the edge: loneliness, fear, arrest, pregnancy, addiction. They'd been tied together by shared bad luck, a tether that Blue had seen as unbreakable; if one stood, or one fell, so would the other. As it turned out, that had been just one more of her mistaken beliefs.

She planned to make the call right after Branford, due in for a four-thirty meeting, left her office. Her secretary announced his arrival.

Branford, who must be in his fifties, always looked shorter than she remembered, with deeper lines in his forehead, and less hair.

"Well," he said, walking up to where she stood at her desk. He clasped his hands in front of him. Calm. Reassuring. If only he could inject her with those elements so that the effect would remain after he left.

"Let's sit over there." She pointed to the chairs grouped near the windows. Outside the nearer window was her access to the fire escape. At the center of the round coffee table in front of the chairs was her bird, the painted bunting.

"Well," he said again when they were seated. He leaned forward, elbows on knees, hands clasped. He had more hair on his knuckles than on his head. She stared at it, waiting for him to say more.

"Well?"

He looked up. "Well, she said she got through the funeral all right, with the help of God's grace and her church community. She's had visitors, and has been going to the homes of her friends for meals and prayer meetings, but she finally had a minute to go into her mother's basement and thinks she's seen the right box. She hasn't dug it out, mind. But it looks like it could be the right one."

"Call me jaded, but does it sound to you like she's asking for a bit more persuasion?"

"She's a receptionist for a well-digging company. Her mother had no life insurance policy," he said.

"I guess it's hard to want to dig through boxes of medical files when you are overcome by grief, and life."

"It is."

"Really, I don't mean to minimize her loss, but we already paid her pretty well."

He nodded. "She bought a lovely casket and got extra engraving on her mother's grave monument."

Blue chewed the inside of her lip, then said, "Okay, offer her ten thousand to get the box out and carry it to wherever she can open it and view its contents. If she happens to discover something of value, she'll get fifty grand more. God, I feel sleazy—I can't wait for this to be resolved."

"Odds are good that this will do it."

Odds. Like the odds of a girl with irregular periods getting pregnant

by accident? Like the odds that someone without strong religious conviction would still elect not to abort? She was not fond of playing the
odds.

Her email pinged. She stood up to go to her desk, saying, "Meantime, let me pay you what I owe you." At her desk, she unlocked a
drawer and took out a plain white envelope. He joined her there and she
handed it to him. "You know how much I appreciate your efforts."

"Hey, to me, it's a privilege. It's not easy being you, I know that.
People like you need people they can rely on. I don't mind saying I take
pride in what I do—even if, you know, I can't exactly brag about it all to
my friends."

He left, and still she put off calling Mel. In a perfect world, she and
her sister would be the closest of friends and, if not quite that, then good
friends and spirited debaters of their differences. They would talk often,
commiserate about men and children and in-laws and their mother—
who had decided to be married at the next full moon in order to give the
couple, in her mother's words, the most auspicious start.

She and Melody, in that perfect world, would meet for lunch at the
Park Grill and speculate about their father's identity over jumbo scallops
and French onion soup. *I think his name is Linus,* she might say, *and he
was a wealthy, married man with other kids and a passionate wife who'd kill
him if she knew about us.* Melody, being more like the Mel of their
younger years, would protest, *No, his name is Luis and he was in the country illegally—from Portugal—but he was a communist, and before Mom
could marry him he was arrested and deported.* They would sit beneath the
colorful umbrellas and discuss whether the park's *Cloud Gate* sculpture
was best enjoyed while under the influence—of wine, like the Zinfandel
they'd be drinking, or something a little more illicit. And Blue would be
able to talk about *how it had been,* that year she was away.

In a perfect world, she would have felt able to tell both her sister and
their mother about her pregnancy when she first discovered her condition. Like Stacey, from the show last month, she would have owned up to
her mistake. She would have gone to her pastor—if she'd had one—or
priest (even less likely, all things considered), and asked to be forgiven.

God, how stubbornly certain she'd been that none of those kinds of people were capable of fixing the mess she'd made. More than that: she couldn't bear the thought of anyone seeing her as vulnerable and unwise.

Had she made any progress in all these years?

She had been the even-keeled one in the family, the one who was going to outsmart poverty and disadvantage—so how, after years of lecturing Melody on her wild behavior, could she with her growing belly have faced Melody, who by that time was engaged to Jeff? How could she, after a year of crowing to her mother about how perfect the Forresters were, and later, how she and Mitch had their future mapped out—how could she reemerge from months of willful exile, pregnant and destitute, and say to her mother, *Now what should I do?*

The only solution, then, had been to undo it all before she was found out—far easier then than now. Now, so many keen eyes were tracking her every movement that she often felt pinned, a butterfly in a lepidopterist's display. *Look at those colors, that pattern! Oh, but wouldn't she be even prettier if that orange area were yellow? If the black was purple? What was she doing, flitting on* these *bushes when her type are supposed to enjoy* those? *How could she let herself be netted—isn't she smarter than that?*

God, she hoped so.

Turning her attention to her email, she saw a message from Marcy— *Your Trip Itin.*—confirming her trip back to Key West next Friday evening. She counted on her fingers: nine days away.

There was an email with an attachment from Mitch: *Lions prospectus and pilot,* which she'd asked for. She was forwarding it on to Harmony's production head when there was a new ping, and a new email appeared, from a sender whose name was a cryptic series of numbers and letters. This email had an attachment, too, and the subject line read, *You might like this one.* It had to be junk. *This one* would be a Rolex, an erectile dysfunction medication, a Mexican vacation offer, a device guaranteed to increase penis size. She went to delete the email, then held off; their spam filters had been so good lately that she wasn't getting junk anymore.

She picked up the phone and called Erin, their techie, getting her voicemail. "Erin, it's Blue. Would you stop by and let me know if it's safe to open an email? Thanks." Paranoid as she sounded, the last thing she wanted to deal with now was another computer virus that would grind their system to a halt.

Now, for Melody. With phone in hand, she went to the window, opened it, and climbed out onto the fire escape.

Below, the street bustled with delivery trucks, cars, pedestrians with jackets unzipped to better appreciate the warming day. The sound of a man singing opera came from up the block. A woman on a rooftop to the east stood before an easel, painting something Blue couldn't make out from here. The picture might be a roofscape, it might be the rusting bicycle leaning against the roof's lip—or maybe something from the woman's imagination. Suppose she yelled across, *What are you painting?* Would the woman be flattered by *Blue Reynolds's* attention, or would her concentration, her creativity, be ruined?

And if the woman's could be, might Mitch's? Maybe she was wrong to have meddled in what he, and Julian, were so capable of doing on their own. Everyone wanted to do things *bigger*, make them *more*—she was guilty of succumbing, guilty of nodding yes, of signing off on the next new strategy to seduce more advertisers, grab more viewership. She had nothing against success; she just worried about what might be getting lost if in making *more* a person ended up with less.

Blue sat on the sun-warmed stair, drew in a deep breath, let it out and dialed her sister.

Four rings, then Jeff answered.

"Hi, Jeff, it's Blue. How are you?"

"Hi, Blue. Not much new here. They got the beans in, but we're short on rain so far this year. Mel's still out," he said before she had a chance to ask. That was Jeff, quick and to the point. "Girls' lunch with the knitting crowd," he explained. "You know how it is."

Could he really think so? She said, "Oh, all right. When's she due back?"

"Hard to say. They get to yakking, I sometimes have to make my own supper."

"Well, you know how women are."

"That I do. I'll tell her you called."

"Thanks."

"No trouble."

After hanging up, Blue stayed on the fire escape step a minute longer. *Girls' lunch with the knitting crowd.* The closest she'd come to that kind of thing was a fund-raiser she'd attended for women in Nepal, to buy them sturdy fine-wool sheep from which they could sustain their own livelihoods.

Not quite the same.

Which was okay. She had plenty of worthwhile things filling her time. With a last look at the roofscapes around her, she climbed back inside her office.

Erin arrived a few minutes later. "Got your message. What's up?"

Blue waved her over to her desk. "I got an email with an attachment, and I don't know who it's from."

"Did you do the preview pane?"

Blue drew a blank. "The what?"

"Here." Erin sat down at the desk and in a quick couple of key-strokes had the email program set up so that it displayed a bit of the message text without her having to actually open the message. "See? This way you peek in and, if you can tell it's legit, open the message." As Blue was about to peek in as suggested, Erin clicked open the security program and spent another minute tinkering. Then she got out of the chair. "Okay. You're all updated."

"Good, thanks."

"Absolutely," Erin said. Blue hardly heard her; her attention was already on the email and the bit of its message she could see

Hey--
    Dad gave me your email address for Lions business.
    Hope you don't mind my using it for something unrelated.

Julian. A funny prickle ran up the back of her neck. "I should mind," she said, clicking the message open, "but I don't."

The attached files are pictures of a bird I thought you would appreciate. I took them right after arriving here in Iraq. (Sorry, can't be more specific on where.) It's a Blue-cheeked Bee-eater, a really useful bird.

I trust everything is going well with Dad.

--Julian

She trusted, too. When she talked to Mitch last night, he'd been warm and reflective, good-natured about David Letterman's recent quip: *This Mitch Forrester's a lucky guy, isn't he? He does her show, she takes him dancing—I was going to call the guy and suggest he also buy a Powerball ticket, but this week's jackpot is only a hundred eighty million.*

She opened the first picture file to find a vibrant green bird filling the frame. Its blue cheek was the least of it; its black eye stripe is what stood out, a stripe like Zorro's mask. She opened each of the four other photos. How clear they were, how detailed—he was so obviously gifted.

Less obvious was why he'd decided to email her. Presumably it was a straightforward friendly gesture: he knew she liked colorful birds, he'd seen and photographed one, he'd shared the images.

If the gesture was so straightforward, why was she clutching the mouse so tightly? Why did it make her stomach fluttery, a little nauseated maybe? Why, at the same time, did it make her smile?

That she was smiling made her frown.

"I'm too old for this."

Whatever *this* was.

She closed the images with five quick clicks, then closed the message with one more.

Then she opened it again. She couldn't *not* reply; he'd be sure to interpret that as disinterest or disdain or some other *dis,* and that would perpetuate their rough start, which would only mean more tension for Mitch.

Reading through the message once more, she tried to gauge his tone for a clue about how best to respond. His salutation, *Hey--* was so casual. But casual was good, it was fine. And there was no sign-off at all, not even the generic *Best* or *Thanks*. Was he saying he'd taken the photos *because* he thought she'd appreciate the bird? Or was it that he appreciated the bird and, incidentally, thought she would too?

She clicked REPLY. "Does it matter?" she said as she began to type, denying the possibility that it did.

25

When Blue arrived at her mother's apartment building Saturday afternoon, Melody opened the door and said, "Yellow."

"Call me Blue."

"Hi, Harmony Blue," Mel said. They hugged, a quick and dutiful embrace. "The dress—I'll wear the yellow dress."

"Why didn't you call me back?"

Mel shrugged and led the way to the rooftop-access door. "She looks wonderful. Calvin gave her the ring last night, she can hardly wait to show you." She paused at the doorway and turned around. "Isn't this something, her getting married?"

"I guess it's time."

"I guess we'll be showering you next, eh?"

"Have I told you how good you look?" Blue said, reaching past Mel to open the door.

"What, aren't you excited about finding Mitch again?"

Mel's perceptiveness caught Blue short, warned her that her defenses were down. She remedied that, standing straighter and smiling at Mel. She said, "I am. No need to rush things, though."

"How long since you've been in a serious relationship?"

"Long," Blue said. "I don't have time to get serious."

"So it's all just weekends on yachts and, like, trips to Jamaica with— who was that last guy?"

"His name is Lou Patterson," a financier she'd met at a Cubs game two years before, "and yes, that kind of dating works best." Until she got bored with jet-setting, as she inevitably did, and bowed out.

"Works best for what? Sex?"

Blue said, "I don't want to get into it. You wouldn't understand."

"I expect you're right about that."

They went up the stairs to the rooftop, where caterers had transformed the garden space into a lattice-covered wonderland of ivy and violets and lace. Mel said, "Mom told me this is all on you. It's beautiful. You really do right by her." Her tone was almost grudge-free.

"She worked so hard for us," Blue said. "I'll just go say hi."

She found her mother directing three women in violet aprons in the just-so arrangement of finger sandwiches. When the caterer had suggested doing the shower like a themed afternoon tea, Blue liked the idea but had expected her mother to pass. Instead, she'd taken to it wholeheartedly (*like a duck to bugs*) and in her invitations directed the guests to dress accordingly. Her mother's own interpretation was a lavender chiffon dress printed with tiny green vines, a green cashmere cardigan, and lavender tights that ended at the ankle above lavender satin ballerina shoes.

Blue kissed her cheek. "Hi, Mom—you look marvelous, like you just stepped off the runway." Her hair was back in a loose French braid and her usual peace-sign earrings had been replaced with small dangling strings of silver and green beads.

"You're not exactly chopped liver," her mother said, holding her by the shoulders and looking her over. Blue's dress was a belted peony print, Carolina Herrera, meant for Monday's show. "You either," her mother said to Mel, who'd come up behind Blue. Mel's dress flattered her, a red, white, and brown abstract print with an A-line skirt. Not cheap, and not matronly, suggesting Mel had put serious thought into her choice.

Mel said, "Show her the ring."

The ring was platinum, with a large, round yellow diamond flanked by a pair of smaller white ones. "Calvin says the middle one is me, I'm the sun; the others are you two, the stars."

"He said that?" Blue asked. "I like him better and better." She liked, too, that his history had checked out. Not only was he who he said he was, his record was clean in every way.

"*She's* the star," Mel said. "I'm the . . . I'm the rhinestone."

Blue nudged her. "Not. You are definitely stellar."

"That's right. You're both stars in my universe," their mother said. "I told Calvin *he* is the middle one, the sun. We had a lively debate and had to settle it in bed."

Mel covered her ears. "I'm not listening. La la la la."

Their mothers' friends began arriving, women from the bookstore, women from the co-op, the gardening club, the arts center—they were all ages, all sizes, colorful and eclectic in some cases, simple and quiet in others. All of them shared an affection for their generous, forthright Nancy, and all of them were eager to say so.

Seated at round tables of six apiece, each woman told her story of how she'd met Nancy, what she'd thought of her. Blue's mother always made a strong impression, as did the bit of her bio she was quick to share. "I don't think I'd known her ten minutes," said Jill, Calvin's bookstore manager, "when she revealed she was Blue Reynolds's mom. Now of course I was startled—Blue, dear, nothing against you, but it wasn't clear you ever had a mother. You seemed to have appeared from the ethers in whole cloth."

Blue had no idea what to make of this, so she laughed along with the others.

Her mother said, "I always say I have *two* girls, I always name them, and then it's *out there* and we can get on to the important matters, like—"

"Like rutabaga," called a woman from the co-op.

"Like men," her mother said. "Men who like rutabaga."

They ate finger sandwiches of chicken and tuna salad, drank tea or wine or cocktails, and the conversation grew even more relaxed. Blue listened to the women at her table discussing teenagers, grandchildren, organic baby food, hemorrhoids, Viagra, marveling at the openness among these women who had not, in most cases, known one another before today. The inclusiveness she felt in simply being among them was a joy.

All of her tablemates were either married or in a long-term relationship, and four of the five were content that way. The fifth was considering a trial separation from her husband of eighteen years. She said,
"Blue, what do you think? Should I leave him?"

You're asking me? was Blue's first thought. "Well, that depends," is
what she said. "Tell me more about your relationship."

Jill said, "Tell us more about yours!"

"There isn't much to tell." This was true. While the media was abuzz
with speculation about an engagement and tangential chatter about
Mitch's being on *TBRS* and nepotism, practically nothing was going on
between her and Mitch in real life. She was busy, he was busy, they'd
spoken only once this past week.

She said, "I knew his family and him a long time ago, then I ran into
them again in Key West. It was a nice coincidence."

The woman across from her said, "It was fate!"

Another added, "My aunt had something like that happen to her,
only it was when my uncle died, and she went to her class reunion and
her high school boyfriend was there, and he was widowed. Widowered?
Whatever. Anyway, they got back together and have been married now
for eight years."

The others were nodding and adding their recollections of similar
events. They commended her, teased her, made all her business their
business—they made her one of them. The picture they painted of her
happily-ever-after was so vivid and enthused that she could almost step
right into it and be that princess she, too, had imagined, once.

Almost.

"Let's order Chinese," Mel said as they stood on the front stoop waving goodbye to the final guest. "My treat."

Blue was about to protest Mel's paying when she saw her mother's
pointed look. "That sounds great. Mom, what do you think? Chinese
tonight?"

"Excellent plan."

They turned back to the building, a three-story Lincoln Park walk-up from the late 1800s. Blue loved the stone and brick, the character of the arched doorway and bay windows. She'd bought it for her mother—the entire building of three restored units, two of which were rented out—that first syndication-salary year. Bought this place, the New York loft, the Montana spread, and still had so much money left that, in a fit of guilt, she gave three million dollars away piecemeal, writing out checks to more than a hundred different charities in one afternoon. She remembered her hand shaking, the urgency. There was no reason she should have so much money. She hadn't *earned* it, didn't deserve it, found the whole nature of the business she'd gotten into improbable and unreal.

In those first few months, she often woke in the middle of the night and called Marcy, her touchstone. "How did I *do* this?" she'd ask. "How did I get here?" And Marcy would say things like, "I bet Neil Armstrong said the same thing when he walked on the moon. 'All I did was climb into the rocket.' Except, yeah, he was a great pilot and all that other stuff first." And Blue would wonder if Armstrong had looked back at the Earth with a sense of no longer belonging there.

"So, Mom," Mel was saying, "what do you think your most entertaining gift was? My vote is the pink feather-wrapped handcuffs."

Blue said, "I thought you didn't like thinking about Mom and sex."

"I don't. I'm hoping she'll re-gift them to me."

"Let's go inside," their mother said, "so we don't embarrass the neighbors."

When they were upstairs again, Blue said to her mother, "About my present . . ."

"I love the idea," which was to have the wedding and the reception in Key West, travel and accommodations for all the guests paid for by Blue. "Your yard sounds like an ideal setting for the ceremony."

"Jeff won't go," Mel said, searching a kitchen drawer for the take-out menu. "If it was here, we were going to drive down, like always."

"Come on," Blue said. "He'll get on a plane for this."

Mel shook her head. "He won't."

"That's crazy—he's missing out on so much."

Mel looked at her. "Huh. He says the same thing about you."

Blue was stung. "My life is jam-packed. What the hell does he know?"

Mel found the menu and shut the drawer. "He knows that his wife and his sons are the best things in his life. Don't you *want* kids?"

"Girls," their mother said. "Let's order, and then let's talk about how we can organize a plan that will work for everybody."

"I'm not trying to be argumentative, Mom, I just want to know."

And Blue wanted to tell her. She looked at her sister, the person who, of all the billions of humans on the planet, was most similar to her by genetics, by history, and wanted to spill it all. She wanted to tell them both, *I screwed up,* wanted to say she'd been wrong, yet not wrong, and have them understand. She wanted them to *know* her, yet feared it as surely as Jeff feared his inaugural flight spiraling nose-first into the ground.

She said, "I think I'll have the mu shu pork."

*L*ater, when all the lights were off and Peep had climbed into his usual nighttime spot on the chair across from her bed, Blue slid beneath her covers and closed her eyes; maybe the future would appear there and put her mind at ease.

But no, it was the past. That cold day when she'd gone to meet Mitch at the Shedd Aquarium, anxious hope sitting like a stone in her stomach. She'd taken the Metra into the city from Homewood. She should have known he would not have chosen the public setting if what he wanted was what she'd wished for. She should have known there would be no proposal, no ring that sparkled with the brilliance of the sun off the lake's surface. She knew enough to be nervous, but was determined not to let her fear keep her from what might well be the greatest surprise of her life—who could say that wasn't what her sixth sense was telling her? And so she'd taken the train to Roosevelt, emerged from the station and zipped her coat against the wind. Put on ChapStick. Snugged her hat over her ears and walked the quarter-mile with eyes watering. Watched him watching her from the steps, arms wrapped around himself as much because of what he was about to say, she would soon discover, as to keep out the cold. The lake was unbearably blue behind him.

If she'd been wearing her fictitious hindsight glasses that day, she would have spared herself the embarrassment of stubborn hope, not to mention train fare and frozen earlobes. She'd have let him break up by phone—or would have broken up with him—or, if she'd put the glasses on sooner, would never have pinned her stubborn hope on him to begin with.

If she had a pair now, what might she see, and save?

She fell asleep wondering.

Late in the night, she had a dream. She was in the house in Harvey, where she and Marcy had lived with Marcy's boyfriend and his friend, only here the friend was Mitch, and she was waiting for him in her tiny bedroom. Hardly room in there for the old mattress; the walls felt close and the room was shadowy, the sky outside darkened as if preparing to storm. She held a book open in her lap and tried to decipher its words, but each time she started, they changed, became nonsense. Frustrated, she stood up and looked out the window. The view was of a tropical garden, dense with trees and vines; a naked man stood with his back to her, solid, broad shoulders tapering to his waist. Who knew he looked this good? Why didn't he come in? She rapped on the glass and he turned and she saw . . . Julian. For long moments she felt locked in his gaze, felt as if he could truly *see* her. Then she held up her hand in greeting, putting her fingertips to the glass, looking at the spots where each finger made contact. When she looked outside again, he was gone.

She woke in the morning with the dream as vivid in her memory as if she'd taken a literal journey during the night. It *was* a journey—to the truth of what she wanted, *who* she wanted, a truth she'd been ignoring. "Oh. My. God." Her face felt hot, betraying the arousal she would much prefer to still deny. She jumped out of bed, as if leaving the scene of a crime.

"Nope," she said, getting a box of Lucky Charms from the pantry. "Not," she said, pouring a glass of orange juice. "No, I'm sorry. No."

Peep came in and seated himself in front of the refrigerator. Blue obliged him by opening the door and taking out the milk jug. "You, at least, are consistent. I, on the other hand, have been under the misimpression that I had a clue about life and my own best interests."

She couldn't have a romantic relationship with Mitch, a man who inspired in her, at most, sisterly affection. "That's the first part," she told Peep.

"The second part . . ." The second part made her swallow hard. It was a feeling like she'd had that night when she was sitting at the stoplight in the Chevelle, shivering with the cold, looking at the sky and wishing her life were different.

26

"She's something to see, isn't she?"

Julian, foot poised to climb inside an armored vehicle called Golan, had a sense that the "she" in question was not, this time, part of the armored fleet he'd been photographing for the past week or so (along with other static objects, like sandbags, and stones), having been restricted to the base and then given nothing better to do.

He turned around to see who the sergeant meant. Heat rising from the macadam made the entire landscape seem to undulate. He spotted Lieutenant Davies leaving the motor pool office. Julian used the front of his T-shirt to wipe sweat from his neck and ears. "Oh, yeah. Very attractive woman."

The sergeant, who went by the name Sims, poked Julian in the thigh. "Take a picture. Your camera might make it back in one piece even if you don't."

Sims was joking the same way the other soldiers he'd met all did. Gallows humor, to deflect the intensity of a truth that was not too far removed from reality. Julian raised his camera and looked at Lieutenant Davies once again. Her long neck. Her dimpled smile. "Is she attached to anyone?"

Julian swung around and sighted Sims in his viewer. The guy's face was smooth and brown as melted chocolate. Angular. Great bone structure.

Sims tried to ignore the camera but his vulnerable smile betrayed him. "Lieutenant Davies sticks to the fraternization rules, far as I know. I guess she could date another officer, but who'd want to?"

"Right," Julian said, taking one picture, two pictures, before Sims put on a more practiced stern look and began stowing his gear.

He could ask her directly—assuming he got the chance, when they returned from their three days at wherever they were going. They gave him no information up front, a security precaution in case he was overcome by the urge to broadcast the mission details from his BlackBerry or laptop. Photojournalists, and journalists in general, did not rate highly here, considered to be slightly more trustworthy than the local hires whose agendas were similarly opaque.

Maybe he should ask her. It wasn't like he had any sane, sensible reason not to.

He and Sims climbed into the Golan. Sims said, "You take the center row, passenger side."

"What, do you guys have assigned seats or something?"

"We have habits, yeah—but this is for your safety. It's SOP for us to put journalists far enough from the driver to be less of an inadvertent target for snipers, far enough from the wheels that you don't take the full blast of an IED."

SOP. Standard operating procedure. IED. Improvised Explosive Device. Sobering didn't begin to describe the effect of this seat assignment on his mood. That they all approached these things so matter-of-factly told him everything.

Today was Thursday; he'd been here for eleven of the sixty days he'd planned, and without having documented a single mission yet, he was ready to go home.

While he waited, he took out his BlackBerry and tried again to access his email. He hadn't been able to stay connected for more than a few seconds since sending the bee-eater photos last week. If not for knowing that no one he'd asked was having any better luck, he'd think he had jinxed the device.

"What's the deal with service out here? Is it ever reliable?"

Sims watched him. "It's hit and miss, man, be it phones, women, or insurgents. Welcome to our way of life."

"And I thought scorpions would be my only problem."

"You ain't seen a firefight yet."

"Mm," Julian agreed, still trying to connect. "But at least you don't get surprised by a firefight when you're putting on your boots."

"Not usually," Sims said.

Nine hours later, Julian was sure the most serious danger in this mission was boredom. They'd bumped along rutted streets in three nearly abandoned villages so far; his most interesting photo was of a dirty white dog, apparently stranded atop a flat-roofed house. They didn't stop.

Sims sat beside him, legs outstretched, iPod playing just loudly enough that Julian could hear the noise but not the music. He tried checking his email again. This time, it worked. There were twenty-four new messages—he scanned the list, knowing that he was looking for a particular name, hating that he was looking for a particular name . . . there, there it was, halfway down the list. Blue.

She'd sent the email a week ago, apparently right after she got it.

Hi, Julian--

How good of you to send these Bee-eater photos. It is a lovely bird.

Stay well,
Blue

All right then. Okay. Nothing here that he shouldn't be pleased with. Reading it again . . . nothing here that should please him, especially— which was fine, appropriate, not in any way a letdown, why would it be?

He felt the vehicle slowing and looked up. Sims did the same, pulling off his headphones and snapping to alertness. Ahead of them on this narrow hillside road was a short bridge, and two boys near its side, squatting down next to an animal that appeared to have been dead for some time. A trio of crows waited on the bridge's wooden railing thirty feet behind them.

Specialist Parker, riding in the front passenger seat, released his assault rifle's safety, and the rest of the soldiers followed suit.

"What gives?" Julian asked. Already he could smell the sweat of adrenalin, sour in the confined space.

They came to a stop fifty feet or so from the bridge. Sims said, "Looks to be a jackal."

Julian set his BlackBerry aside and switched on his camera, aiming it as the soldiers were doing with their weapons. All thoughts of women, of birds, evaporated.

The boys, dusty, dark-haired kids who were still on the early side of puberty, stood up and waved.

"Watch 'em," Parker said. He fastened his helmet's chinstrap.

The driver, a twenty-year-old private named Barredo, said, "It's a dead jackal. They probably want to take it home for dinner."

"They're not gonna eat roadkill."

Julian kept the boys in his frame, zooming in on their faces as he said, "If they have to, they will." They looked hungry, having left *lean* behind and become *gaunt*. Huge dark eyes in unreadable faces. He widened his view as he shot, saw the boy on the left put his arm around the other boy's shoulders.

"Let's go," Barredo said.

Sims shook his head. "Nah, this doesn't smell right."

"It's roadkill in ninety-five-degree heat, course it don't smell right."

"That's you who don't smell right," Parker said.

The boys remained near the carcass, watching them.

Barredo drummed the steering wheel. "Why don't they move?"

Sims fastened his chinstrap. "Maybe they think we're gonna take their dinner."

"Bullshit," Parker said, scanning the rocky hillside that rose steadily to their left. He opened his door and stepped out a few feet, looking down the road behind them, then back up at the hillside, rifle at his shoulder, finger on the trigger.

Julian scooted forward so he could see whatever Parker saw out the front—which was nothing. Stones and scrubby bits of vegetation and dirt.

The first sound was faint, a small *thwack* like a friend flicking your arm, and then a sharp crack, a rock hitting bulletproof glass. He looked to his left, at the driver's window, still intact but with a dark crater the size of his fist blooming in its center. Curses erupted, his own included, but it was the alarmed gurgle that made him look at Barredo, whose neck appeared to have become a fountain spewing dark blood out its side.

Parker jumped back into the vehicle, slamming the door shut before pressing his hands over Barredo's, which were now clasped around his own neck. The sniper's bullet had sped straight through. Parker's stricken face confessed what the reports would later conclude, that his leaving the Golan's door standing open had given the sniper the shot he'd been hoping for.

"Aw fuck," Parker said. "Aw Jesus. Hang on, buddy. Forrester, get the kit."

Julian had seen blood before, had seen gunshot wounds, had pressed wads of gauze, as he was now doing, to injured men's bodies, his own heart beating double time as if to make up for the slowing one beneath his hands. You kept pressing, and praying, hoping for the miracle that never came. There were no miracles, only luck, and Barredo's was pouring from him despite the pressure, the only mercy being how rapidly it poured.

This is what he was thinking as he looked out the windshield and saw the boys turning, running from the bridge, saw the burst of dust and smoke as it exploded, making the Golan jump. He thought at first that the second boom was in his head, a reverberation, until Sims said, "Oh Christ."

He looked at Parker, then at where he and Sims were looking. The road behind them was hidden in black smoke.

27

After pouring his beer into a pilsner glass, Mitch took it and the draft of his Tennessee Williams script out onto his front porch. The floorboards were chipped and the paint was peeling in some places, stained with mildew in others. He really should get the azaleas under control; they were blooming now in an explosion of fuchsia, pink, and white that threatened to overtake the porch. Fortunately there was room, still, for the pair of rockers he'd bought on his first weekend here; you couldn't live in a North Carolina house with a covered front porch and not put rockers on it. One look at his neighbors' homes had told him that.

He pulled one of the chairs away from the overgrown shrubbery and sat down. It being mid April, the sun had eased back out of the southern sky, leaving his porch shady at noon. If he sat here long enough, he'd see the rich Carolina blue of the sky hold on to its color well into the evening. Then the sky would turn a silky red violet with a sliver of orange glow on the horizon, before the night went fully dark.

He liked that the porch faced west, toward the Blue Ridge Mountains. True, his view was partly obstructed by other bungalows, by pines and magnolias, and by some hundred or more miles of interposed land. Those miles, however, contained the promise of far-off mountains in the rolling hills that he *could* see. In his soul he was a man of landscapes—maybe that was why Hemingway drew him the way he did.

He needed his landscape today, as badly as he needed this day away from the university and the craziness he'd brought to the place after kissing Blue in public eleven days ago. In those eleven days, he'd had to change his home telephone number and make it unlisted; he'd had to withstand his colleagues' questions, his students' questions, the questions emailed to him by journalists, questions left as messages on his office voicemail. Every day, a new magazine or newspaper clipping showed up in his English department mailbox, as his colleagues seemed to be making a *Where's Mitch?* game of finding every published reference to him and Blue.

There was no hope of keeping his or his students' attention on the remaining Wharton reading assignments; he'd dismissed the class with instructions to work on their research papers, and to find him during his office hours if need be. By rights he should be keeping office hours right now, but he couldn't bring himself to face one more question or comment—even a well-meaning one—about what he expected to happen next.

He leaned his head back and closed his eyes, enjoying the melodic singing of a wren that had roosted at the far end of his porch. He heard a car's engine, heard it cut off, heard a door shut, but didn't look up until he heard a voice, Brenda's, saying, "Can we talk?"

Mitch stood up and pulled the other rocker over. "Have a seat. Want a beer? Maybe some tea?"

"I'll have a beer. Inside might be better," she said.

"All right. Come on in."

He led her into the kitchen and took his time getting the beer, opening it, pouring it. "S'posed to get to eighty-three today," he said, as though she would have nothing more pressing than weather on her mind.

She wasn't so reticent. "Our office staff is about to mutiny," she said. "The phones don't stop ringing. Every English-speaking reporter on the planet wants to talk to you, or to talk to someone who knows you. Half of the faculty have turned off their phones. The other half are making up whatever version of Mitch-plus-Blue they think fits and telling it to whoever is on the line. It has to stop."

He sat down. "I'm sorry. I didn't realize—"

"They're relentless. You'd think a person needed to actually do something of import or merit to rate this kind of attention."

"Brenda, I'm *sorry*. I . . . I'll do something. I'll . . . I'll hold a press conference and ask them to lay off."

She sighed. "Don't do that, you'd just be feeding the fire. It'll die out, I know that. This is just a slow news week, they have nothing better to do."

They looked at each other for a long moment, and Brenda smiled. "You should be more careful about what you wish for."

Mitch smiled too, ruefully. "How do people live like this?" He was accustomed to the simple and quiet routine of books and classes, intellectual inquiries about his opinion of Heidegger, or Fitzgerald and the unreliable narrator. "Really, I never imagined . . ." He let the statement trail off. She was nodding. She knew.

"How long have we been friends?" she said. "Fifteen, sixteen years? Here's what I know about you: You act before you think. Sometimes you succeed—*often* you do, often enough for you to keep using that haphazard approach—"

"But sometimes I end up in a *what the hell?* situation," he finished for her. "Like now." He wiped condensation from his glass. "It's not Blue. She's, well, she's as wonderful as ever."

"So maybe when things stabilize, you'll stabilize too." Though her words were supportive, her tone was flat.

"Maybe."

"Or . . . maybe all you really have in common is nostalgia."

He looked up at her. "I've thought of that."

"And?"

"Here's the thing: When I met Blue, I was a mess, but somehow she saw the man I wanted to be."

"That must have been very flattering. Not to mention attractive."

"It was. *She* was . . . and is."

"But?"

"But . . . she's not that same young woman. She seems fond of me, but the chemistry isn't . . . well, forgive me for bringing this up, but it isn't what we—that is, you and I—had. Julian says I don't know her at all, so maybe that explains it."

Brenda's interested expression became a curious one. "*Julian* said that."

He nodded. "We were arguing."

"About Blue?"

"No, about his mother and all that mess, but it started when I asked him if he'd go find some flowers for Blue, last-minute."

"Hold on," Brenda said. "I'm confused. You wanted him to buy flowers for her, and . . ."

"And he resisted. He was saying, in essence, that no gesture of mine could matter to someone like her."

"As though he would know," she said.

"Right, he wouldn't. He was being judgmental."

"And protective of you, from the sound of it, which is sweet, really."

Mitch thought again of the argument. "No . . . no, I didn't get the sense he was being protective of *me* . . ." He brought his hand to mouth, rubbed the haze of whiskers he hadn't bothered to shave this morning. "He was angry at what I'd done to him, way back when, but also about what I'd done to her."

"Ah."

When Mitch looked at Brenda, she wore an expression that matched how he suddenly felt. An expression of discovery.

She said, "Well, Blue makes a pretty strange cause for Julian to take up. And that's interesting . . . But honestly? My concern is you."

He liked those words, liked the way she said them, with warmth and acceptance and, he was pretty sure, willingness to look upon his digression as if it was nothing but back-story that in some ways made her like him better.

"I'm real glad to hear that," he said. "If we're right about Julian, though . . ." He shook his head. "It's hard to imagine a happy ending there."

28

*T*hey had no options except to wait and hope, and so Julian had called his grandparents, only to get their machine. He'd kept his message simple: "Things are not working out as well as expected. My phone's low on power so I'm turning it off, but I just want to say I love you both. Please tell my parents, too."

They waited—him, Parker, and Sims, all three of them silent, no need to state the obvious. Julian was unsure whether he thought the metallic smell, the blood, was the worst of the stink; it was more wrong than the other odors, though, he was sure of that. Sure, too, that a person could not die from nausea, but unsure whether a Golan was so airtight that they might, if they were stuck here a lot longer, have to open a window or else be asphyxiated. Once it was full dark, the risk of that open window would be smaller. Meantime, he pulled his T-shirt up to cover his mouth and nose and waited.

A mix of profound and troubling thoughts tumbled around in his mind, adding to the nausea and dismay. When there was nothing else for it, he turned his BlackBerry on again and began typing.

Nothing like being trapped in an armored personnel carrier with a dead soldier, all adrenalin leached out of your pores, darkness falling, bulletproof glass and door locks the only defense you've got, hoping what THEY'VE got isn't a grenade or rocket launcher, to make you see what matters most to you in your life.

Although he was no writer, and the fading light made it difficult to see the device's keys, the urge to document his thoughts was too strong to ignore. Suppose this waiting was all just a mind game the insurgents were playing with them, a little torturous cat-and-mouse where the mouse was already trapped beneath the cat's paws, exhausted? If that was the case and he didn't take this opportunity to lay down some last words, he'd be gone, and she'd never know.

Maybe it was better that she never know.

Except, if he couldn't live honestly *now,* what hope was there for him if they got out safely? How would he face himself every day, knowing that even when hanging headfirst off a precipice he was inclined to be a coward? It was a matter of principle.

He needed her to know.

Or, would the knowledge burden her?

He set the device in his lap. His palms were stained, despite having been scrubbed against his pant legs.

Pulling his shirt away from his face, he said, "When do you think our guys will get here?" He asked Sims, because Parker wasn't talking.

"Soon." Sims avoided looking Julian in the eye. "Can I . . . um, can I use that when you're done?"

"Sure."

Julian read over what he'd just written. He added,

If I get out of here, I'm going straight to Daniel and Lynn's. I'd like to see you when you're in town. I owe you an apology. We need to talk.

Or maybe they didn't. Christ, he didn't know. He backspaced, deleting the line. What he knew was that he needed safety and comfort, the salty breeze and the blue-green water and the feel of frangipani blooms, thick and silken, between his thumb and fingers while he sipped his famous lemonade. Fresh lemons, sugar, bourbon, ice . . . She'd like the lemonade too, as much as he did, as much as she'd loved discovering the birds that entranced him. Not a doubt in his mind about that.

Plenty of doubt, however, about the wisdom of his feelings, and why he felt the way he did.

It wasn't star worship, certainly, because his regard for celebrity in general could not be much lower. He didn't want anything from her, in material terms. And God knew his attraction wasn't based on any kind of common sense. Chemistry, then? Yes, definitely. More than that, though, or he would not have spent the last hour sitting here weighed down by anger and dread and the certainty of being in love with the woman who was his father's girlfriend. As different as he and Blue seemed to be on the surface, he recognized that underneath they had a lot in common. He really thought they might make a good pair. This truth was preposterous, and yet somehow because it was, it felt all the more true.

Sims's voice cracked when he said, "There's a light."

A bobbing, weaving light, up past the destroyed bridge.

Julian wiped his sweating palms on his shirt, then typed,

I love my father and wouldn't try to interfere with you two even if it was possible.

Glancing up, he saw the small light was closer. He swallowed hard.

I'll trust you to keep this just between us.

On the edge of his awareness was a low, rhythmic noise that seemed to be growing louder.

"That's them," Sims said. "I think."

Parker agreed. "Gotta be. Man, do I need a shower."

The sound became identifiably a helicopter. Julian looked again at the email. When in another minute the small light had disappeared and the helicopter, its searchlight like a path to heaven, hovered above them and rescue appeared imminent, he pressed a button and selected DIS-CARD.

"Don't."

Julian glanced up and saw that Sims was close to him, reading over his shoulder.

"Look at him." Sims gestured toward Barredo's body. "This might not be over. Ain't nothin' guaranteed."

Julian finished the message with a simple *J*. and sent it.

29

*H*eavy gray clouds hung from massive thunderheads when Blue arrived at the studio on Thursday morning. The line of waiting audience members snaked over the sidewalk; she signed autographs with forced cheerfulness, and when a white-haired woman asked if she was feeling all right, Blue said she just really missed her dog. What else could she say? *I'm hung up on my old flame's son?* That was a topic for Jerry Springer if ever there was one.

The day felt wrong in every sense, from her dread of this morning's meeting where they would talk, ad infinitum, about how to make next season better than this one, to the way her hair insisted on frizzing up, to the sight of pregnant women seemingly everywhere—along the streets, in the audience line, working in the office . . . To her eyes, they all appeared beatific, a joke at her expense.

Unlike those women with their rounded bellies and secret smiles of optimism and contentment, her future contained an unending string of days that would be more or less exactly like the last several had been, not to mention most that had come before. Yes, she had the new house now, and she would use it as much as possible. At best, though, it would be an infrequent exclamation point in a long, long series of dull words, white space, and commas.

Branford's call came in just as she was returning to her office after the Season Eleven planning meeting. As always, he called her cell phone. As it rang she told her secretary, "I'm not available," then shut her office door.

She answered the phone. "Massachusetts."

"I hate to call with so little to report," he began.

"But?"

"It's the daughter," he sighed. "She took the ten grand and now when I call she won't answer, and she doesn't call me back. I sent an associate over to both her house and the mother's, and there's nobody around. The neighbors don't know anything. One says she's gone to visit a sister, one says she's on a church retreat. Hell, one says she saw her getting her mail yesterday afternoon. Nothing checks out."

"She can't just disappear."

"Not permanently, maybe."

"Do you think she scammed you? Maybe there was never any file box at all. Or maybe . . . maybe she's taken it hostage! I bet that's it. She'll let us sweat and then demand more money."

"No offense, but that sounds like a bad TV show. My theory is, she got cold feet and now she's avoiding me. Good Christian that she is, her conscience said not to give out the information after all."

"While she keeps the money you already paid her?"

"That would surprise you? Hey, for all I know, the plan is still on and she just doesn't share our sense of urgency. Could be she's in Vegas right now playing slots."

Yes, and it could be that all of this stress, all the wondering and hoping and believing that if she could find her son, she'd right every wrong in her life, was bullshit. She'd had her chance to be a parent. It was folly—or worse, hubris—to be trying to buy it back now. Even buying only the answers to who he was, and where, was an exercise in self-gratification.

She could call it off right now. She thought of it: no more anticipation, no more fear, no more waking up in the morning and wondering if *this* was the day she'd hear something. It was tempting . . . But no, no, not when they were as close to the answers as they might be right now. She'd see this through. Get the information, if it could be gotten, and then be satisfied with that.

She said, "Okay, so what do you suggest?"

"We wait."

Blue closed her eyes and nodded, waiting for the pressure in her chest to decrease. "Fine. Call me when you know something."

The rumble of thunder drew her to the window. She unlocked it and pushed it open, then climbed out. If anyone on the street below noticed her standing on the fire escape, face turned to the sky, she was not aware. If they did see her, and wondered what would happen if she decided to jump, well, she was wondering the same thing.

She sat down on the step and called Marcy.

"If I jumped off the fire escape, would I, you know, splatter?"

"Pardon?"

"It's nine stories. That's just break-all-your-bones-and-kill-you height, right?"

"I know Peter was boorish this morning, but I don't think it's worth killing yourself over. Where are you?"

"Out here on the fire escape."

"Don't jump. I'll be right there."

Less than thirty seconds later, Marcy climbed out. She looked annoyed. "You're *sitting* here."

"Yeah, now. I was standing."

Marcy sat down next to her. "It's starting to rain." Fat drops, spattering the steel and making small *ting* noises.

A drop hit Blue's forearm and she watched the water split and slide off. "It's only noon, and already I've had a hell of a day. All I want to do right now is twitch my nose and be in one of those zero-gravity chairs on my Key West patio—would you call the decorator and have her add a couple of those to my list? I'm thinking teak, or maybe bamboo."

"Sure thing," Marcy said. "Wait: Do they come in bamboo?"

"A weekend in Key West is going to help a lot, but let me tell you, in my vocabulary, hiatus is a synonym for heaven."

"So what's the deal?" Marcy said. "What do you hear from our favorite PI?"

"Nothing of substance."

"Well . . . maybe you should take a page from old Marcy's book and distract yourself with your man."

"I wish I could, but it's not going to work." Right tactic, wrong man.

"What, not at all? What happened?"

"More like, what didn't happen."

"Well . . . there's always Viagra."

Blue gave a half-hearted laugh. "Not for this kind of dysfunction."

"Oh," Marcy said. "I get it. Sort of. Want me to handle it for you?"

Yes. "No, I think this needs to come from me."

A half-hour before showtime, as Blue tried to decide exactly how to break off a relationship that had never really gotten off the ground (again), her phone rang, with good news for Mitch: Her production team was prepared to make an option offer.

Perfect; now she could call on an *up*beat, one of few in her day so far. She offered to deliver the news, hung up, then dialed Mitch immediately. Momentum was everything.

"Hi, Mitch, it's Blue. You won't guess why I'm calling."

"You've had second thoughts," he said.

This stopped her. "Wow. Talk about taking the wind out of someone's sails . . ."

"You *haven't* had second thoughts?"

She laughed. "Actually, yes, I've had some, but I wasn't going to start the conversation with them! What I *wanted* to tell you first is that we're ready to make you an offer on *Lions*. You should hear from my producers shortly with all the details. I just volunteered to ring the bell."

"I'm—this is terrific news, Blue. I'm ecstatic, truly." He paused and she waited while he processed everything. Then he said, "However . . . I'm not so clear on whether or not you're also dumping me."

"You don't sound especially crushed by the prospect."

"And you don't sound especially worried that I might be crushed . . ."

"Which pretty much says it all, doesn't it?"

He said, "It does. And I'm sorry about that—but to tell you the truth, I'm not cut out for life in the spotlight anyway."

"Few are," she said. "So no hard feelings, then?"

"Not a one. I'd say I wish you all the best, but I guess for you that's redundant."

Not so much as you'd think.

𝒯his afternoon's audience was a difficult group, peevish and damp after waiting outside in bad weather. The front sidewalk was covered but the wind had blown the rain in on them. They grumbled during commercial breaks and had to be coaxed to laugh at the young comedienne who Blue hoped had gotten a better response from the audience watching at home. *The Blue Reynolds Show.* What a thrill.

Peter caught up with Blue backstage. "It'll be better tomorrow. The forecast is good, and the lineup may be our most crowd-pleasing of the season."

"Remind me," Blue said.

He frowned at her. "Do the remaining *American Idol* finalists ring a bell?"

"Don't use that tone with me. I have a lot on my mind."

He raised his hands in supplication. "I was trying for levity, geez. I think I'll go find our comedienne and knock back a couple empathy drinks."

In her office, Blue cancelled her gym session and got ready to head home. A hot bath, two glasses of wine, and a review of her Idol file was her plan—there were worse ways to spend an evening. Tired as she was, before she left she spent a few minutes watching the contestants' recent performances online and tried to commit faces, names, and songs to memory.

Finally, she checked her email and saw the odd numbers and letters that she now knew identified Julian, standing out amidst the dozen other sender names. There was nothing in the subject line, no attachment—no more bird photos, too bad.

She clicked open the message. There was no salutation, either, which she thought odd—and then she read,

> Nothing like being trapped in an armored personnel carrier with a dead soldier, all adrenalin leached out of your pores, darkness falling, bulletproof glass and door locks the only defense you've got, hoping what THEY'VE got isn't a grenade or rocket launcher, to make you see what matters most to you in your life.
>
> If I get out of here, I'm going straight to Daniel and Lynn's. I'd like to see you when you're in town. I owe you an apology. I love my father and wouldn't try to interfere with you two even if it was possible.
> I'll trust you to keep this just between us.
>
> J.

No salutation was the least of it.

She read it again, then clicked REPLY, hands poised on keys as she watched the cursor blinking, blinking, on the white screen. But she could not write back when her heart was in her throat and her hands were shaking, when the things she yearned to say would be as confusing and upsetting to him as they were to her.

She printed the email, folded it and put it in her bag, and then when she was in the car a few minutes later, she took it out to read again.

If I get out of here, he'd written. *If. If* was not possible. *If* she could not bear.

Please, God.

On first read, she'd interpreted *what matters most* as referring to his relationship with his father. And he didn't want his negative attitude about her to be a wedge between her and Mitch. He wanted to apologize, wouldn't interfere with them even if it was possible—in essence, he saw her and Mitch as a fated pair.

On this read, that meaning wasn't so definite.

I'd like to see you . . .

Suppose . . . suppose *what matters most* meant *her?*

But how could it? His disdain was no secret.

Still, she read the printout again, the paper trembling in her hands.

No. No, she had it right the first time—much as she wished otherwise. Such wishful thinking was foolishness, a rapid and direct path to humiliation both private and public; she could not afford to be a fool again.

She folded the paper and pressed it between her palms, a prayer for his well-being, and hers.

*B*lue paced her apartment Thursday night feeling powerless, unsettled, unable to distract herself with a book or the TV. She couldn't call Mitch to find out Julian's status without raising unanswerable questions and abusing Julian's trust. And she had no other legitimate reason to call.

There was nothing more she could do, so she went to bed—but her mind refused to rest. Surely Julian was fine. Surely the danger was less than it seemed. She might have misinterpreted everything. Maybe the danger was already past when he sent the email. Maybe *If I get out of here* meant, if the Army sent him home sooner than planned.

There were so many possibilities.

And so few.

She sat up and rearranged the pillows, straightened the blanket, straightened her nightshirt. Laid down again. Examined how the dim light from the nighttime city made a long line across the ceiling. Counted sirens wailing. Counted buttons on her shirt. Counted her breaths, in, out . . . She did not *want* to think of him; she could not drive him from her mind.

When she finally closed her eyes, tears leaked from them. Whether they were for Julian or for herself, she would not have been able to say.

At three AM she gave up on sleep. At three twenty she gave up on pacing. At three forty she searched all the drawers in her kitchen and then the ones in her den until she located the Yellow Pages. She couldn't recall which charter company they'd used for the trip to Key West and so she chose the one with the largest ad; in ten minutes she had a confirmed departure time of five thirty AM.

At nine o'clock eastern time, she was on the phone with Lynn Forrester, asking for landscaper recommendations. "I'll be down over the weekend to start making plans," she said, which if not the full truth—she was there already, taxiing to the terminal—was not exactly a lie. "And listen, I want to apologize for having brought such chaos into Mitch's life, especially now that we aren't, you know—"

"Yes, he told us. No need for apologies," Lynn said. "He's fine—and as I told him, I'm sure a little more name recognition will only be a good thing later on when the series is made."

"That's magnanimous, thank you." This all seemed good. Lynn wouldn't be chatty if Julian had been harmed. Still, she needed to be sure. "Incidentally . . . what do you hear from Julian?"

"Seems he ran into a little trouble while out on a patrol—we don't have too many details. He gave us a scare, but apparently he's all right. He says he is." Her tone said she wasn't convinced. "It's been quite the week for the Forresters."

Blue closed her eyes, cool relief filling her. "I'll say."

"But all's well that ends well, right?"

Part 4

Make the most of your regrets . . .
To regret deeply is to live afresh.

HENRY DAVID THOREAU

30

*O*n Friday afternoon, Key West welcomed Julian with soft rainfall. The air was rich with the smell of it as he got out of his grandparents' car. Everything was so lush, so green that he wanted to cry.

Water dripped from the heavy palm fronds overhead and he stood still, letting it stream down his hair and into his collar. A pair of Saffron Finches flitted past him, landing on the porch rail and shaking the water from their golden feathers before flitting off again.

"Coming, J?" Lynn asked, standing beneath her umbrella.

"In a sec."

"All right. I'll tell Daniel we're here. Come in whenever you're ready."

He feared he would never be ready, that he would lie down on the flagstone driveway and close his eyes and when they came to find him later, he would have melted away.

Wishful thinking?

There had been, after all, no reply from Blue.

He'd heard she would be here for the weekend to start planning the work she wanted done to her house. Lynn said they'd spoken early this morning, that Blue had inquired about him.

He was glad of that, and glad that she had, apparently, kept his email in confidence. It was even possible she'd never received it. His hope that she'd never received it was almost as strong as his fear that she had. From the moment he'd sent it, he'd vacillated about whether he'd done the right thing. It had seemed right when he didn't know for certain he'd leave that Golan alive. It seemed less so when he was strapped into the helicopter for the long, loud ride back to the base. What had he hoped to accomplish, really?

Rain was dripping from his nose; how long had he been standing here? He should get his gear and go in. He looked toward the house and saw Daniel waiting there on the porch, watching him.

Daniel said, "Wha'cha doing?"

"Nothing."

"That I can see. Lynn's got a towel warming in the dryer for you."

Julian wiped the rain from his face, slicking his hair back. "Tell her I'll be in soon. I . . . I think I'm going to take a walk first."

"Right now? I thought you might want to call your dad. Hey, did your grandmother tell you that your dad and Blue—"

"I just need to get a little exercise," he interrupted, heading off any chat about Blue. "Too much sitting, you know?"

"All right, then. Take an umbrella."

Julian shook his head. He was already backing down the driveway. "This feels good to me."

"Well, you have to do what feels good, I've always said so, haven't I?"

Julian nodded, waved, and turned to go.

Daniel's support was the thing that had many times before kept him standing, moving forward. Sometimes that forward motion was down a questionable path, yet Daniel had let him go, trusting him to know his own mind or to be able to determine it along the way. It had worked before; now, though, he half wished Daniel would lasso him and pull him back because he could see already that the path was entirely dark.

He went anyway.

As he left the driveway and began walking west, he tried to let go of the questions in his mind and just absorb the warmth and weight of the falling rain. The questions, however, would not let go of him. What, for example, was he doing with his life? Yes, he was a working photojournalist; he was, sometimes, a documentary filmmaker. What he'd been

doing, though, was roaming from one natural disaster or political or social train wreck to another, documenting, cataloging, moving on, sometimes illuminating things for others but never, it seemed, for himself.

All these years he'd been photographing people in order to connect
them with others, all the while remaining disconnected himself. There
was, he thought ruefully, something wrong with that picture.

And this bit about Blue: wasn't that just one more example of how
he set himself up to remain disconnected? A psychiatrist—or Alec,
who'd been as good as one over the years—would probably say so. An
attraction to yet another woman with whom there was no chance of
forming a permanent bond, or at least not the sort of bond he'd had in
mind.

He crossed a street, not avoiding the puddles, hardly hearing the
rooster crowing from a nearby shed's roof. He wiped the water from his
face and walked on, thinking that his attraction to Blue might be an un-
conscious strategy of distancing himself from his father—maybe he'd
created a certain impossibility that guaranteed he'd *continue* to keep
away, and for what? He thought he wanted to be closer to him, but if that
was true, how could he have let himself fall for Blue?

If he could answer that question, he might be able to escape the lu-
nacy that had him out here psychoanalyzing himself in what was now
rumbling thunder and a steady rain.

Not until he heard a squawk, saw the flutter of bright red wings as a
macaw disappeared into a nearby tree, did he see that he'd come to the
corner across from Blue's house. The macaw, possibly the one she'd
mentioned before, perched itself on the high branch of a mango tree in
the middle of her yard. He crossed the street slowly, keeping his eye on
the macaw, wishing he had brought his camera. The bird's colors were
as vibrant and saturated as he could ever hope to make them appear after
the fact.

The wall surrounding her yard, when he was next to it, was too high
to see over, so he went to the gate—and discovered he was not the only
one watching the bird.

There was a moment, then, just before Blue, on her porch, turned and saw him. A moment when he might have been able to back away without being seen. A moment when he had a clear and brilliant view of where that escape path would lead. A clear, brilliant view, where there was nothing to see.

31

She couldn't hide her surprise and didn't try. "What are you doing here?" It came out sounding all wrong, like an accusation. It was the shock of it, the assault to her senses; he was drenched, and gaunt, and more beautiful, with those wide, searching eyes, than she recalled.

"I had the same question for you. I'm sorry—I didn't mean to intrude. I saw the macaw, and—well, I'll leave you alone—"

"No, it's okay," she backpedaled. "You startled me is all." Her cell phone was ringing inside the house. She ignored it.

"Right," Julian said. "I mean, who'd be out in this weather?"

And why? "Come on," she waved him in and watched the flex of his bicep, his shoulder, revealed under his soaked tee, as he lifted the gate's latch. She noted the trim taper of his waist down to solid hips, muscled thighs hinted at, inside clinging wet jeans, as he came up the path. He was so . . . alive. Tangible. Present.

It was all right to admire and appreciate him, to feel affection toward him, especially after what he'd been through—a person would have to be heartless not to. Everything else she felt for him had to be dismissed, and if she couldn't manage that, disguised. Her reaction to him, this warmth in her belly, this urge to pull his T-shirt over his head and lap the water droplets from his skin, this was more the result of her long-running sexual drought than anything about *him*, surely. It was infatuation at most. A resistible whim. Was that plausible? She needed it to be plausible, or how could she be near him and not betray herself?

As he climbed the steps to the porch, she avoided his eyes, turning away and going for the door. "Come on in, I'll see if I have anything you can use to dry off."

"Thanks, but I don't want to get your floors wet."

"Oh, right, okay, I'll be right back." Inside, she was away from the edge of the abyss, she was safe.

"You playing hooky today?" he called through the screen.

"You could say that."

Peter had been dumbfounded when she'd spoken with him this morning, said she'd come down to Key West, told him to cancel today's show. Then he recovered enough to sputter, "You need me to do what?"

"Peter, I'm calling in sick, all right?"

"No! Today's show took *four months* to coordinate—I'll never be able to get it together twice."

"Then it just won't happen," she'd snapped. "Get over it."

Briefly, she'd had second thoughts, third thoughts, even, but dismissed them. It was her show. She could take an unscheduled day off for her mental health. The world would not stop turning just because *TBRS* had broadcast a rerun without warning.

She checked her phone: Marcy—Marcy could wait. Then she searched the cabinets, closets, and pantry and found nothing more absorbent than a can of Ajax. Julian would just have to drip-dry.

He was sitting on the porch step when she went back outside. "I hate to say it, but unless you want to roll around on the bedroom carpet, there's not a thing inside to dry off with." She regretted the words the second they were out; she sounded *lewd*. This was how her subconscious worked?

"Thanks for checking anyway," he said, either not noticing, or pretending not to.

The macaw remained in the tree, preening. "He's so gorgeous." She sat down, leaving two feet between herself and Julian. If only the steps were wider.

"Your garden here must be part of his territory."

"Mmm. I only hope my cat won't scare him away when we're here for the summer. Peep—my cat—and me, that is." Smooth. "I'll have to think up a name for him. The bird, I mean." She knew she was jabbering, and pressed her nails into her palms. Having him this close, where she could smell the rain and the musk on his skin, made her heart pound, truly *pound*. It was crazy.

It was wonderful.

She wanted to feel his arms wrapped around her, his hips against hers, his hands in the small of her back. She wanted to know everything about him, down to the smallest details: How often did he trim his toenails? What did he think of the current president? Was there phantom pain where his finger was missing? Had he ever read *Gulliver's Travels*? Did he think baths were only for women? Had anyone ever told him a person could lose herself in his eyes?

Her nails dug into her palms.

She could hear her phone ringing again, and let the call go to voicemail. This might be her last chance to be this close to Julian, one final happy accident of crossed paths before they went their separate ways.

He seemed preoccupied, which was lucky for her. They might yet get through this encounter without her embarrassing herself and, potentially, annihilating her relationship with Daniel and Lynn, which was the one gift that she could keep. She'd essentially ditched their son, but she was sure no one was going to hold that against her. They would not so easily get over hearing she was infatuated with their grandson. Their *grandson*. God help her.

He said, "I heard about *Lions*. I guess my father's pretty excited."

"You haven't talked to him?"

"Not yet. In one of his emails he'd said he might be coming down with you—"

"No," she said, probably too quickly. "There was some talk, after the benefit dance. But he and I, well, we decided we weren't . . ."

"Compatible." he said.

"Right."

"Yes, my grandmother mentioned that too."

She waited for some criticism, some chastisement for having led Mitch on. All he did, though, was nod thoughtfully.

"So . . ." she said, "is your schedule all cleared to shoot more of *Lions* this summer, or . . ."

"Actually, I'm not certain that's what I want to do next."

"No? Well, I imagine you have all kinds of options . . ."

He turned to look at her, biting on his thumbnail as he did. "You get my email?"

Startled, she nodded. Not only had she gotten it, she *had* it, folded into a square and tucked in the front pocket of her shorts. "I was—" *terrified* "very concerned for you. I'm so—" *grateful* "glad you all got back safely."

"Not all," he said, looking away. In a careful, even voice he described for her the narrow hillside road, the boys on the bridge, the single sniper shot, the helplessness. "I . . . I wasn't sure who would get there first."

"Oh, Julian." She wanted to hold him. Why couldn't she hold him? What sort of cosmic joke was this? The impossibility of the situation was torturous.

She had to get hold of herself. "Well," she said, "it was generous of you to send that email. But really, you didn't need to apologize. I understand how strange it's been for you, my interfering with *Lions* and," she glanced at him; he looked puzzled. "That is," she added with less confidence, "it's natural to be protective of your dad—"

"Right," he said. "Sure, protective." His voice lacked conviction, and he wouldn't look at her.

"I'm sorry—am I being presumptuous?"

"No. It's not that." Looking out into the garden, he was silent for a long moment, and then he said, "I was sitting there in Iraq, in the truck, composing the email . . . because, the thing is, I may not have much, but I do have my principles . . . and, I decided, I couldn't risk you not knowing how I felt. Feel." He looked at her again. "So let me just say—"

There was a flash, then, that she mistook at first as lightning, accompanied not by thunder but by banging on the gate that made them both jump.

"Ms. Reynolds! Your reaction to the Drudge Retort?"

Icy dread washed over her. She stood up, shielding Julian from the view of a man with a camera, and his companion, a woman with a thick ponytail and an expression she knew well as one she'd worn herself, in her hungrier days.

She tried to look composed as she said, "I'm sorry?"

The woman shifted her umbrella so that she could make a note on a small pad. "You're apologizing for attempting to bribe your midwife's daughter into turning over confidential records?"

What? Blue's every nerve thrummed as if the flash really had been lightning striking nearby. She stepped to the edge of the porch and said quite calmly, "No, *I'm sorry* that I don't know what you're talking about—neither Drudge *nor . . . who* did you say?"

Julian came up behind her and put his hand on her arm. The camera flashed again. "What's this about?"

"Nothing. I don't know. Stay here."

The woman made another note as the camera flashed again, and again as Blue left the porch and walked toward them. Despite her instruction, Julian followed, so she let him; now was not the time to make a scene.

"Ms. Reynolds—or do you prefer *Kucharski?*—are you confirming or denying the report?"

"I truly don't know what you're talking about. I haven't seen any of today's news." Thank God for the rain; in better light they'd see the vein throbbing on her temple and the flush rising on her skin.

"According to Drudge, who followed up on another website's report, you offered one hundred thousand dollars for the names of the couple who adopted your son when you were nineteen."

Not one hundred, and how in the world . . . ? "I wouldn't know anything about that," she said evenly. Her stomach churned, and she felt as if she might vomit at any moment.

"And nothing at all," the woman continued as the rain that was soaking Blue drummed on her umbrella, "about the website's photographs of you at approximately seven months pregnant," she held up a copy of the photo but Blue couldn't make it out, "or your son," a second photo, "shortly after his birth."

Photographs. She could feel the hook pricking her flesh and yet she could not stop herself from going to the gate for a closer look. The reporter continued to hold them up—out of reach, of course.

No question, the frizzy-haired pregnant girl was her. Presumably the other photo was the real thing too.

He was so tiny . . .

She kept her face blank and turned back toward the house, taking Julian's hand when she reached him so that he'd come too. Already he was closer to the gate, to the photos, than she liked.

The reporter banged the gate's latch. "Come on, Ms. Reynolds. It's *Drudge* on your tail. Why not let me quote you as apologizing—it'll go a long way toward making you look sympathetic."

Her mind raced. She stopped and turned. "Oh. My lawyers will want to know the website those pictures are on; would you write it down for me?"

The photographer smirked. "A shorter list would be the ones they're *not* on by now."

"Originally," Blue said.

The reporter was giving nothing away. "You'll want to know that someone's unhappy with your," she glanced at her notebook, " 'over-liberal, soul-damaging beliefs and the terrible example you set for today's youth.' "

"Look, Ms.—"

"Dana Coogan."

"Look, I know you're eager to scoop an interview here, but I have nothing to say. This is all baseless, and until I get to the bottom of it, my official comment is 'no comment.' "

It took everything she had in her to turn slowly, to walk past Julian and back up the steps, to go inside without appearing to be upset or hurried. She was Blue Reynolds, not some intimidated, angered easy mark for a wet-behind-the-ears reporter.

Blue Reynolds was in trouble.

32

$\mathcal{B}$lue's measured, silent retreat into the house made it clear she had nothing more to tell the reporter. Julian, fighting his confusion, strode to the gate.

"What the hell kind of person are you, ambushing her that way? Get out of here."

"We're not trespassing," the reporter said. "Your name, for the record?"

"Fuck off."

"Charming," she said, but she wouldn't meet his eyes. "Let's go," she told the photographer. "That's enough."

"That's right," Julian said. He had the primal urge to throw himself against the gate in a show of aggression, even as he had, too, the unsettling fear that he was shielding Blue from some threat that he absolutely needed to see.

He walked back to the porch, replaying the scene. She'd denied everything, but he'd had a good enough view of the photograph to know its subject was a dead ringer for a teenage Blue Reynolds. It *could* be her . . . And if so, she had a kid somewhere in the world, a kid who would be about ten years younger than himself.

He stopped on the second step. Ten years. The age he'd been when she was seeing his father. "Oh, no . . ." He leaned against the handrail and closed his eyes for a moment. His judgment could not be that lacking, could it? She could not have kept that kind of secret from all of them . . .

When he tried the door, he found it locked. He raised his fist to knock, then stopped and let his hand drop to his side. The locked door was itself an answer, wasn't it?

*H*e parked himself on a hard bar stool in the Green Parrot, thinking he had a fair idea of what was what. Or might be what. Thank God he hadn't finished what he'd been about to say to her, there on the steps— that his email was much more than an apology. A small grace, and he should try harder to feel grateful for it.

Wouldn't he have known if he'd had a half-brother? Sensed it, somehow?

Blue's child, and his father's. It could be true. It could be true that his instincts were so sucky that he'd fallen for his own half-brother's mom.

What he wouldn't give, just now, for a hot shower.

A hot shower, and the answer to how much of Blue's generosity toward his father—if any—stemmed from guilt over the secret she'd kept all this time. He took out his BlackBerry and pulled up his father's number.

"What can I get you?" the bartender asked.

Nothing I want. "Captain Morgan's, double."

He hoped Blue had something at hand to smooth the edges from her day, too. What must she be doing, locked up, all alone? Would she call someone? Her mom? Marcy? She shouldn't be trying to deal with this all on her own, but she obviously didn't want to let the privilege fall to him.

He called his father, listened to the line ring. When his father answered, Julian had no preamble, he simply said, "Blue had a kid back in the eighties. Is it yours?"

"Wait. What?"

Julian filled in the details, then said, "I need to know."

"Good God. No. She had a *child*?"

"Apparently."

"I never imagined . . . But no, J, it's not mine."

"How can you be so sure?" Julian asked, taking his glass from the bartender.

"We never, you know, we didn't get that far."

"Come on."

"I'm completely sincere. What's happening there? Is she all right?"

"I wish I knew. I'll talk to you later." Julian ended the call, then downed his drink all at once.

"Set me up," he told the bartender. One more, for clarity, or courage, or something.

So the kid wasn't related to him; that at least was clear. Everything else, though? Not so much. Twenty minutes ago he'd been convinced he should tell Blue about his feelings, that the timing was right, that everything was converging into a moment of truth and, if nothing else, he'd walk away knowing he'd done the right thing.

Then he'd walked away and now had no idea if he'd done the right thing.

Daniel and Lynn would be wondering what had become of him. He knew he should call, but had no answer to give them. What *had* become of him since he'd left Iraq eighteen hours earlier? What would?

Eventually he would have to step back into his life, figure it all out, make some choices. Soon, he would have to make some plans, some decisions more difficult than whether to have a third drink when the one the bartender was pouring was gone.

The bartender set his drink in front of him, then a moment later laid a Green Parrot T-shirt next to it. "From the ladies at the pool table." He inclined his head, and Julian looked that way. Two twenty-somethings, with over-dyed hair and enough extra cleavage exposed by their bikini tops to make another woman or two. The women waved and smiled.

SLICE OF LIFE, read a banner painted across the beam above them. An American flag hung from the beam's center.

One of them called, "We don't want you to catch cold!"

He raised his glass in a salute, then turned back and rested his elbows on the bar. He thought again of how he'd felt sitting next to Blue on her porch, the fear and wonder of possibility. Maybe it wasn't rational, but it was real. He'd thought it was real. Wasn't it possible that it had been real?

"Nah," he said.

The bartender, who was stowing clean glasses nearby, asked, "Did you say something?"

"I said my imagination's running away with me."

"Happens to a lot of guys when those sorts of girls are around. Looks to me like your two might be happy to oblige you."

Julian nodded as though they were talking about the same things. The bartender continued to look at the girls and grin.

Even after draining his second glass of rum, Julian felt short of answers to the hard questions. He tried one more, then put money on the bar, stopped in the bathroom, and left for today's version of home.

The rum that had seemed to have no effect while he was sitting on the bar stool became a little more effective as he'd made his way through dark streets in rain that had slowed again. Traffic was light, owing to the rain and it being too early for the crank-up of Duval Street's revelry. His main danger, while walking along some of the alleyway cut-throughs, was that he would fail to see a chicken or a dog or a tabloid reporter in his path, and fall facefirst into the dirt.

His feet and his pant legs were soaked when he got to the house, entering through the back door. Daniel set down the book he'd been reading. Lynn did the same, and got up from her seat at the table, where a loaf of French bread and a cutting board full of cheese said they'd waited dinner for him. He put a hand against the kitchen door for balance and attempted to take off his shoes, saying as he did, "I have some news." He had to tell them what was going on; his photo and the Forrester name was about to be everywhere times ten.

Lynn went toward the hallway saying, "There will be no dissemination of news until you're dry. Wait there."

He concentrated on pulling free the knot in his left shoelace and thought about the word *dissemination*. It had a vague sexual quality, like, taking away semen—castration would be a synonym . . .

"Julian?"

He was drifting. "Hmm?"

"Where ya been?"

"Oh. Well, I wanted to take a walk, you know, after spending all day in coach class. I had a window seat from Berlin to Miami—"

"Here you go." Lynn brought him a warm towel—what a wonder she was!—and draped it over his shoulders, then shooed him out, saying, "Daniel already put your things out in your room. Come right back, and then you can share your news while we have dinner."

Inside the guest cottage was a wall of photographs he'd made in the first few years after Daniel got him started with a 35mm point-and-shoot. Everything that moved, and most things that didn't, had been targets for his enthusiasm. There were pictures, here, of tree trunks and bike tires and clouds; there was a collage of feet photos, every kind of footwear imaginable. His first bird photos were here: gulls, herons, and one of his favorites, an Oystercatcher, vivid in its black and white plumage and orange beak.

This was a bird to admire; it didn't take the easy route the way the other birds did, surviving opportunistically on bugs and worms and fish. No, it was named for its habit, and to see it living up to its name was to witness an impressive feat.

He dried off and changed clothes, thinking about it. Alec had said he was like the loners of the aviary world, and he had been. Now, though, he would rather be like the Oystercatcher, engaged, purposeful.

Simple, elegant nature . . . It was so much easier for the birds, which simply were what they were, no effort, no forethought, no second-guessing involved. No deliberate cruelty, no artifice.

If God *had* created mankind, he'd done it on an off day and was now simply waiting for the species to give way.

33

*L*ight hardly traveled faster than sensational news. As Marcy would soon report, the story of the ambush was all over the Internet before Blue had risen from the middle of the parlor floor and finally answered Marcy's panicked call—her seventh attempt, according to the cell phone display. Blue had heard the phone ringing again and again, had noticed the day growing dark, but only vaguely. She could not recall how she'd gotten inside the house, or what had become of Julian. She recalled only that feeling, that strange yank to the edge of the abyss, and the relief she felt when going over—and, once in, how vast and empty it was.

Marcy was saying, "Oh thank God, *there* you are."

"Yes, I'm here." The sound of voices outside drew her to the window. A sea of umbrellas was outside the wall. Where had they all come from? It must have been a race from all points north the minute Drudge began banging his drum.

"So it's out, like, everywhere, as you know." Marcy sighed. "God damn it all. Are you okay?"

"I'm okay . . ."

"You don't sound okay. Hey, did you tell a reporter that Julian was your boyfriend?"

"Did I what? No."

"I couldn't imagine, although the pictures on *TMZ*—"

"What pictures?"

"Of you holding hands—these people work *fast* . . . And there's one of him behind you on the porch; he's holding on to your arm. What's up with that?"

Bastards.

Blue said, "Any names—you know, *his* name, parents, anything?"

"Nothing. No, here, I'll read you the statement from the site where this all started. It's that woman, Meredith's daughter. She found the picture of you, and then I guess busted a gasket. Listen:

A woman trying to find a child she gave up offered me one hundred thousand dollars if I would give her my mother's private medical files. I considered it because it would be her own medical record and maybe I would be doing the Lord's work in reuniting a misguided soul and her child. I would not have taken any money at all, and I took only a fraction, because I had to pay for my mother's funeral and all the associated expenses incurred in doing other tasks.

I found the file and looked inside to see if my mother had included the information on the closed adoption, which is all the type of adoption Mother did until about ten years ago when she found God and saw the error of this terrible practice that destroys the souls of women and children. There were some pictures (see below) who I quickly identified as Blue Reynolds, also known by her real name Harmony Blue Kucharski.

"Oh for God's sake," Blue said.

"Exactly. Wait, this is the thing:

I did not find out who Mother placed the child with so I can't help that child (an adult now, born 12/19/86). All I can say is, it is because of Blue Reynolds's lying about her life and not learning from her mistakes, and the terrible example she sets for today's youth by encouraging them to have sex before marriage (see as

one example March 21st, the day of a pregnant girl, Stacey, and
the Reverend Mark Masterson) that I feel I must reveal the truth
of Who She Really Is. Special thank you to Reverend Masterson
for giving me a way to make this statement known to his congre-
gation and if you wish you may share this information with your
family and friends who will want to stop watching her show as I
am going to do and should have done sooner.

"Peter called Masterson and tried to get it yanked. No surprise, he got
nowhere." Marcy added, "So there you have it: Another happy *TBRS*
viewer, another happy *TBRS* guest."

"I can fix this," Blue said. Her voice sounded stony, seemed to echo
inside her head.

"How do you mean?" Marcy's voice grew cautious. "Are you all
right?"

"Fine." She flipped the switch for the overhead light. "I'm going to
figure things out."

"Blue, the networks are calling, the paparazzi are swarming . . . And
God, the website headlines . . . they're making it look like you're sleeping with Mitch and Julian at the same time. What *are* you doing with Julian? *TMZ* says he tried to attack the reporter—the pictures they
posted—Christ, what a nightmare. It's too late, we're sunk on this
one."

Julian. Mitch. The Forresters. She blinked away the images. There
was nothing to be salvaged there.

She would think only about the show. She said, "No, not sunk, I
won't let that happen." They were all depending on her, everyone at
TBRS, Marcy, Peter, Todd, Elena, Marcus, Shawn—whose wife was
about to have triplets, she couldn't let them down. "I can fix it . . ."
Somehow. Ideas streamed through her mind. "I'll put things right and
the show will be okay, it'll be safe . . . I . . . let's see . . . Okay, I know: I
just need a small crew to go with me to Provence."

"To go *where*? You're not making sense."

"I am." She began pacing the room's perimeter, treading a single plank like a balance beam as she walked toward the windows, then, when she turned right, avoiding the cracks until she was across and could take a single plank again. "I'll say . . . I'll say I asked Julian here to discuss his work on *Lions*. Then I'll . . . I'll make a statement about my giving up a child for adoption, and then I'll go to Provence, to, you know, talk to Angelina Jolie about how adoption's good for some kids. Will that work? I think they're still in France. Get Peter on it. When I'm back we'll do a whole week just on, on, on teen pregnancy and desperation and adoption. Do I need to get a visa before I go, or—"

"Even if all this was possible, you can't just run off to France. Your mother's about to get married."

"Not until next weekend."

Blue heard some rustling and a voice, someone talking to Marcy. Then Marcy said, "Where are you right now?"

"In my house." She wiped her nose on her shirt hem and went to the kitchen to check her purse for her passport. "Why?"

"Stand still."

"What?"

"Whatever you're doing, just stop and stand still and listen."

"We don't have time to debate this, Marcy." She began to dig through her purse. "I need you to find out if I can get into the country without a visa. Then I need you to charter a plane—wait, do that first, and get me a car to the airport, and then check on the visa, and then—" okay, there was her passport, good—"get in touch with Angelina's publicist and—"

"Blue—"

" . . . and see if we can broadcast from their villa—"

"Blue—"

"So that—"

"Damn it, Blue, would you shut up for second and listen to me?"

"No, come on. I'm pretty sure we can get away with reruns next week as long as we're doing good promos for the special, daily. Peter will know how to work it. See whether any of the other celebrity moms who have adopted are willing to book last-minute."

Marcy gave an exasperated sigh. "Blue, stop! Just . . . just *stop*. It's too late, it's too big to shut down."

Blue's hands were trembling. She tightened her free one into a fist and still it continued, her whole body beginning to shake. "You don't know that for certain. Maybe there's something else. A benefit concert. We could get Barbra, or Madonna."

"Blue, it's done. Yes, you'll own up to it and we'll keep doing damage control. But you aren't going to be able to make this go away."

Blue wrapped her arm around herself, gripped her shirt at the waist. Her mind raced on, trying to find another way to plug the dyke, trying . . . and failing.

It was no use. No matter what tactic they used, no matter how sincerely she wanted to help someone, somewhere, they would not outspin the celebrity smear sites, the fundamentalist Christian groups, and all the Internet joy-riders who spread gossip as a sport. As huge as her viewership was, it didn't begin to approach the combined viewership of celebrity news shows, late-night TV, and the Web. What point in even trying?

What point was there in any of it anymore? The pressures, the pace, the persona . . .

Marcy was saying, "Sit tight. I'm sending a car."

"No car," Blue said wearily, heading for the door.

When she appeared outside the gate, it was as though an invisible force field kept the crowd of reporters and photographers a uniform twelve feet away. Their distance was a favor, based solely on her having given them so little reason to harass her in the past.

What must they think of me now?

She said, "Where's the woman who was here earlier? The reporter? Is she here?" Blue shaded her eyes and looked at the faces of the reporters, all of them holding tight to their umbrellas, while she stood in the rain with their photographers' flashes lighting up the night around her.

"Ms. Reynolds, why did you give up your child?"

"Ms. Reynolds, where is the man who was with you earlier? Is it true that he's Julian Forrester, your lover's son?"

"Are you sleeping with both of them?"

"Who is the father of your baby?"

"What would you say to being called a hypocrite?"

"Why didn't you have an abortion?"

She had her own questions. Where was Julian? Was he this very moment telling the Forresters what a fraud she was, making them regret having welcomed her back into their lives? How ludicrous to imagine she had any place with them, *any* of them . . .

The reporter from earlier came up to the front of the group. "Have you decided to make a statement?"

Blue said, "Who do you work for?"

"I freelance."

"Ah. So you hoped to score big today. Imagined the bidders lining up."

The reporter looked away. "I have to pay my rent."

"How much did you spend on that last-minute air fare to get here?"

"Twelve hundred."

"Wow. Just on the chance you might get to Blue Reynolds first. How much did the photos go for?"

The reporter shrugged defensively. "My split will cover my expenses."

"That meager, huh? You and your photographer friend sold me out for . . . three grand."

"I'm trying to build a career, just like you did."

Blue nodded. "I know." She raised her voice and said, "Everybody listen up: I'm going to make a statement. Are you ready?"

She waited, letting her silence build their anticipation, hearing the rain on their umbrellas like a drumroll, and then she said, "*The Blue Reynolds Show* is off the air. I've had enough. I quit."

The reporters were still yelling out questions when Blue returned to the house, found her phone, and called her mother. She did it without thinking through what she would say, because if she thought too much, she might not call at all. A simple delivery of the facts was what was needed: *I had a child. I lived a lie. I was scared to tell you. I'm sorry.*

Her mother's generous reply: "I'm on my way."

"No, Mom, not yet. I need some time to . . . to just be here, okay?"

"I love you. Call me any time. *Any time.*"

"I will."

She called Marcy next and told her what she'd done. "Call Peter, call my lawyer, and tell them no, I wasn't kidding."

Marcy said, "Can I do anything for you? Do you want me to come down?"

"I could use a towel, and a pillow."

"I'm on it. Now I have to ask—because they'll all be asking me: What are you planning to do? You know, next?"

Blue looked out the window; most of the crowd was gone. Off to upload their photos, to write and file their stories. "It's going to be a firestorm."

"Uh-huh."

"I'm not cutting you loose, don't worry."

"I'm not worried about me. Do you have a plan for you?"

"No," she said, walking to the sliding door and looking out into the rainy garden. "But I'm hoping to find one here."

After hanging up, Blue listened to the rainfall for a little while, soothed by the sound, the smell. What did she want to do next? What sort of options did she have? Who was she now, besides the former host of *TBRS*? Who did she want to be?

There was no rolling thunder of approval, no sign from the universe that she'd done the right thing in quitting. Only the sensation of a bit less weight now on her shoulders, and the far-off barking of a tree frog, and the steady patter of rain on the leaves.

A few minutes later, there was a banging on the gate, a voice calling out, "Delivery!" Blue went outside, permitted a pair of men to bring to her porch a cot, linens, and four bags of supplies. "I'll take it from here," she said.

When she had locked up the house and made her bed, she lay down in the dark, thinking about what would be happening at news stations and on websites while she was here in this empty house, disconnected, unplugged from all of that. The rumors. The lies. The analysis and speculation.

The media would be telling her story in every sensational way they could construct, the way she had always let them do. When that story had been both impressive and favorable, she'd been content to stand on the sidelines, calling out the plays only once in a while. She had, in so many ways, let the media shape who she was, let it determine who she would become. It had created her reality.

And now here she was.

She sat up, then she got up and found her phone, to call Marcy and get the phone number of the editor-in-chief at *Time*. She may have walked away from *TBRS* but she was still of the media; it was time she created a reality of her own.

34

*J*ulian avoided most opportunities for firsthand media exposure in the days afterward—as Blue was apparently doing, given that there'd been no official word from her since Friday. He kept away from the TV, the phone, and the Internet and within the confines of the house or yard. A few stubborn reporters remained camped out near the driveway even after they'd been told there would be no comment from him, or Daniel or Lynn.

Still, he couldn't avoid his grandparents' ongoing discussions. From them he knew that much was made of the pictures of him and Blue together. A lot more was made of that photo of her seven months pregnant. Depending where you looked, Blue was being portrayed as a cradle-robbing incestuous slut, a liar, a hypocrite, a coward, a baby-selling criminal, and a church-shunning sinner who deserved what she was getting after trying to buy her way to the son she hadn't bothered to keep. Daniel read the headlines aloud whenever he came across one: *Daytime's Angel Falls from Grace. Mamas, Don't Let Your Babies Grow Up Like Kucharski. Take Two: One Man Is Too Few for Blue.*

Julian's father was the Jilted Lover and he, Julian, was the Traitorous Son.

"What a load of horseshit," his father said, on speakerphone Tuesday evening. "I keep telling them that it's all out of context. Why is it that now, when I have something to say, nobody wants to hear it?"

Lynn said, "And why isn't Blue out there defending herself? She's shut herself in, no word to anyone." All they knew was that supplies and furniture had been delivered to her house. She wouldn't starve.

" 'The Jilted Lover,' " his father snorted. Julian, knowing his own label had nearly fit, kept silent.

"Aren't we the notorious group now?" Daniel said, but kindly.

Julian was pruning the climbing oleander from the side-yard fence Friday afternoon when the mail was delivered. Before bringing it in, he finished his work and got the wheelbarrow and rake, stopping outside the shed to observe a Red-bellied Woodpecker that hung from the feeder he'd built and mounted at the edge of the backyard. The design was simple; essentially a box, with a lid that was also an overhang and a base that was also a tray. He'd covered the tray with crosshatched wire to keep the squirrels out, and added a suet cage to the side, to attract woodpeckers like this one and the Red-headed and the Downy. There were Mangrove Cuckoos in the vicinity, too; he'd heard the guttural chuckle-like call several times in the past few days. He'd managed to lure a few to his feeders in years past with the fruity suet the Red-bellied was enjoying just now, and hoped he would again. It was an elusive bird; not flashy but handsome, one of the few Keys birds he hadn't managed to photograph yet. Getting its picture was his singular goal; a man needed something to occupy him, after all.

Scrounging up the materials to build the feeder had occupied him all day Monday. Tuesday morning was taken up with the construction itself, and Tuesday afternoon, he'd dug out the lawn mower manual and spent the remainder of the day tuning up the machine. Wednesday he'd cleaned the pool. Yesterday he and Lynn painted the two main-house bedrooms, each a different powdery pastel. In the evenings, after dinner, he'd talked some about his experience in Iraq. He gave snapshot accounts but held back most of his thoughts, said nothing at all about the email. Generously, his grandparents held back the question they were surely wondering about him, *What next?* He had options; Alec and Noor were off to China and said there was work, too, for him; four editors had pitched him assignments—and only one of them had been au-

dacious enough to make the assignment Blue. He knew people everywhere, yet wanted nothing more than to just stay put right here on this
four-by-two spit of sand and rock and coral.

After he finished raking up the oleander clippings, he went to the
mailbox. Amongst the letters and ads was *Time* magazine, on which
there was a compelling photo and the headline, "*Harmony, Blue?*"

He opened to the article and read it on the spot.

Who is Blue Reynolds?

We in the press would have you believe she's a spoiled celebrity
completely lacking a moral compass. She did, after all, give away
a child it turns out she could easily have kept, then followed that
with bribery and recent bed-hopping with an old lover and his
son—or so the story goes. She's been advised not to speak to the
potentially criminal matter of bribery, but about the men she
says, "I think it is safe to say that neither of them did or would
have me."

"Maybe safe, but not completely accurate," he said.

"Julian," Lynn called to him, "I'm off to Publix. What do you need?"

"I need a life," he sighed, well out of earshot. "Lemons," he called
back. He read on.

It looked as if she would pass the baton to an up-and-comer from a
network affiliate in Miami. For now, they'd run canned shows for the
last two weeks of the season, and that would truly be the end of *The Blue
Reynolds Show*.

Rest in peace.

She has no idea what to do next, yet the prospect of getting out of
television is not all bad. "Some people go into this business because they're chasing a dream. In my case, the dream was chasing
me, and all these years I've felt like I was staying barely a step

ahead." With the show derailed by her own hand, perhaps she can stop running.

About her secret being outed, she says, "I don't have to ask Ms. Harper what makes her believe she had the right to flay me publicly; she made that clear. I would ask, though, 'Who did I harm?' and I would ask, 'How would you feel?' "

Julian was startled to find his grandmother next to him. "Is it an interview?"

He said, "Yes. I guess she's having her say after all."

"Good for her."

Daniel joined them. He tilted the magazine so that he could see the cover. "Nice picture. She just gets better looking, don't you think?" He was looking pointedly at Julian.

Julian looked pointedly at his rake, where he'd left it propped against the fence. "Sure."

"So what's the holdup?" Daniel asked.

Lynn said, "Now, you said you weren't going to bug him."

"I changed my mind."

Julian stared at them. "You're not suggesting—"

Daniel said, "More like directing. Clean up your mess. Take a shower. Put on some cologne. A housewarming present is always a good excuse for dropping by."

35

$\mathcal{B}$lue took the issue of *Time* from her mother and opened it to the article, scanning to make sure the copy had run as she'd approved it.

"They did a nice job," her mother said. "You've vindicated yourself. Now we can all get on with things." She peered through the parlor windows as the crew they'd hired to transform her garden to a wedding chapel was outside putting the finishing touches on their work.

All week long the crew had gone about their business as if there was no self-exiled celebrity in the house watching them erect an arched arbor and weave into it yards of white grandiflora vine called sky flower. Watching them string tiny white lights into her lemon tree. Watching them put a second arbor just before the gate, where they hung a series of wide white satin ribbons with shining yellow and fuchsia beads weighting the ends, to make a sort of wedding-day bead curtain.

"How bad is it out there? Outside the gate, I mean."

"What, paparazzi? Five or six guys with cameras. Nice bunch. Haven't you made friends yet?"

"I haven't been out."

"Not once?"

Blue shook her head. "I've . . . I don't know. I wasn't ready. And you know, I was thinking, maybe it'll be better for you if I don't go to the reception tonight."

"Hold on, Harmony Blue. Here—I've brought fresh oranges and pomegranates. Did you know poms are a symbol of righteousness?" She handed Blue a mesh grocery bag. "I understand Melody's reluctance to show up, but you're used to the limelight. Isn't it time to get out of the house?"

She was used to the limelight in her talk-show-host guise. This week, knowing the *Time* article had yet to run, she'd felt too defenseless. She'd needed a little time to grow a thicker skin.

"It's not that I'm worried about me, so much; I don't want what should be a wonderful, joyous evening for *you* to be a circus." She set the bag on the counter. "In fact, it's not too late to reschedule the whole wedding."

"Now I know you've been shut in too long." Her mother emptied the bag, got a knife, and began slicing oranges. "Do you have a juicer?"

"No. I barely have the basics in furniture, and I'm still working on a list for the kitchen." She found two glasses, then began squeezing the oranges by hand, saying, "There are some really wonderful private islands in the Caribbean. It wouldn't take too long to make new arrangements—we could have it all in order by tomorrow afternoon."

Her mother opened the sliding door to the patio. "I have no reason to relocate or reschedule."

"If you go through with it here, you and Calvin will be in every tabloid—"

"Good! Let everyone celebrate with us! Come on outside, it's lovely in the shade."

Blue followed her mother out to one of the tables that had been set up for tomorrow's pre-wedding breakfast, watching for photographers. "Do you see anyone in the trees around here?"

"I don't care if they hang from them like monkeys. I have nothing to hide."

"I'm just trying to protect you."

"For this minute—but then what? How will you keep hold of the reins when I leave here? When Calvin and I are on that cruise ship tomorrow night? When we're back in Chicago and some customer comes into the store and says, 'Hey, you're the mother of that heathen slut, Blue Reynolds.' How will you protect me then?"

"I—"

"Can you control the entire media?"

"No."

"Do they say false things even when they know the truth?"

"Yes."

"Then I advise you to stop worrying about it." Her mother looked at her watch, then stood up. "Oops, you'd better give me the grand tour; I'm going to have to run soon. Calvin's playing host to our guests over at the hotel and I'm heading back to the airport to pick up your sister. We have the most amazing menu for tonight's meal, and there will be plenty of champagne. Music, too. It was a good idea, scheduling our dinner reception for tonight. What couple really wants to hang around after the ceremony, right?"

"You're asking the wrong person," Blue said, following her inside.

She took her mother around the house, pointing out its features and telling her what changes she was planning. New fixtures in the bathrooms, new appliances and skylights in the kitchen, plantation shutters, refinished floors.

"It's going to be marvelous," her mother said as they stood in the parlor. "It is already. So what's the verdict—will you be joining us?"

"I don't know, Mom . . . I hate thinking how it would distract from the party's purpose."

"People will be talking about it either way."

"Not as much. I really want it to be *your* night."

"Without you there, it would be my *incomplete* night. My *somewhat sad* night. I want to be with all the people I love. And look, the wedding tomorrow's not going to be any different. Don't try to tell me you're also thinking of missing that."

"No. I'm sorry. You're right." She sighed. "I just want it to all be perfect for you."

Blue followed her mother to the door, feeling so much the way she had when she was small and watching her mother head out on a date. She said, "How do you know, really know that Calvin is The One? How do you know that what you feel isn't, say, infatuation, or a whim that will pass?"

"We like the same things, and we want the same things."

Blue waited, but her mother said no more. "That's it?"

"Think about it. It's not as simple as it sounds. But yes, that's it. So: I'll see you at eight o'clock."

Blue rubbed at a spot on the wood with her toe. "Yes, okay."

"Honey."

"What?"

"It's a gorgeous day. Get out of this house. Do something. *Live.* Honestly, it's like you're waiting for an engraved invitation from God and let me tell you, it's not going to come."

After her mother left, Blue sat in the kitchen wishing she had Peep there for company. That had to wait, though, until the renovations and decorating she was planning for the house got done. A few weeks, maybe a month from now, it would be all set, and she and Peep could have exactly the summer she'd envisioned.

She went to the windows to admire the wedding preparations. The crew had gone, and the breeze played on the beribboned arbor, making the strands sway. For just the briefest moment, she saw Julian there in the garden, the image from her dream, and then like a passing shadow it was gone.

It really was time to get on with things.

She went for an elastic band, bound up her hair, grabbed her sunglasses, and went outside to the carport. The old bike still sat where it had been when she first saw the house. After pulling out the bike and brushing off the cobwebs, she began walking it down the driveway toward the gate just as a FedEx truck pulled up to her curb.

The driver waved his greeting, then climbed out carrying a business-size envelope. "Here you go," he said, handing it over. "Take it easy."

Take it easy. Perfect for Key West. In Hawaii they probably all said "Hang loose."

Take it easy. Ha. Her heart was already racing from surprise and anxiety. Who was overnighting things to her *here?*

The sender's name was *Branford*.

The truck rumbled off. Photographers called to her. Cameras

flashed. She ignored it all as she parked the bike back under the carport and went inside.

Maybe now that her secret had been outed, Branford felt free to bill her directly. Maybe instead of calling he was sending his condolences. She leaned against the counter and opened the envelope. Inside was a small white piece of paper and a rubber-banded file folder. There was a single line written on the paper, underlined for emphasis: *Call me before you open the file*.

She was tempted to open it immediately, regardless. Why call first? What if he wasn't available right now—was she supposed to wait? Besides, she didn't have her code-word list. She'd forgotten it in Chicago, had no cause to use it in the week since.

The folder was slight, and held closed by two pale green bands. She slid one of them off and started on the other . . . then, nervous, she set the folder down on the counter. Branford had a reason for his request. He never did anything without a reason. She took her phone from her shorts pocket and placed the call.

He answered right away and she said, "I don't know the word, but I got your note."

"What was the previous word?"

"God, I don't know! But it's me, I swear."

"What's your mother's middle name?"

"*You* don't even know her middle name," Blue said.

"That's right! Good. So, you got the file."

"Yes. What is it?" He could just tell her, and defuse the growing pressure in her head, her chest, her gut.

"I can't believe you really didn't look—but I'm glad you didn't, because I need to set this up for you, and I didn't want to risk putting it in writing. I'd have called you before, but—well, when I tell you what's going on, you'll see why I waited."

"*Tell* me, for God's sake."

"Okay, sorry."

He'd been angry, he said, at how the Harper woman set Blue up, at the woman's self-righteous attitude. If Blue was going down, he was going to do whatever he could to make sure the woman did, too. He went back to her town to dig around a bit more, and while digging heard a rumor: she hadn't revealed everything to Masterson after all.

Blue took a second to process this. Her voice caught as she asked, "What else does she know?"

"She had the parents' names. She just didn't want *you* to have them—according to a source who had a different definition of *Christian duty*."

Blue looked again at the folder. "So you found out their names? How?"

"Those nice utility company folks who were inspecting her mother's basement fuel oil tank—the house is going on the market, you know—offered to also check hers, free of charge. Good people over there, decent, eager to earn a few extra dollars and serve a good cause."

Blue had no words. She could only stare at the folder.

"So when I got back home, I connected some dots."

"And . . . ?" she whispered.

"And you should open the file. I didn't put any identifying info—name, address, you know—in case the envelope went astray, but I have it right here in front of me."

If he hadn't included *that*, then . . .

She reached for the folder, slid off the other band. "So all you sent is—"

"A picture. Grab a pen, I'll tell you the rest."

"Wait." She put her hand on top of the folder. Her blood rushed in her ears, in her neck; she could see her T-shirt pulsing against her chest. "Wait. I don't know, yet . . ."

He was real.

He could be found, be photographed. Be contacted. Be known.

She cleared her throat, then said, "Just tell me the basics. Don't . . . I mean . . . does it seem like he's had a good life?"

"Pretty ideal. Respectable family. College education. Are you looking at the photo? He looks great."

"No, no, I haven't looked yet."

"Here, just write down the address he's using now, and then you can decide what you want to do next."

His address. How to find him, *where* to find him. Would she be able to resist the powerful pull of a house number, a street, and city name? What would it mean for him to know he was her son? How would it feel to be the child who was Blue Reynolds's rejected, shameful secret, revealed?

"Just tell me his name. His *first* name," she said.

"His name is Ryan."

"Thank you." She hung up.

Her entire body trembled as she opened the folder. And there he was.

The photo was of a young man sitting at a polished oak bar in some trendy urban eatery, a beer and a ball cap on the counter in front of him. He had sandy brown hair and trimmed sideburns, and he faced a blond young man whose back was to the camera. *Ryan.* Ryan wore a yellow Lacoste shirt, untucked over blue jeans, leather flip-flops on his feet. On his left wrist was a yellow rubber bracelet. He was sweet-looking, and handsome.

He was laughing.

And though there were tears streaming down her cheeks, so was she.

36

$\mathcal{B}$lue wheeled her bike down the driveway and stopped at the code box. She pressed the numeric keys in the order that would swing open the gate, and then, with a deep breath, wheeled the bike out onto the street.

Photographers. Questions. She waved just as if this was the everyday routine for all of them. Then she climbed onto the bike, put her foot on the pedal, and pushed off.

The first thing she noticed was that the bike's tires needed air. Still, she wasn't turning back. Not when she'd gotten this far, not when the warm air, the breeze she made by riding, felt so good against her face. No one was looking for her here, like this.

As she rode through the blocks of Old Town, cars passed her without slowing. Closer to the main streets, she cruised past groups of pedestrians on their way to dinner or to Duval, no one much interested in the ordinary woman on the bicycle. She was factually, blissfully anonymous. In a fit of daring, she turned the bike onto Duval Street and began riding toward the port. When she stopped at Southard Street to wait for the light, she kept her head down and hoped that with all reports saying she was holed up, no one would imagine they might see her here. She was just a chick on a bike, not an uncommon sight in the slightest.

To her left, she remembered, the street made a short trip through the Truman Annex to the submarine basin, passing the Green Parrot on its way. How long ago that night at the Parrot seemed. Julian so edgy, until they'd gotten out into the night, alone, and then he'd shown her a side of him she suspected few ever saw.

How preoccupied she'd been at first, waiting to hear from Branford. Well, if nothing else, Meredith's wonderful daughter had relieved her of that stress.

She hadn't been so preoccupied that she didn't notice Julian—for what little good it had done either of them. It had been a nice walk in the mist, though.

The light changed and she rode farther down Duval, then right onto Greene and up to the marina. A flock of catamarans and ketches bobbed on calm, turquoise water, masts and ropes cutting vertical lines in the blue sky. A small crowd was milling near the dock; she sat on her bike and watched, curious, but nothing appeared to be happening.

"Still room, miss!" she heard from nearby, on her right. A weathered, fiftyish man inside a tiny white booth waved to get her attention. "We got room, yet. Thirty-nine dollars gets you the Snorkel and Sunset, free wine, beer, champagne, soda."

"Oh, thanks, but I don't snorkel."

"Don't, or won't?" the man challenged. "Thirty-*five* dollars, let's call it. We got all the gear, we'll teach you on the way. Flotation devices are included, vests, noodles, no charge. Every day we got kids going out, families, first-timers. Every day. Key West has the finest reefs in the northern hemisphere. Now's your chance to see the coral, see the colorful fish."

He was as amusing as he was annoying, but the best part was that she knew this was the spiel he used on *everyone*. All day, from this booth, he enticed tourists to part with their money and get on a boat. He didn't watch daytime TV, he didn't read the tabloids, he didn't surf the Web. He didn't recognize her.

"I don't have my swimsuit," she said, shrugging.

"Can you have one in ten minutes? Bikinis aplenty down Front Street or Duval. *Thirty* dollars, call it, Snorkel and Sunset. You'll love it. Three relaxing hours. Free beer, wine, champagne, soda."

She laughed. "Does anyone succeed in resisting you?"

"Why would they want to?" He smiled, a rakish smile that she imagined he used quite successfully in other places and for other purposes. Little slowed him down.

She thought of her son's smile—*Ryan's* smile. He certainly didn't seem to be the type to hold himself back. She said, "You know what? I'll do it, I'll go." She leaned the bike against the booth and bought a ticket, already thinking about how she would tell her mother this tale later. "Now I have to get a swimsuit—don't let them leave without me."

At the first shop she came to, she hurried inside, paying no attention to who else was there; she scanned the racks and racks of bikinis, every color, every style from full coverage to thong. A red floral print caught her eye; not knowing what size would fit, she took down four suits in her best-guess range and bought them all, plus a towel and sunscreen—but not the T-shirt that read, "For my next trick, I need a condom and a volunteer," tempting as it was. Maybe tomorrow night she and Mel could browse some shops and have a few laughs. Better than old times.

The sales clerk chatted loudly using an earpiece phone, never looking at Blue as she took her credit card, processed it, and bagged the purchase.

Fabulous.

The crowd that had been milling by the dock was now milling onboard a catamaran accented in vivid orange, red, and gold. Blue left her bike at the booth and went to board, with more than a little trepidation. A lone woman was sure to be noticed no matter what. A lone woman who was also a newly fallen celebrity was sure to be apprehended; she could only hope the bold apprehender, or apprehenders, would not be obnoxious.

Besides, no one could talk with their face in the water, so how bad could it be?

She managed to get on the boat, get her gear, and find a seat, all before she sensed she'd been recognized. Her sunglasses were a welcome shield while the boat motored away from the dock and a tanned, shirtless crewmember, blond hair pulled back and tattoos in full display, briefed the twenty or so passengers about safety, and toilets.

An hour out, an hour there, an hour back. The sun would oblige them by setting on their return, and then, just as evening got fully underway, she'd hurry back home (*home!*) to change and join her mother's reception, which would have only just started.

Excepting the contortions it took to change her clothes in the storage-bin-sized head, the sail out to the reef could not have gone better. Two women, look-alike dyed blondes with wide designer sunglasses and the barest signs of stretch marks on their sunburned bellies, spent the time that wasn't used by the crew for snorkel instruction and shark jokes telling her how much they admired what she'd done. Adoption, career, retirement, all of it. They had kids, they said (back at home, with the husbands) and there were plenty of times they'd second-guessed their choices. "Hell, I want to give away my four-year-old at least once a week," one said. Blue did not visibly flinch.

When the captain, a dark-haired, dark-tanned, jolly guy in hibiscus-print shorts announced that they had reached the reef and it was time to gear up, she tried to quell her sudden panic. In almost every direction as far as she could see, there was water. Beautiful Disney World water, but water—ocean—just the same. Land was the briefest sketchy line on the horizon, an hour's sail behind them. An hour's *sail*. And now she was meant to put on a thin vest, rubber fins, and a face mask, stuff a tube in her mouth, and climb off or jump off a perfectly good boat?

Her new friends were at the bow waving their encouragement. She waved back and slipped the vest over her head. "Go on, I just need to . . . er," she grabbed the small plastic tube that protruded from the vest. "I'll be there in a minute." The tube was for inflating the vest, which would somehow keep her buoyant but not too buoyant; too much and she would flip belly-up like a stranded turtle.

The blond crewman saw her and walked over. "Need help?"

"Will you snorkel for me?"

He laughed. "Pull that bit up, there, then blow into it until you're just the littlest bit fluffy."

He watched while she tried it. She felt idiotic, unsure whether she was now fluffy enough. "Good, thanks," she said, to make him go away.

Up front, kids, old ladies all were hopping into the sea with the enthusiasm of a Cousteau crew. She carried her fins and got in line for the stairs. She repeated the actions of the people ahead of her, positioning her mask and snorkel, sitting on the top step, putting her feet into the fins. Down the center stairwell she scooted, and down, and down while the boat was heaving left and right—to and fro? Fore and aft?—water sluicing across the stairs. One sharp dip to the left and she was pulled suddenly into the chilly waves.

Pulled under, salt water rushing into her snorkel, her mouth, her mask where it wasn't seated well against her face. She came up gasping, kicking, but the fins felt wrong, foreign, impossible for treading water. The vest was doing nothing for her. Water washed over her again. She went under, bobbed back up, tried desperately to get her arms and feet coordinated, to lay on the water the way they'd described. Through the sloshing water in her mask she could see the boat's hull about twenty feet away, the boat suddenly enormous and towering above the water's surface, the sun behind it, blinding. She'd bobbed off to the side of the boat, away from the group. Her arms flailed; she thrust up her chin— forget the snorkel—struggling to keep her nose and mouth above water. Another swell dunked her and she was pulled down into the cool, blue emptiness, water filling her nose and mouth, and she knew without question that she would die here.

She would not see Julian's face again. None of the past week's crisis would matter. In a few days or a week, it, and she, would be old news, archives on a Web server, a name carved into granite. Nothing left behind but footage of her encouraging someone to talk, observing while someone else cooked, or sang, or stitched, or joked, or danced, or loved, or suffered, all in front of a studio audience. Centuries from now, archaeologists would uncover the footage and think, Now where was that filmed? Where did she live? Only to discover upon closer examination that in every important way she hadn't.

She bobbed back up, coughing and gasping.

"You okay down there?" a voice called from above. She pushed her mask up and looked in the voice's direction, straight into the sun.

She coughed. "Define *okay*."

"Here, this will help." A foam noodle landed on the water near her. With a black spot in the middle of her vision she reached for it, noticing the hull was now just five feet away. "Lay on the water," the crewman called. "Let it be your lift."

With the noodle under her armpits, she fixed her mask, cleared her snorkel, put it into her mouth. She'd be damned if she'd drown out here, not if no one else was drowning, not if the friggin' boat wasn't going down.

She challenged herself: *Lay* on the water. *Arms out, legs out, move them from the hip. Breathe with your mouth. Lay* on the water.

Lie on the water, wasn't it?

Whatever, she was doing it, lying, breathing—sounding like Darth Vader after aerobics—breathing, seeing! A school of cobalt and yellow fish, with a black dot in the middle! A green fuzzy donut-looking thingy on the ocean floor, with a black dot in the middle! The black-dotted ocean floor! Her mask was fogged, but she was seeing! Praise-the-good-lord-jesus-buddah-allah-krishna-hallelujah-amen.

37

Blue toweled off after her shower. The salt water and sunscreen were washed away now, but the feeling of accomplishment remained.

Without the daily deliberations of product and flat-iron and stylist, her hair was reverting to nature's intended curls. She bound it up in a loose twist and put on the one dress she'd packed when she thought she was coming down for only last weekend. A pale green cotton sun-dress—a daytime dress for a nighttime event. A fashion violation that she was pretty sure would violate no one who'd be at the reception.

It looked good on her less-exercised, slightly softer body. So did the low-heeled sandals she wore with it, and the everyday diamonds, which were the only jewelry she'd brought. She was rosy-cheeked from the sunshine, something that had become all too rare for her in past years. Even at garden parties, even on yachts, even on those weekend trips to Jamaica where she'd sunned beside a pool inside a walled estate, she'd taken pains to keep the sun from actually reaching her skin.

Tonight, she felt like she was imbued with sunshine.

The photo of Ryan waited on the kitchen counter, tempting her to bring it for her mother and sister to see. She'd meant what she told her mother earlier, though; the focus should not be on her life but on her mother's and Calvin's. She tucked the photo back into the envelope. It could keep until after the wedding tomorrow, and then she would show it, proudly.

Progress.

The paparazzi, embodied now in only three photographers, waited dutifully outside her gate. They seemed bored as they took her picture climbing into a cab. Where was the news? Where was the drama? She heard one of them say, screw this, he was going for a drink.

Me too.

Except her stomach was still a little queasy from so much swallowed salt water; she would go easy on the champagne tonight.

Two photographers patrolled the lobby doors at the Ocean Key. In darkness, with so many tourists thronging the Mallory Square area, she thought she might pass them and use the entrance off the pier, but no such luck. They saw her. They yelled. Their cameras flashed. At one time she would have acknowledged them with a smile or nod—good press, always. Now she ignored them as she passed. Disdained them, in fact. Who chose such a job, and why? There were so many better ways to be a photographer. Take Julian, for example.

Julian. How was he managing the media chaos? He'd had wounds to lick already; she hated that she'd made it all worse. She hated the idea that he might hate her for it. She hated not knowing for certain how he was doing or where he was.

A hotel clerk spotted her passing the desk. "Ms. Reynolds! Welcome, uh, back. May I—"

"Thanks, I'm all set." She continued into the hallway leading to the elevators. It charmed her every time she was here. Some brilliant designer had created a tunnel of white lattice, with wide-striped blue and yellow fabric hanging overhead like a circus tent. The elevator's doors were blue on top, yellow on the bottom, with white herons in the center of each side's upper section and pineapples below. They opened, and she stepped into a chamber of mirrors.

"Good evening," she practiced, speaking to her reflection. "It's wonderful to see you!" And, "I'm doing well, thank you. Never better, in fact. Tell me, how are you?"

On the door of the Hot Tin Roof restaurant was a subtle placard, *Dining Room Closed for Private Party.* Inside, she was greeted by a handsome Latino man who bowed and extended his arm toward the warmly lit room, where calypso music and the breeze coming in off the ocean set the mood just so.

Mel saw her first. "Harmony Blue . . . What a week—it's good to see you in the flesh." Mel hugged her, then stood back to study her. "Eh, not too much worse for the wear."

"So you won't disown me, then?" Blue tried to sound light-hearted.

"Is that an option?" Mel joked, then grew serious, saying, "At first I kept thinking, Why didn't she ever *tell* me? I wasn't exactly there for you, though, I know that."

"It's done," Blue said.

"Guess what?" Mel said, brightening. "Jeff did it—he flew. He's over there—" she pointed. "He said your courage shamed him into doing it."

Quitting had not been so courageous. She'd done it only after she was in free fall anyway. She'd done it knowing that the rest of her life was so well-funded that, even if she never earned another dime in salary, she could live lavishly every day. *Every day.* And even then she would have spent only a fraction of what was there.

The thing she was most afraid of doing was so much riskier than quitting her job and so much harder to accomplish. Unlike Jeff with his flight to Key West, she couldn't buy a ticket to Julian.

Her mother saw her with Melody and came over, pulling Calvin with her. "My girls." She kissed Blue and took both daughters' hands in hers. "How wonderful is this?"

"Quite wonderful," Blue said. Everyone looked beautiful, the room was beautiful—polished wood, palm-shaped light fixtures, lush palm murals on the ceiling; everything was so perfect-seeming that Blue tried to dismiss the odd feeling of being in the wrong place.

For more than an hour she mingled with the other guests, fielding questions and working, always, to steer the conversation back to the occasion if it got too far off-track. "Tell me how you and Calvin got acquainted," she'd say, or, "I did a show, once, on tattoos, but I've never seen anything as elaborate as yours. Did it hurt?" "The dress my mother's wearing tomorrow is vintage—you should ask her about it."

She'd thought she would tell her mother her snorkel story during dinner. She waited until they were seated together at a white-clothed table. The story would be an entertaining tale to anyone listening in, and at the same time a way of telling her mother, *I did it, Mom, I got out, I took a risk, I lived.* Since talking with Mel earlier, however, the message felt like a false one. Here were Calvin and her mother, bold in their love and sure in their belief that when it was real, you didn't wait. Seeing them sitting at this table, radiant, assured, delighted, she understood that love was always the riskiest proposition—and promised the biggest pay-off.

As the salads were being served, she leaned close to her mother and said, "There's something I have to do."

"What is it, what's wrong?"

"I'll explain later." She left the table, left the restaurant, took the elevator downstairs, walked back through the lobby and out into the busy plaza, and stopped to get her bearings.

Duval was packed with weekend revelers, so she took Front, intending to weave her way up to the Forresters' house in the hope of finding Julian still there.

She took her shoes off at the corner of Simonton. Ahead on the right was the little shop she'd visited on her first day here, the bird shop. She should see if there was something small she could bring him, a *gesture,* her grandmother had called such gifts. Gestures would, she'd told Blue and Mel, help them make new friends.

Blue recalled being at a tiny IGA grocery store once, where the selection of inexpensive children's gifts was slim, and boring. She'd wanted to skip it and leave, but her grandmother urged her on.

Gestures show that you have the person in your thoughts, that you like them.

Don't they know that, if I'm there?

If you never presume, you won't ever be mistaken.

Tonight she wanted very much to be clear.

The shop was open, the wind chimes ringing on the softly lit porch. A group of women was leaving as she was coming in. They paused, but she continued inside. If she waited on every person who waffled, deciding whether or not to speak to her, she'd spend a great deal of time waiting—and she'd done too much of that already.

A Blue-cheeked Bee-eater would be the perfect gift for Julian, connecting them in a way that would always please her, regardless of what did, or didn't, come afterward. She scanned the first display cases and, not seeing one, went around a tall shelf toward the back corner of the shop, to find the artist or a clerk.

She found two people, one who looked as startled as she was.

"*Julian.* You're . . . here."

"*You're* here," he said.

They stared at each other until the shop owner, the artist, said, "I thought you'd be back."

She looked at the artist. "Because you said my Bunting needed . . ." She stopped, suddenly spooked. *A partner.* "Julian, do you have a few minutes to talk?"

He followed her outside and said, "Are you okay? I saw the *Time* article. That was nicely done." He looked worried but also pleased, which made it easier for her to answer.

"I came here to find you a gift, an apology."

"None needed," he said. "I came here to find you a housewarming gift."

"You're kidding."

He shook his head. "I thought you might be staying awhile."

The moon was full and rising, white and clear against the blackest star-filled sky. "It really is glitter-strewn," Blue said, staring upward. She made a quick wish for fortitude. "I read that, *glitter-strewn sky,* in a guidebook." Looking at him again, she thought he was the more compelling sight. She said, "Do you want to walk? Let's walk."

They walked along Simonton in silence. On any other night with any other man, she would have waited for some overt sign that what she wanted to say was going to be well-received. Tonight, with him, she felt impatient and powerless at the same time, pulled again to the edge of the abyss. The idea was not so frightening, though, as it had once been. She recalled the wish she'd made from the balcony of her hotel suite not so long before: *Ease.*

She stopped walking. "So be it," she said. "I'll do it right here."

Julian stopped too. "You really don't need to apologize. It must have been hellish for you, but I think you're handling it—"

"That's not it," she said, looking up at him.

"No? Then what—"

"I never imagined I'd be standing here, holding my shoes, saying . . . I mean, my plan originally was, you know, to get you a *gesture,* a bird—a Bee-eater. And if you were there at Daniel and Lynn's house, I was going to give it to you and say, 'I'm really sorry you got pulled into the mud with me.' And then, before I lost my nerve—because I'm not good at this kind of thing at all—I was going to tell you—even if your grandparents could hear me—I was going to say something that probably would have come out all hokey, like, 'I can't stop *thinking* about you,' or, 'I wish there was some way you could feel like I do.' " Hearing herself, she stopped abruptly. There were limits to how ridiculous she would let herself be.

Silence.

She ventured a look at his face. He was staring at her. He said, "Like you do?"

She could only nod.

He held onto the fence beside them for balance and took off one shoe, then the other. This was so unexpected that she had to laugh. "What are you doing?"

With his shoes in his hand, he said, "It's been a long week, hasn't it?" His expression was thoughtful. Sympathetic. A man like him would have a lot of experience in putting off love-struck women.

"The longest," she said, her voice thick with emotion she wanted so much to suppress.

He said, "Blue? That email I sent you, from Iraq, that was more than an apology. It was me saying—or trying to say, 'She'll know the truth so that, if I die tonight, at least I'll have said what needs saying.' Which is my still not very clear way of saying, well, of saying . . . I don't, I *can't*, think of anyone but you."

"You don't?"

He shook his head. "And I'm pretty sure I feel like you do."

"You do?"

He dropped his shoes, then took hers and dropped them as well.

She said, "Are you going to kiss me? Because if you feel like I feel, you'd kiss me, quick."

He did; a tender, testing kiss that encouraged a soft, deep one, and then he folded her into his arms.

On any other night, with any other man, she would have invited the man to her place for only drinks and conversation. She would do the balance-sheet calculations, pluses and minuses, and consider the possibility of getting together again, when her schedule was clear, maybe. She might call her mother—as she had just done—to say all was well and they'd speak soon.

She would not do what she was doing with Julian: walk past the lone remaining photographer with her arm wrapped around Julian's waist; leave the lights off after they'd come inside; push him against the wall and kiss him until she was breathless and he was, and then kiss him like that again.

It was not her style to pull a man into her bedroom and take his clothes off him as if unwrapping a fragile gift. There was nothing fragile about him. He was the vision from her dream, made real, made warm, made panting softly when she slid her hands over his bare chest, his waist, the expanse of his back. He was a man who, when she found his appendectomy scar and traced it with her tongue, found every way to return the favor.

She would not have made love with naked passion and abandon, but she did now.

And she would, she hoped, again; maybe before the night was through.

.   .   .

*W*hoever had built her house must have been an early riser, a person who didn't want to waste one moment of the day; the sun, now higher than the garden walls but lower than the trees, poured through the eastern windows and set the bedroom ablaze with color. With Julian still sleeping beside her, Blue sat in the light with her eyes closed, absorbing it, until it was swallowed up by the trees.

"Good morning," Julian said. He tugged her down onto him. "In case you're wondering, my shoes are still off."

"In case you're wondering," she kissed him, then rolled off him, "there will be caterers here in about fifteen minutes."

"In case you're wondering," he sighed, sitting up, "I'll be making the coffee and waiting for my turn in the shower."

"Just Lucky Charms for me," she said.

He grabbed her hand before she climbed out of bed. "I need you to know something. This, us, it's real. For me. I'm done roaming, in every sense."

She said, "I'm older than you, you know." As if that were the most of it.

"Do you have a point?"

"If . . ." She could hardly find words for the feeling that made her throat tighten. She cleared it, and tried again. "If this *is* real, I'm done too." She had wishes for her future, wishes she'd never been brave enough to make, before. "There are so many things we can do together. I'd like . . . I'd like to make a difference in the world. We could, you know."

He nodded. "Kids?" he said.

She tilted her head and smiled at him. "I think so."

After her shower, she sat on the porch steps feeling purely happy to be looking out into the garden, the sun dappling her legs and the ground in front of her as though she was any old girl on any old porch on any old tropical morning. If you took away the ribbons and the light strings and the vine-and-flower-covered arbor where her mother's wedding vows would be said, there was nothing at all exceptional here. A woman in love was as common and unremarkable as the green of a lemon tree's leaves—until it was your lemon tree, and you.

She heard a car stop at the gate, and Calvin's voice thanking the driver in his I'm-sure-from-the-Upper-Midwest way. Her mother came through the gate trailing a garment bag and suitcase, as did Calvin. They were halfway up the path before her mother saw her, time enough for Blue to see more clearly than ever the difference Calvin made on her mother's posture, the composition of her features. It was as though there was less gravity at work on the pair of them. Blue felt a bit like that herself.

"Harmony Blue! Good morning." Her mother pulled her into a hug. "I've got your dress right here with mine."

"Happy Wedding Day," Blue said.

"It certainly is. I see we beat the caterers; are any guests here yet?"

"Only one," she said. "Julian Forrester."

Her mother's raised eyebrows and wide smile said everything.

They greeted Julian as if it was routine to see a damp, half-naked man in her kitchen picking the marshmallows out of cereal he'd just poured. "I'm counting my lucky stars," he joked. "And then I'll get out of everyone's way."

"Why?" her mother asked. "Stay. Better yet: go, and bring your grandparents back with you. We'll have a buffet available to anyone who was able to wait to restore their energies—and we'd love to meet them."

"They'll be delighted," Julian said, and Blue believed him.

Watching Calvin and her mother at the altar two hours later, Blue imagined how their wedding announcement might read:

The bride wore a white silk tea-length sheath, her silver hair piled on her head and held by seed-pearl combs. Matching heart-and-vine tattoos were visible on the bride's and the groom's left forearms. The groom wore blue linen trousers and a white silk guayabera shirt. None of the wedding party wore shoes.

She held Julian's hand as she stood behind her mother, white lights twinkling all around them in the shady garden, and listened to the judge, who happened to also be the mayor, intone the words that would bind her mother and Calvin for as long as they chose. Melody stood on her other side, wiping at tears just as she was, as this well-deserved moment in their mother's life unfolded.

"Above you is the sun and below you is the earth. Like the sun, your love should be a constant source of light, and like the earth, a firm foundation from which to grow."

It was a good start.

Epilogue

With the house filled to bursting with his brother, his sisters, their friends, his friends, and relatives from both sides of the family, the young man had to wait until after two AM to pull his baby book from the library shelf and sneak it up to his room.

The book was a long shot. He'd already scanned all the photographs displayed throughout the three-story house. Every tabletop, every wall display, the mantles in the den, living room, and family room, even his parents' bedside tables and bureaus. Hundreds of photos of him and his siblings, but none that matched the one he'd seen online—and in line, in the grocery and convenience stores' magazine racks. A scrunchy-faced infant in a blue knit cap and a mint-green shirt, with a little bit of striped pastel blanket showing.

Generic baby.

He didn't know why he was so intent on confirming that he was not one and the same as the scandal-child. The smarter thing would be to get some sleep before tomorrow, when he was graduating from the University of Chicago. It was a temporary ending; he'd be back in the fall to turn his anthropology BA into an art history PhD. His mother didn't mind a bit that her youngest wanted to stay close to home for a little while longer—though she was not as thrilled about his summer plans: ten weeks biking across Europe with his pals Collin and Beck. The party tomorrow night was a celebration and a bon voyage, and was certain to last pretty much all night.

Still. Knowing that his birth date was the same as Blue Reynolds's son's was a coincidence he needed to investigate so that he could put it out of his mind. The baby book was the last record he could check without alerting any-

one to what he was doing. *If there was no matching photo there, he would put the issue behind him.*

With the book under his arm, he used the back stairs to get to his room, creeping as quietly as he could manage and listening to make sure he wouldn't run into anyone in the hall. If his brother caught him with his baby book, he'd never live it down. Pat would never admit that, in his position, he'd be pulling out his own book to see if he was the one with celebrity blood in his adopted veins. And his sisters—well, more likely either of them would turn flips at the prospect of being Blue's child. What could be more glamorous? Jill would probably sell out completely if she thought their parents wouldn't mind.

The thing was, their parents *would* mind. They'd arranged four private, closed adoptions, with deliberate emphasis on *private* and *closed*. It was their belief—a belief he'd shared until he saw the Blue Reynolds mess—that the only family that mattered was the one that chose the child. They weren't callous people, just practical, and protective.

At the top of the stairs, he stopped and turned around to go put the book back, hesitating on the step. If he never looked, he'd never have to deal with the question of what to do if he *was* the kid. The grandfather clock at the opposite end of the hall ticked, slower than the thumping of his heart. *Look. Don't look. Look. Don't look.*

Suppose she *was* his birth mother. He didn't need anything from her. He didn't even *want* anything from her. He wouldn't have to tell anyone; it might be enough to just *know.*

He took the book to his bedroom.

Before opening it, he logged in to his computer and went to the website that had published the photos first. The way this whole thing had come down really pissed him off. His family was Christian, and these extremist people offended him way more than anything Blue Reynolds had done, ever. If she thought she couldn't take care of a kid, then she couldn't. If she thought kids should be educated about sex, well, if he hadn't been, he might have been a father at seventeen. Studying anthropology had taught him a lot of things, but nothing bigger than the importance of being open-minded.

He scrolled down to the photos. She was so young then—younger than Jill *and Jess, who weren't either of them mature enough to handle motherhood. In his opinion, at least. What would his parents have done if one of them had gotten pregnant?*

And . . . there was the baby picture.

He opened his baby book.

Even as he turned the pages to the one announcing First Photo, *he knew what he would find. It was going to take some time, though, to decide what he would do.*

Acknowledgments

This, my second novel, was so much a labor of love: Love for writing and for telling a story that engaged my imagination so thoroughly; love for my profession and all the excellent people who publish my work; love for the readers whose responses to my first novel, *Souvenir*, have humbled me beyond words . . . To *Souvenir*'s readers I send my most heartfelt thanks, and to those beginning with *Reunion*, my warmest welcome.

Second novels are, they say, the hardest to write. The quandary is in deciding how similar the second book should be to the first. I decided to approach the matter much the way a singer might when selecting which songs to record for a new CD. Listeners don't want the same song on every track—yet they do need to recognize the sound as uniquely that artist's. Consider this book my track #2, a contemporary, slightly up-tempo offering that I hope is as captivating as readers and reviewers say the first track is.

Novelists work on faith. We sit at our keyboards day after day hoping that what we have to say will be things our readers want to hear. It is my good fortune to have the guidance of a publishing team that can and does steer me so capably as I make my way through to each story's end, and beyond. I'm grateful to Linda Marrow, Libby McGuire, and Gina Centrello, whose faith in me is invaluable. Wendy Sherman, who has championed me from the beginning, is tops. I appreciate so much the efforts of the crew at Ballantine: Brian McLendon, Sarina Evan, Kim Hovey, Katie O'Callaghan, Christine Cabello, Junessa Viloria, Kate

Collins, Dana Isaacson—and Charlotte Herscher. No less valued are Jenny Meyer and Michelle Brower. It takes a village . . .

I treasure the camaraderie and support of my writing pals, who know better than anyone else the struggles that take place at the keyboard and behind the scenes.

Most of all, I treasure and thank my enthusiastic family (and not only for the unpaid publicity efforts!). My husband, Andrew, and our four boys get both the pleasures and the pain of living with a "creative type," and seem to love me just the same.

About the Author

THERESE FOWLER is the author of *Souvenir*. She holds a BA in sociology and an MFA in creative writing. She grew up in Illinois, and now lives in Wake Forest, North Carolina, with her husband and two sons.

About the Type

This book was set in Centaur, a typeface designed by the American typographer Bruce Rogers in 1929. Centaur was a typeface that Rogers adapted from the fifteenth-century type of Nicolas Jenson and modified in 1948 for a cutting by the Monotype Corporation.